"High-class suspense."
—*The New York Times* on *American Quartet*

"Adler's a dandy plot-weaver, a real tale-teller."
—*Los Angeles Times* on *American Sextet*

"Adler's depiction of Washington—its geography, social whirl, political intrigue—rings true."
—*Booklist* on *Senator Love*

"A wildly kaleidoscopic look at the scandals and political life of Washington D.C."
—*Los Angeles Times* on *Death of a Washington Madame*

"Both the public and the private story in Adler's second book about intrepid sergeant Fitzgerald make good reading, capturing the political scene and the passionate duplicity of those who would wield power."
—*Publishers Weekly* on *Immaculate Deception*

ALSO BY WARREN ADLER

FICTION

- Banquet Before Dawn
- Blood Ties
- Cult
- Empty Treasures
- Flanagan's Dolls
- Funny Boys
- Madeline's Miracles
- Mourning Glory
- Natural Enemies
- Private Lies
- Random Hearts
- Residue
- Target Churchill
- The Casanova Embrace
- The David Embrace
- The Henderson Equation
- The Housewife Blues
- The Serpent's Bite
- The War of the Roses
- The Children of the Roses
- The Womanizer
- Torture Man
- Trans-Siberian Express
- Treadmill
- Twilight Child
- Undertow
- We Are Holding the President Hostage

MOTHER NILE

WARREN ADLER

RosettaBooks®

NEW YORK | 2016

MOTHER NILE

Copyright © 2016 by Warren Adler

ISBN (EPUB): 978-0-7953-4964-5

ISBN (Paperback): 978-0-7953-4963-8

Produced by Stonehouse Productions

Cover design by Alexia Garaventa

Cover images © Shutterstock

Published 2016 by RosettaBooks

www.RosettaBooks.com

RosettaBooks®

To Sunny who was by my side in Egypt and everywhere

CHAPTER ONE

THE DARK-SKINNED CONCIERGE at the Hotel Genaina rubbed his moustache with the crook of his finger, contemplating the young man with shrewd, dark eyes. With his other hand, brown gnarled fingers poking out of the sleeves of his faded blue djellaba like chicken legs, he circled the approximate location of the necropolis, the City of the Dead.

To the older man, who had, at first, frowned to the rim of his gray woolen skullcap, it was obviously an unprecedented request.

"There is nothing to see there," he had assured the young man, who, in jeans, T-shirt, and sandals, still had the air of an American tourist.

"Nevertheless, that's where I want to go," Si Kelly said in Arabic, underscoring the original request and displaying his mastery of the language. The accent, he knew, was distinctly foreign. But Cairenes were used to all accents. The man showed him a row of rotted teeth and busily sketched the route.

"Muhammad Ali's mosque in the Citadel is a good landmark." Then he paused. "No more than fifteen minutes by taxi."

Si Kelly thanked him with a ten-piastre coin—"baksheesh"— and the older man's hand opened and closed quickly, a snapping maw. But he could not resist his curiosity.

"A relative?"

Si Kelly nodded, closing his eyes, deliberately illustrating the solemnity.

"May Allah grant eternal life," the older man said respectfully.

"Thank you," Si said, turning and heading through the dank lobby into the people-clotted street.

What greeted him was an unprecedented assault on his senses. Engulfed in a soup-like smog overheated by the mid-July sun was a hodgepodge of vehicular traffic moving like a river of molasses around Ezbekieh Gardens, a dust-coated green spot in a vast sea of crumbling brown and gray buildings. Scrawny donkeys pulling flatbed carts competed for space with ramshackle buses choked with people, trucks belching dark exhaust, cars of every vintage, motor scooters, bicycles, barefoot men on little gray donkeys, and human-propelled transport as well, the young dark boys in filthy pajamas pushing huge nondescript burdens, cigarettes dangling from their lips. In all, a giant swarm of refugees escaping, it seemed, from some monstrous persecution.

The images drained his energy, and he stood in the shadow of the hotel entrance, unable to find his bearings. On the edges of the vehicular swarm, people moved like a pencil scribble

out of control; women in clothes that described five thousand years of women's fashions, chic girls in high heels side
by side with bulky women in long somber black abayas, burdened with children and packages; barefoot boys in ragged
pajamas, men in sleek French-cut fashions as well as every
style of djellaba, turbans, and woolen skullcaps. Animals were
everywhere; dogs, cats, donkeys, goats, and sheep.

The initial assault on the eye masked the attack on the ear,
rising like a symphony orchestra tuning up. No car seemed
to be able to function without perpetual horn blasts; vendors
hawked, children shouted, babies howled, radios blasted
Arabic and Western music. The nose, too, did not escape. Gas
fumes permeated everything, and a saffron-coated chickpea
stink laced with vague odors of human waste larded the air.
A single inhalation, and it could be tasted like some noxious
medicinal brew. He was now digesting Cairo, and it lay like
lead in his gut.

Gathering his courage, he moved into the current, retreating again to a slatted chair of what passed for an outdoor café,
a dingy hole in the wall where men sat around smoking water
pipes, playing backgammon, or arguing. Others sat staring
into space. Kayf, his mother had called it. Looking into the
eye of emptiness. He had seen her doing it many times. It was
a talent he would have liked to call upon at that moment.

He ordered a Turkish coffee, brought by a man in a tattered
djellaba who patted his arm as he laid the cup on the table.
Si noted that everybody seemed to touch each other in this
human warren, as if the connection of the flesh was not merely
accidental, but necessary.

3

Could this be the Egypt of his mother's memories? he wondered. In her green eyes, which he had inherited, he had assumed that he could actually visualize what she persistently refused to reveal of her early life. Because she wouldn't discuss it with him, he had to invent images of this strange land for himself. Feluccas, like graceful swans slipping soundlessly along a green Nile, depthless and flowing, a mirror of those eyes; sun spangles on the minarets, the soft colors of an orange sun against an azure sky, timeless and beautiful.

And more. The blue Mediterranean kissing the golden sands of Alexandria. Morning dew on the wadis. The perpetual rhythm of the Archimedes' screw worked by the blindfolded water buffalo, lifting the life-giving water of the river to the verdant soil, the soft plaintive rhythm of the tarabooka floating in the perfumed mysteries behind the Mashrabiyas, the latticed screens that hid the curious veiled women. And dominating all, the glories of the ancient monoliths, the old kings and queens of the timeless kingdoms, sitting solidly on their stone thrones, living proof that they had conquered time forever.

Seeing what he saw now, Si learned what really had been in the crucible of his mother's dying brain. Certainly not his romantic speculations. She hadn't given him a clue. And he had gotten it all wrong.

"What was it like?" he had asked her, a perpetual refrain.

"What?"

"Egypt. Your childhood. Growing up."

What she had given him, he knew finally, were evasions, stuff that he extracted from books. The temples of Karnak and the Valley of the Kings wasn't her Egypt. Abu Simbel wasn't her Egypt. Ramses II, his domains and megalomania, wasn't her Egypt.

"Tell me what it was like, for crying out loud!" he had remonstrated. He knew she had grown up in Cairo. She had admitted that. She'd had to, because he'd needed to provide his family's background information for school. Mother's birthplace: Cairo, Egypt.

"What do you know about it?" he had asked his father many times.

"Nothing, kid. She doesn't talk about it."

"Why not?"

His father had wrinkled his Irish thin-skinned freckled face into a broad sunny smile. "Who gives a damn?"

His father had met his mother in Tripoli in 1953, while he was stationed there before Qaddafi had kicked the Americans out of Wheelus. She had been a belly dancer in a nightclub.

"You should have seen her," his father told him often, usually after he had drained two six-packs or a fifth of whiskey.

"You should have seen her up there on that dance floor with those veils floating around her and the music pumping out the Arabian beat, and her long black hair flowing. Poetry. The first time I saw her, I said to myself, 'Tom, you black Irish bastard, there's your mate.'" He stared inward and shook his head, as if in disbelief that he had won her. "She was something."

Si could never imagine her that way. By the time he'd arrived, she had grown plump. Occasionally, she had performed for them, briefly and privately, just to please his father.

"You should have seen her." His eyes would grow moist, wistful. "Up there in front of all those gaping guys. God, I

5

love that woman." His mother had giggled when he said this, thumping him playfully.

She had taught Si Arabic. It had annoyed his father.

"He's an American," he would tell her gloomily when mother and son chirped together in that alien language. It had been a needless concern, and when Si finally started school and did well, his father let them talk together without commenting.

They had named him Osiris Sean Kelly. His father had always called him Si, but his mother never used the diminutive. It wasn't an embarrassment to him until the other kids taunted him.

"What kind of stupid name is that?" some kid invariably said when a teacher called it out in class.

"Egyptian," he would say aggressively in self-defense. Later, he would learn it was the name of an Egyptian god, but he would never tell them that.

"They call me Si," he would say. "Only my mother calls me Osiris," he would explain.

"He was the most important Egyptian god of all," his mother told him. It was only later that he found out about Isis.

Because he was an only child, she smothered him with maternal excess, invoking a thousand don'ts, can'ts, and be carefuls, as if he were perpetually walking a tightrope across some dark abyss. Danger was everywhere, except near her watchful eye. As he grew older, he became guilt-stricken because he was vaguely ashamed of her. The Arab woman, they called her behind her back. She hadn't made much attempt to assimilate. Even his father had abandoned any attempt to help her achieve that, although he'd tried to make Si a Roman

Catholic. But his mother's invocation of Allah confused him and finally became the despair of the priests.

"When he gets old enough, he'll choose for himself," his father said. By the time he was old enough, he forgot to make a choice, preferring to be nothing.

"Praise be to Allah," his mother would say often. "For giving me the gift of Osiris." She could never get enough of touching him, watching him, fussing over him. That, too, embarrassed him, especially if others were around, particularly his friends.

"Allah, shmallah," his father would say, mimicking the stereotype.

They were an odd triumvirate. To most people, he was a Mick, and he liked it that way. The Israeli victories had made the Arabs seem like bumblers. For most of his life, the Egyptians were pariahs. Only when King Tut's treasures made their rounds and Sadat went to Jerusalem did it become acceptable to be an Egyptian. He made a point of telling people that he was, as he called it, a half-breed, an absurd combination at that.

Farrah, his mother, had olive skin. Her green eyes were almond shaped. She had bequeathed that to him, along with her jet-black curly hair and wide mouth. He'd gotten his height from his father as well as the wide shoulders and thin hips. His nose was a hybrid, straight like his father's, with flared nostrils like his mother's.

But most people took him for an Irishman. He was, after all, a Kelly. And he had long since stopped asking her what it was like in Egypt.

Then, suddenly, it became the most important thing in his life.

Her Allah had picked a terrible time for her to die. Worse, he had made the going painful and consuming. Si was certain she was thinking that, sitting propped up in the bed they had moved to the sunniest spot in the living room of their little apartment in Brooklyn Heights. He had come down from Cornell in the spring, just two months from graduation, hoping that the deathwatch would not inhibit his preparation for finals.

"I can't sit up there, knowing what is happening," he told his father, who had lamely protested. The distraught man was glad that Si came, although his getting his degree meant a great deal to his parents. Tom Kelly had never gone to college, and Farrah could barely read Arabic, no less English. He had promised them both that he would study and take his finals.

"It's only a B.A. in liberal arts," he told them, not daring to reveal that it didn't matter much to him. He was swimming in indecision.

There were other things he could not tell them as well. He felt, as he put it to himself, estranged. For some unknown reason, he could not run with the crowd, could not find peers. He felt foreign in what should have been his own milieu. It wasn't thrilling to douse his mind with pot or booze, or his body with indiscriminate sex.

He tried to put up a brave facade of evaluation. But that grew difficult and boring. He blamed it on the times, then on himself. Perhaps, he decided, he needed something to prove himself, to display his courage, his martyrdom for a brave cause, his superior goodness. Something!

How could he tell them that?

By the time he had arrived home, his mother's skin seemed to have turned to thin gray paper. Her eyes had sunk into their almond-shaped hollows, although, when the sun filled the room, the green shone like emeralds. They had placed two chairs beside the bed and took turns embracing her, sitting on the bed, while she remained lost in a perpetual kayf, a blank mental haze. Now it was drug induced.

"She was something, Si," his father repeated as they sat in the quiet room, as if she weren't present at all. "Standing up there on that stage, a soft lovely beauty, like a flower. I was so proud of her. So damned proud." Then he turned to her and caressed her hands, squeezing them. "You were something, baby." It had been his "moment," the high point of his life.

Grief consumed him now and, already, there was a hint of his future as he sipped whiskey endlessly, giving in to the curse that somehow she had helped him avoid until now. In many ways, Si had thought her passive in her relations with his father, and only now could he glimpse her silent power over him. They belonged to each other. His father had actually said that many times, but, up to then, he hadn't absorbed its meaning. *So that is love*, he thought.

When her mind was lucid, she spoke very little. He knew she was resigned to death. Yet something he saw in her nagged at him, some shadow, even stronger than the specter of impending death. Occasionally, in her pain-racked sleep, she would mumble a single Arabic word, *"Battal."*

"What did she say?" his father asked.

"I don't know," he lied. *Battal* meant bad. She was too young to die, forty-three. To Si, she had been a good, blameless, and loving woman. Watching her now, he realized how little he knew about her. Except that she loved him and he loved her. Yet even as he observed her agony, he felt that she had cheated him, had left him too much in the dark about herself.

When she emerged from her drugged kayf, he tried to ease the anguish with talk of the future.

"When you get better, we'll go to the Tut exhibit at the Metropolitan Museum. The whole town has Tut fever," he had told her that day. He had been surprised at the interest, but had postponed going himself for fear it would leave him unmoved.

She smiled and nodded.

"Egypt is in. Between Sadat and Tut, the eyes of the world are on Egypt," he said.

She looked at him for a long time, until tears spilled over the lower lids onto her cheeks. Coming close, he kissed her and gently wiped away the tears.

"Isis," she whispered, her lips quivering.

"Isis?" The word was certainly clear. He had, by then, stopped explaining his name to others. Most people thought it had Greek origins. But Isis?

Isis, he had learned, was the goddess of heaven and earth in Pharaonic times, wife of Osiris, god of the underworld and judge of the dead. It was Osiris who decided who would or would not have eternal life. He had always snickered at that. Osiris was the son of the sun god Ra, supreme arbiter among the bickering gods. Set was Osiris's brother. Set murdered Osiris, cut him into fourteen parts, and dispensed the parts throughout Egypt.

The fourteen parts signified the fourteen provinces of Egypt. But his beloved mate, Isis, was determined to put him back together again. She searched everywhere for his missing parts. But all she could find were thirteen. The missing piece was Osiris's sex organs.

They never found those. The myth always embarrassed him. "What a ridiculous name," he had protested.

"It is a necessary name," his mother had said, which always puzzled him. Osiris and Isis were like two halves of a riddle.

"I'm Osiris," he reminded her gently that day, misunderstanding. He thought her mind was slipping and she had gotten confused.

"My baby," she said.

His father was not in the room then. She started to speak, in Arabic. His father would not have understood in any event.

"My baby, Isis," she repeated.

"I don't understand, Mother." He thought she was hallucinating. She had gripped his arm. Her fingers were like claws, digging into his flesh.

The spring sun was setting, and the shadows were lengthening across the bed. The fading light made her gaunt face skeletal, eerie. She tried to rise from the bed, frightening him, since she was too frail and weak. The cancer had almost consumed her. Embracing her, he tried to force her down against the pillows. Oddly, her strength persisted.

"What is it, Mother?" he cried, feeling the panic begin. He could feel death in the room. Looking into her eyes, he could see that they were surprisingly clear. Her gaze turned on him like a blinding floodlight.

"You have a sister, Osiris."

"A sister?" Then it came to him.

"Isis?"

She nodded.

The power of the revelation seemed to erupt inside of her. She was forcing it out of herself. Her chest was heaving with the effort, and her breath came in short gasps. She struggled to expel it.

"In Egypt?"

She nodded again. He knew she was dying now, but could not bring herself to go with this thing embedded in her.

"I left her in Cairo, the City of the Dead. In the tomb of the family Al-Hakim. Come to my sanctuary."

"I don't understand," he cried, embracing her. She was gathering all of her strength as she tried to control her speech.

"There was no other choice. He would have killed my Isis, my baby. So I left her with the woman in the tomb of the Al-Hakim family in the City of the Dead. 'Come to my sanctuary.' Above the entrance. It is written."

His mind was clogged with questions. But he dared not broach them. There didn't seem time. She had begun to perspire, struggling for every moment of life.

"She was born the first of December 1951 in Alexandria," she panted. "Isis." He felt her sinking. The sudden burst of strength was all she had left. Watching her face, he saw her lips open, her eyes narrow; an attitude he had never seen before, as if she were poised to spit out some horrible curse.

"Zakki," she cried, clearly, in a voice he had never heard, a curse crawling out of the smoldering pit of her anguished soul.

Then she sank deeper into the pillows, slowly closing her soft lips again, forming a sweet, contented smile, while her eyes looked upward, sightless, into the void.

"Mama," he cried, embracing his dead mother's body.

Sometime later, he felt his father's hands touch his shoulder and gently move him away.

They buried his mother in a Roman Catholic cemetery in Brooklyn. It seemed an incongruous setting for her burial: dour pink Irish faces watching tearlessly as the priest offered the blessings of Jesus. Dust to dust. Ashes to ashes. The exit seemed contrived, fraudulent. For his father's sake, he protested only in his heart.

The Kellys had had little to do with her. Not that they hadn't tried. But she was always that strange Arab woman that Tom had married. There was no enmity, only indifference. She had, after all, made Tom Kelly happy.

They went, father and son, back to the apartment, feeling lost in the emptiness. She had not said much, but the presence of her love for them had filled the place. Si's father brought out a bottle of whiskey and filled two tumblers. He picked his up, lifting it upward in acknowledgment of his son, then put it down again, unable to hold back the quaver in his voice.

"She had no right to go first. You had no right," he said to the walls. Si felt his heart break for him.

"She was something," his father said, when he had controlled himself, repeating his mantra. "We belonged to each other." He lifted the glass to his lips and swallowed the liquid in a long greedy draught, his pale gray face flushing quickly.

"She said nothing? She mentioned nothing?" Si asked. It was his litany now. He had told him about Isis.

"Not one damned word."

"Why?"

"Guilt, maybe," his father said after a long pause, refilling his glass. "Hell, it wouldn't have mattered. I'd love her any way, any time."

"All those years. Living with that." They sat for a long time in silence.

"She loved you, Si," Tom Kelly said, his tongue thickening. "She wanted more kids. But it was just not in the cards."

"And she never talked about it? Hinted? Never spoke of her past life?"

"It wasn't important."

"But it was," Si protested.

"She just never mentioned it."

"All that brooding. All that kayf. It wasn't emptiness at all. She was thinking about Isis. My sister." He tried to drown the word with a gulp of whiskey, but it burned going down and he coughed, nearly spitting it up.

After a while the alcohol turned his father maudlin. Si suffered it as long as he could, then went out.

He never went back to Cornell. Instead, he roamed the streets and tried to cajole his father into not being dependent entirely on the crutch of alcohol. He didn't help much.

"How else can an Irishman drown his grief?" Tom Kelly had cried, pouring another deep drink, wallowing in the cliché.

"She wouldn't have wanted that."

"I know. You don't know about love yet, son. It's like belong-
ing. Like your place." Tears brimmed in his eyes. "I've lost my
place. I'm nowhere."

Si reached out and touched his father's shoulders. "You've
got me, Dad," he said, feeling foolish.

His father nodded. Si knew it could never be same.

He stood in line for hours at the King Tut exhibit. Moving
slowly in the line, he listened to the effusiveness of those who
viewed the objects. What right had they to comment, he told
them silently, maliciously? *They have no connection with it.*

He studied the golden death mask of Tutankhamun,
imagining the youth's face stripped of its false beard of majesty.
The slopes of the eyes, downward toward the flared nose,
were outlined with thick black lines of eye liner. In their
centers the upper segments of the pupils were lost in the
upper fold of their almond shape. He knew those eyes. They
were his mother's. His own. He shivered and coughed to
hide his confusion. The lips were wide, sensual. Like his? He
was sure he was fantasizing, and he ridiculed himself and
moved on.

His namesake, of course, was there, in color photographs, a
mummified figure, complete with striped headdress, greeting
the boy Pharaoh in the glorious afterlife. He carefully read the
text, explaining how the boy king was "given life forever and
ever." The idea moved him, and his knees shook. What was he

feeling, he wondered. Kinship? The boy had died more than three thousand years ago.

He bought a poster of Tutankhamun's golden face, excited with a strange idea that had surfaced in his mind. He went into a drugstore not far from the museum and bought eye liner, pancake makeup, and lipstick. He could think of nothing else on the subway ride back to Brooklyn. He rushed into the apartment, unfurled the poster near the hanging mirror in the living room, and mounted it with clear tape on the wall beside it. The apartment was empty, although his mother's presence, her scent and spirit, still seemed to permeate the place.

Working carefully, through trial and error, rubbing off the makeup with a moist towel when he made a miscalculation, he applied the pancake and the eye liner until he had it right. Then he painted his lips lightly with the pink lipstick. Taking a dish towel, he fashioned a headdress as best he could. A reddish beam of the setting sun reflected itself in the mirror and bathed the room in a faint orange glow. The face in the poster was gold, which he could not match, but as the sun faded and his eyes probed the face in the mirror, he was sure that he could see the resemblance.

"I am your seed," he whispered.

He studied this new face in the mirror for a long time, trying to create within himself that sense of kayf that was his mother's refuge. But he could not find it. His mind raced with thoughts. Perhaps he had overintellectualized it. He felt embarrassed. Finally, he washed off the makeup, unfastening the poster and rolling it up again.

When Si's father came home, his eyes were rheumy with weariness, grief, and alcohol. They sat in the living room for a long time, not speaking, letting the darkness hide them, hoping that the woman, Farrah, wife and mother, would come back and turn on the lights.

"I miss her, Si," his father's voice croaked out of the silence.

"Me, too."

"She wasn't talkative. I never really knew what she was thinking. But she was there." He was silent again. "You know what I mean."

"And she never told you any of it?" Si asked, again. It was still incredible to him that she could live with him for a quarter of a century and tell him nothing about it, the old life. Isis.

"It didn't matter," he said again.

"Maybe because she bottled it up, it killed her." He knew it was stupid when he said it, and it set off a long silent pause of brooding.

"I've got to go there, Dad," Si said. The pronouncement neglected all practical considerations. They hadn't much money. Whatever his father had, had gone into his education.

"Where?"

"Egypt. To find..." His tongue seemed to choke him. "Isis." The idea rose out of the depths of himself, surprising him as he had not been conscious of its percolation.

"I knew you would," his father said. "Maybe that's why she told you and not me." Did Si detect the faint jealousy? His father stood up shakily, and went to his bedroom, coming back with something wrapped in tissue paper. He unwrapped it and held up a gold coin on a thin gold chain. It was the thing she wore around her neck. It had become so much a part of her, he had forgotten to notice it.

"She wanted you to have this." He dangled it in front of him. "It's supposed to be worth something. An old coin. She never told me where she got it, but she was wearing it the day I met her. She never took it off."

Si took the coin and rubbed it between his fingers, searching, perhaps, for some vestige of his mother's old warmth.

"Take it to a coin dealer," his father said, sitting down again.

"She wanted me to go, Dad," Si said after a while. He was sure of that now.

To his surprise, a Manhattan coin dealer gave him three thousand dollars, explaining that the coin might be worth more in the future, but was still fairly common, minted in the last years of the Ottoman empire, about 1912. Immediately, he rushed to the airline office, bought a ticket to Cairo, round-trip, with the return open, and applied for his passport.

For the first time in a long while, he felt he had shed his ennui. He had never really come to grips with it, although he could sense the same affliction in many of his fellow students. Sometimes, he felt as if his whole generation was in a swamp of indecision, isolated, alone, like himself. A number of his classmates had taken refuge in some of the various cults that had sprouted up on the campus. He had resisted that as well, and all the other "-ologies" and causes that were then fashionable.

Now, suddenly, his mother had given him a cause, a mission. To find Isis. But why? He decided not to answer that question. *She wanted me to do it,* he convinced himself, excited by the potential adventure, a search for something.

"Don't worry about me, Dad," he told his father as they embraced at the airport. He could smell the whiskey breath. "And you take care of yourself."

"Be careful, Osiris," his father said, turning away tear-filled eyes. He had never before called him that.

CHAPTER TWO

H IS HAND BRUSHED THE coffee cup, spilling the black liquid, rattling the saucer, and hurling him into the explosive present. He was conscious again of the amorphous movement of the traffic, human, animal, and vehicular. The cultural shock, he decided, was beginning to subside, and he began to individualize the images before him, recognizing bits and pieces of the helter-skelter moving mass.

He observed how cabs, operated like jitneys, passengers solidly packed, were hailed. It was a precarious operation with hopeful riders lunging like fanatics toward the crawling vehicles without regard for personal safety. He observed, too, the methods of boarding the rattling ramshackle buses, few of recent vintage. A hand reached out to grip metal or human. Some people managed to insinuate themselves into the tightly packed mass. Others hung out of the doorless openings, while ragged kids in pajamas or djellabas hitched on the rear.

Leaving five piastres on the wooden table, now bathed in blinding sunlight, he rushed headlong into the ant herd. The art of getting a taxi would take more practice, he decided, when his first three attempts ended in failure. He opted, instead, for the bus, one that headed vaguely in the direction that the concierge had described. His main landmark would be the Muhammad Ali Mosque in the Citadel, the highest point in Cairo.

Grabbing a handhold on the edge of the doorless opening of the first bus he saw, he hoisted himself aboard, pushing himself into a stench of pulsating bodies. Fearful of being pushed into the interior, he hung partially outside, watching for the mosque. The bus lumbered haltingly through streets teeming with humanity. The bazaars were jammed, saleable goods lined up on the thoroughfares in patternless disarray. Over the stink of smog and food grown gamey in the heat, he caught the familiar whiff of hashish among the distinguishable effluvia. Even the odors were becoming individualized in his mind.

Incomprehensibly, all traffic suddenly stopped dead in its tracks as a barefoot shepherd holding a withered stick herded a flock of sheep across the road, leaving a trail of black pellet droppings in its wake.

Finally, the traffic moved again, and he noted that it was heading upward, snaking through the crowds, past dreary open storefronts, tiny dank coffee shops and cubicle factories where workmen, oblivious to the crowds, plied their various crafts. Bolts of multicolored cloth, throne-like chairs trimmed in gilt, hanging carcasses of lambs, blue and flyspecked in the sun, shared the narrow streets with halfnaked babies, sleeping dogs, goats, donkeys, and mothers whose heavy breasts nursed the eager mouths of their offspring.

The mosque came into view, the tip of its dome glinting in the sun, as it towered above the brown formidable stones of the Citadel wall.

Ahead, he knew, remembering the map, was the vast necropolis, the City of the Dead, just across from the old Roman aqueduct. He had no idea what to expect. Cemeteries to him were neat silent monuments to the dead, studded with polished granite stones, like the place where his mother was buried. He had learned that the population explosion had brought people from the villages into the city. Since housing was impossible to find, they had simply moved into untended mausoleums and had actually begun to establish some sort of living society among these relics of the dead.

He saw it, stretching beside the wide road that ran parallel to the aqueduct, in the center of which ran a green electric tram, surprisingly modern, although already revealing the first signs of poor maintenance. As far as the eye could see, stretching almost to the foot of the high Muquatt Hills, their sides showing the stone cuttings of distant centuries, he saw long lines of attached mausoleums whose walls, neutered by time, crumbled in the mist of dust and heat.

Puffs of smoke floated over the mausoleums' domes, attesting to the existence of pulsating life within. The skeletons, he imagined, slumbering beneath the ground in their dark sepulchres, seemed incidental, intruders actually, in the mundane pursuits of the living.

People walked the narrow rock-strewn streets, going about their daily chores, just as they did in the nearby high-rise slums, where sheep and goats poked their heads over the balconies between the banners of drying wash hung like welcoming pennants exhibited to greet a conquering army.

Jumping off the bus, he walked under a crumbling gate, where a crowd watched two youths attempt to repair an aging motor scooter. He followed a narrow road deeper into the necropolis. Some of the mausoleums were locked, showing the attempt by some families to retain some dignity for their dead. In open spaces behind the mausoleums were grave-stones marking sepulchres of families who could not afford mausoleums. Over each stone and mausoleum were faded markings indicating family names, dates of death, and, above these, a Koranic inscription.

He remembered what his mother had said about the inscription above the entrance to the Al-Hakim mausoleum, "Come to my sanctuary." Moving deeper into the necropolis, he soon realized that he was in an impenetrable vaporous maze. Even the brown Muquatt Hills seemed barely distinguishable in the distance. He wandered aimlessly, studying the inscriptions on the mausoleums.

He moved through disparate groups of people. Goats, sheep, and dogs crouched near the walls, husbanding thin slivers of shade. Occasionally, he would glance inside a mausoleum where humans and animals crouched in the darkness. Once, a woman appeared with a battered pot of murky liquid, throw-ing its contents on the dusty road.

Searching the faces he passed, he was unsure who he might ask. Finally, he spotted an older man in a red djellaba. He was not certain whether it was the color or the man's lined and ancient face that provided the visage of authority.

"The mausoleum of the family Al-Hakim," he asked. "Do
you know the way?"

The man watched him thoughtfully, stroking his chin with
inspective curiosity. Si sensed the look of a baksheesh solici-
tation and put his hand in his pocket.

"Al-Hakim," the man repeated, making much of the inquiry.

"'Come to my sanctuary' is the inscription over the doorway," Si pressed, looking for some sign of recognition in the
man's lined face.

To spur the man's memory, he extracted a roll of bills and
handed him an Egyptian pound, knowing it was far out of line
in terms of baksheesh value for such a casual encounter. He
would have given a hundred times more for the correct answer.
The man smiled, showing a mouthful of pink gum. His brown
fingers scooped in the pound.

Sensing someone nearby, Si noted that two young men had
watched the transaction and were eyeing the roll of bills in his
hand. He quickly thrust it into his pocket.

"In that direction," the man said with solemnity. "About
a kilometer." He pointed vaguely down a narrow road that
threaded its way endlessly along the crumbling rows of mausoleums. When Si turned again, the man was gone.

As he walked, he knew he was being followed. Turning, he
saw a group of smiling teenagers in filthy patterned djellabas
watching him, making no attempt to hide their interest. When
he moved, they moved in tandem. The deeper he ventured into
the necropolis, the more disoriented he started to become.

"The mausoleum of Al-Hakim?" he asked a youngish woman.

She held a naked baby on her hip. Flies swarmed around the
child's eyes, nose, and mouth. The woman made no attempt

to shoo them away. He repeated his inquiry, but he could not resist scattering the flies on the baby's face. The woman looked at him as if he were mad and flounced away, indignant.

Stumbling into an alley of makeshift shops set up in the doorways of mausoleums, he saw a man slicing a carcass of bluish fly-encrusted lamb. A woman squatted in the shade of a broken wall near a pile of shriveled oranges. A young man scooped brown beans from a sack into a funnel of newspaper. Turning, he glared openly at his pursuers. They were relentless now. It was impossible to dismiss the growing sense of danger he felt.

The sun rose higher through the smog and he felt it burn his forehead and nose. His T-shirt was soaked with perspiration and the dust began to cake on his exposed feet. He felt as if he were "it" in some bizarre game, the object of which was to taunt him with confusion and fear.

When he turned a corner, they turned a corner. There were about six of them, stalking him. The danger was now as tangible as the oppressive heat.

He was tempted to shout, "*Bolis*," the Arabic word for police, but the lack of any authority and sense of anarchy were too compelling.

The tug on his sleeve startled him. He had just flattened himself against a doorway, a futile action, since it seemed to make him even more conspicuous. People looked at him strangely. Every person in sight was a potential beacon. There was no way to lose himself, and the tug on his sleeve seemed like the first onslaught of his pursuers.

He found himself looking into large luminous brown eyes set in a smooth coppery, high-cheeked face. It belonged to a tallish, slender boy with curly hair cropped close to the skull. Si grasped the boy's upper arm, feeling the thin bones beneath the pajama-striped djellaba. His grip tightened and he was sure he was hurting the boy, who bore the pain without acknowledgment.

"Follow me," the boy whispered in Arabic. There was no time for any decision, and Si responded mechanically to what seemed like a sympathetic imperative. He released his grip and the boy flashed by, loping, graceful as a deer. Si's reaction was mindless, automatic, and he followed the striped djellaba. It looked like a billowing sail in a heavy breeze.

Giving himself up entirely to the boy's whim, Si followed swiftly, turning, crouching, moving along a low wall of crumbling stones, then into another narrow alley lined with small mausoleums. The people he saw were always the same in texture, color and odor, as if the same group had been assembled and reassembled, like a traveling road show.

His heart pumped heavily, spurred by the heat and exertion, but the boy was relentless, never pausing, never looking back, always that wisp of striped sail just ahead. Occasionally, he disappeared. But soon the tug on his sleeve signaled him, and they were off again, as if the djellaba sail was tacking on a spurt of strong wind.

Time seemed suspended. The fiery disc of sun was paralyzed in space. The brown hills of Muquatt disappeared completely in a shimmering heat fog. The sliver of billowing stripes suddenly burrowed into a low tunnel, and Si followed without hesitation. It struck him suddenly that he was Alice following the White Rabbit. He smiled at the image.

Crouching, he moved along the dark tunnel, which continued interminably, following the sound of the boy's crunching step ahead of him. Then there was only silence.

Hesitating, he lowered himself into a deeper crouch, testing the blackness with his hand, which he moved like a flap over his eyes. An acrid, dusty flavor coated his tongue and as he tried to swallow it away, a burst of light brightened the tunnel's edge and he hurried toward it.

The boy was sitting cross-legged in a vault lined with rectangular stones, the upper walls of which were lined with a deep shelf. A candle rested in a depression on the stone floor, feebly illuminating the small chamber. The boy, he realized, had fixed it up into a kind of all-purpose room with a straw pallet and a potpourri of cast-off household objects, a chipped plate, a dented metal cup, a battered basin, and a pile of dog-eared Arabic paperbacks. Si could not stand to his full height, finally squatting to face the boy.

"This is my place," the boy said, proudly. Si looked around, letting his eyes roam the squared walls, grateful now for the instinct that made him follow the boy.

"Better for the living than the dead," the boy said. Behind the words was a faint, lilting good-humored giggle. "Robbers have been pinching the bodies for years." The space was obviously an abandoned sepulchre, the shelf reserved for bodies.

"You live here?" Si asked.

"Welcome to my house," the boy said, his full lips curling over perfect white teeth. Si wondered if the boy was teasing him. But the boy's good humor was disarming. Si put out his hand and the boy took it, revealing a supple strength.

"Trouble was looking for you, my friend," the boy said, releasing Si's hand.

"I wasn't looking for it. I was stupid. Tempting fate. What would they have done?"

"At best, a tap on the head and you would be parted with your wealth."

"Wealth?" He patted his pants pocket. He had cashed fifty Egyptian pounds out of his five hundred dollars' worth of traveler's checks, which he had pasted under the baseboard of his hotel bed.

Suddenly suspicious of the boy's motives, Si waited for the outstretched palm. He was being set up for some baksheesh, he decided. Nevertheless, he was grateful for the rescue. The boy was obviously streetwise, a survivor. In the candlelight, his face looked delicate, the chin rising gracefully from a perch above a swan-like neck.

"I am an honest businessman," the boy said.

"That figures," Si said, happy to have the transaction in the open. "Hell, kid, I'm grateful. I wasn't getting anywhere." He recalled his sense of mission. "I'm looking for the Al-Hakim mausoleum."

The boy grew thoughtful, rubbing his chin in concentration. "Al-Hakim," he repeated. "Al-Hakim."

"'Come to my sanctuary' written over the tomb," Si offered. Having seen the endless lines of crumbling mausoleums, Si was now beginning to despair of ever locating the place. Besides, he had no idea what he might find. Still, it was the only starting point he had.

The boy continued to rub his chin. Then he nodded tentatively. "I might know it," he said.

"Might?" It seemed like a ploy.

"On the western side. Closer to the hills." The boy nodded, reaffirming his knowledge. "Many children. An old woman who cares for them."

Remembering the old man who had misguided him, Si was suspicious. The boy must have seen his doubts.

"I live here," he explained. "I know this place. I know the mausoleum of Al-Hakim. It is not as mysterious as you think." He paused. "I will take you there."

"And how much will that cost me?"

The boy stood up and paced the stone crypt. His height just missed the roof.

"I work by a time factor," he said solemnly.

Si resisted a compulsive giggle. The boy seemed quite serious now, businesslike.

"Like a taxi," Si muttered.

The boy nodded.

"And the meter is running?"

The boy stroked his chin.

"Already you have engaged five piastres' worth of time." Si reached into his pocket, but the boy's hand stayed him. "I trust you," the boy said, smiling. Then he turned toward the tunnel exit, stooped, and was off again.

Soon Si was once more following the moving striped sail, heading toward a dot of sunlight in the distance. The light was blinding and he had to press against his eyeballs with his fingers, opening them gradually to admit the piercing brightness. When he could see, he noted that the boy was waiting, his graceful neck twisting like that of a cautious bird.

Moving with difficulty through the narrow crowded "streets" of the necropolis, they found little refuge from the relentless sun. There seemed no pattern to the boy's journey. But then there was no pattern to anything in this place. Even the edges of mortality seemed frayed and ill-defined.

He found himself searching the faces of the women they passed, particularly those who might be about Isis's age. But even the differences between various ages seemed blurred as well.

They moved for what seemed an eternity. Occasionally, the boy would stop, survey a line of grim mausoleums, and move on. Si followed obediently.

A visit to the main branch of the Brooklyn Public Library had offered some sketchy information on Muslim burial habits. Wealthier families built mausoleums over sepulchres, not only to house the dead but the living as well. Relatives paid their respects by visiting and sometimes spending the night. Many had paid caretakers to guard the mausoleums, but as the families died out, mausoleums were abandoned and quickly occupied by an army of dispossessed, impoverished settlers from the countryside, who were lured to the city by the promise of a better life.

Now, the vast necropolis was a squalid slum, housing hundreds of thousands of people. The government, obviously beset by an impossible housing situation, looked the other way. Cairo had been built to house a million people, not the eight million who lived there now. To many, it was still, obviously, a burial place. But, to those who lived there, it was home.

Si had looked into many of the mausoleum's dark interiors crowded with people and animals. Ubiquitous, smiling, dark, flyspecked children and scrawny animals wallowed together on the stone or hard mud floors. Some of the mausoleums, oddly, had television antennas poking from crumbling roof-tops, like rotting cornstalks in half-harvested fields.

Incongruous as that was, the sound of blaring pop music— the Bee Gees, Si noted—screamed out from one of the open interiors. Was this the past or future? he wondered, spitting a wad of saliva into the brown earth as if to validate the present. Occasionally, Si sensed that the boy had made a wrong turn, retracing his steps. He did not let him out of his sight, fearful that he might never find his way out of this place.

"There. That one," the boy said, pointing. At the entrance stoop, an ancient woman in an incredibly filthy black malaya squatted, surrounded by a group of half-naked children. Ignoring them, Si moved closer and inspected the faded stone facade, his fingers tracing the Arabic words engraved there. His heart pounded as he saw the words "AlHakim. Come to my sanctuary."

The children reached out to touch his legs as he moved past the old woman into the dark inner chamber of the mausoleum. The boy followed. A drowsing old man lay in a corner, indiffer-ent to their entrance. A young woman sat on the floor nursing a baby, while three preadolescent girls sat cross-legged on the floor weaving mats.

Beyond, in another chamber, a group of dark adult male faces stared at a flickering television set on which a bearded, turbaned man read passages from the Koran. The faces turned toward him briefly, unmoved from their solemnity, and he felt the sense of harsh intrusion. Over everything hung the smell of rotted fruit, unwashed bodies, a persistent stink of body wastes and the acrid odor of hashish.

The only alert eyes in the darkened hovel were those of the young woman nursing the baby from a flaccid breast. As the baby nursed, she patted its buttocks and smiled. Always the smiles. It was unnerving. What was there to smile about here?

"Is this your house?" he asked the nursing woman gently, watching the boy's face for signs of disapproval. In this atmosphere, he sensed, tone and protocol were important.

She looked toward the drowsing old man, whose heavy lids occasionally opened, watching them with little curiosity. He was obviously ill.

"Have you lived here a long time?"

"Always," the woman said, giggling suddenly, contemplating Si as if he were an idiot. Was this Isis? he wondered, searching the woman's face for some characteristic feature of his mother. But her face was too dark, hinting at splashes of Nubian blood.

"I'm looking for someone who lived here in 1952," he asked politely. The question seemed ludicrous. These people had no sense of time. "She was a baby then. My sister."

The nursing child must have pinched the young woman's nipple and she slapped its behind. It let go of the breast and squealed. She squelched it by stuffing the nipple back between its lips.

"Ask the old man," she said, pointing. The three girls weaving on the floor laughed, mocking him.

Si squatted beside the old man and the boy did the same. The people watching television paid no attention. The sudden interest in him seemed to rouse the old man, and his wrinkled chicken-skin eye pouches opened to semi-alertness. Straightening a dirty knitted skullcap, he rose to a sitting position and leaned against the wall.

"Sheikh," Si began, using the respectful word, watching the old head cock toward him. Si raised his voice. "Sheikh," he repeated.

The old man nodded. Si hesitated, annoyed by his own loud voice. The three weaving girls watched him, eager for the diversion. The nursing lady began a rhythmic slapping on the baby's buttocks. From the other room, the monotonous recital continued.

"Did you live here in 1952?"

The old man frowned, but the expression in the eyes indicated that the man was quietly calculating. "Twenty-seven years ago," Si added to buttress the flicker of recollection. The old man nodded. A group of children clustered in the doorway, watching them.

"Do you remember a girl baby? Isis?" Si's eyes, now accustomed to the dim light, watched the old man's face. It was impassive, perhaps from habit. He shook his head.

"My mother brought her here," Si pressed. "Her name was Farrah."

Behind him, the old woman who squatted in the doorway seemed to stir, shifting closer. There was, he knew, an absurdity about the idea, a mad presumption that there was any reasonable connection between these people and what had occurred twenty-seven years ago. Still, he persisted. One had to start somewhere.

Squatting there, Si watched the old man, uncomprehending, irritated by his invisibility. In the other room, the recital continued without pause. Even the children who had filled the doorway had wandered out again into the dusty sunbaked yard.

"No," Si mumbled. *Something, indeed, is wrong,* he thought.

"If you know something, you are doing a cruel thing," he said. But his voice was a whisper and he was certain the old man did not hear him. A wave of frustration overwhelmed him and he stood up.

"Where the hell is that little bastard?" he shouted in English. The faces in front of the television set turned toward him, their features lost in the shadows.

"You're all assholes," he said, as if he were intoning some abiding truth. "To accept this shit." He whispered the last statement, struggling to tamp down his anger. He felt put-upon, victimized, by all of them, by this preposterous place.

Stepping outside, he scowled at the old lady and the half-naked children. But he reserved his coldest contempt for the boy who had led him here. He had not paid him. It was comforting to remember, somehow softening his rage. He stood in the blazing sun, confused, unable to act.

"Go away," a cracked voice said from behind him.

Turning, he confronted the old woman's face, haggard, wrinkled like a prune. One eye had a cast to it. The other, squinting and black in its wrinkled sack, seemed like the evil eye of his mother's earliest admonitions. "You must avoid the evil eye," she had warned when he was a boy, invoking an image that had once frightened him into submission.

He recalled how much he had feared such ideas, the evil eye, the wrath of Allah, the sting of the unseen cobra. When he grew older, he had admonished her. He was sure she believed it.

"Superstitious camel dung," he shouted at the old woman, feeling now the cutting edge of his own exhaustion, consumed by the dust and heat and squalor, the jet lag, the stink, the hopeless illogic of it.

"Listen, you witch," he hissed. "I'm not afraid of you."

"You will never find her," the old woman said. A dribble of spit lingered on the lower lip of her toothless mouth.

"So you do know something."

Two younger men came out of the other room and came toward them.

"He comes to make trouble," the old crone cackled in an angry voice.

"Trouble?" The idea was confusing and he wanted to protest. The sense of menace was pervasive. It was time to retreat, to sort things out. He hadn't expected this.

"I'll be back," he murmured, moving away, refusing to run, hoping that his slow withdrawal would show them his determination.

He was soon bobbing again like a piece of flotsam in this river of misery, totally disoriented. Stopping people to ask directions on how to get out of this mad hellhole, he received conflicting information. Nothing was visible in the distance. The brown hills of Muquatt were completely obliterated in the shimmering polluted heat. He was lost in nowhere.

Yet even that sense of floating rootlessness was less troubling than his confrontation in the Al-Hakim mausoleum. There, he had felt a sense of psychic danger. Physical danger he could understand, and strangely he felt immune to that. What did it matter how he felt? He was a sitting duck for anyone taking it into his head to be belligerent. He did not look behind him as he had done earlier, oblivious to being followed, pushing forward relentlessly, determined to get loose of this place, the living and the dead, and get back to his hotel.

The recollection of his shabby urine-smelling room, with its peeling green wallpaper and opaque glass wall designs of ibis-headed gods, was almost comforting. He had not slept well, tumbling into the rickety bed after his flight from London. The outside din had been relentless. Obviously, he had learned the hard way, the city never slept. Inside, the ceiling fan screeched on its faulty bearing, while the toilet dripped and faceless guests pursued noisy nightmares.

Then, suddenly, the boy appeared in front of him. He had found a comparatively shady alleyway where the mausoleum walls were high enough to create an envelope of shadows. The boy was actually leaning against a wall, graceful as a high-legged bird, his long neck stretched in an elastic furtive gesture, as if he were looking about him at all sides at once. He had, it seemed, deliberately chosen this spot.

"I should break your ass," Si said, but the benign, smooth face with the enigmatic smile had already disarmed him.

"I keep my word," the boy said, straightening and urging by his look for him to fall in step.

"You owe me one helluva explanation."

"Later."

The boy held a tapered finger to his lips, then moved swiftly through the crowds, taking unexpected turnings to avoid curious onlookers. Si discovered that they were surprisingly close to the edge of the necropolis, and in a remarkably short time they had passed through a crumbling archway and were moving swiftly down a wide traffic-choked street.

They walked along the edge of a ruined aqueduct for some time, then turned into a warren of narrow streets lined with decaying buildings. As before, the boy moved swiftly and Si had to jog to keep up.

In the midst of a crowded, noisy bazaar, the boy stopped.

"Where are you staying?" the boy asked.

"Hotel Genaina." The boy recognized the name and gave him careful instructions.

"We do business now," the boy said when he had completed the directions.

"Not until you tell me what was going on back there."

He watched the boy's eyes grow inert, peering outward through a self-protective glaze, not unlike that of the old man. It reminded him of his previous frustration and made him angry.

"Dammit. I have to know," Si said.

"We must continue the original business," the boy said quietly. Si watched him, shook his head, and threw some coins onto the ground. The boy looked at them, stooped, and gathered them up.

"I'll see you around, kid." He took a few steps and, for some reason, could not resist a last look at the boy.

A gust of breeze had flattened his djellaba, and the background of sharp sunlight made the material translucent. He saw the distinct unmistakable outlines of high small breasts. The boy was not a boy at all.

CHAPTER THREE

Mocked by the ibis-headed god on the translucent panel that separated the toilet closet from the sleeping portion of his hotel room, Si lay in a pool of sweat on the bumpy bed. They had not changed the sheets or made the bed properly, and when he turned restlessly, he could see the edges of the stained mattress. The ceiling fan squeaked and labored ineffectively. From the streets rose the perpetual din. Auto horns tooted like irrepressible bratty children vying for attention. Noxious fumes seeped into the room, adding a choking pall to the overheated air.

Too many people, he thought, glimpsing an image of a slithering mass of humanity locked in a snake pit. Why had his mother left Isis in this cesspool? Twenty-seven years was a nodule on a pimple on the ass of time in this weird shithouse of a country. He acknowledged that he had deliberately sought out the lower depths to spare expenses and the visit to the strange necropolis was obviously inhabited by the poverty stricken, random squatters and lost souls.

Whatever wealth existed was in the hands of those who lived elsewhere. But why would his mother leave her child in such a squalid environment? Perhaps it might not have been as bad then. Had his saintly mother deliberately abandoned her baby? It was completely out of character. Then why hadn't she gone back to claim her child? It puzzled him. Tears welled in his eyes.

The sweat pools in his bed gave him the sensation of melting while the fan on the ceiling pressed on valiantly, its rhythmic screeching like the dying gasps of a faulty heart.

He tried to shut out the sounds and smells, to concentrate only on actualizing the image of his half sister. He tried to fathom the connection. Wasn't that what his mother had intended? Isis and Osiris. Like Damon and Pythias, Romeo and Juliet, the sun and the moon.

What did she look like? Was she black-haired, fair-skinned like him? What did she feel? Had she brooded, searched for, yearned to touch her lost mother? How much pain was there? Pain of loneliness? Pain of loss? Pain of abandonment? It was then he felt the corrosive power of guilt. Had he taken away all of Isis's mother love?

A sharp stab tingled the flesh of his lower thigh. He slapped and crushed a fat insect. It had bitten him and he felt the welt rise and an itch begin that destroyed his drowsiness. His eyes remained shut, but his ears could not close themselves to the sounds.

Finally, they became indistinguishable, like a vast symphony orchestra straining for a single effect. A discordant note intruded, a scratching sound. It seemed like some animal, a dog or cat. He sat up, listening. He was on the floor above the street. A doorway led to a small narrow balcony. Apparently, the price of the room was directly related to the distance from the human swarm. He had deliberately taken the least expensive room.

Padding silently toward the slatted balcony door, he peeked out through one of the many busted and awry slats. A person was out there. No animal.

The door opened and the streetlights' reflection sketched the unmistakable outlines of a human being. Si stepped farther into the shadows.

It was only when the presence was halfway into the room that he lunged, locking on to a surprisingly wiry figure who struggled fiercely against his hammerlock.

Dragging the silent grunting carcass, he kicked a light switch with his elbow, and a naked bulb brightened the room.

"Not you!" he said with some disgust when he recognized the face of the girl. Seeing that it was Si, she stopped resisting.

"What the hell..." he began in exasperation as the girl slipped downward, out of his grasp, squatting against the wall.

Moving back, he sat on the bed, suddenly aware of his nakedness, gathering a sheet to cover his exposed genitals. When she raised her head, he noted a bruise around one eye, dried blood near her nostrils, and a swollen upper lip.

"Did I do that?" he asked. She shook her head, obviously too upset to talk. Still holding the sheet in front of him, he drew her a tumbler of water from a green-encrusted wall sink. Her shaking hands reached out and she managed to tip the glass against her swollen lip for a brief sip.

"You also in the thief business?"

She took a deep breath, determined to calm herself, obviously embarrassed by her predicament. Backing toward the bed, he sat down again and watched her.

"I wasn't sure this was your room," she whispered. "The concierge wouldn't let me in."

Crumpled against the wall, she looked pitiful. The naked light made her djellaba seem dirtier than it had looked at the cemetery. Raising her eyes to him, she squinted into the bulb and covered her injured face. Now that he knew she was a female, he detected a note of vanity in the gesture. In deference to her discomfort, he got up and flicked off the switch. A glow of streetlight through the still-opened balcony door illumined the room. The softer light apparently made her more comfortable, and she removed her hand from her face.

"They beat me." She raised her chin pugnaciously. "But I told them nothing. Nothing." He detected her pride in that.

"What was there to tell?"

"Your hotel. Why you were looking for her." She paused. "Isis." She spat out the name like a curse. "I didn't know it was that Isis. Not until I felt it in that place."

He was totally confused.

"Felt what?"

She looked up at him with obvious rebuke.

"That you were looking for Zakki's Isis."

More confusion. He suppressed the questions, waiting for her to gather her thoughts. But the name jogged his memory. Zakki! It was his mother's death rattle.

The girl began, "He is a very important man. Very powerful. He comes frequently in his big car, sitting in the backseat, watching. Always watching. Searching. Everyone knows he is searching for Isis. They say that all the hashish is his. He is very powerful. And guarded by dark, cruel men. He has always come. Everyone will tell you that." She squirmed and probed her bruises with her fingers. "There is no place to hide from him. His men beat me." She lapsed into silence.

"Why?" He could no longer keep it contained. She shrugged.

"No one knows."

"Is he her father?"

She looked at him with sudden alertness, her eyes open now, like big puddles.

"You said she was your sister?"

She seemed to shrink back, in confusion.

"Half sister. We have the same mother."

Frown lines formed on her forehead.

"I've come to find her." He hoped she wouldn't ask why. There would be no adequate way to explain it. Not now. She spared him the explanation, and if she turned the question over in her mind, she avoided giving voice to it.

"They offered money," she said, defiantly.

"You should have taken it." So they would have found him. He refused to show her his fear.

She looked aghast.

"They are cruel men. They kill. There is no way to resist." He wondered if, for some reason, she was overdramatizing, although he felt some self-rebuke in his lack of trust. She was, he already knew, not what she appeared.

"You resisted," he said. It added fuel to her obvious exasperation.

"And look what I got for my troubles," she spat angrily. "I came here to warn you."

"About what?"

She began to sulk.

"Look, I don't know any more about where Isis is than they do," Si explained. "I don't even know what she looks like. All I know is that she was born in December 1951 in Alexandria. That she was left with people in the Al-Hakim mausoleum. Long before both of us were born." He looked at her, trying to appear compassionate. "They know more than I do." He deliberately told her nothing of the last word his mother had uttered.

She remained silent for a long time.

"You're stupid. You don't know a thing. They are not looking for this Isis... this half sister of yours... out of love. You have only to look at them."

"So they'll bang me around a bit. That won't solve anything." A confrontation was inevitable. Perhaps this is what explained his mother's fear. Her silence.

"You're an idiot..." Her voice trailed off. With some difficulty, she edged up the wall and started toward the open balcony door.

"Where do you think you're going?"

"Away from here. From you." Despite her anger, her appearance of defenselessness moved him. "You've caused me enough trouble."

"You better rest," he said gently.

"If they find out that I came here and talked to you, they will break my legs."

"They said that?"

"That's their business. They are very powerful. I believe their threats."

"You'd better rest first."

She clutched her stomach, revealing the full extent of her beating. She had not exaggerated their cruelty. Reaching toward her, he grasped her shoulders. She shrugged him loose.

"You can't go now. You're hurt."

"They could have done worse."

"I know," he said, gripping her arm. She tried to break free, but his hold was strong and her strength had waned.

"Get on the bed. We'll decide in the morning."

"Decide what?" Her terror was palpable as she looked toward the bed.

"I won't rape you." He held her now in a tight embrace, feeling the unmistakable outlines of her slim woman's body. She stiffened, started to protest, then surrendered.

"It is easier to be a man," she murmured.

"Don't be so sure."

"You don't know this land." She was obviously too exhausted to explain further. He lifted her and put her on the bed, placing a pillow under her head. Then he lay down beside her and watched her face. In silhouette, the illusion of her maleness faded.

"How old are you?" he asked.

"Seventeen," she whispered. Her eyes were closed, and she sighed.

"You won't tell."

"Your secret is safe with me." He hid his smile behind his hand. She nodded.

"You're one gutsy little lady," he said.

"Maybe like Isis," she whispered.

"Maybe."

He watched her slip off. When he was sure she was asleep, he leaned over her and kissed her forehead.

Now why did I do that, he wondered?

CHAPTER FOUR

THE DRESSING ROOMS ASSIGNED to the six background belly dancers of Auberge des Pyramides was an accurate measure of their status in the pecking order of entertainers in the big, ornate, Hollywood-fantasy-style nightclub that sat like a brassy whore on the road to the Giza pyramids. The girls were crowded into a hot, semi-partitioned cubicle furnished with six chairs and a sliver of cracked mirror that had to accommodate all of them, despite the fact that their livelihood depended on an elaborate preparation of makeup and costuming.

The state of emotion was one of nerve-racking chaos as the girls approached the zero hour of their performance, the first of two that they would have to do that night. The room was permeated with the odor of female sweat, cheap perfume, and cigarette smoke.

Since it was her first night, Farrah had little experience in coping with these new conditions. Now she had to elbow her way through the wall of flesh to get even a cursory peek at her face, hair, and costume.

Not that it had been much different at every Cairo nightclub that she had played since she was fourteen years old. She was eighteen now, seasoned by a special strategy of survival, which demanded a hard, arrogant crust and an imperious air.

Her father had brought her to the Auberge when she was a tiny girl. Not inside. In the parking lot, where he rubbed the dust off the beautiful cars for baksheesh, most of which went for hash. She didn't know that then, enjoying the sights of the glittering people who went into that magical place and the show people who lingered there between the performances. In the glow of the parking lot's string of colored lights, she resolved to be a dancer. Her father prevailed upon the lounging girls to teach her the complicated routines.

She was not considered an especially gifted belly dancer. But her wide eyes, with big puddles of green, peering out of her oval face like giant emeralds, her luminous black hair, long shapely legs, and glowing olive skin edged her a hairsbreadth over the line that separated the inept from the mediocre.

The impresario, she believed, hired her on merit, although there was the implication that she might have to be especially friendly to the club's most important customers. Being especially friendly while avoiding pregnancy or disease required, she had already learned, far more talent than the dance.

It was better than being, like her mother, a stevedore at the Rod El Farag market, unloading wicker crates of tomatoes for a pittance, while her father spent his days playing backgammon with his cronies at the coffee shop, sucking hash smoke from his water pipe.

Her mother was shamed by Farrah's dancing. But that did not extend to refusing to accept a weekly stipend to feed the ever-burgeoning army of squalid children that fell from her mother's fecund womb. With that, and her father's increasing dependency on his hashish dreams, there was almost nothing left of her salary.

The impresario's tyrannical assistant barged into the dressing room and clapped his hands.

"Hurry, ladies. Hurry now. Highness has arrived."

"Old fat ass," one of the girls grumbled, audible enough to engage the assistant, who treated the dancers like a herd of sheep.

"He is your king, you bitch," he hissed. Despite the power of delegation, he was an object of ridicule. He pointed a finger at the offending girl's nose.

"And when you dance, I want his royal cock to tingle."

"Nothing can make the dead rise again," another girl said.

"Except maybe his tongue," the first girl said with obvious reference to the assistant. He glared at her arrogantly.

"There's not a good fuck in the crowd," he muttered, surveying their state of readiness and moving off.

Farrah listened but said nothing. She liked the idea of the king watching the show. It would certainly be a step up from her usual audiences, a leering mob of businessmen, bent on experiencing the famous fleshpots of the orient. Not that she did not enjoy their admiration, especially during the routine. There was something enormously fulfilling being the center of attention.

The musical cue began and the girls made their last-minute corrections in their makeup and costumes and elbowed their way out to the stage entrance. The assistant checked them out and they moved into the spotlight, an undulating mass of spangles, silk, and female flesh.

They were the warm-up act. The real attraction was the European stars that would follow.

King Farouk was sitting alone at a large ringside table. She could almost touch him, a huge mountain of a man in a red fez, wearing a dark striped suit with a white flower in the lapel. On the table in front of him was a huge silver tray of pastries from which he would delicately pluck one with his chubby fingers and drop it whole into a gaping mouth, washing it down with a glass of cola. At other tables, placed on either side of him were his notorious Albanian bodyguards, alert and watchful over their charge, and a motley group of fawning retainers.

Although she was only one of the six dancers in the opening act, she sensed the flattery of his special observation. Farouk looked heavier than his pictures, if that were possible. But what struck her, more than his physical appearance, was an aura of loneliness. He sat there like some overstuffed, neglected child, an illusion fostered by the fact that his chair was double the proportions of the others.

When their routine was over, the girls gathered in a little courtyard outside of the club, set aside for the entertainers' leisure until the next show began. The management also provided dormitory-style rooms for those girls, like Farrah, who chose to live there rather than home.

It was January and cool and the girls huddled in their light wraps. But it was more comfortable than the steaming dressing rooms or stuffy dormitory. Farrah listened to the girls' gossip, mostly about people she did not know. It was of little interest to her and she made no effort to join in. Besides, she was a loner and few people had ever earned her trust. Her father had come the closest. But in the end, he had betrayed her with his habit.

A man appeared in the entranceway. He flicked a spent cigarette on the hard dirt floor of the courtyard and ground it out with his heel. The gesture told everything about him, arrogance and guile, cruelty and theatrics. He was squat, like a block of solid energy, with a bull neck that held a sallow face out of which dark little eyes peered, mocking and contemptuous. A crooked smile, nothing more than an empty show of teeth, spread over the lower part of his face.

"Zakki," one of the girls whispered.

"Look," the girl closest to Farrah hissed. "The king's pimp." The girl sighed, showing the mixture of resignation and contempt in which she held him.

Surveying the girls as if he were looking over prize dogs from the king's kennels, he walked over to Farrah, bowed mischievously, showing a full head of shiny brilliantine hair parted dead center, and handed her an ornate candy box. On it was the king's crest.

"Compliments of His Majesty," he said. Then he looked at each girl in turn, showing his disdain. "He hopes you will join him at the cabaret after the last show. I'll come and escort you to his table." She felt his arrogant, lustful gaze wash over her. She had no illusions about what that look meant. She had seen it many times.

When he left, the girls turned toward her, not with the glow of envy as she expected, but with disdain. A girl named Tina, her dark skin showing its mark of Nubian antecedents, was quick to voice her opinion.

"It's the hazards of the occupation, my dear. The king's pimp has chosen." She spat out the words sarcastically.

"She'll be riding the pyramids tonight," one of the other girls chuckled.

The reference inflamed her. Not that she was beyond reproach, but she had, above all, clung to a sense of dignity. A man's needs were his own business and submission was a tactic employed when all alternatives to avoid it failed, which was not often.

"It's not all that bad, kid," one of the girls chirped. She was the heaviest of the group with huge breasts that hung like melons over a rippling, fat-layered belly. "He's like a big Teddy Bear, generous and gentle. He likes his food and his pussy, in that order."

"I can picture you both. Two fat goats in rut," Tina snapped harshly. "When I think of you together, I could retch." Now that she had the group's attention, there was a malicious pause as she gathered her venom. "Of course, that's ancient history. Who would look at you now?"

"She's jealous," the big girl said, as the eyes of the others turned toward her. "She's beneath his royal dignity. He wouldn't go near her black hide."

"At least I didn't have to suffer the humiliation of that grease-ball," Tina bellowed. She jerked a finger toward the entranceway through which Zakki had just passed.

The last remark, delivered with raw malevolence, dampened the conversation, and the girls drifted silently into their own thoughts. Zakki's entrance and departure was like a black sandstorm. He had, Farrah knew, extracted his admission charge from each of them.

Farrah opened the chocolates and picked one, offering the rest around.

"Have a sweet," she said, hoping to take the gloom out of the atmosphere. But Tina would not be pacified, refusing her haughtily.

"That's the way it is with them as well," she said, looking at the preferred candy box. "They make a selection and it comes out without resistance."

"You wish it were you, Tina," the big girl said. "Too bad they don't like chocolate."

The remark drew laughter. Tina stood up and quickly ran through the door.

"She's too sensitive," one of the other girls said, directing her remarks to Farrah. "What the hell. At least he's the king."

"Some king," another girl said. "That's why Egypt is a sewer. What can he do for his people in nightclubs and gambling casinos, making an ass of himself with girls?"

"Like you," the big girl said. "And me." She laughed. "I suppose it's not easy being a king. He needs relaxation. So we are doing our patriotic duty. At least one gets laid in a palace."

"And the royal cock doth rise, thank Allah," the big girl said.

The girls laughed at her joke, breaking the tension. It was no good being serious, Farrah realized. Better to flow with the tide. One did not control events, especially a woman. Not in Egypt.

The king was still at his table during the last show. The pile of pastries had dwindled, but the face, heavyjowled and impassive, watched the proceedings without the slightest show of emotion. She knew he was observing her. Zakki sat at another table, grinning, exhibiting his empty smile. He seemed to embody something greedy, unclean. She had not yet defined it to herself as hate.

CHAPTER FIVE

Z AKKI WAS WAITING FOR her outside the dressing room, leaning against the corridor wall, a cigarette dangling from his lips. Like the others, she had dressed quickly, eager to get out of that stifling atmosphere.

"You were good," he said. "I liked watching you."

"I wasn't my best," she admitted, anticipating what she might have to say to the king. She expected a barrage of flattery and platitudes from Farouk, and had decided to treat him like any other important customer. She had learned that the fantasy and illusion of the cabaret world faded quickly once the stage lights were turned off and the costumes put away. She was hardly as interesting as the dance implied. But the fantasy, she had learned, continued to dwell in a man's mind.

Zakki grasped her under her arm and led her along the corridor to what she thought was another entrance to the cabaret. Instead, he moved quickly into a small dimly lit room. It took her a moment to get her bearings. The room contained a low couch, a table and dusty mirrors, obviously an old dressing room.

"The king really likes you," he said, sitting down on the couch and patting the pillow beside him. "I think you should consider yourself quite a lucky lady." She held back, more curious than frightened. He was quite repulsive. Pathetic, she decided, with his clumsy attempts at ingratiation.

"It's not everyone that gets chosen by the king himself." His crooked smile looked like it was being held there with enormous effort.

"All right. I'm flattered," she said, assuming a hardcrusted pose. It seemed the only response. He patted the pillow next to him again.

"Come. We will talk. I want to get to know you." She started to back toward the door, turning the knob. It was locked and he held up the key, laughing.

"You said we would meet the king at his table."

"And we will. We will." His tongue, like a cobra's, seemed to lash out over his teeth onto his thickish lips.

"Now come here. Don't be a silly girl." He reached out and she stepped back, feeling the cold breeze of his movement. Her agility obviously annoyed him. The smile drooped and he stood up and pressed her body to the wall.

"When Zakki says come here, you come here."

Against her, his body felt like cold stone. Gripping her shoulders, he began kissing her neck and breathing heavily into her ear, while his hands roamed her buttocks. She let herself hang against him, inert, groping for a solution.

"Finished?" she asked, contemptuously. The remark seemed to dampen his ardor and he moved away. But her momentary relief was short-lived. He grasped her arm, dragging her along to the couch, tossing her on it with great force. His smile was gone now, his face flushed. Suddenly, he reached into his pocket and withdrew a pearl-handled knife. He pressed a button and the blade jumped out.

Her options, she knew from experience, were quickly narrowing. She could, of course, submit. But that was always a last resort. What she feared most was disfigurement. Not pain.

But he did not make any move for immediate gratification. Instead, he began to calmly clean his nails with the blade of the knife.

"There are many doors in life," he said, not looking at her. "You can take the door to kingly favor, which has its special rewards. He is very generous if he gets what he wants. Or you could take the door to obscurity." He looked up suddenly and surveyed the room. "This is considered a pretty good place to work, don't you think?"

She didn't respond. He had made his point.

"Zakki is the keeper of the key. You must always remember that. But Zakki demands his admission fee. You understand."

There seemed no other choice than to nod agreement. Looking at him, she shuddered with revulsion. There was something so palpably repelling about him that she decided that even access to the king, whatever that meant materially, wasn't worth it. Yet now was not the time to make that decision. The blade of his knife was a firm persuader.

She prepared herself to do anything, to steel herself, not for the sake of the king, but for herself. It was pointless to be a heroine. To a woman, the theatrics of refusal had dire consequences. Suddenly, he looked at his watch.

"You've wasted time. We could have been finished by now," he muttered. So, she thought, hopefully, he is afraid of the king.

He put the knife away and opened the door with a courtly display of feigned politeness, although he squeezed her breast as she passed to claim his title of possession. She made no protest.

The king turned to her as she approached, his impassivity melting. She noted that all the cakes on the table had disappeared. He did not stand up to greet her, offering her a seat beside him, a gesture of special honor. Beneath the kingly air, she detected again the pain of his loneliness. The fat seemed a shield. Behind the jowls, she sensed an innocent boyishness.

Perhaps it was the contrast with Zakki, who had taken a seat at the next table with the Albanian guards, but she felt oddly comfortable.

"You've a smashing figure, Farrah," the king said, smiling.

"Thank you, Your Majesty," she responded, lowering her gaze. She felt all eyes on her. The proximity to him gave her special status.

"I used to have quite a figure myself." He patted his belly, recalling pictures she had seen of the handsome boy king. "Would you like a sweet?" he said. A waiter had placed another tray of cakes on the table. When she refused, he lifted one and popped it into his mouth.

"Very wise," he said. "Very wise." Without taking his eyes off her, he chewed the cake.

"I haven't seen you here before," he said.

"This is my first night, Your Majesty."

He lifted his glass of cola.

"My compliments to the management." He sipped his drink. "Nothing on earth is better than a pretty woman." He reached for another cake. "Or a good pastry. In the end, what else is there?" He held the cake delicately in his chubby fingers. His smile disappearing as his thoughts turned inward again. Abruptly, he stood up. The Albanian guards rose en masse. Offering his arm, she took it and the retinue passed quickly through the cabaret, like a formal parade.

His white Rolls was waiting for him and she was surprised to see that Zakki was already seated in the front seat. So he is only his chauffeur, she observed, with relish. The car shot forward and moved swiftly through the city, followed by two other cars packed with his guards.

"Do you like to gamble, Farrah?" the king asked. He sat in a corner of the rear seat, taking her hand in his.

"I don't know," she said. "I never have."

"You'll bring me luck." He squeezed her hand. "Everything is chance." Again, he seemed to slide back into himself, sighing lightly. In silhouette, his profile gave away hints of his youthfulness. He had, she knew, just passed his thirtieth birthday, an odd paradox because his pictures made him seem much older. He had been divorced from the Shah of Iran's daughter for nearly three years, which seemed to anger many people, despite the fact that the marriage had long ago disintegrated.

The white Rolls stopped before the canopied entrance of the Royal Automobile Club. Zakki got out and opened the door, and the king playfully jabbed him in the ribs as he got out.

"This is the meanest Arab in captivity," he quipped. "A dark bastard with a black heart." Zakki bore the remark with his now familiar fixed smile. "Every good king needs a trusted lackey." The king laughed, turning to Farrah, who was uncertain how to act, sensing that Zakki was seething inside, but had obviously, long ago, worked out a strategy of dissimulation. *Let him*, he seemed to be saying, although his eyes glowed with hate. Farouk either ignored it or did not understand.

The club was crowded with players in formal dress. They looked up only briefly from the chemin de fer tables and roulette wheels as the king strode to an oversized chair reserved for him at the roulette tables. One of his Albanian guards placed piles of chips in front of him. A high chair was brought for Farrah, who sat beside him.

"You will be a lucky charm." He patted her thigh. "What is the month and day of your birth?"

"March 5," Farrah said, flattered by the question.

"One thousand on the three. One thousand on the five," he told the croupier. Two other roulette games were in progress nearby, and the croupier sent a messenger to place the bets on all three. The wheels spun, the steel ball rolled. She could not understand the game, only that the pile of chips dwindled and the little ball never clicked into the holes of the three or the five. Apparently this was also true of the other tables as well. Through it all, the king was stoic, unemotional, watching the play without comment, mesmerized by the moving ball and the constant movement and counting of the chips.

She felt the contained excitement of the atmosphere, masked by the steady hum of the gambling machinery, the click of the steel ball, and the call of the winning numbers called out in French by the croupier.

"You are not so lucky, my sweet." It was Zakki, whispering in her ear, his breath hot with an odor that must have come from his bowels.

The king pressed on. Piles of chips paraded before him in endless quantities. He never touched a single chip, his pudgy hands clasped over his enormous belly, as if he had to press himself together to keep everything inside from spilling out. He smelled of light perfume, and she noted that his hands, clothes, and shoes were immaculate.

Then it happened. All three tables won at once. The din was electric with tension as the three croupiers counted out the winnings. Then two tables hit again and more chips passed in front of the king. Messengers from the other tables carried handfuls of chips and put them on the table in front of him and, for the first time, the king relaxed, smiled, unclasped his hands, and caressed Farrah's arm.

"All good things come to him who waits," he said, the jowls on his face rearranging themselves into a broad smile. Then he stood up, and while the eyes of the players turned, walked slowly out of the club, Farrah on his arm. Zakki scowled at her as he moved ahead of them to the exit.

Back in the car again, the king moved closer to Farrah and put his arm around her, stroking her shoulders. They did not drive for long. The door opened and they stepped into the star-filled night to a little dock that led to a small yacht whose motors were already revved up, anticipating the king's arrival. He led her to a divan in the stern where a uniformed waiter brought two cups of Turkish coffee and the inevitable pastries.

The air was cool, and the king threw a fur wrap around her shoulders and held her hand as the boat moved effortlessly forward. She saw the dark hulks of Cairo's tallest buildings, the lights brighter than stars. A few cars moved soundlessly along the Corniche. For some reason she wanted to shout out to them. *Look at me*, she wanted to tell them. *I am with the king.*

The air was soft, scented with the moist sweetness of the river plants.

"You don't see it from here," he said softly, his voice youthful and melodious. The night hid his grossness.

"What?" she asked.

"The corruption. I am the fifth king. The King of Merde."

His attitude confused her. He giggled like a child.

"There is the King of Hearts, the King of Clubs, the King of Diamonds, the King of Spades, and the King of Merde." Reaching out again to the tray of pastries, he took one, and she could hear the chewing, like that of an animal secretly munching away in the darkness. The thought brought an image to her mind of a restless bull, circling his pen in frustration, greedy with ungratified impulses.

"We will see who wins," he whispered to himself.

"Wins?"

He turned and looked at her in surprise, as if it were the question he were asking himself.

"It's a race. Will they do me in? Or will I? The question is who will derive the greatest pleasure." His hands caressed hers and he moved them over her breasts, opening the wrap and the front of her dress. She offered no resistance, moving her body to help him, looking downward, watching her breasts glow in the delicate light of the stars, their fullness the color of pale ivory. She felt the steady movement of the boat, the faint splashing as its bow cut through the calm Nile waters. He lay his head against her naked breasts and she stroked his cheek. For a long time, he did not move. She felt like his mother, felt the sadness of him, the lost boy.

The boat moved gracefully upstream beside the Corniche, then turned and moved again toward Cairo's center. In the distance, she could see the lights of the bridges, like a string of pearls.

In the soft air, Cairo seemed like some slumbering princess, the Nile a quilt of silk. It was not the Cairo she knew. Not the squalid crumbling pen of the old city with its faded minarets and the perpetual sounds of its street merchants and pajama-clad boys taunting each other in the alleys. Not the Cairo of her parents' misery. Perhaps what she saw now was the Cairo of her father's hashish-induced dreams. She was surprised to be thinking of her father.

He once said, "When I smoke, the minaret rises high into the blue sky. And when the smoke is gone, it crumbles into the filth."

How she loved him! His grandfather had been a French major who had passed through their village briefly, leaving a pair of green eyes. Perhaps it was that legacy in her that had made them so close.

She breathed deeply, trying to chase the thought. Her father was lost, another dead dream. The light heave of her chest stirred the king, who had dozed. Then the boat drew close to the dock and she covered her breasts.

Zakki, who apparently had been in the cabin, was the first to reach the shore, opening the door of the Rolls while the king helped her inside. The stars were fading, and in the east the faint glow of dawn's beginnings could be seen, outlining the jagged edge of minarets.

The Rolls moved through the empty tree-lined streets, preceded by the two cars of the Albanian guard. They honked their horns at the mass of donkey carts that had already begun the early morning scavenger ritual through the streets of Cairo. The automobile caravan reached the gates of the Qubbah Palace, which opened quickly, and the Rolls veered off and sped past the guardhouses along a winding road that snaked through the property's manicured gardens.

As familiar as the Nile, the palace was a city landmark that had become anonymous in her mind. It was simply there, barely noticed in the daily routine of the ordinary Cairene. It occurred to her how isolated it was from the Cairo she knew, and she felt herself entering a foreign land.

Doors were opened automatically for the king by bowing, ever-present servants. He still held her arm, followed by Zakki, a ubiquitous shadow, like the dog that slavishly follows its master. Detesting him thoroughly, knowing what was really going on in his mind, Farrah had the impression that her role here was being totally manipulated by him, recalling again the derision of her fellow dancers. The king's pimp. As for Farouk, he seemed kind and gentle. She hoped he liked her.

He led her up a wide staircase, through endless corridors, passing through high mahogany double doors engraved with plaques bearing the royal crest, to what was obviously his private apartment. They moved through the main foyer of his quarters, to a series of adjoining rooms. She followed him past vast rows of books, art objects, displays of stamps, coins, paintings, and prints.

"He collects," Zakki whispered. The words were expelled with heavy contempt, as if to influence her judgment of the king, to characterize him as a mad fool. "Coins, books, stamps, matchbook covers, even metal household objects, like scissors." He jabbed her in the buttock. "And pussy." He disgusted her. She refused to show any reaction.

The king moved ahead, lost in contemplating his various collections, touching the books lovingly, stopping occasionally to ponder a case of coins or stamps. After a while, he rediscovered her presence, and patiently explained the significance of many of the objects, describing their history and commenting on the value of each. She had already borne witness to his greed for food. It seemed quite natural to see it again in his passion for collecting.

The glow of dawn was brightening the eastern windows and she was beginning to feel fatigued. But the king was still wound up, pacing the length of his collection rooms, a mass of restless energy.

"But I must be boring you..." She felt that he was trying to remember her name, groping in his memory. She followed him back to a low divan in an alcove and he leaned back and removed his fez, revealing his nearly bald head covered with a thin mist of perspiration. Without the hat, he looked like a dimpled fat pink baby.

"Will you be needing me, Majesty?" Zakki asked, winking at Farrah. So he was still playing his little game, she thought.

The king looked at Farrah, perhaps waiting for some reaction, as if she had the option to leave on her own. But the thought of having Zakki take her back to the nightclub, and all that it might entail, made her cling to the king's arm. He

65

smiled, and patted her shoulder, enjoying the display of affection.

"Crawl into your hole, Zakki," the king snickered. It was obvious that one of his enjoyments was to ridicule his chauffeur. It seemed to form the true basis of their relationship.

Zakki fawned, but beneath the pose was not devotion, but the hard steel of hatred. *Pamper the fat bastard*, his eyes told her. *Zakki takes his commission.*

When Zakki left, she relaxed, nestling into the soft flesh of the king's chest. He shifted slightly and pulled a draw cord, which operated a curtain that swept back, revealing a shelf of books. He slipped one out and opened it on his lap. The subject matter startled her, drawings of naked bodies in various stages of sexual activities. He held her in the pit of his shoulder and eagerly turned the pages, occasionally stroking her hair but saying nothing. Sometimes he pointed to a particularly bizarre performance and sighed.

"I envy them their pleasure," he finally whispered. She looked at the pictures, curious but indifferent. He seemed wistful, like someone revisiting the pictures in a family album. He loved it, showing his pleasure. "This is the best of it," he said. She had no illusions about her role. She nodded.

"Will you dance for me?" he asked, looking up briefly. He had opened the front of her dress again and was caressing the nipples of her full breasts. They had hardened, but she felt nothing. "Naked?"

She discovered then that she had actually been jealous of his concentration on the pictures, and while she might have protested coquettishly, she somehow welcomed the idea, as if he had set up a competition between her living flesh and the picture-induced fantasies. He watched her as she undressed, his eyes wide-open and glistening as they roamed, caressing her body. She began the dance to a rhythm tapped out in her mind, watching his face, determined that her undulations would monopolize his concentration. He was, after all, the King of Egypt. Farouk! Or was it merely a romantic image in her mind? What she saw was a sad, lonely man, unable to concentrate on anything but pleasure.

As she danced, he stood up and slowly undressed, kicking away his clothing, then sitting down again. He seemed a white mass of rippling flesh, cascading in long rolls that looked like dripped candles. A flaccid, half-erected organ peeked out from under his huge belly as he began a rhythmic manipulation of it with his fingers. Watching her, he was a sad, ridiculous Buddha-like figure.

She enjoyed his attention, exhibiting the full range of sensuality that the dance implied. The rhythm of his hand grew more frenetic, sending a deep flush to his face as perspiration rolled down his cheeks. His expression seemed glazed, joyless, although the organ rose finally to a more erect state under its shelf of flesh.

She did not feel demeaned by his actions, but rather strangely proud, although she felt tentative in her role, not knowing what to do beyond the undulation of her movements.

"Please," he cried, suddenly, a pleading whine, as he beckoned her closer with his free hand. "Like this," he whispered, pointing to a picture in the opened book at his side, showing a man mounting a woman from the rear. Obeying the request, she kneeled on her hands and knees, feeling his weight against her buttocks as he entered her. She felt the pressure of his wheezing

bulk as it moved against her, forcing a painful contortion of
her body, although she ignored the pain, hoping, as she always
did, that it would end quickly. The sheer physical difficulty presented by his demanding, enveloping flesh, was tormenting and
she bit her lip to prevent herself from crying out.

He was relentless in his attempts to squeeze a maximum
pleasure out of the activity, and when it finally came, he fell
against her. His pores had opened and his perspiration felt like
mucilage on her body. Yet it was not disgust that she felt. Nor
abuse. A woman's body was meant for this, she told herself.
He was, after all, the king.

When he disengaged, he lay back against the divan's pillows,
gasping and spent. The flush had paled to ghastly whiteness.
His eyes were closed and his huge belly rose and fell with the
effort of his breathing. She was surprised by her overwhelming sense of compassion for him, and she moved closer and
curled beside him, feeling an odd comfort in the proximity to
this mountain of human flesh. She had heard stories that he
was a sated, evil man. *He is just a man*, she thought.

CHAPTER SIX

W HEN SHE AWOKE, SHE discovered that someone had covered her with a soft woolen blanket. Farouk was gone. A yellowish brightness penetrated her closed lids. Someone, she sensed, was watching her. She deliberately kept her eyes closed. From the sweetly sickening odor of his cologne, she knew it was Zakki. He made no move to disturb her, but even this quiet inspection seemed an obscene violation. She prepared to scream if he should touch her. As if to protect herself, she opened her eyes.

"Sleeping beauty awakes." She saw Zakki's thick-featured face, his greased hair glistening, his bull neck bulging with heavy whiskers.

"The king?" she said, rubbing her eyes, feigning sleepiness.

"The tub of lard is restoking the fires," Zakki snickered. He held a silver kettle, from which he poured heavy black Turkish coffee into a small white cup. He handed it to her.

"You must need this," he said. His clumsy attempt at ingratiation only added to her revulsion. "Once he's fucked himself out, he hates to sleep with anyone."

She resented his coarseness. Sitting up, she threw off the blanket, exposing her nakedness. His gaze washed over her like a bath of corroding acid. She ducked under the blanket again. Zakki clicked his tongue.

"Such modesty," he said.

A door opened, and a liveried Nubian servant passed through the room, ignoring her, nodding at Zakki. She sipped the scalding coffee and tried to reconstruct her sense of place. The events of last night seemed to have occurred to someone else, although the soreness of her body denied it.

"You had better get dressed. It's nearly five in the afternoon. This is not a rest house. I have to get you out of here. He hates to see the night's dung in the daylight."

She ignored the obscene image, surprised that it was so late.

"In his world, everything is backwards." He seemed delighted by the pun. "Come on. He will be up soon and he will expect you to be gone and me to be ready."

"Ready for what?"

"For anything. For the night. Egypt"—he swept his hand through the air as if to indicate the entire country—"is a contrivance for his gratification."

"Does he know how much you despise him?" she asked between clenched teeth. He threw his head back and uttered a croaking laugh.

"You saw him. All he thinks of is his stomach and his cock." He grabbed his genitals. "Zakki does a far better job of it." He had put the kettle down and moved toward her. Jumping up, she grabbed the kettle and raised her arm. He backed off, looking at her malevolently. Then, rearranging his features, he lifted both palms toward her.

"I wouldn't dirty myself in his leavings," he said, pausing. "But don't get any ambitious ideas. He collects things. You are a thing and he has collected you." He shook his head. "You have a high opinion of yourself."

"Much higher than of you," she snapped, getting up and searching for her clothes.

"You could at least turn your eyes," she said, assuming the arrogant air that typified the king's abuse of him. But he did not turn away. She collected her clothes and began to get dressed. Watching her, he grew silent. She hoped he was titillated. Let him wallow in his deprivation. The king might command her, but this monster had no rights to her body.

When she was dressed and had made herself presentable in one of the numerous mirrors—the king apparently collected mirrors as well—she followed Zakki through a maze of unfamiliar corridors to a rear entrance. She passed more Albanian guards and armed soldiers who watched her impassively. It hurt her sense of dignity to speculate what they must be thinking. Another whore being spirited away after a night of forbidden pleasure for the sated king. The imagined slight depressed her.

In her heart, she was not a whore. Indeed, she took little pleasure in it. But she could not deny that she enjoyed attention and kindness. The king had been kind and she had repaid that by providing herself for his pleasure. She must not find guilt in that, she told herself. She hoped she had pleased him.

Zakki made her sit beside him in the front seat of a small car, an arrogant reference to her status without the king's favor to protect her. Gunning the motor, he maneuvered the car through the palace gate and inserted it into the languid traffic.

"So you can tell your children that you have experienced the great Farouk," he said, sarcastically, eyes darting periodically toward her.

"I don't intend to have children," she replied, though her lack of precaution the evening before now assaulted her memory. "I was amused and he was very kind," she said, dismissing both her fear and her involvement.

He became silent as he drove the car through the wide streets toward the Giza Road. She welcomed the silence, although she was curious.

"So it is like this every night," she said. It was obviously a question begging for an answer, although she feared anything that might set up an involvement with him. He did not respond for a long time.

"He is like a locomotive," Zakki said finally, as if her presence were superfluous. "Always on the same rounds. Night after night. Sometimes he changes nightclubs. Sometimes he gambles all night, until everyone else is exhausted. But on he goes. Round and round. The same in Alexandria. He moves from the Ras El Tin Palace to Montazah. From Montazah to Ras El Tin."

Farrah nodded to acknowledge that she was listening.

"When he was sixteen years old, he rode in an open carriage through the streets of Cairo. He was the boy god, the great king come to deliver this filthy land from all the plunderers. I saw him then and I cried with joy. I was twenty and I vowed then that I would dedicate my life to his service." He looked at her suddenly. "You don't think it is possible for me?"

She couldn't tell whether or not this was another attempt to slyly pose as a human being or merely to paper over beast-liness with a pose of dedication. For a moment, she decided that both conclusions must be correct and, briefly, her attitude softened.

"Through an odd stroke of fate, I have wound up as his pimp and his yes-man. Zakki, the dirty Arab." He stabbed a thumb back toward the direction of the palace. "He is a mix of Albanian, Circassian, French, and Turk. There isn't a drop of Arab blood in his veins. Not a drop. Yet he wants them to make him officially the direct descendant of Mohammed." He mumbled a curse under his breath. "The army plots against him. He knows all about that, but does nothing, as if he wants them to nail him. He is content instead with his own greed, his collections, his pleasures. Pastries and pussy."

She winced at the reference, but remained silent.

"Good for him. Let him piss on Egypt. What is it but a way-side brothel. Everyone has raped it. Why not him? Why not everybody? He is a good teacher." The reference confused her. Teacher? But he was quick to explain, as if it was necessary.

"He has taught me the true meaning of greed. Take as much as you can cram in. Take everything." He suddenly acknowl-edged Farrah's presence again, and he looked at her, revealing his own frustration. "He cannot get enough possessions. Everything. Everybody."

"Then why isn't he happy?" she asked, annoyed that she could attribute a measure of wisdom to this man whom she despised.

"Because," Zakki said solemnly, "it is impossible to get everything. There is always more." He sighed. "I loved him once," he mumbled. She knew it was not intended for her ears, and he coughed as if to mask the reference.

He remained silent for a long time. The car moved steadily, crossing the flowing slate-colored Nile at El Gamma bridge, swinging past the zoo, through El Gaza, on to the sparsely settled Giza Road. His political references were beyond her, she decided. Better not to think too deeply.

"Don't expect this to happen every night," Zakki said, breaking the silence. It annoyed her to have such a prominent place in his thoughts. "He is predictable to a point. Of course, he can be directed... manipulated." There it was again, she thought, the implied threat. She knew what was coming next.

"I can help you, not only with him. There are lots of ways."

He seemed to be retreating, showing some diffidence. Perhaps he was mistaking her silence for acquiescence. He moved a hand across the seat and stroked her thigh. She quickly removed it as if it were carrying some disease.

"I'm a better man than him," he whispered. "I can help you." She detected, for the first time, a sense of weakness, and she enjoyed the observation. "I can be negative as well. The sword cuts both ways."

She moved as far away as possible, pressing against the door.

"Sooner or later it will happen," he said.

"I'll tell him."

Zakki croaked out a smug little laugh.

"He expects it. We often compare notes. He will mock you. That is, if you see him again. You are all interchangeable little cunts to him. Just cunts. One is like the other. Don't flatter yourself." His voice rose, and he gunned the motor in a tantrum of anger.

The car shot forward out of the line of traffic onto the grass shoulder, actually hitting the flank of a donkey, who screeched out in pain, toppling a flatbed little cart. An old man fell to the ground. Zakki paid little attention, directing the car back into the lane. The incident seemed a deliberate illustration of his threat, and she shuddered. What frightened her most was not his sly transparent pursuit. She had a sixth sense about that. Her profession, she knew, encouraged, activated the fantasy of sexuality. But his craving seemed beyond that, as if she were a stalked animal in his gun sights, and he had a finger on the trigger.

"You can let me off here," she said, seeing the club in the distance. He did not slow the car. "Here," she demanded.

"Afraid someone will see you with Zakki and surmise that you are the king's new whore?" He enjoyed the articulation of the accurate insight with obvious delight. "You have too much pride. Someone will have to beat that out of you."

She decided that any attempt at retaining a special dignity had vanished last night when she sat down with the king in the crowded nightclub.

He deliberately pulled the car up to the front entrance where the employees and some of her fellow dancers milled about, casting discreet, knowing glances. Dipping a hand into an inside pocket, he pulled out an envelope. Tapping it against the wheel, he ripped it open.

"A fifty note," he exclaimed. "You must have pleased the lard-assed bastard." He tossed the note onto her lap. "You have won his balls, my dear." He chucked her under the chin.

"Pig," she cried, the anger running through her like flaming oil. She crumpled the note and tossed it at him, then opened the door and slammed it hard. Curious eyes turned to watch. He opened the window of the car and tossed out the crumpled note as if it were garbage. It fell at her feet. She stood rooted to the spot, feeling humiliated, her pride spent.

At the edge of the parking lot, squatting in the dust in his tattered djellaba, she saw the gaunt gray face of her father. He had come, as always, to collect his weekly stipend, the key to unlock his dreams. He watched her, his eyes empty with futility and the agony of his cluttered mind. A little breeze caught in the folds of the crumpled bill, carrying it rolling along the mist of dust. Running after it, she retrieved it. Zakki sped away, leaving her to wallow in her humiliation.

CHAPTER SEVEN

THE KING'S ATTENTION TO her persisted and she took pride in that. Perhaps Zakki was wrong, she decided. Perhaps she meant more to the king than simply an object of his pleasure. Yet when Zakki's eyes caught hers, she felt his sarcasm. "Sooner or later it will happen," he had said.

Farouk would sit at his regular table every night at the Auberge des Pyramides looking very much like the mischievous, sad little boy she knew he was. As always, Zakki, surly and arrogant, when out of the king's sight, would collect her after the last show and the little troupe of flunkies and guards would proceed on their restless orbit.

"You are not the only one," Zakki would tell her at every opportunity. "There were two this afternoon alone."

When she looked at him incredulously, he would retort: "Pigeon juice." He laughed his croaking obscene laugh and explained, "Pigeon. The great aphrodisiac. He keeps one chef busy all night melting down the juice of thirty-six pigeons.

Then he drinks it for breakfast. Makes the cock crow, Farrah. Who would know better than you?"

It was futile to react. It was enough merely to try to avoid his relentless pursuit.

"Sooner or later," he would say. It was his litany.

The group would spend the better part of the early morning hours gambling at the Royal Automobile Club. Farouk was, Farrah believed, convinced that she was bringing him luck, to the point that she began to watch the little steel ball with growing anxiety, as if a long losing streak would spell the death knell of his interest. What money the king offered her, through his agent, Zakki, was quickly soaked up by the sponge of her father's habit. Of course, she knew that Zakki always took his cut.

The people at the nightclub, she noted, began to treat her differently. The continued liaison with the king gave her status. Even the arrogant assistant who lined them up nightly seemed deferential, and the other girls became standoffish and silent, all except the Nubian, Tina, who could not contain her contempt.

"It won't matter," she would say in a meant-to-be-heard whisper. "She will still wind up with the river rats."

Farrah ignored her, trying to dispel all the imagined implications and jealousies. She tried her best to ignore Zakki, but that was increasingly difficult. In her life, the selfanointed king's pimp was ubiquitous, a leering sinister shadow of doom. Nor did she dare make the king aware of his conduct as if his role in the king's favor was clearly and secretly defined between them.

And, yet, even in Zakki's threatening, cruel taunting, his arrogance and crudeness, he provided her with insights into

Farouk's character and habits, as if he were preparing her for the end. Although she was passive in accepting her relationship with the king, she became better adept at reading his moods, helped by Zakki's steady barrage of gratuitous information. In her mind it was as if she had accepted a role in a bizarre play, knowing it was both temporary and dangerous, but keeping up the pretense for the benefit it could provide.

"The bastard is in deep political trouble." That was Zakki's favorite theme, and he delighted in recounting it, between his tormenting pursuit and insults. "The day will come when he'll be lined up against the wall and shot. Me with him and all the other flunkies... and cunts like you."

She had, she thought, steeled herself against these references, but they always inflamed her when he uttered them. On her part, she had stopped threatening to tell the king, not wishing to disturb the situation. Besides, she was not sure of what the king's reaction might be. He and Zakki had an odd love-hate relationship, and she began to view the king's almost sadistic abuse of Zakki as an accepted method of communication between them.

"Dirty Arab," Farouk would rail at him at every opportunity. "Dung of a camel."

It confused her at first to hear the King of Egypt use *Arab* as a term of derision. Egypt was, despite its Christian Copts, an Arab country. Once, she asked Zakki what it meant.

"The fat bastard's a European, an aristo. He would have loved to be a Brit. It's the mentality he hates, himself as well."

She did not understand. Nor did she dare press further to decipher what it meant.

But, despite the barrage of insults that Farouk rained on Zakki's head, the bull-necked chauffeur was always the first man he saw when he awakened, and the last man he saw when he went to sleep. Zakki bore it all with outward stoicism, except when he was out of the king's presence. Even his pursuit of her took on the quality of competition with the king. He had, she knew, approached that point when rape alone would not have satisfied him. He wanted an offering, a gift of herself, a capitulation.

Deliberately holding back taunted him. That knowledge relieved her, since she would never willingly give herself to someone so repelling and stomach churning.

"Isn't it time for a real man?" he would say. Always, when it came like that, it seemed more furious and obscene than his usual attacks. "Why settle for gruel when you can get caviar?"

"I'd rather take poison than you," she would answer boldly.

In the king's presence, Zakki's dark covetous eyes pursued her, and even when she was alone with Farouk she could not shake the idea that Zakki was watching them play out the king's fantasies.

Once he stopped the car and pointed to two dogs fornicating in the street. "Familiar, eh," he said, pinching her arm. "Short and quick." She turned away in disgust, although she had flushed with her own sense of overwhelming shame. The fact was that she had become adept at dissembling.

"Zakki's day will come," he muttered. *Never*, she vowed.

When the king talked politics, and those moments were rare, he seemed incomprehensible. Sometimes he would get angry and fling a newspaper in front of her.

"You see. They accuse me of corruption, when they are more corrupt. Ten times, a hundred times more." Since she could not read, she merely nodded in sympathy. "What good is a king who cannot punish his enemies?"

"He is growing angrier and angrier," Zakki confided. "Naturally, he resents their corruption. Only he, the king, is allowed corruption. That is the royal province. He has his fingers in everything. The smuggling, the arms, the hashish, the brothels."

But Zakki's drumbeat of vituperation did not disturb her own view of Farouk, the vulnerable boy king who had determined that pleasure was a goal of life. Perhaps this is wisdom, she told herself, although she could not understand even the concept of pleasure.

"When it comes, the revolution, they will have their revenge on everything he ever did or touched," Zakki warned, hoping to frighten her. She listened with indifference. What did all this mean to her?

She reveled in the king's attention, and its monetary rewards, which she turned over to her father.

But she did not know really how the affair was being observed by others until two men arrived at the club one night and insisted on speaking with her.

The king was not present, and although it was no longer obligatory for her to be nice to the customers, she consented, more as a break from the chatter of her fellow dancers than for any other reason.

Joining the men at their table, she ordered a cola and observed them. They were both about the same age, forty-ish. One of them, Thompson, was an American, a weary parchment-faced man with an air of knowing cynicism, perhaps emphasized by the contrasting personality of the other man, a "Dr." Ezzat. He had an alert and pedantic air, very intense, with dark eyes that seemed to burn with penetrating fire and tension. His spare, aesthetic face looked as if it would break if he smiled.

"I'm a kind of freelance journalist," Thompson said, after he had run out of a long string of platitudes.

"Dr. Ezzat here is a professor of archaeology at Cairo University."

What do they want with me? Farrah wondered.

"I hope you won't be insulted," Thompson said. He seemed very uncomfortable, out of his element, but he spoke Arabic very well. "I hope we can count on your confidence."

"Secrets?" she asked, startled. "From whom?"

"Farouk," Ezzat said. He seemed embarrassed and looked helplessly at Thompson.

"You see, Farrah, I'd like to do your story. You and Farouk." He lifted a hand and pointed a finger to the ceiling. "Not necessarily now. But the time will come when you might like to tell it. We would, of course, be generous in our payment."

"Payment?" She hovered between being insulted and purely curious. "I don't understand."

"You see," Thompson said, interrupting Dr. Ezzat, who was winding up to speak, "people are very interested in Farouk, his style of life, his habits. And the impressions of a young girl, who was having a... a liaison with him... would be terribly interesting to the readers of many publications."

"I don't see why," Farrah said. She looked at the men for some hint of humor. Certainly, it was a joke.

"You just give it some thought," Thompson said, obviously backing off.

"I don't think I would be interested, gentlemen," she said. "No. I don't think so." She shook her head vigorously.

"Not now, of course," Thompson said, delicately.

"No. But perhaps you will change your mind in the future," Ezzat said. He did not hide his disappointment.

"I don't believe so," she said politely.

Thompson groped in his pocket and pulled out a white card, handing it to her.

"You might wish to call me sometime," he said pleasantly. "You never know about the future."

"I really don't think so," she said, looking blankly at the card.

"So be it," Ezzat said, slapping his thighs and rising, obviously dissatisfied with the interview. Thompson scowled at him, visibly annoyed by his display of impatience.

"I know you will keep this between us," Thompson said softly. "It would do none of us any good to mention it. Especially yourself."

"Of course," she nodded. He was certainly right about that.

She watched them thread their way through the aisles lined with tables. Being illiterate, she could not read the card, although she slipped it in her bodice. Undressing later, she saw it flutter to the floor, and she put it carelessly in her purse without giving it a moment's thought.

"They are crazy," she decided.

CHAPTER EIGHT

THE KING DID NOT come every night. When he stayed away for long periods, a week or two, she detected a difference in the attitude of people around her. Little things. The impresario's assistant would be surlier. Tina, the Nubian, would snicker sardonically. "The novelty has worn off," she told everybody in her perpetual stage whisper. And Mimi, the heaviest of the dancers, would expound on the fickleness of man's lust. "A woman's body is a backgammon board. When the game is over, they fold it up and put it away."

It did, of course, burst the bubble of her secret illusion that she was more than just another "cunt," that she was a person, and that the king saw in her more than sexual fantasy. Hadn't she pierced his crust, become his companion, his friend? Perhaps, in her wildest dream, a queen.

"Don't get too comfortable, Farrah," Zakki had said with his usual poisonous tongue. "His attention span is limited.

Ultimately, he grows bored with everything. Everything. Especially women."

"You think I don't know that?" she had responded belligerently. But she still harbored secret dreams.

She had always feared her own wish-fulfilling dreams, and because of that, she expunged them as fast as they surfaced in her mind. Instinctively, she understood the dangers of obsessive aspirations although she failed to resist them. That she had gotten from her mother, whose single dream in life seemed to have been to have an indoor sink. "If only I can have an indoor sink." She could remember the litany as almost her earliest recollection of her mother, a woman who seemed always a stranger.

When Farouk did come again to the club, her status once again changed, at least for a while.

One night, after they had made love, he lay back on the pillows and she nestled against him. It was then that her most illusionary secret dream was expunged for all time.

"I will marry again soon," he said. It was not meant as a confession. He might have been talking to the air.

At first, she did not comment on the announcement, nor did he have any inkling, she was certain, that the news meant more to her than the unconscious flicking away of a persistent fly.

"Do you love her?" she asked after a long pause. It seemed an appropriate comment. What else was one to say? Besides, her own aspirations were an absurdity. She was merely a vessel for his lust. For her part, she submitted but felt nothing.

"She has good teeth," he said, suddenly erupting in laughter that shook the flesh of his enormous body.

She pondered that later, prompting a timid question as Zakki drove her home.

"He means she will be a good breeder. He wants a son. The next King of Egypt." There was no need to belabor the fact that his first wife had given him only daughters. What use were daughters? It was also her own mother's plaint.

"In my grandfather's time, they would dump the baby girls into the Nile," she had told Farrah. Nothing had changed, Farrah had determined that at a very early age. Indeed, there were moments when she considered such a fate a preferred outcome.

"You could have told me," she said, curious that Zakki had not been the first harbinger of the bad news. There had been ample opportunity earlier in the evening.

"I didn't want to be indelicate," he said, looking at her archly. His response seemed completely out of character.

"Zakki," she taunted, "you are getting soft in your old age."

He pulled the car to the side of the Corniche overlooking the Nile, then turned and faced her. It was midday and a film of sweat lathered his forehead and upper lip, although the air was cool.

"Maybe it's time for both of us to take a queen," he said with effort. He was less clumsy when he was mean. She dreaded what was coming, praying she might hide beneath her skin.

"What are you talking about?"

"Us. Farrah. Us."

"There is no us," she said with brutal finality. "No us at all."

"I know I have seemed mean."

"Seemed. You have always revolted me." She threw back at him his original proposition. "Zakki is the keeper of the key."

She laughed with contempt. "Not to mention that little drama with the knife."

He lowered his eyes and looked down at his rough hands.

"That was only a game," he mumbled. "I never hurt you." Then suddenly, his eyes misted, confusing her completely. Was this beast capable of tears? "I have a heart, Farrah."

"I never doubted that," she said haughtily. "A black one."

He ignored her attack, humbled by his own confession. She knew now what had always lain beneath the surface, and she was determined to beat it back at all cost.

"You think it was easy to endure. You and him, while the king's lackey..." His thick lips trembled and the cobra tongue came out to lick them. He seemed, suddenly, to contemplate a new thought. "His bride-to-be was taken from another man. She is engaged. He simply says: 'I want you.' And the engagement is broken. He doesn't love her. He is not capable of that. He will never be faithful to her." He was silent for a long time, as if he resented the king's intrusion. "If you would only let me prove to you—"

"Zakki," she said with total indifference, "it is not becoming. Just take me back to the club."

"I will marry you. I will take you away. Believe me, I have lined my pockets. I can take care of you. And I will love you."

His revelation seemed to trigger some particularly venomous streak in her.

"Love me," she spat. "The king's cunt." She could not help herself, persisting in the sarcasm. "I would rather marry a camel."

For a long time, he sat watching her, looking pained, forlorn, the way he must have looked as a poor boy roaming the slums of Cairo. She saw the image, glimpsed it briefly, and felt guilty for not feeling any pity at all. In fact, she welcomed this opportunity to taunt him, to be cruel.

"You've only seen one side of me," he begged, as if he were peeling away his own skin. "I have deep feelings." Tears flooded over his cheeks and his shoulders shook in a convulsion of hysteria. She watched him for a while, suspicious still. *Is my heart supposed to melt?* she wondered, angered at his display of emotion.

"Take me to the club, Zakki," she said, turning away, concentrating instead on the feluccas that looked like listing swans moving gently in the Nile breeze. The agony of his hysteria sputtered and she knew that he was concentrating on reassembling himself, drawing the layers of his old self-protective veneer around him. She had been foolhardy, she realized now, surrendering herself to pure vengeance. She knew he would not forget his humiliation.

The car moved, swerving as it jumped the curb, kicking up a cloud of dust as the wheels gripped the hard ground. When she looked at him again, his eyes were dry and the cobra tongue again licked the thick dry lips, curled now in a mocking half-smile.

This Zakki was familiar. But it was the other one she feared.

CHAPTER NINE

S HE SUSPECTED THAT SHE was pregnant just about the time that Cairo's frenzy and good feeling about the king's impending marriage was at its height. For some reason, Cairenes had interpreted Farouk's decision to marry again as a kind of renewal. The bad boy king, the voluptuary, was turning over a new leaf. Egypt would be saved from its degradation, the British would be expelled, and this ancient land, the cradle of civilization, would regain its shining glory.

What it meant to Farrah was that the king was now simply more discreet, although his meetings with her were less frequent. Zakki, still the faithful intermediary, would drive her to and from the king's presence, maintaining a surly indifference, barking occasional insults. She knew that the memory of his humiliation lingered, and she tried to avoid any conversation with him.

The king enjoyed his clandestine indiscretions and their logistics reflected his nervous meanderings, the designless pacing and huffing of the penned bull. He would have Zakki deliver her to a nondescript villa in Heliopolis, a posh suburb in the northwest part of the city, which he owned in the name of a fictional bohemian rug peddler.

"I am Omar Natachian." He winked, greeting her in the strange setting, a room authenticated by his own bizarre imagination of how a bohemian rug peddler might have lived.

Sometimes, they flew in one of his private planes to his summer palaces at Alexandria or Montazah, spending part of the night there and, in the early morning hours, taking a sunrise cruise in the royal yacht *Mahroussa*, which lay at anchor on the clear sparkling Mediterranean.

Mostly, the game plan was to have her driven to the Qubbah Palace after the last show, where the king awaited her in his private quarters. He no longer appeared in nightclubs now, one of the few concessions to his fiancée. Sometimes they would watch Hollywood westerns, or play backgammon, or she would sit silently as he gorged himself on food, concentrating on his ingestion until the blood rushed to his cheeks and the sweat poured off his forehead.

Her role, she knew, was to provide him with continuing accessibility to her person and her time. She no longer harbored any illusions that went beyond that. Wasn't she lucky to have engaged the king's attention? It gave her status. A mistress to the king! She knew she was merely an occasional diversion for this obsessive man who could not bear to be alone with himself. Zakki would never let her forget that she was just one in a sea of royal cunts.

"Tomorrow is Lily's turn," he would snicker as he shuttled her back and forth. "Or Margo's, Tutu's, Ellan's." She never gave him the satisfaction of responding.

Besides, she was absorbed in her own problem, searching
for the perfect moment to announce her predicament. In a
month or two, it would be impossible to hide the fact from
the people at Auberge des Pyramides. And, she realized now,
that Zakki had been right about her false pride. She simply
had not figured on such an eventuality.

When Farouk told her that he was planning an extended
honeymoon on Capri and the Riviera, she knew she had no
choice. He would be gone for months. He might even remain
faithful to Narriman, his new wife, become a devoted doting
husband. If that occurred, she was certain, he would never
take responsibility for his paternity.

She decided that she had to see her father. They seldom
talked now. Even his weekly appearance to accept her largesse was a cold, empty transaction. Although he was not
yet forty, he looked twenty years older. But she still loved
him, cherishing their earlier years together. She hoped that,
pressed by this crisis, his mind might clear momentarily, and
offer some wisdom. He had fawned over her as a girl, much
to the irritation of her mother, who, in the end, ignored her.
It hardly mattered now, since her life had become a treadmill
of childbirth and simple survival.

It was her father, too, who had urged her to escape from the
predictable drudgery of a slum woman's existence. That had
been wisdom, and she was grateful for it.

"You must leave this, Farrah." He had encouraged her to
become a dancer. "Teach my daughter," he had begged the
dancers, who took their leisure in the Auberge parking lot.
Responding to his tenacity, they'd begun to oblige and soon,
Farrah was dancing for piastres in the streets, a beautiful,

coppery-skinned girl with green eyes. What did it matter if her father took the money to buy hashish? She loved him and he loved her.

Her dancing became the principal source of irritation between her parents, and their arguments reverberated through the filthy slum building. It had been built for ten families. Now it housed forty, a stench-ridden snake pit filled with people, animals, and despair.

"You are making her a whore," her mother would cry.

"A dancer," he would mutter.

"It is against the will of Allah. It brings shame on our family. Allah will punish us all." Her mother would be sitting cross-legged on the floor, a child in her lap, another suckling at a wrinkled breast. Her father would be leaning against the wall, his legs stretched out on the chipped floor, a water pipe at his side, drawing in the fumes of the hashish, lost in a kayf. The acrid sweetish odor dominated all other effluvia in that barren, dank, empty room.

"There is no worse sin than to be a whore," her mother would rail.

He would lift his eyes dreamily and look at his wife, a black-draped raven-like creature to whom the present had no meaning.

"It is Allah's will," he would mock. He had long ago lost his trust in Allah.

"Well," her mother greeted her when she arrived at their crowded ruin of a home. "The king's whore." She had expected such a reaction, and that was probably the real point of the expedition in the first place. Perhaps she needed to take another quick look at the abyss.

There was her mother, surrounded by the squalor of a doomed life, howling half-naked brats, and the stink of putrefaction; trapped by ignorance and the appalling weight of reproduction.

"How can you live like this?" she whispered. It was, she knew, the litany of hopelessness. She looked around the room. Her father was gone.

"Allah will provide," her mother said with a sigh. The poor woman had just returned from a day hauling tomato crates and was too exhausted to continue the combat. She was nursing her latest baby, and the child was protesting the meager milk supply in the woman's shrunken breast.

"Not in this world," Farrah observed gloomily. Her mother shrugged helplessly.

The biological connection, the knowledge that she was spawned here and had deserted them, filled her with a gnawing sense of guilt. She wished she could find the child's lost maternal love. Had she ever loved this woman? she wondered.

Her mother's head dropped, and she backed away, moving down the garbage-strewn steps choked with children and animals. She wondered which among the shabby children were her brothers and sisters.

She found her father in the back of a dingy coffee shop, sucking on the inevitable water pipe. He lifted his dreamy eyes and watched her approach. She did not sit beside him, knowing that the other men in the shop would be offended. This was the domain of men, only men.

"I must talk with you, Father," she implored. Through the haze, he must have sensed her anguish. He took a deep, lung-swelling drag on the water pipe, then stood up. He followed her out into the narrow, crowded street.

"The king has made me pregnant, Father," she said. He had once been alive, alert. Now he peered at her face through bloodshot, glazed eyes.

"You know what I'm saying, Father?" she asked softly.

He nodded slowly, avoiding her eyes.

"I don't know what to do. If I tell him, he will be angry. It will be a burden, a complication."

"He will provide," her father said thickly. "He is the king."

"Soon I won't be able to work," she said. "I will need every piastre."

"Then Allah will provide."

"Allah?" She looked at him curiously. *Allah!* Was he mocking her now?

"I can't go back to this, Father. Never."

"No, you mustn't."

Then what shall I do, she wanted to ask him. His face was a mirror of futility. She needed wisdom now and he was incapable of providing it.

"Soon there will be no more for you," she said, gently. But he was far away, nervously looking toward the coffee shop, beyond comprehension.

"I must go," he said.

She sighed and touched his gaunt face.

"I love you, Father," she whispered. His eyes misted, and he turned away. She knew she was alone now. Perhaps she would have been better off not knowing a different life. It was too late for such thoughts, she decided.

CHAPTER TEN

S HE SAW THE KING again at the Qubbah Palace on the
   eve of his wedding. He had sent for her, as Zakki had
explained maliciously, for her farewell "hump." But by then
she had made allowances for his crudeness, knowing that she
had transcended them. Determined not to let the evening pass
without a discussion of her predicament, she was crestfallen to
find that the king was totally consumed by plans for his wedding. Between bites of pastry, he explained what was being
planned.

"The noise will blast these dirty Arabs from their hovels.
A hundred-and-one-gun salute, each blast a signal to send
the king presents. Lots of presents. Gold, preferably. Then
Narriman will come in a motorcade of a dozen Rolls-Royces,
twenty-five motorcycles, five red Cadillacs. It will be fantastic.
Fantastic."

She nodded, hoping that his euphoria might dissipate so
that she might get on to her problem. But he rambled on.

"I've reserved a hundred and fifty rooms at the Caesar Augustus Hotel in Capri," he said. "They will see that the King of Egypt is no third-rater."

That night he consumed more pastries than she had ever seen him eat, an endless parade of sugar that seemed to feed his nervous energy and goad him into a talking fit.

"This will be a whole new phase. When I come back, I will whip those political bastards into bringing this sewer of a country into the twentieth century. And I'll expel the British shits. I'll be able to govern then. I'll be a real king."

He stood up and began pacing the ornate room. It was curious that his bulk did not physically slow down his movements. He waved his hands. "Somewhere out there is the blood of the Pharaohs, enough of the old genes to resurrect this dung hill. Egypt's glory will live again. Once and for all we will be the guardians of the gateway to the Middle East and Africa. Our own masters at last. No more foreign dogs to tell us how to conduct our affairs. I will build my army, not the bleating bastards that couldn't wipe out a few Jews. Brave men with modern weapons. Weapons that work. And I will cut off the balls of every lousy politician." She had never seen him so wound up. His eyes blazed with his words. "You will see. Before I am through, I will be the great king of the Middle Eastern empire. I swear to the heavens that I will toss those British dogs back into their filthy kennels. I will build a great army and I will expand my rule. No more will we pay those filthy Arab and piss-ass sheikhs to keep things quiet. It will be Egypt, and Egypt alone that will control the waterways to the east and the land bridges to the west and south. What Hitler did not do in Europe, Farouk will do in Africa and the

East." He patted his bloated belly. "I will make bulk fashionable. Everybody will want to be like Farouk."

Suddenly he became aware of Farrah watching him and he smiled enigmatically.

"You've never seen me so..." He paused, showing the boyish uncertainty. "So kingly?"

She nodded vigorously.

"I am Farouk of Egypt," he said. "I will be greater than the second Ramses."

He stopped, growing pale, and leaned back on a clutch of pillows. She knew what that meant, and she undressed him. His speech had already excited him and his organ was hard, twitching. As he watched it, his eyes glowed with pride.

"Am I powerful?" he cried, patting her head, diverting her. She caressed the organ with her tongue. A film of sweat flowed from his huge bulk, as his breath labored and his flesh grew hot with pleasure.

"Is it strong and hard and beautiful?" he gasped.

"Yes, Majesty."

"I will be greatest of all Egypt's kings."

"Of course."

He was particularly satisfied with his pleasure and surprised her by slipping a gold chain around her neck. Attached to it was a gold coin. "A special gift," he whispered. She thanked him. For a moment she was happy and she determined to take advantage of his mood.

"I am going to have a baby," she whispered, watching his closed eyes for some reaction. He yawned and rubbed his nose.

"May it be a son," he mumbled.

"Yours," she said.

"Talk to Zakki," he said after a long pause.

Zakki! A dark hand grabbed at her insides. Was he going to throw her on the mercy of Zakki? Sooner or later, Zakki had said. Was this what he meant?

"Very efficient fellow. He will do what is necessary," Farouk muttered.

In his mind, it was obvious, her predicament was a vague detail. He did not want to be bothered. She felt her anger rise, filling her with a sense of her helplessness.

"What can he do?" she managed to ask, but her throat was constricting as the image of her parents' hovel rose in her mind.

"Whatever! Money." Then he slapped her bare buttock play-fully. "If it's a boy, keep it. If it's a girl, throw it into the Nile." He enjoyed his little joke and his flesh jiggled.

So he was washing his hands of her, she thought, throwing her to the mercy of her nemesis Zakki.

"You can't do this, Majesty," she said, summoning her cour-age. "Not Zakki."

"He is an expert at these matters," the king said, growing annoyed, waving a hand as if swatting a fly.

"He wants to marry me," she blurted. The king sat up, his big belly exploding into ripples. From deep inside of his bulk, she could hear the boyish laughter begin. Finally, his eyes were watering with the effort.

"Marry you. That sly, dirty Arab," he said, choking with glee. Calming finally, he said, "See. You are a lucky woman. We will have a double wedding. You can join us all on the honeymoon.

Fantastic. We'll be able to play this little game forever." He shook his head with satisfaction. "You should be smiling." He chucked her under the chin.

"I won't do it. I just won't do it," she cried. He stood up and put on his velvet robe hanging nearby. He hated disobedience. It destroyed the fantasy of his domination, and she saw, for the first time, the tantrum of the inner child. He pressed a nearby button. Zakki, she knew, was being summoned to pick up the pieces.

"But it's your baby," she said.

"A whore's bastard," he hissed, his lips curling into a tight, cruel smile. "What has it got to do with me?" He turned and walked slowly to his bedroom, slamming the door.

"Fond farewells," Zakki smirked as he pressed the accelerator of the big white Rolls.

"Pig," she hissed.

"So, it's ended with a little tiff," he said, watching her, as the car moved slowly into the Cairo streets. It was still dark. "Of course, he's a pig. What do you think I have been saying for five months?"

"I meant you as well," she said.

"That was established long ago. So it's over. You are a free woman."

Her fists clenched in frustration.

"I'm pregnant," she cried. "And he wants me to marry you."

He pulled over to the curb and stopped the car, turning her roughly by the shoulders until she faced him.

"You little bitch. You told him. You told him about me."

"About wanting to marry me? Yes. I told him." What concerned him most, she knew, was whether or not she had described the scene. "Not everything," she admitted. "Just that."

It seemed to placate him and he started the car again.

"And did you agree?"

"To marry you?" She paused, watching his dark, repellent face. "I'd rather die."

"Maybe you will," he muttered, again pulling the car to the curb with a screeching stop. He opened the door.

"Get out," he said. "Have your baby in the gutter."

"He said you would know what to do," she said, suddenly panicked.

"I know what to do," he said, his eyes shining with anger and malevolence.

"Money," she blurted. "He said..."

"Money. Money," he shouted. "You filthy whore. Dung. That's what you will get."

"He said..." she began, realizing suddenly that she had foreclosed on any help from him.

"It's his as well," she cried, her voice rising.

Zakki looked at her, his lips forming a sinister smile.

"But how will I manage? The baby. It will grow in me." She could not find the words, knowing that he would pocket whatever the king would provide.

"You want my advice, whore?

"A girl. Into the Nile. A boy. Cut off its head."

He opened the car door and pushed her out. She fell on the road.

"Cunt," he spat, gunning the motor. She rose then turned away, determined not to show him her tears.

The next day, King Farouk married Narriman Sadek. The hundred-and-one-gun salute rocked the city and the pageant of Narriman's entry to the square outside Qubbah Palace and later to Abdin, where the royal couple was married in the ornate Ismal Room, was viewed by thousands. Fireworks showered the city until the early hours and Auberge des Pyramides was filled with festive crowds.

As for Farrah, the buoyancy of the crowds and the sound of the guns and fireworks only acerbated her gloom. To make matters worse, she was, as she hurried along the backstage corridors after the early show, confronted again by Thompson. His eyes, as before, rheumy and bloodshot with alcohol, offered again the same lugubrious view of the world as before. Only this time, it reflected her own mood.

"Well, the old boy wasn't kidding," he said, with obvious mockery. Farrah shrugged and tried to pass him, but he blocked her way.

"There's money in it," he said sadly. "Good money. My people will pay well."

"How much?" she asked. Thompson's eyes opened wide.

"So you are interested?" he asked, obviously surprised.

"That would depend," she said, cautiously. She couldn't imagine that her story had any value at all. Everybody knew Farouk's habits.

"What would you write?" she asked.

"I'm in a shit business. All the gory details. Gluttony. Greed. Satyriasis."

"What?"

He chuckled.

"The screwing part."

"Leave me alone," she snapped, turning away, carrying with her the shreds of her wounded pride. Doing it was one thing, talking about it another.

"I'll be out there all night. In case you change your mind." Beyond his voice, she could still hear the sound of the fireworks. His presence seemed to have been perfectly timed.

Before the last show, the impresario's assistant called her into his office.

"Sorry, kid, we're cutting the line." He handed her an envelope.

"Many are called. Few are chosen," he said. She stood before him. He seemed to enjoy seeing her suffer. "Live by the royal sword. Die by the royal sword," he said.

She wanted to curse him, but she knew he was merely an agent. Zakki had worked fast.

Only Mimi, the heavy dancer, showed her any measure of compassion when she announced to the others that she would be leaving as of tonight. They avoided her, as if somehow proximity might bring them bad luck.

"The bastards." She whispered the epithet in Farrah's ear.

"I'll try the Hanya Palace," Farrah told her bravely. The Hanya Palace was a competitor of the Auberge des Pyramides, although less large and classy. Farrah knew she had little chance there. Or anywhere. Zakki had undoubtedly passed the word around. Besides, she would soon be showing her pregnancy and that would be the end of dancing until after the birth. She had decided that under no circumstances would she abort the baby.

"See. It's not the end of the world," the heavyset girl said.

"But it is," Farrah cried. Tears misted her eyes and the women embraced.

"Nobody escapes," Lily whispered.

Farrah knew what she meant.

CHAPTER ELEVEN

Z AKKI HAD EFFECTIVELY STOPPED her employ-
ment at all the major clubs of Cairo. But the king and
Zakki were away now on the king's honeymoon in Europe.
Alexandria, she hoped, might still be open territory for her,
at least for the time being. She also calculated that she might
be able to hide the fact of her pregnancy, at least for the first
weeks of the season.

Anything, she reasoned, would be better than having to
return to her parents' hovel, to the double misery of her
mother's recriminations and her father's disintegration. She
resented him now for having siphoned off the money she
might have saved, although she directed much of her disgust
and aggression against herself. She should have gotten more
money, demanded a whore's profit. Her mother was right.
There were no illusions left. She was a whore.

She was a fool, she knew, goaded by pride and some ridiculous false image of herself. She was simply the teenaged cunt

toy of the debauched king. By now, he had probably forgotten her name. Still, she did not yield to self-pity. The memory of her early life and the present horror of her family provided her with the impetus to rise above these temporary circumstances. Once the baby was born, she decided, she would find some new path to respectable survival.

Landing a job at the Dancing Dolphin within a few hours of getting off the train in Alexandria lifted her spirits. She'd deliberately picked a second-rate club, one that would not be in the king's orbit if he returned earlier than expected to Alexandria. He had his favorite haunts there as well. Mostly, the patrons were foreigners on short vacations, visiting Alexandria because it was still cheaper than the Côte d'Azur.

The proprietors of the Dancing Dolphin, an Italian couple named Vivanti, gave her a little cubicle at the rear of the building, which she used as both living quarters and a dressing room. She soon discovered that the Vivantis waged a perpetual war with each other. Usually, the woman won. To everybody, she was the boss. Indeed, the woman's proprietorship extended over the customers as well.

"This is a cabaret," she would say. "Not a bordello." It was her principal admonition. Farrah's belly dance, twice nightly, was the major entertainment.

"She should talk," her husband would whisper slyly to his favorite customers and cronies. "Where do you think I met her?"

Mrs. Vivanti was a swarthy woman with a thick moustache and a surly, sarcastic tongue. She never smiled, although Farrah suspected, and later confirmed, that she was softer inside than she appeared. Her principal activity, besides watching the cash register, was bullying Mr. Vivanti, who scowled at her all day long, whispering counter insults to third parties.

"Vivanti, you filthy wop. We're running short on beer," she would shout, disregarding the customers. Their battleground was everywhere. Sometimes, their arguments stretched long into the night, concluding temporarily when they would drop off with exhaustion.

"His brains are between his legs," she would shout, although to everyone Vivanti's real interest lay in cheap red wine, gallons of it.

"Better than the filthy bottomless ditch between her legs," he grunted in retort.

But despite their mutual enmity, they both treated Farrah with protective solicitude, keeping the lecherous customers at bay.

"She is for sale as a dancer only," Mrs. Vivanti would declare for all to hear. Farrah liked that, although Mrs. Vivanti's scrutiny often irked her.

The Vivantis were beached in Alexandria by Mussolini's dreams of glory. They had followed the Italian troops to Libya, where they opened a bar and enjoyed some success until it became apparent that the Italian army in North Africa was doomed.

"We were the first to desert," Mrs. Vivanti told her. "We came across the Libyan Desert on a camel dressed as Arabs. Montgomery didn't stop us at El Alamein." She growled approval of what she must have thought was a wry joke.

Farrah spent a great deal of time with Mrs. Vivanti. She envied her strength.

"The principal business of men is war and screwing. The trick for a woman is to avoid them both." This was the bedrock of her philosophy.

She was impressed by Farrah's apparent celibacy and her indifference to the customers' blandishments.

"Live without them. It is healthier. You'll live longer." She firmly believed that sex shortens a woman's life, although she was perfectly content to have men pay for the titillation brought on by liquor and Farrah's dancing.

"They watch you and heat up. May it shorten their lives."

Mrs. Vivanti had many eccentricities. Her first name was Maria, but none, including Mr. Vivanti, dared call her that. Her dislikes were gargantuan, particularly contemporary men, animals, and countries. She had hated Italy and Libya, but her loudest recriminations were for Egypt and Egyptians.

"Once they were organized, prosperous, hardworking. But that was thousands of years ago. They had something. Believe me, what they have now is a pale shadow of that." She grew uncharacteristically wistful, describing her visits to the temples of Karnak, the Valley of the Kings. Abu Simbel. She knew their history and could catalogue their many gods. "Even their gods made sense. Now they have Allah. Male gods." She spat.

"What about your Jesus?" Farrah would ask. She had a dim idea of Christians. Even the Copts were a mystery.

"Him!" Mrs. Vivanti said with contempt. "Only a fool would believe the circumstances of his birth."

"You will go to hell," Mr. Vivanti cried when he heard such blasphemies.

"I am in hell," she would respond, coldly.

"That belly is not from pasta," she said to Farrah one night, pushing a finger in her navel. "Some brat is growing there." She especially hated children, including her own, who had apparently all gone back to Italy.

"I'm sorry," Farrah said, as if somehow her condition was an offense to Mrs. Vivanti.

"Raped, no doubt," the Italian woman said with sarcasm.

"In a way."

"Stupid fool," Mrs. Vivanti exclaimed. "Who is the lucky father?"

She looked across the room at her husband, who was playing dominoes. "Not him, thank God." She shook her head, her anger directed now at her husband. "Besides, his thing is like a dead snake." Then she looked at Farrah.

"Coglioni," she spat. "They will destroy the human race." The men playing dominoes hid their smiles.

Later, when her anger abated, she asked Farrah, "What will you do?"

Farrah shrugged.

She hissed, "Fool. With me, they always paid for their pleasure."

Mrs. Vivanti let her stay on even when she could no longer dance. Farrah paid for her board by doing odd jobs around the place, although she had to sleep on a pallet in the corridor.

As near as she could calculate, the baby would be due before the end of the year. She was not yet sure what she would do with it.

Mrs. Vivanti continued to observe her, shaking her head in despair as she watched Farrah's growing belly.

"The father must pay," she would say. "Make him pay. Farrah. Don't be an ass."

"Someday," Farrah responded, more to placate Mrs. Vivanti. How does one make the all-powerful Farouk pay?

When Farrah finished her work, she roamed the city and walked along the beaches. In the distance, she could see the palace where she had stayed with the king, and that spot in the sea where the shiny white yacht was kept at anchor. It was not there now. The king had apparently taken it on his honeymoon.

Alexandria, with its art deco buildings ringing the Corniche, its babble of foreign tongues, its elegant casinos and restaurants, and its nightly round of lawn parties, seemed to lie on another planet, a forbidden island.

For Farrah, the hardest part was holding back resentment. She would see pictures of the king on his honeymoon, glaring out from the newspapers. Invariably, he was photographed in a white dinner jacket and baggy silk pants with Narriman beside him wearing the same ridiculous costume. She tried to find the humor in it, but her condition made it impossible to laugh. Besides, her pregnancy was not an easy one.

Perhaps this was the punishment her mother had always predicted for her. She wondered about what name she would give the child.

"It must have a name, a family name," Farrah confided to Mrs. Vivanti.

"Use the father's."

"I can't."

"Why? To protect the bastard. I would have snipped off his cojones like ripe grapes."

When the labor pains came, Mrs. Vivanti summoned the midwife and stayed with her during the birth.

"A girl," the midwife announced as the baby slipped into the world.

"A girl," Mrs. Vivanti exclaimed with uncharacteristic disdain for that sex. "Your Allah has pissed on you."

The midwife, an indifferent leather-faced woman with tough sinewy arms and clawlike hands, wrapped the baby in swaddling clothes and placed it beside Farrah.

"Green eyes, like mine," she said with uncommon joy, as she felt the baby's warmth against her breast.

Even finding a first name for the baby gave Farrah trouble. She consulted Mrs. Vivanti, who, true to her hatred of the contemporary, offered a fertile suggestion.

"Isis would be my vote. An Egyptian goddess. She had a husband, Osiris, who wound up without his cojones. But she knew what she was about."

Farrah thought about the name, whispering it to the baby. A goddess. She was, after all, the daughter of the king of Egypt.

But the child's illegitimacy gnawed at her, and she confided her fears to Mrs. Vivanti.

"Find the father, then. Make him give her his name."

"It is impossible."

Farrah continued to brood, and Mrs. Vivanti finally took it upon herself to act. As usual, she laid the chore on her husband. After considerable argument, he registered the child's birth in the city hall.

"We've made her a wop," Mr. Vivanti said. He did not tell her what name he had used.

Farrah called the child Isis. After a while it didn't matter about the family name. There was no need for it. After all, she was a genuine princess. Nothing could change that.

When Farrah's figure had snapped back and some of her strength had returned, Mrs. Vivanti gave her her old job.

"Don't grow too attached to her, Farrah," Mrs. Vivanti urged. "Give her away... to some good family. She is too much of a responsibility for a young girl alone."

"Never," Farrah said, clutching the child protectively.

Mrs. Vivanti shook her head.

"The stupidity of human nature," she muttered. She detested motherhood as well.

Farrah got her old cubicle back and fitted the drawer of an ancient bureau as a crib for Isis. Lying awake in the early morning hours, too exhilarated from her dancing to sleep, she would wait for the baby to awake for its nightly feeding, draw it close to her milk-heavy breast, and connect it with this life-stream of herself. She felt wonderful. Now she had someone to love, a creation of her own. She could never give her away. Never!

But the baby developed some discomfort, perhaps a colic, and would cry continuously. Nothing would placate the infant, and her screams echoed through the club and living quarters.

"If you can't shut the brat up, you'll have to get out," Mrs. Vivanti ranted. The crying had made them all edgy. By the time it had gone on for three days, Mrs. Vivanti was urging that she give the child away.

"Never," Farrah said, glaring with determination.

"It's stupid," Mrs. Vivanti responded. "It will only hold you back."

"Never," Farrah repeated.

"It is ruining business," Mr. Vivanti said.

Finally, Mrs. Vivanti came to her one morning. Her features seemed inert, as if she was having difficulty keeping herself under control. She edged herself into her chair near the register and poured herself some tea.

"I'm sorry, Farrah."

"She'll behave. You'll see."

"No, Farrah. It won't work. Vivanti is right. A baby is a burden, in any event. It destroys the illusion."

There was no ultimatum. The alternatives had been clearly stated. Give away the baby or get out.

"I can't be responsible," Mrs. Vivanti muttered, as if to convince herself. "He wants you to go," she said, pointing to Mr. Vivanti, who sat at a rear table, looking glum and sipping wine. Turning her eyes away, Mrs. Vivanti unfolded a newspaper. Beyond, they could hear the sounds of the crying baby. Farrah's eyes drifted to the paper. There was the king, holding a newborn baby in swaddling clothes. She could not read the words.

"Well, the fat one has got his wish," Mrs. Vivanti said, her thin lips curled in a sardonic smile. "A crown prince." She held up the picture.

She saw the gloating face of the fat king, his young bride, and the contented smugness of the baby. Suddenly, she remembered Thompson. She ran to her cubicle. Isis was crying pitifully. Without attempting to quiet her, she rummaged through the drawer where she kept her possessions, finding Thompson's card. For some reason she had kept it. Although she could read the numbers, she had never used a telephone.

When she returned to Mrs. Vivanti, she thrust the card in front of her.

"Call him, please," she said.

CHAPTER TWELVE

T HE TRAFFIC SEEMED MORE unruly than usual as
she elbowed her way through the crowds of downtown
Cairo, in the direction of Shepheard's Hotel.

"The police are on strike. Things are a mess. Let's meet at
Shepheard's. In the lobby." Thompson's clipped British accent
and high telephone voice made him seem younger than he
looked. Mrs. Vivanti had been generous in her severance, and
the two women had embraced in farewell. There was even
a film of moisture over Mrs. Vivanti's hard eyes. She had, of
course, turned away in embarrassment. To her, nothing in this
world was worth tears.

Farrah took the train to Cairo, holding Isis on her lap during
the sweltering journey. At the train station, she splurged and
took a droshky to her family's place.

She decided to leave the baby with her mother while she
talked with Thompson. The confrontation was predictable, as
was the stench, the noise, the horror of their existence. She

avoided all explanations. The family had sunk deeper into decay. Her father sat listlessly against the wall, lost in a stupor. His hooded eyes offered hardly a flicker of recognition.

"Whore," her mother said. The baby's presence was sufficient confirmation of that.

"I'll be back before the day is over," Farrah said, counting out ten pounds. "Baksheesh," she said, unable to hide the contempt for this life. *Anything is better than this*, she thought, buttressing her resolve to stay as far from it as she could.

Before she left, she bent down and kissed her father's forehead.

"Your grandchild is the daughter of a king," she whispered. He was beyond comprehending.

"You have disgraced us," her mother said as she hurried away. But she held Isis with instinctive care. Farrah had learned the power of that. Her baby, at least, would be safe.

Shepheard's Hotel was a refuge for the British, and the swarm of tourists who continued to view Egypt as an antiquity and the people of the present day an incidental annoyance. Liveried employees and the pink arrogant faces of the guests eyed her suspiciously as she walked up the ornate portico into the large neat lobby.

"The natives are restless," Thompson said, his half young, half middle-aged face forcing a brave thin smile. His once elegant striped suit was creased and shiny as he led her to a little table. Sitting down heavily, as if weariness was about to consume him, he snapped his fingers and without asking her preference, ordered two Turkish coffees. Then he lit a cigarette and puffed deeply, blowing the smoke out of his nostrils like a dragon.

"The place is erupting," he said, turning his rheumy blue eyes on her, the veins like red tributaries. "Your fat friend may not make the month." He looked through a window into the crowds outside. "Maybe not the day. The students are agitating. All sides are foaming at the bit. The Commies. The Fascists. The Moslem Brotherhood."

"What do they want?" she asked. She was ignorant of political matters.

"Want?" he said, smiling broadly now. "They want"—he waved his hand, sweeping it around the lobby—"what these people have. They want what they have not got.

"The haves against the have-nots. It's an old story. What they have here now is someone on whom to focus their hate. Our fat friend. And, of course, the British." The waiter brought the coffee. "What they need now is someone else to love, someone to galvanize events. There is talk that the army is getting ready to uproot him." He looked at her. "I expect there will be lots of bloodshed. Maybe even yours." He said it bluntly, as if she were an inanimate object.

"Mine?" The idea frightened her. She shivered and thought of her baby.

"You, my dear, are a symbol of his decadence."

She didn't know what that meant.

"I'm not afraid," she lied. "He deserves whatever happens."

"Good girl. Good girl," he said in English, patting her arm. She assumed it was a form of flattery. Yet she was concerned that he had not broached the matter of the story. Had he forgotten? "The fact is," he said, as if interrupting his own thoughts. "Everything will be the same. The Brits will go.

Farouk will fall. Only the faces will change. Most of the haves will still have. Most of the have-nots will still have not." He sighed wearily.

"I have his baby," she said, suddenly, the words impelled on their own. Gulping his coffee, his Adam's apple seemed to have stuck in his throat. When he recovered, his smile was boyish. He did not hide his delight.

"And is this little bonus a boy or a girl?"

"A girl. Six months old."

Counting blatantly on his fingers, he shook his head in mock disbelief.

"Farouk's?"

She nodded.

"That big bastard. He was exercising the old royal... prerogative, while he was engaged. And he sent Narriman to Rome to teach her a little finesse." He chuckled. "That's rich."

The crowd outside seemed to grow noisier, more unruly, and many of the guests crowded the portico to get a better view. Suddenly, the outside world was intruding, although some of the guests, older British-looking men, continued to read their newspapers, lost in the calm of their privileged world. What had events outside to do with them?

"Okay, Farrah," he began again, after a brief deflection of interest in the rising noise. "We'll want pictures of you and the baby and, of course, your story of your meetings with Farouk... the whole affair." He rubbed his hands again. "They'll eat it up. Not that anything he does or did will surprise anybody. It will simply underline the moral decay of the man." He shook his head. "You can't imagine what it was like sixteen years ago, when he assumed the crown. Cairo was ablaze with optimism. He was like a god. The happy smiling crowds."

"Yes. He told me," Farrah said. The noise outside was continuing to increase, and even the calm newspaper readers took notice. The manager and a troupe of liveried servants began to shutter the windows.

Suddenly the panicked doorman ran into the lobby.

"They're burning everything. Fires are everywhere."

At the mention of fire, some of the women screamed and the people began rushing for the street. The manager, his face flushed and sweating, ordered the desk clerk to ring the alarm and more people began pouring downstairs and out of elevators.

"Where are the soldiers?" Thompson asked, grabbing the manager by his arm as he passed.

"They've joined the crowds."

"And the king?" He looked at Farrah.

"The king," the manager said with hissing contempt, "is having a little soiree at the palace in honor of the birth of the crown prince. Cairo burns and he celebrates."

"Like Nero," Thompson said, wearily, rising.

"The hotel is burning," someone shouted, running through the lobby.

"Armageddon," Thompson said, displaying his weary cynicism. He guided Farrah through the panicked crowds into the street, where angry men were setting fire to everything in sight. Bodies lay in the street. Caught in the chaos, holding tightly onto Thompson's arm, she could think only of Isis.

"My baby," she screamed as the crowd surged and ebbed in their "danse macabre" of destruction. It seemed like the end of the world.

"Why can't they stop this?" someone asked.

"Because Farouk is a fool," Thompson said, vaguely answering the person who had spoken. "Because all the politicians are fools. Because the Brits are fools. I can see them all licking their chops, hoping that they will each benefit when the smoke clears."

"We must get my baby," Farrah screamed, leading him now through the crowds in the direction of the old city.

It took them hours to finally reach Farrah's family's street. Looking back, they could see the fires burning in the distance. But in this neighborhood all was as before. The orange glow in the distance seemed like the setting sun.

Thompson followed her into the crumbling building and up the stairs where the children crowded around them. He threw a handful of coins on the steps, scattering them. In her family's room, Isis slept peacefully on a dirty pallet in the corner. Farrah's mother lay sleeping in the darkness. Slumped on the floor, Farrah spied her father, his body like a discarded sack, lying inert, face turned as if in shame to the wall. Sets of children's eyes opened sleepily.

"Here," she said, gently lifting the baby. "Farouk's bastard."

"Give me money, please," Farrah said. Without hesitation, Thompson dipped his hand in his pocket and brought out a twenty-pound note.

"On account," he said.

She put the note in her mother's hand. The woman stirred, clutched the money, then fell off again.

Farrah took one last look around the place, knowing she would never see it again.

"Nothing will change here in this pig sty," she whispered with disgust.

CHAPTER THIRTEEN

T HOMPSON BROUGHT HER TO his cluttered apartment in a seedy building overlooking the Nile and cleared a space in his gloomy study filled with moldy books for her and the baby.

"You will stay here. We have work to do together. We will decide what to do once we have done the job. I will take care of both of you." He shook his head. "You needn't worry. I will not harm you in any way."

She did not question his judgment. It was the best alternative for the moment. Besides, Isis was with her. Nothing else mattered. Besides, he had promised that she would get five hundred pounds as soon as the story appeared, a fortune for her, enough for her and Isis to live for a long time. That was all that mattered.

Not all of Cairo burned, as she discovered the next morning. She found Thompson in the parlor, the sun streaming in on the heavy nondescript furniture, his face buried in a newspaper. He did not look up when she came in carrying Isis.

"Only fifty Egyptians killed," he murmured, "seventeen foreigners. They burned Shepheard's, three other hotels, a British club, of course, an office of the Moslem Brotherhood, several department stores, seventeen cafés and restaurants, eighteen cinemas, a Jewish school, and seventy other commercial establishments. Not bad for a single day's work."

"And Farouk?"

He put down the newspaper, and let the baby grip his thumb.

"Daddy lives. All's well in paradise."

The telephone rang and he answered it, spoke in whispers, then came back to the table.

"Now for work," he said, clearing the table of everything but a pad and pencil.

She worked with him for hours telling of her relationship with Farouk without emotion, as if it had happened to someone else. She told him about Zakki. He questioned her on everything: Farouk's collections, his eating habits, his clothes, his body, his sexual proclivities. Unsmiling and attentive, she told him everything she could remember. Thompson seemed to cluck with joy every time she offered what he seemed to think was a new revelation. It was all rather boring to her.

"Will it hurt him?" she asked at one point.

"It obviously won't be the coup de grâce. Just another little annoyance to further the process along."

"Where will it appear?"

He named an Egyptian newspaper and others in other countries. It did not occur to her to ask him why he was doing this, although he took the time to explain that he was a freelance journalist who had lived in Egypt for more than ten years and that he was an American.

As if to prove his sincerity, he gave her fifty pounds, and she immediately went down to the Khan el-Khalili bazaar and bought herself and Isis decent clothing. Once she was finished with Thompson, she vowed, she would go out and find a good job and a decent place to live. For the first time in her life, she was thinking ahead.

Occasionally, he went out, returning early in the small hours of the morning. Sometimes, he had people in, but always sent her off to the converted study with Isis.

Because she was bored and Isis was asleep, she would put her ear to the door. Frequently, she recognized one of the voices, the man she had first met with Thompson at the Auberge des Pyramides, the intense man with the dark eyes. A Professor Ezzat, she remembered; a pale ascetic face. Their conversation seemed repetitive.

"...sometime in the next six months. They are not sure. There is only agreement, Farouk must go," the professor said as she listened one night. He spoke swiftly, expelling chunks of language like staccato hammer blows.

"It has been going on for years, Ezzat," Thompson interjected. "His pressure for help by our government is increasing. Acheson won't budge. They keep asking: When will it be? When will it be?"

"His position is untenable. The joke is, he is easy to discredit. He made an ass of himself in Europe. The story of this girl and her baby will be another nail in his coffin."

"He is so easy to discredit. His honeymoon was a public farce. Every night at the nightclubs, then the gambling tables.

Somehow, things appear more dissolute in a luxury hotel setting. The silly ass doesn't understand how his antics are fodder for propaganda. Image is the word they are using now. He has an absurd image. A lecher. A voluptuary. Ridicule is a powerful tool."

"But the pot must continue to boil. People forget." Ezzat's voice rose. "And, imagine, the crown prince and the other were born only six weeks apart. More grist for the mill."

"It's a dirty business, Ezzat."

"Your government should be quite pleased with you."

She heard a long pause. Thompson must have told him to be quieter, and she had trouble listening for a while. Then the professor's voice barked again.

"The British are finished here, as everywhere," he said. "But if you think these soldiers will give you a glorious democracy, you had better think again. It is merely a first stage. Topple the king. Nothing will change under the army. They are naive. Inexperienced. Corruption will continue. As always the men at the top will corrupt eventually although there might be a grace period. They claim idealism and democratic intent. Perhaps for a while at least they won't have their hand in the till. Not like the fat one with his grubby fingers in every filthy enterprise. Arms. Smuggling. Whorehouses. Hashish. Not to mention kickbacks everywhere."

"There will always be that. All sides have that. It is part of their filthy culture."

"It is a pity that we must rely on these silly soldiers with their romantic macho dreams," Ezzat said. "But they have the weapons and they seem to have convince people that they are honest, if that is the right word. Power greed is a worse affliction than material acquisitiveness, don't you agree, Thompson?"

Thompson mumbled what Farrah took for assent.

"They are the sons of clerks and fellaheen. Nasser, Sadat, the others. It is not that they are so efficient at secrecy. It is simply that no one, the king included, wants to acknowledge their existence. It is an old Egyptian habit. Deliberate blindness. It is more comforting never to tell ourselves the truth." Ezzat groaned as if the revelation gave him pain before continuing, "Maybe the fellaheen will gain in the long run."

"The fellaheen! All they will gain will be knowledge. Then misery. The land gives them their strength and their meaning. Unfortunately, they will have to bite the bullet. It is the way of evolution. Yet it is sad."

"Well, then, why do you advocate the revolution?" Thompson asked. "Why do you work with them? Why do you help us?"

There was a long pause.

"You may rail against it. Howl in anger at the moon. Curse whatever god your myth demands. But irreversible entropy carries with it a living horror. Pain. Misery. Nothingness. Who knows that better than the Egyptians. Ruins everywhere!"

"So, if the king goes, what do you think you'll gain."

"Ferment. Revolution brings ferment. We must shock this country into the twenty-first century."

"The twenty-first?"

"We have already lost more than half of the twentieth."

"You're too cryptic for me, Ezzat. I suggest we just concentrate on the immediate future."

"Yes," Ezzat said. "That is the fatal flaw of you Americans."

"Please, Ezzat. Don't make me defend our mistakes."

"I'm sorry. But you people are such a tempting target with your fierce optimism and naïveté. You haven't had enough blood soaked into your soil. We've been bleeding now for five thousand–odd years. The Syrians, the Persians, the Greeks, the Romans, the Arabians, the Turks, the Marmalukes, the French, the British. They all come and go. They rape this old Egyptian whore. But still she lies there, legs wide, showing them her gaping, depthless, erotic, tantalizing, bottomless allure."

"You do get carried away, Ezzat."

He laughed drily.

"Yes. Another Egyptian pestilence. We lose ourselves in rhetoric."

Farrah heard the clink of glass and another long silence. She imagined they must be looking at the sparkling lights that lined the bridges over the Nile and speckled the tall buildings as they sipped their drinks.

"Deception breeds deception, however you look at it," Ezzat said, ruefully. "The king stinks. The soldiers stink, but slightly less. We will have to suffer them for a while. Perhaps some good will come of it."

"First things first," Thompson said, his words beginning to slur. "Discrediting the king is like taking candy from a baby. Farrah's story should put a little icing on the cake."

"The man is his own worst enemy," Ezzat said.

"Every little bit helps," Thompson said. "Besides, I'm beginning to think he's deliberately looking for a way out."

"Well, then, maybe he is not so stupid, after all."

"At least the wife is beautiful. And the girl who will as I said put the icing on the cake. Quite a beauty. He has good taste."

Farrah could not contain an errant shiver of pride at the compliment. Inside herself she did not feel beautiful, although others told her so.

"Maybe we are all looking in the wrong direction," Ezzat mused. "Perhaps we are all pursuing pleasure in one form or another. It comes in many forms, you know."

"You sound envious, Ezzat."

"Not really. I think I am getting pleasure from this."

There was another long silence. "Well, it's no pleasure for me. I hate to think what the notoriety will do to that girl."

"Why, she'll be a heroine," Ezzat said. "A great patriot."

"Innocent victim," Thompson snapped.

"Like Egypt."

Farrah listened, unsure of their meaning. For a while, she lost the thread of their conversation.

"There are no quick and easy solutions. Not for us. Our destiny, Thompson, is in our geography."

"Intellectuals..." Thompson hissed.

"...we are the geographical lynchpin that holds the world together. Gateway to Africa and the East..."

"You exaggerate your national importance, Ezzat. To us, you're just another banana republic on the verge of a revolution, an illiterate swarm, and I'm just a goddamned spook bureaucrat doing his job." Thompson's voice had grown husky. The words were getting thicker, slower in coming.

His voice trailed off, and in the long silence that followed Farrah grew drowsy and her attention drifted.

Then Ezzat spoke, his voice clear with cunning and rebuke.

"Your problem, Thompson, is a problem that comes to all who meddle with us... you have become emotionally involved."

CHAPTER FOURTEEN

D AYS DRIFTED INTO WEEKS and still Farrah's story did not appear. Thompson worked diligently at his typewriter, but she was not sure whether he was working on her story or something else. They settled into a kind of domestic rhythm. She began to prepare the meals. He bought a perambulator for Isis and they took long walks along the Corniche, spending hours sitting on benches, watching the graceful feluccas moving up and down the Nile.

Thompson was a moody, inert man, given to long silences. He seemed burdened by a pervasive weariness.

"When will the story come out?" she would ask.

"Soon."

He confided nothing. Sometimes, he would spend hours just watching her. Actually, she enjoyed his contemplation of her, as if he were trying to see beneath her skin. It seemed protective, and, for the first time in her life, she felt secure.

He stayed away for two or three nights at a time, offering no explanation. When he was gone, she found she missed him around the apartment. He was especially kind to Isis, and his absences seemed also to be felt by the baby. He bought her toys, bounced her on his lap, and made her giggle by tickling her stomach. Occasionally, he would even diaper her. It seemed odd. She had never seen men in Egypt spend much time with babies.

One day he came home with a basic Arabic school reader and began to teach Farrah to read, patiently pointing out each letter. She had never equated her illiteracy with ignorance. None of her family knew how to read. It had never seemed to matter. Now it became, next to Isis, the most important thing in her life.

"You are very kind to me," she told him after she had proudly read an entire page without making a mistake.

"Not really," he said as he sighed. "Knowledge doesn't bring happiness."

"Well, I'm happy now."

She wondered about his life, but could not muster the courage to ask him about himself. Nor did she ever ask again when the story would appear, fearful that its appearance would mark an ending in their closeness.

She knew he had to be into his forties. He had graying sideburns and crow's feet deepening at the edges of his dark, pained eyes. A woman's picture stood on his night table, a blonde lady, neat and pinched, without softness.

"Who is that woman?" she asked him one day when she could no longer resist her curiosity.

"She is my wife," he said. He offered nothing more.

Ezzat visited often. He was always polite, very correct, although Farrah could sense an antagonism toward her that seemed to grow with each visit. Obediently, without Thompson's having to ask, she retired to the study with Isis. Most times she went directly to sleep, but on one particularly hot night, when it was impossible to sleep, she stood near the door and listened.

"You know, Thompson, what you're doing is absurd."

"What is?"

"Her."

"It's not time yet."

"Not time. It will never be more perfect. What remains of the government is in turmoil. Nasser must be prodded to act. The fat fool has actually been declared a direct descendant of Mohammed. Not bad for a man without a drop of Arab blood. If we don't encourage events, they will drag on forever."

"It will happen without her. Why put her in jeopardy. I mean her life. She's not that important. The message of the king's peccadillos has been burned into people's minds. Why tamper with her reputation?"

"Reputation," Ezzat exclaimed loudly. "She was the king's whore. That baby is his bastard."

"It will happen without this," Thompson mumbled. "It's inevitable."

"Your job is propaganda," Ezzat said in rebuke. "The more he is portrayed as a bumbling incompetent lecher, the faster the atmosphere for revolution will be created. That's your job."

"But I've planted many discrediting stories already."

"More is never enough."

She could sense the tension in the tone and pitch of the men's voices. Another long silence, and Thompson spoke, the words layered with antagonism.

"And you, Ezzat. What's your game? A student of Egyptian antiquities, a man from another world. This is not your Egypt. None of the present players gives a rat's ass about your Egypt. Why, then, should you care? You should be like the fellaheen, indifferent to all this political horseshit. What difference does it make to them? Or you? Millenniums between your world, the fellaheen world, and ours..."

Thompson's words trailed off, lost in a thin whisper. "That, Thompson, is the heart of my own dilemma." She had never heard Ezzat so hesitant and unsure.

"What, after all, is the fall of another dynasty, considering the thirty-two dynasties of that other world. Why did they fall? We don't know that answer. Perhaps there were men like me who had decided that their ruling blood had run too thin. Perhaps I am trying to find out how dynasties end..."

"You're too abstract for me, Ezzat," Thompson interrupted. But Ezzat had apparently not finished the thought.

"Perhaps it is pride in being an Egyptian... in wanting to control our own destiny. We must kick out the British. They are the last invaders. Always in my studies, the fact of our rape fills me with rage. Imagine, there are more obelisks outside of Egypt than inside. British, French, German, Italian museums are filled with our spoils. Mummies have been stolen from their tombs for centuries—"

"Death worshippers. You are a nation of death worshippers. When you put your wealth in graves, what would you expect?

King Tut and all that buried loot..." Thompson's tone was sarcastic and contemptuous. Ezzat ignored the interruption.

"Or perhaps it is the desire to prove that we can do it again. Organize ourselves into a great society, the flower of civilization."

"Even the modern Romans and the Greeks have lost that dream."

"Not the Egyptians."

"You are a foolish romantic."

"All revolutionaries are foolish romantics," Ezzat said, finally running out of steam. Thompson returned then to the matter at hand.

"She is an innocent..." Thompson murmured.

There was a long silence.

"You are the innocent, Thompson. Frankly, I never figured you for such a letch."

"Damn you, Ezzat..."

Farrah felt her heart pound.

"I'm sorry, Ezzat," Thompson murmured, as she strained to hear him. "I'm afraid in this case she's more like a daughter. We lost ours, Babs and I. But that's another story. If you really want to know, I'm scared shitless for her."

"Perhaps you should ask for a transfer."

Thompson sighed. "No. I always finish what I start. I guess I just needed someone to validate my priorities again."

"She's just caught in the crossfire," Ezzat said. "One more Egyptian body thrown on the pyre."

"Two," Thompson said. "That's the hell of it." Farrah had begun to perspire. She lifted the baby from the perambulator and carried it to bed with her. For a long time she could not stop herself from shivering.

The story appeared in early July in Cairo's leading daily and, simultaneously, in many other publications throughout the world. Earlier, Thompson had arranged for a photographer to come up to the apartment and take pictures of Farrah and the baby.

He paid her in cash, American dollars, which he counted out on the study table. She rolled the bills in a little cloth sack and attached it to the gold chain she wore with the coin around her neck.

"Gift of the USA," he said. "Guard it well."

To her joy and surprise, the appearance of the article had not meant an end to their arrangement, and life went on as before.

"You must not leave the apartment, Farrah," he warned. "When I am out, lock the door... Open it for no one. No one." Offering no protestations, she obeyed. He had a cleaning maid who came twice a week. He discontinued her services, and Farrah contentedly filled the gap.

He spent more time than usual in the apartment, using the telephone frequently, talking in hushed tones. Once, when he was out briefly, she looked through his papers, curious to see the story for which she was so well paid. Not a copy could be found in the apartment.

"You wouldn't want to see it," he said when she had continued to press him. "People will forget. Besides, the dam has broken. The man's become a paranoid and is sinking in quicksand."

"What will happen?"

"Things will get worse. It will be very dangerous as he is pushed to the wall. He will react. Things will get bloody. Then will come the coup, a military coup. A revolution. More bloodshed. It goes on and on."

It was obvious that he was not sleeping well. His world-weariness deepened, etching deeper shadows under his eyes, carving new lines in his temple. Yet he still found the patience to continue her lessons, and she was beginning to move to more complicated books.

"You're doing great, Farrah," he said, patting her hair. She welcomed the fatherly affection, and his interest in the baby.

"Would you like to come with me to America?" he asked one day. It was July, and they sat framed by an open window, trying to coax the tiniest breeze from the sweltering air.

"Of course," she said. She studied his face. Perhaps now was the time, she thought.

"But what of your wife?"

"Babs." A frown passed over his face. He had told her very little about his wife and their dead daughter. He shrugged. "Who knows, it may bring us together. Ready-made family. People to love." Then he stood, as if the gesture was required to dismiss the thought.

Ezzat came one night, puffing and sweating. The elevator was not working, and he'd had to walk the five stories. Farrah went into the kitchen to mix him an iced drink.

"Next week," he said excitedly. "All is set for next week." He no longer seemed inhibited by Farrah's presence, and he raised his glass to her.

"You have done well, my little lady," he said. Then, turning to Thompson: "He is wriggling like a python, and has sent a note to Heidar, the army chief, to get rid of conspiring officers. And they, in turn, have drawn up a liquidation list. It will be a miracle if the surgery can be completed without bloodshed."

She went into the study, but did not listen to them talk. They continued on into the night. Finally, she went to bed, but slept fitfully. When she opened her eyes, the edge of dawn was on the horizon. She could still hear their voices. She went to the door and opened it a crack. Ezzat was standing near the outer door.

"It wasn't your responsibility," he said. "And you can't guarantee her safety. Unfortunately, she is a marked woman for either side, a symbol of the king's excesses. To the king, she is a betrayer. To the others, a collaborating whore. Take your pick. Toss a coin."

"Don't be so damned casual about it."

"You are a fool, Thompson, disobeying the caveat of your profession. Send her away."

"Never," Thompson mumbled.

"Idiot."

Ezzat squeezed Thompson's arm, then opened the door, cautiously. She could hear his footsteps as they descended the stairs.

Thompson came into the study, surprised to see her sitting on the bed.

"I don't want you out of my sight," he said.

They moved into his room that night. He gave her his bed, and he slept on a mattress on the floor, awakening at every sound, pacing the room, moving restlessly from mattress to chair. She noted, too, that he had a gun holster strapped to his chest.

She felt no danger, more protected than ever, and she liked the new arrangement. Perhaps, she mused, she had found a new father. Perhaps, she fantasized, he would take her to America. The idea gave her renewed hope for the future for her and the baby.

He used the telephone sparingly, talking briefly. He would leave the apartment only after giving her elaborate instructions.

"When I close the door, I must hear you draw the bolt and the chain lock," he told her. She would make certain that it made a loud enough sound for him to hear.

Despite all the warnings and precautions, she did not sense any danger. When the furtive knocking began, she was more curious than alarmed. But obeying Thompson's instructions, she did not respond. Then she heard her name.

"Farrah, open up."

She recognized the voice instantly. Fear, moist and hot, gripped her insides. It was Zakki.

"You must open," the voice entreated. "I am not going to hurt you. It's for your own good. And the baby. Please. You must open this door."

She did not respond. Her breath came in gasps, and she could not quiet her shaking limbs and chattering teeth. "I can easily break in the door. I know you're in there. There isn't much time."

She listened, hearing his breathing through the door.

"It is finished with Farouk. I am here to protect you," he whispered.

She was confused. She needed Thompson to tell her what to do. To compound her confusion, the baby began to whimper in the bedroom.

"I'm here to help you. To save you and the baby," Zakki pleaded. The mention of the baby stirred her fear. Perhaps, too, she was moved by his disembodied voice and the absence of his sinister face, his cold, cruel eyes. Confused and uncertain and as if in a trance, she unlatched the chain and unbolted the lock. He came in quickly, disheveled, unshaven, an ominous presence filling the room, and she immediately regretted her action.

Ignoring her, he relocked the door and ran through the apartment, opening doors and closets. In his hand, she saw the barrel of a revolver.

"When will he be back?" he asked sharply.

"I don't know," she responded, her voice quivering. The baby's squeals grew louder. Farrah ran into the bedroom and picked her up. Zakki followed her.

"I drove all night from Alexandria," he said. "Ras El Tin is surrounded. The fat bastard is finished." He displayed a thin ominous smile as he observed her. "Mother and child. How domestic. Your face is plastered everywhere. He didn't think it was funny. But, I must say, my dear, it helped me get the hell out of there. I promised him I would send you both his regards." He hefted the gun in his hands. "I had to bribe one of the officers. Baksheesh always works. The right palms are everywhere. Besides, I knew all the secret ways out."

"How did you find me?" she murmured, tightening her hold on the baby.

"We always knew you were here," he said wearily. It puzzled her and, as always, he felt the compulsion to prove his insight. "You think the lackey Zakki was letting grass grow under his feet. I told you he was doomed."

"Why have you really come?" That was the principal question in her mind.

"For you, Farrah," he snapped. "I got away because I promised to put a bullet in your head." He pointed the gun to the baby's head. "And hers." She froze. Her heart lurched. Then he waved the barrel of the gun toward the door. "And him, as well."

The trembling increased in her body; her breath came in short gasps. The baby's whimper rose, as if she had sensed her mother's fear.

"I've come to save you, Farrah," he said, softly now. "If things get out of hand, they will make you a public display. They've made you the symbol of his lechery, the embodiment of his endless line of whores." He smiled, but it could not disguise his twisted, pent-up rage. She felt the old revulsion sweep over her, almost as debilitating as her fear.

"You will be grateful to Zakki," he murmured. She recognized his futile pose of ingratiation. "I'll hide you until things blow over. It's hard to tell how long. You will see. Zakki will protect you. I have also bought our protection for the future. Zakki knows how to survive." His squat body stiffened, showing his puffed pride. "You're the one that made yourself a target. It was stupid. Foolish. But you're lucky. Lucky, Farrah. You have Zakki. You'll see. You will learn respect."

It was then that they heard the knock on the door, the fumbling of keys.

WARREN ADLER

"Farrah, please open the door," he cried. "Are you all right?"

Zakki put his finger over his lips and shook his head.

Farrah turned toward the door. Thompson's banging grew louder.

"Farrah," Thompson cried. "Speak to me. What is happening? Are you all right?"

He began to kick at the door, which was heavy and secure.

"I will break it down," he shouted.

Her throat constricted with a choking sensation, and she had to swallow hard to keep her windpipe open. Zakki must have assumed she was about to scream, but she was simply incapable of action. To be sure of her, he put the barrel of the gun to the baby's head, propelling Farrah forward by gripping her upper arm.

She held back, resisting, her motor reflexes rejecting his prodding. She heard a faint metallic click in the gun and the baby's squeal, perhaps reacting from the pressure of the gun on her temple.

Farrah's trembling made it difficult for her to move, and she let Zakki drag her forward, until she reached that spot in front of the door just beyond the periphery of its inward swing.

Quickly he pulled the deadbolt, removed the chain and stepped back, standing behind her now, the gun barrel still pointed to the baby's head.

The door opened. Thompson entered swiftly, a look of dark concern on his face. When he saw her, he started to smile, then noted Zakki and the pistol against the baby's head... Zakki's foot pushed the door closed, and the point of the gun barrel shifted now to Thompson's midsection.

140

Her mind struggled to make sense of what was happening. Thompson stopped any movement, rooted in his tracks.

"Don't hurt them," he whispered, nodding in surrender. "They're—" But the crack of a single shot shattered the sentence into gurgled incoherence, and his body seemed to fold, the seamed face resigned to his fate. She was shocked into incoherence, holding her whimpering baby, her thoughts barely registering.

She was pliable and unresisting now, as Zakki led her around Thompson's body, reopening the door. He listened for a moment, then slipped the revolver back into his pocket. The crack of the bullet seemed to have ordered the silence. Nothing stirred in the corridor. Even the baby suddenly quieted.

Holding her arm, they walked down the stairway into the bright sunshine of an ordinary, lethargic Cairo day. On the Nile, they could see the feluccas, indifferent to death and revolution, floating with their graceful elegant sureness. She felt inert, beyond feeling, clutching the baby, as if that mass of breathing pink flesh were her only bridge to reality.

Zakki opened the car door for her. She slid in holding the baby on her lap. She had no sense of reality. Soon he was beside her and the car was gliding along the sparse traffic of the Corniche, a world of surrealistic indifference to her personal anguish. "That," he said, jerking his thumb over his shoulder as if to punctuate the horror, "was for the fat bastard."

She could not fully understand the comparison.

"Zakki is your guardian angel," he whispered, nodding his head.

CHAPTER FIFTEEN

FARRAH FELT SUSPENDED IN a vacuum in which there was no time or space. Images swam before her, but she could not distinguish them. Sometimes they lost focus. Glittering spangles of light bounced off the minarets. Lines of wash, looking now like abysmal banners of defeated armies, lined the narrow streets as the car moved cautiously through the motley crowds. Zakki spoke occasionally, a hoarse, low muttering, but he seemed far away. Everything was far away, lost in timelessness.

The car swung through a wide avenue, then into a vast crumbling cemetery. Vaguely, she recalled her father had once taken her to a funeral here. The landscape was bleak, the mausoleums in disrepair, abandoned by families who had dwindled, forgotten, or lost faith with the dead.

They passed a procession of mourners, shuffling wearily behind horse-drawn hearses, which moved laconically through narrow rock-strewn streets.

Mausoleums stretched as far as the eye could see, interspersed with squares filled with cluttered gravestones. Some mausoleums were two-storied, edged with iron gates, proclaiming wealth. Here, relatives were supposed to gather on death anniversaries to pay tribute to the memory of their ancestors.

Now, ragged children played in the puddled, pitted alleys, and black-garbed women prowled like eerie scavengers among the deserted caverns of the dead. Only they were not all deserted. In some, whole families resided, many of them caretakers, charged with guarding the mausoleums, surrogate families to ease the conscience of their employers.

Zakki stopped the car in front of one of the mausoleums.

"Stay here," he ordered Farrah. It would not have mattered. She was unable to act on her own. Her will was gone. Nothing mattered. She felt as inert as the dead that lay in the sepulchres. Isis had fallen asleep, oblivious to the horror she had to have witnessed.

Zakki got out of the car and swaggered to the mausoleum's iron gate. She noted the name Al-Hakim carved into the stone plaque, and above it, the words "Come to my sanctuary." How she wished there were a sanctuary for her and Isis.

A heavy woman with a dark, ageless face emerged from the gloomy interior, knee-deep in half-naked children, all of them females. She held two infants on each hip as she leaned against the doorpost. Zakki lit a cigarette and talked to her for a while, gestating toward the car. Farrah could not hear what they were saying. Nor did she care.

The woman clutched the children with brown bony fingers. She wore a black malaya that covered her completely, except for her face and hands. Occasionally, she would turn sternly toward the children. One of her eyes seemed glazed and blinded.

Behind the woman, revealed in the dim light, sat two men, dour and indifferent, who played cards and sucked water pipes. Finally, Zakki thrust his hand in his pocket and pulled out a wad of money. The woman's hand reached out and her fingers closed over them. She nodded her head. Something in the transaction shocked Farrah out of her trance. She felt fear stirring again and drew the sleeping baby closer to her body.

"She'll take the kid until we get set," Zakki said, returning to the car, reaching to take the child. Farrah quickly moved the child out of reach, as if his hands contained some fatal contagious disease.

"Never," she cried.

He reached into the car and grabbed her hair, pushing her head back. She could feel his hot noxious breath on face.

"You listen," he said between clenched teeth. "I've risked my ass. You're the one that marked yourself and her." He jabbed a finger into the baby's soft body. The child awoke with a yelp of pain.

"You think they're playing games. We've got to hide. At least for now. She'll be safe here."

"No," she gasped. "Not my baby. Do whatever you want with me. But not my baby. Please."

His response was an obscene curse. The baby began to howl. He took hold of her clenched hands and began to pry loose her grip on the child. His strength was too much for her.

Extracting the baby, he lifted her out of the car and held her, dangling, as if she were a piece of hanging meat.

"I could just as easily smash her brains out," he said, lifting Isis over his head. "It's his kid. Don't think I won't enjoy it." She watched his face, knowing he would do it, remembering Thompson. What could she do? She lowered her eyes in surrender.

He nodded, pleased with her docility. Then he carried the baby to the woman, who took it in her arms and turned toward the gloomy interior. Seeing them move into the darkness, Farrah sprang out of the car, leaping past the startled Zakki. The woman did not resist, handing the baby to Farrah, watching her. She held up her hand to the pursuing Zakki.

"Let her," she said. Zakki grumbled and lit a cigarette, leaning against the wall of the entrance.

Clutching Isis, Farrah held her, caressing her head, kissing her face and eyes.

"Mama would never hurt you. Never," Farrah cried. "My baby." The tears blurred her vision, ran down her cheeks. Zakki turned away, puffing impassively. Farrah began to rock the baby in her arms.

Zakki watched her, scowling, until he had smoked his cigarette to a stub. Then he threw it angrily to the ground.

"That's enough, Farrah. We'll be back to get her."

He entered the mausoleum and extracted the baby from her grasp. The woman helped him. Farrah's strength left her, and she submitted to being led back to the car. She felt lost now, dazed.

"You'll be thanking me, Farrah," Zakki said, starting the car. "That's his kid. If things get sticky, they might take it out on her as well."

Nothing penetrated her gloom.

"Trust Zakki," he said, patting her knee. Her body recoiled from his touch.

CHAPTER SIXTEEN

"THE REVOLUTION IS PROCLAIMED. Farouk is finished. Long live Naguib."

The words screamed at her from everywhere. Newsboys in tattered djellabas hawked the news. Everyone in Cairo seemed to be parading in the blazing heat-misted street.

It became impossible to drive, and he had to abandon the car. Dragging her out, he held her arm as they moved into the massive wall of people. Everyone was festive, smiling, obviously certain that the fall of Farouk would signal a new day. Poverty and despair would disappear now. A miracle has been proclaimed. Hunger, disease, corruption were to be banished. It was the end of misery. Hail Naguib! She felt nothing but despair.

"Idiots," Zakki muttered. "Nothing will change."

Clots of people assembled in the streets around various speakers. All offered their messages of hope. They heard bits and snatches of their orations. "We demand vengeance for the royal theft from the people. Kill them. Kill them. Death to the king and his cohorts."

"You see," Zakki whispered, moving arrogantly through the crowds. "They're calling for our blood. I told you."

They pushed through the crowds at the Khan el-Khalili bazaar. Metal shutters were down, while merchants stood beside them, watching the restless people with fear. All goods had been cleared from the streets. Zakki ducked into a narrow alley, and they moved through lines of ramshackle buildings.

"No one will find us here," he said, as they stopped at the heavy wooden door of a nondescript building. He banged his fist against it with a deliberate rhythm, unmistakably a signal.

A shutter in the door snapped open. Bloodshot eyes peered out, blinked, and the door opened. A tall, muscled Nubian studied them and nodded. "Ahmed," Zakki said. The man backed away as Zakki proceeded down a dimly lit corridor. He moved ahead, and she followed his silhouette toward a distant brightness. The thick sweet odor of hashish filled the air as they came into a room lit by a single shaded bulb. A plump woman sat on a brocaded pillow smoking a thick odd-shaped cigarette. She looked up and acknowledged Zakki's presence with heavy, hooded eyes.

Half-naked children, all of them prepubescent, lay around on carpets and pillows like discarded dolls, their faces heavily painted with exaggerated emphasis on their eyes and lips.

"Ali," Zakki ordered. "I want Ali."

The plump lady's eyes, dreamy with euphoria, moved languorously toward a beaded doorway. Zakki turned toward Farrah. A film of sweat coated his skin, glistening in the reflective light.

148

"Stay here," he ordered.

She leaned back against the wall, slipping exhausted into a squatting position. The girls watched her impassively.

"You want," the plump lady asked, the smoke curling from her mouth, as she offered the cigarette. Farrah shook her head. The woman's eyes had the same look she'd seen so often in her father's.

"Nice," the woman said with a sigh.

From the beaded entrance, she heard a rasping, angry child's cry. A naked child came out, rubbing her wrists. She wore bracelets on her legs and arms, and, like the others, her face was hideously painted. A fat oldish man came out of the beaded entrance, fastening the belt of his trousers. He said nothing but threw a wad of cash on the woman's lap and proceeded toward the exit door.

The woman beckoned and the girl came toward her, still rubbing her wrists. Tears glistened in her eyes. Nestling against the woman's ample bosom, she continued to whimper, calming finally as the woman stroked her thin shoulders. Then the girl groped at the woman's bosom and removed one fat bloated breast and began caressing the nipple with her tongue. The woman lay her head back, her eyes half closed.

Men's voices rose from room that Zakki had entered.

"He's finished, you scum." It was Zakki's voice, cruel, merciless. A cry of anguish pierced the air. The girls cowered toward each other, huddling together like frightened helpless animals.

"You obey Zakki. Zakki. For you, the king is Zakki." Again, a scream of pain filled the room.

Farrah heard the crinkle of beads and saw a frightened short man emerge with Zakki behind him. Blood had trickled down the front of the man's shirt. One eye was closed and bleeding and the man's nose was a bloody pulp. Zakki pushed him roughly and the man fell to the floor. He kicked him in the groin and the man screamed again.

The plump lady opened her eyes, pushing aside the naked child.

"You understand that, whore," he snapped, looking at her. The woman nodded, euphoria draining out of her. She buttoned her blouse and scrambled to her feet.

He turned to the man on the floor, "I am the king here now," he cried.

The man lay writhing on the floor. Ignoring him, Zakki lifted Farrah to her feet and led her down another darkened corridor to a small room with green walls. On one side was a large bed, on the other a sunken, much abused upholstered chair. He sat in it heavily, legs apart, eyes watching her as she squatted against a wall.

"Now you're safe," he said quietly, kicking the door closed with a sharp movement of his foot. He watched her. There was no way to evade his stare. She felt helpless, a fly stuck on flypaper.

"You should be grateful, Farrah."

She was unable to respond, looking instead around the dismal room. He took her gesture for a question.

"The fat bastard melted down whatever gold he had into ingots and stuffed them in whiskey cases. I've taken two cases. Mine now. He had his fingers in everything. But this was my idea. Actually, there is a string of places like this. The commodity is flesh, all kinds, all ages." He smiled, emitting a low, croaking laugh. "Like a traveling road show. Boys as well. For every taste. And the hashish."

He punched a thumb into his deep chest. "Of course, only Zakki would dip his finger into the slime. The king wouldn't let them see this part of the picture. Your friend, Thompson, should have written about all this." He shrugged. "You would never see his fat ass in this place. He was clever about that, and other things as well. But he never refused the money." He looked at Farrah. "Now I don't have to share it, Farrah. It is... ours."

His inclusion of her made her gasp, and she turned her face away, but too late. He had seen her reaction.

"It means nothing, Farrah? What I did? The risks?" he asked.

Why me? she thought, trying to calm herself. Her head was clearing now. She needed time, she decided. She must save Isis, get away. The thought of her baby being left in that terrible place sickened her. She had to shake off the terror. Be clever, she begged herself. Lowering her eyes, she looked at her hands, more as a diversion to keep him from seeing her expression.

"I do appreciate it," she said, wondering if it might placate him, at least for the moment.

"Well, thank you, Your Highness," he sneered. He was silent for a moment, then a hand reached out and caressed her cheek. Her flesh revolted, but she did not turn away.

"Perhaps gratitude might one day turn to love," he murmured, teetering cautiously on the edge of his own obsession. She sensed again the old power.

"And Isis?" she whispered.

His lips tightened into an uncertain smile. His eyes probed her face.

"She will be fine for now," he said, his hand caressing her face, cupping her chin. She wished she could remove herself from her body. "I told you. We will get her when things settle down. In the meantime, we're going to stay here. And there is always the possibility that they might come here looking for me. Or you." He paused. "Ali out there. I had to impress him with the need for silence and obedience. I think he was getting his own ideas."

"When?" she asked, forcing her pleasantness, referring to the original question about Isis.

"We will have to see. It is too early to tell. One thing is certain. The fat bastard is finished."

"What will they do to him?"

"Kill him, I hope. Better yet, cut off his cojones. That is something we could all enjoy." He paused, contemplating the sentence he had imposed.

For a long time, he was lost in his own thoughts, then he looked at her again. Getting up, he moved to the bed and sat down, watching her.

"You must trust Zakki," he whispered, reaching out his hand again. "He will be good to you." He searched her face and she forced herself not to turn away. *I must find a way to get out of here, to find Isis. Flee! I must hold myself together, watch for the moment.*

"Beautiful green eyes," he said. "So now they are looking at Zakki. Only Zakki." His face seemed to be melting before her eyes. "Acknowledge me, Farrah. I have saved you and your child. See me. I command you to see me."

She turned toward him, but forced her eyes into blindness, viewing him through a black screen, willing all sensation from her body. She was someone else, she assured herself. *I am nothing now. I do not exist.*

She let him lift her to the bed. If not for Isis, she would gladly die. Gladly! How did it come to this? Her fate emerged now as a sentence of servitude. Allah's wrath. It was time to accept her punishment. She did not resist now. In her mind, she had already been violated.

Suspending any sense of herself, she felt his body reaching into her like a hot dagger. She welcomed the pain, as if somehow it might cleanse her. She felt her body turn, as if it were on a spit, roasting on the fires of hell, the dagger piercing her in every orifice of her body. Because she was removed from herself, she allowed her body to suffer every penetration. It was a violation, but only of her flesh. He did not seem human as he ripped through her, a relentless monster, his breath roaring out of him like the fumes of some hideous beast. Biting down on her tongue, she did not scream out. Even when he forced it open and entered her there as well, she did not scream.

Time stopped completely. Death could not be worse, she told herself as he became the embodiment of everything she had ever feared in her life, every phantom and nightmare, ever atrocity or evil. Only the image of her child, Isis, sustained her sense of living. He was, she was sure, peeling away her flesh, bit by bit.

She must have willed herself into semiconsciousness. She could not call it sleep. His relentlessness continued even when his body, finally, collapsed with surfeit or exhaustion. She hoped it was death. He was inside of her somewhere, attached by some hideous umbilical cord. She lay in a pool of moisture, fetid and noxious, the meltings of his beastly flesh. The room seemed to hang suspended in a pall of stale air, and she felt her lungs gasp and her stomach churn.

When her alertness returned, she painstakingly extracted herself, bit by bit, fearful that she might awaken him. His breathing was heavy, like a relentless pumping bladder, but it allowed her to gauge his consciousness. She had to get out of there. She had no idea how long it took her to move slowly out of his grasp, then, holding her clothes, to make it across the room. Slowly, she dressed and, still holding her sandals, cautiously pushed aside the bolt.

The door squeaked on its hinges, and his breath sputtered. Then its old rhythm returned. Closing the door behind her, she tried to get her bearings, hearing only faint mutterings beyond the thin walls as she cautiously felt her way along the darkened corridor into the room where she had seen the woman and the half-naked girls.

Pale shafts of pink light filtered through high windows. Hugging the walls, she moved through another darkened corridor that she sensed might lead to the entrance. The Nubian who had let them in was asleep on a chair, his head leaning to one side. Fearful that her beating heart would wake him, she stood frozen until she was certain he was asleep.

Watching his face for any signs of movement, she padded past him. Slowly, she reached the door. Her hand groped for the deadbolt, touching the cold metal. It did not slide easily. Grasping it with both hands, she pushed against it. The Nubian stirred, but not to full alertness. Sensing that it was too late to stop, she tugged at the bolt with all her strength now, feeling it move at last. She grasped the knob and the door swung open. The Nubian grunted and jumped from the chair. She dropped her sandals and began to run through the alley, oblivious to the pain as her bare feet moved over the rough stones.

CHAPTER SEVENTEEN

HE WAS BEHIND HER, moving steadily, and it was only when she turned the corner into the deserted street that she saw him. There was no time to think, to plan. All of her energy flowed into her legs as she ran toward Ezbekieh Gardens. The roads that circled the gardens were already filled with donkey carts, the dawn procession of scavengers and garbage collectors.

Bending, oblivious to the danger, she threaded her way through the maze, occasionally rising over the neck of a donkey to observe his pursuit. The mass of carts had confused him. Suddenly, as if she found herself in the vacuum of his inattention, she instinctively jumped and rolled into the back of one of the carts. The driver, an old wizened man with a gray face, turned. But something in her manner, in the way she transmitted her fear, conveyed the danger, and he whipped the donkey forward to the center of the traffic.

She lay in the cart's pit, hidden by its low walls, ignoring the smells and slime of old garbage, oblivious to anything but her fear and the determination to get to Isis. Huddling in a corner, she listened to the clip-clop of the donkey's hooves as the old cart carried her to what she hoped was Isis and freedom.

At last, the cart came to a halt. Lifting her head, she saw that they were in a narrow alley, typical of any slum street. The old man looked at her.

"It's all right, child," he said. "This is the street on my rounds."

She rose cautiously, sure now that she had evaded her pursuer.

"I must get to the cemetery," she said. "The old one, near the ruined aqueduct."

The old man shrugged.

"I'm sorry. I have my work."

He seemed kind, apologetic, but preoccupied with the chores demanded by his marginal existence.

"My family must eat," he said sadly.

Remembering suddenly the American money she had tied in the cloth around her neck, she reached into her dress and pulled it out, untying it. Miraculously, Zakki, in his sexual ferment, had missed it.

"I have money. American money. Please take me. I must find my baby."

The old man scratched his head, startled by the money thrust in front of him. Thompson had taught her how to read the numbers on the face of the bills. She unrolled a ten dollar bill and handed it to him.

"That is a great deal of money," the old man said, apparently recognizing the denomination. His reflexes were slow and he looked at the crumpled bill in his hand. Then he shrugged, nodded, and slapped his whip against the donkey's rump.

She lay at the bottom of the cart, feeling every squeak and hoofbeat as the old man whipped the donkey forward. She did not raise her head until the cart stopped again.

"We are here," he said.

The sun had risen over the minarets, promising another scorching day. She had difficulty getting her bearings, since she had paid little attention when Zakki had driven her there the day before. At her direction, the old man guided the cart through the broken streets, while she searched for some familiar sight. Around noon, she found the mausoleum.

The heavy woman stood in the entrance, fanning herself with a piece of cardboard and watching a group of children playing in the yard. She did not see Isis. *She must be inside*, Farrah thought, rushing into the mausoleum where, as before, two men sat at a ramshackle table on which stood a flickering candle.

They were, as before, sucking on water pipes and playing backgammon. They ignored her as she explored the dreary interior. Two babies were asleep in a makeshift crib fashioned out of boards. She was certain that one of them was Isis. The men looked up indifferently as she ran to the crib and inspected the two sleeping babies. Neither was Isis. Certain that she had not missed a square inch of the interior, she turned toward the woman.

"Where is my baby?" she screamed.

The woman watched her impassively, the face encased in a burnished mask, but the eyes darted nervously toward the men.

"My baby. Isis. Yesterday," Farrah sputtered, unable to form a coherent sentence, her chest heaving. The woman continued to fan herself. From his donkey cart, the old man looked at her, puzzled. She had told him to wait in the road. He nodded, then lowered his head and closed his eyes.

"You must know," she said, confronting the woman, holding back the panic. Perhaps it was the wrong place. She looked again at the name engraved on the stone: "Al-Hakim. Come to the sanctuary."

"You are the same woman. Zakki was here. He carried my baby to you."

A tic attacked the woman's lower lip, betraying her, and she looked again at the two men, one of whom looked at her sternly. The communication was not lost on Farrah.

"You must tell me. Where is my baby?" She groped at the woman's malaya. The gesture alerted the men and one of them stepped out of the mausoleum to where the women were confronting each other.

"Go away," he said, making a shooing motion, as if he were dispersing chickens.

"Where is my baby?" Farrah cried. Nothing on earth would intimidate her now. The tic in the woman's lip had spread to her chin, causing the lower part of her face to tremble.

"Please," Farrah begged. "Tell me where she is."

The man glared at her, picking up a rock.

"Go away," the woman said. The man who held the rock projected menace.

"Get her the fuck out of here," the man said, addressing both women.

"You must help me," Farrah said.

"I can't," the woman said, her eyes furtive, heavy with fear as they danced nervously between the man with the rock and Farrah.

"There is no baby of yours here," the man said. Farrah did not look at him, staring, her eyes misting.

"Go away. You make trouble, they will kill us all," the woman said, moving closer to Farrah and stretching out her hand as if to restrain the man with the rock.

"I want my baby," she whimpered, oblivious to threats and warnings. The children, some of them still in diapers, cowered in the mausoleum's entrance like frightened animals.

"If you come here again, they will kill her. I know they will kill her," the woman warned, her voice rising.

"I want my baby," Farrah said. It became a mantra. Farrah fell to her knees and grabbed at the woman's garment. The man shook his head, and spat into the dirt.

"If you value her life, go away," the woman said. "What you see here is a farm for their business. You make trouble, they will kill her."

The woman's words hit Farrah like hammer blows. Watching the woman left no room for doubt. In the place where Zakki had taken her, she had seen the children's fate with her own eyes.

"Please. Go away," the woman cried. "You will be making trouble for all of us. Believe me, they will kill your baby."

"Let me deal with this bitch," the man cried, slamming his fist into Farrah's face.

She fell backward. Then he lifted the rock and sneered at Farrah.

"I warned you, whore," the man grunted.

"We don't play games here," he cried.

She watched his hands, the dirty fingers tightening on the rock. He stared at her as she rose. Her face ached from his blows.

"Go away, whore. Never return here."

"But my baby," she whimpered.

"Forget her." He spat into the ground. "You're lucky."

"Lucky?"

"Your baby will live," he said, observing her through narrowed eyes. The woman nodded.

Farrah rose to her knees. The man watched her impassively, and spat a bubble of saliva onto the dust then smiled ominously showing rotted teeth.

"You had better be gone," he croaked, watching them from the mausoleum's entrance.

"You must go," the woman warned.

"Where have they taken her?" Farrah begged.

"Forget her," the woman said. "I can do nothing to help you."

Farrah managed to stand up. Her knees shook.

"Will they bring her back to you?" she asked, trying desperately to clear her mind.

"Only if they are sure you have gone," the woman replied, bending and whispering in her ear. "Zakki said the message must be clear to you. If you ever try to contact her, if you ever show your face again, they will kill her. It is not an empty threat. They have done this before."

"Kill her?" The words froze in her throat. "Kill my baby."

Again, she tried to hold back the wave of hysteria, searching her mind for some thread of hope. Thompson, her savior, her protector, was dead. Her father was beyond reason, her mother, a virtual enemy. Farouk, the Vivantis... all had rejected her. Perhaps she should throw herself on Zakki's mercy, become his harlot. They had stolen her daughter. She summoned up images of the children in the brothel. Her stomach churned.

Then she remembered Ezzat, Thompson's friend.

"Will you remember this name?"

The woman shrugged. The man, who had gone back into the mausoleum, reappeared in the doorway.

"I warned you." He came toward them.

"Dr. Ezzat. Cairo University. My name is Farrah. Can you remember that name?"

"Dr. Ezzat. Cairo University. But I can do nothing. Nothing."

The man roughly gripped Farrah's shoulders and threw her bodily into the back of the cart, like a lump of garbage. The old man stirred and whipped the rump of the donkey and the cart chugged forward.

Farrah lay inert in the cart, feeling its movement, hearing the squeaky wheels and the rhythmic clop of the donkey's hooves. The sun was high, blazing. She let it burn her, welcoming the pain. Was it possible to will herself to die? She yearned for it, wished it. But the idea lost its impact suddenly. Would death, she wondered, shut out the memories? How awful it would be if death wasn't the end, after all.

CHAPTER EIGHTEEN

S I LAY NAKED ON the bed, his face turned toward the wall. He sensed that she had been watching him for some time. Not wanting to embarrass her, he kept his eyes closed until he heard the squeak of the faucet and the splash of water in the corner sink. When he was certain that her back was turned, he discreetly pulled the sheet up to his waist.

"I must have been sleeping like a dead man," he said. She lifted her dripping face from the bowl, then rubbed it dry with a threadbare towel. Her bruises were quite visible in the bright morning light, and she winced as the towel passed over the bruised side of her face.

"They did a job on you," he said.

"I am a little sore here and there," she said, showing a broad smile, which faded as she watched him. She squinted into the sun. "It is a good day to leave Cairo."

"You leaving?" he asked, sitting up and cracking his knuckles. His sleep had been deep and his mind was just emerging from a dreamless murk.

She shook her head.

"You had better," she said.

"I might," he murmured. "If I finally understood what is going on."

"What is there to understand?"

He observed her carefully, wondering how he could have been taken in by her masquerade. She was too delicate, too graceful, thoroughly female.

"Mysteries," he said. He was being deliberately cryptic. He felt himself on the edge of some unknown universe, and it excited him. "I have to go back there," he said.

"You're crazy."

He tossed the sheet aside, turned away from her, and pulled himself into his jeans.

"I'm sorry you got banged up over me," he said. "You're free to go."

"It's your life." She shrugged, obviously frustrated with her inability to transmit the danger.

"One man's meat is another man's poison," he said, sliding his T-shirt over his head. "At least I know I haven't taken this trip for nothing." Oddly, he had always been sure of that.

Before they went out, he bent under the bed and removed the traveler's checks. Somehow, her presence removed any sense of security in the room. This country was not a place to be short of funds, he decided.

She started on him again in the outdoor café, where he ordered a brioche and Turkish coffee for both of them. The coffee tasted of curry. As always, the streets were a mass of crowds and color.

"Why is it so important?" she asked between bites of the brioche, which she ate ravenously. He also noted that her eyes searched the crowd, like an animal watchful for predators.

"To them as well," he said. "Why is it so important to them?" It seemed the heart of the puzzle.

"A rabbit doesn't question the fox," she said.

He liked the analogy as well as the revelation of her intelligence. At least she had not tried to deceive him about that. He looked into the crowds, surprised how he was now able to separate the street images.

He watched a barefoot boy push an incredibly large wheelbarrow load of kerosene cans, a cigarette dangling from his mouth. A goat roamed aimlessly in front of a dingy barbershop, where a barber in a dirty striped djellaba shaved an old man who slumbered during the process on a broken chair. A sleeping dog lay not far from where they sat, his mangy coat covered with flies. *This land is mad*, he thought, as his attention wandered again to the girl. She, too, was an enigma.

"What shall I call you?" he said. "A name."

"Abdel."

"That's a boy's name."

"My name is Abdel," she repeated, dipping her face into the coffee cup.

"And you think I'm crazy," he said.

"If you go back there," she said.

"I have to."

"In that place, one body more or less won't matter. Especially a foreigner, a stupid American."

"Now I'm stupid." Despite her bruises, her concern for him seemed exaggerated. Besides, he felt a lingering distrust of her story.

"You are dealing with people who are very powerful. They do what they want. The government does nothing. The police look the other way."

She bent closer to him. "Many things here are not legal." She held her nose in the air and sniffed. "Hashish," she said. "It is everywhere."

"A body needs some pleasure, some respite from"—his eyes swept the streets—"from this."

She looked at him blankly, not comprehending, and he saw how wide the gulf was between them.

"Look," he said gently. "Thank you for warning me. I'm also real sorry you got involved. But I think you had better walk away. It's not your affair."

She stared at the black grounds in her coffee cup, and began to pout.

"No need for gloom, kid. You do your thing. I've got to do mine."

Dipping a hand into his pocket, he drew out a roll of bills and peeled off an Egyptian pound, putting it on the table in front of her.

"For services rendered," he said. "Now we're even."

"You are very stubborn," she replied, lifting the pound note as if it carried some disease and placing it on the empty plate that had held his brioche.

"Crazy. Stupid. Stubborn," he said sarcastically, standing up. He had had about enough of it. "Then pay for the damned breakfast," he snapped, moving off. He hadn't wanted to be so abrupt, but it seemed the only way to get rid of her.

He looked toward Ezbekieh Gardens for his bearings. Soon, she was beside him again.

"The old woman who was sitting in the entrance," she said. "She was angry with them for hurting me. She was not as afraid as the others."

He ignored her, and began to move through the traffic. A bus slowed nearby and he ran for it, grabbing a handhold and hoisting himself up. She jumped after him, using his shoe as a foothold. The bus lurched forward.

"You don't give up?"

"Maybe I'm crazy, too," she muttered.

"No maybes," he said. He tried to make it sound like a joke. She did not smile.

"Without me, you won't even find the place."

He groaned and shook his head.

"I speak the language," he snapped.

"It will be like yesterday," she said, her voice rising above the traffic din.

The bus chugged forward, stopping frequently as crowds shoved and clawed their way through each other on the moving vehicle. He studied her battered face.

"It's not your show," he said finally. "I don't want to expose you. Really, Abdel." He ignored the incongruity of her name.

They were passing the Presidential Palace, Abdin, a huge somber structure surrounded by a fence. Soldiers in black unpressed uniforms and bared bayonets guarded each entrance.

"I don't want you on my conscience," she said belligerently.

They dropped off the bus near the old aqueduct. Crossing the street, they entered the cemetery. The gloomy aspect of the mausoleums, their faded sameness, recalled his previous confusion. But he did not want to show her that he had lost his bearings, and strode forward resolutely.

"Why do you insist on being stupid?"

"Why don't you just bug off?" he said, turning toward her.

She looked down at the ground and kicked the dust with her worn sandals. He wondered if she were about to cry.

"It's none of your business," he said, too gently, hinting at his lack of conviction. Ragged children smiled at them as they milled aimlessly in the blazing sun. A sheep baa'd persistently. The loud beat of rock music blared from a rubble-strewn alley.

"You'll never find it," she said. "You'll just wander around until someone decides to rob you."

She repeated the admonition several times as he pressed forward again. After a while, he stopped and faced her in exasperation. She looked back at him, dry-eyed, tightlipped, smug.

"Just point the goddamned way," he said. The heat and his confusion increased his irritation. "And beat it."

"It is not so simple."

"Shit," he spat, disgusted with himself, with her, with the idea of his so-called mission, with this filth, with Egypt.

"You are going in the wrong direction," she said quietly, standing her ground. Shaking his head, he offered the most reluctant nod of assent he could muster.

She moved ahead of him, now sure of his consent. Occasionally, she looked back over her shoulder to be sure he followed her.

They walked for a long time, slower than yesterday's frenetic pace. She was being more cautious, watchful. She paused in a narrow, dusty alley and pointed to an open area several yards beyond. He saw the mausoleum. The old woman was sitting on the threshold, surrounded by the children.

"If you are smart, you will talk to the old woman alone. Without the men inside seeing you. That will be healthier for you."

He started to move away from her, ignoring her warning. Her fear seemed abstract. Then he reluctantly decided she was right and checked himself, moving to the protection of a ruined wall.

"How?" he asked. Abdel squatted against the wall and he crouched beside her. She sighed, emphasizing her own exasperation.

"She will go to the water faucet. Sooner or later."

"Suppose she doesn't?"

She looked up at him and scowled, showing her authority. Obediently, he sat beside her, his fingers circling in the dust, watching the mausoleum. The woman could not see them.

The wall gave them some protection from the sun, which baked relentlessly through the smog. He forced himself to sit there, annoyed at his dependence. The place was a wasteland, a moonlike landscape where even the living had the aspect of moving cadavers. Was this a preview or afterview of his own world? It was inconceivable that his mother could possibly have left a daughter here. He tried again to summon up some image of her. Isis!

How had his mother lived with it all these years?

Sitting there in the fetid air, he groped in time for the sparse bits and pieces of this land his mother had recalled, bits and pieces of images she had inserted in his mind when he pressed her. The pyramids are not Egypt, she had told him, inexplicably. Nor the Sphinx. They mock us, she had said. Well, then, who put them there? he'd asked. Egyptians? Strangers?

What did these people in the City of the Dead know of the pyramids, the Sphinx? He wondered how he would have reacted if his mother had confessed that he had a half sister living in Seattle, or San Diego, or on the other side of Manhattan.

Abdel stirred, touching his knee. The woman had risen and was moving, like some broken antique machine. A motley group of her tiny wards followed her. What was she, he wondered, a nanny, a baby sitter? He stood up.

"Wait," Abdel whispered. She seemed more alert than him. They watched the woman move away from the mausoleum. Abdel rose and loped along the shadow of the wall, then turned in the opposite direction, beckoning him to follow.

They moved into another street, confronting the woman head-on as she turned the corner. Abdel hung back. The woman, coping with the inevitability of her entrapment, looked around her, then faced him, her one good eye peering at him from its wrinkled chicken-skin sack.

"I told you," the woman said with a sigh. "It is trouble."

"Why trouble?" he asked, his voice deliberately flat and menacing. But the woman was not intimidated. She opened her mouth, showing the stumps of teeth on a bed of pink, empty gums.

"You will bring only trouble. To her as well," the woman whispered.

"Isis?"

The woman nodded.

"You know where she is?" The one good eye opened as wide as it was able, swimming in its sack, observing him with ominous foreshadowing.

"Always the same question? Where is Isis? Where is Isis?"

"Who asks?"

"He." Her good eye moved as if to signify some vague direction.

"Who?" he pressed.

"Zakki." She hissed the name. "He cannot forget." She looked at her gnarled fingers. "He thinks she will come back to old Herra someday. Never."

She talked haltingly.

"She was left here by her mother?" Si asked. "Why?" It was his private enigma. But it did not seem to have the same relevancy for her. She nodded. It did not answer his question.

"Why?" he repeated. Her good eye stared at him.

"She was your mother as well?" the woman said, scrutinizing him. She nodded her head and showed her awful smile. "The same eyes."

"You knew her?"

She nodded her head.

"It was not her fault," the woman said. "She had no choice."

He had not expected this defense of his mother's motives. He felt suddenly closer to the woman.

"She died. In America," Si said. "She was a good mother. I loved her."

The woman watched him and her aged face seemed to grow darker, the wrinkles deeper etched. "Then why does it matter?" she asked. Beyond the parchment face, her mind was alert.

"It matters," he said.

"Let the old dogs sleep," she said.

"It is too late for that." He felt suddenly that he had passed some Rubicon, had proceeded beyond the point of no return.

"Why does he want Isis?" he asked, knowing it was, for her, the heart of the matter. She bent closer to him and he could smell her stale breath.

"For what she did to Zakki. There is no forgiveness for that." A croak bubbled up from her throat. She put a gnarled finger up against her closed lips.

"I had better be silent now," she said, softly.

"You can't," he pressed.

She started to move away, but he blocked her path.

"I must find her," he said.

"If Zakki can't find her, no one can."

"I can," he said with theatrical bravado. She surveyed him again and shook her head.

"You will be worse than dead," she hissed.

"Worse? What is worse?"

She turned suddenly, and the ancient cords of her neck tightened as her head moved like a lighthouse beacon, surveying the indifferent faces on the street. She turned to him again.

"You had better go home," she said. "Or perhaps they will settle for you instead."

Settle? He was chilled by the assertion. What did she mean? A prod in his ribs made him turn. It was Abdel.

"Him," she said, calmly. "Don't look. The man who beat me last night. We must go." The old woman sensed the surveillance.

"You had better heed the boy," she said.

"No," he said. "I'm not afraid. And I won't go until you tell me something." Abdel tugged at his T-shirt. The old woman contemplated his face. Again, her one eye turned in its sack. Her voice grew lower, barely perceptible, and he had to cock an ear to hear.

"She is safe now. She came to me that night. She was alone, afraid. I brought her to him at the university."

"To whom?"

The woman's voice dribbled off, and she began to walk again. Abdel prodded him.

"To whom?" Si pressed. He reached out and grasped the woman by her shoulders.

"I have never told a living soul," the woman said. The words had been expelled in a tiny whisper and her single eye became blurred with tears. "No," she said, her voice rising now, as if the confession had exploded something inside of her. "I brought her to him. And he took her away. From them."

"But where? Where is she?"

"Go away. You can only hurt her."

"But I must know." The woman's face grew blank.

"Please," Abdel pleaded. Some sense of an alien, potentially harmful danger asserted itself. Turning, he saw the man, a huge black man with a bulbous face and tiny, sinister eyes. He watched them blatantly, keeping his distance.

"She is right," the old woman said. "You don't know them. Life means nothing."

"Where is Isis?" he persisted.

A dark pall descended over the woman's face. Her eye looked beyond him. Turning, he saw that the man was moving toward them.

The sense of danger overwhelmed him. It was time to go.

For now.

CHAPTER NINETEEN

H E LET ABDEL PROPEL him forward, until they were running as fast as they could. Sweat oozed from his pores, soaking his clothes. He ran beside her like an automaton, his mind turning over what the woman had said. *I brought her to him at the university.* It meant nothing.

They reached the outside of the cemetery, crossed the train tracks, and proceeded swiftly into a warren of highrise slums that began on the other side of the old aqueduct. Animals and people crowded the narrow streets. Incongruously, many of the faces were smiling, as if all this frantic scrambling for survival was a vast entertainment. For a moment, he thought he was in an amusement park. Disneyland of the Middle East!

They reached a huge bazaar. He bought two oranges from a vendor and gave Abdel one.

"The woman knew," he said.

He rolled it over in his mind. What she had said cast a long shadow, the edges blurred and unfocused.

"I have to go back," he said. There were too many unanswered questions. He cursed his ineptness at this business. He saw the girl's frightened perspiring face. She shook her head.

"They'll hurt you. I know they will."

The danger she transmitted was visual, and he felt its strength. But she said nothing.

"Later," he mumbled. "When it gets dark."

They finished the oranges and edged their way through the crowds of the bazaar. He bought them some helpings of steaming ful from a yellow-toothed street vendor, who spooned the mash of beans, rice, and lentils into a large circular bread loaf. They ate it as they walked. The bazaar thinned and they passed the old Mamluk tombs to the high stone walls of the Citadel built by Saladin. Climbing the hill, they entered the Citadel itself in which Muhammad Ali, in a fit of devout megalomania, had built his incredible mosque.

He purchased two tickets and they entered the huge courtyard, moving to the stone balustrade that surrounded it. Below them, from this highest vantage point in the city, they could see Cairo simmering in the heat and smog. Miraculously, in the distance, the Pyramids of Giza caught the sun's spangles.

"Makes you feel like the most inconsequential speck of bacteria," he said.

She looked at him, uncomprehending. He turned toward the high dome of the mosque, recalling the Allah occasionally invoked by his mother. Praise to Allah. He recalled her voice. *Why praise?* he wondered, turning again to view the umber city in its dusty halo.

A group of squeaky clean Japanese tourists led by a guide holding a little Japanese flag stopped by what looked like a well not far from where they stood.

"Allah," the guide yelled down into the well. "Allah," the voice came back in a booming echo.

"There's your Allah," Si said to Abdel. "An echo."

Abdel looked at him curiously. She turned to watch the city. He observed her. A breeze had caught a loose curl and he could see, clearly, the feminine outlines of her face, a visage that she had, so assiduously, tried to hide. She must have felt the penetrating observation, turning away to hide her face.

Sound suddenly exploded from the minarets, a clarion, it seemed, announcing the falling sun.

"There is no god but god. Come to prayer. Come to salvation," a scratchy loudspeaker voice intoned in Arabic.

They watched the spangles on the minarets grow orange. Crowds of the faithful began to enter the mosque.

"I must go back now," he said, adding quickly, "I think I can find my way." He was trying to pry her away gently.

Outside the Citadel, he took a more direct route. In the distance, the hills of Muquatt were suddenly visible again, their vertical sides, from which the ancient Pharaohs had carved their limestone blocks, showing red and pink in the diminishing light. Still, she would not leave him.

"Now who's stubborn?" he asked. But he did not protest.

By the time they reached the City of the Dead it was pitch-dark, and they could barely see the outlines of the mausoleums. Only the glow of cooking fires, some in the streets, while others peeked from murky interiors, marked the way through the maze.

The darkness provided security and they reached the Al-Hakim mausoleum without incident. Si's mind was filled with potential questions. He knew he had to lure the woman out alone, but he had postponed any specific plan. Perhaps, too, the men would be gone.

The area around the mausoleum was eerily quiet, and the interior was strangely dark, showing no signs of life.

"Where is everybody?" he whispered.

From somewhere down the narrow street came the sounds of voices, the clash of metal, shuffling footsteps. Then, coming closer, the clip-clop of a donkey cart and the inevitable squeak of an unoiled wheel. Si and Abdel moved deeper into the shadows.

The donkey cart came to a halt in front of the mausoleum entrance. A group of people milled about, adults and children carrying a variety of burdens, including the pots that had been clanking. The driver of the donkey cart alighted and walked slowly into the apparently deserted mausoleum. When he emerged, he carried what appeared at first to be a sack on his shoulders.

"Her," Abdel said, her words frozen in the air like an icicle stabbed into space. His eyes had become accustomed to the dark and he saw the old woman's dangling arms reaching lifelessly for the hard ground. The man threw the body in the back of the cart, as if it were a discarded mattress.

"Neck broke," they heard the man say, as if it were necessary for him to provide the diagnosis to the circle of spectators.

"Where do they bury them?" Si asked.

"Not here. In a public pit. Many who live here wind up there."

178

A shred of resignation had crept into her voice. They watched incredulously as the donkey cart moved away and the spectators began moving into the mausoleum, obviously co-opting the site for their new home.

The fact of death passed quickly, and soon the children became animated and the adults began conversing in excited tones, congratulating themselves on their good fortune. Si started after the donkey cart. It was only when he felt the restraining pressure of her arm that he stopped.

CHAPTER TWENTY

E VERYTHING IN THE HOTEL room was awry. Whoever had done it was very thorough. Not a single object in his suitcase had escaped inspection, and the suitcase itself looked denuded, its sides torn out, its framework revealed. The mattress had been overturned. Even the sink had been dismantled and put together again, although the mechanics of this operation had obviously baffled the intruder.

The balcony door was open, showing, unmistakably, the mode of access.

"What the hell were they looking for?" he wondered aloud, patting his jean pockets, where his traveler checks and passport remained intact, grateful for his foresight. The concierge had asked for his passport to be held at the desk, but he had refused, placing a pound in the chubby hand, heeding some vague warning that he had overheard on the trip from London. "Your passport is your life. Give it to no one."

Abdel said nothing, staring blankly at the mess. They were both exhausted, having walked most of the way from the cemetery. He had looked forward to a night's sleep, time to restoke his mind, which seemed unable to grasp what was happening.

"Well, they know where we are," Abdel said, moving toward the open balcony door. "They are surely watching."

"Watching what? Us? Me?" He looked around the room. "All they had to do is ask me. I have no secrets." His voice rose, as he remembered the old woman. "They must have broken her neck. Can you believe it? Over what? Why?"

Abdel shrugged, squatting on the floor. The mattress was leaning against the bed frame. He pulled it down to the floor, then lay on it, looking at the ceiling.

"They know where I am. Why don't they come?" he said, clenching his fists. He resisted running to the balcony and screaming out his anger.

"I told you," Abdel said, wearily. "Go away."

"Away from what?" *Why is everything a question?* he wondered.

"From them," she whispered.

"Them?" Earlier he had dismissed her fears as a fantasy of the powerless. To a child of the streets, almost anyone might seem a menace. He had finally gotten her point.

The connective link between the old woman and his mother chilled him. His mind buzzed with suppositions.

The blurred image of Isis surfaced in his mind, the edges becoming more distinguishable. Yet she was still out of focus, still struggling to emerge.

"Maybe we should go to the police," he said. In America, that would be his instinctive reaction. She raised her head and looked at him as if he had gone mad.

"I know," he said, remembering her earlier admonition: "They keep order. They don't redress wrongs. Besides, what would I tell them? And they would say to me, 'Why did you go to the City of the Dead in the first place? Americans do not go to that place.' I would wind up the guilty party. Perhaps they will deport me."

"Well, then," Abdel snickered. "They will give you sensible advice."

"You're not so smart yourself," he said, finding just enough humor to break the tension. "You had a good deal going until you met me."

He closed his eyes. He wanted to sleep, but he couldn't.

The past gnawed at him, as if in recalling it he might understand the present. His mother had been protective, smothering sometimes, and even now, he felt the terrible loss of her.

"Let the boy go," his father had urged when he had determined to go to Cornell. It had not been easy for him to make that decision. "He's not your baby anymore, Farrah. He's a man now. Someday we won't be around to protect him."

He heard Abdel stir, reminding him of his loneliness.

"Come here," he said, patting the mattress beside him. "You need rest."

He sensed her hesitation, then patted the mattress again. Soon he felt her weight beside him. From her breathing, he knew she was not sleeping.

"What would it have been like for her?" he asked.

"Her?"

"Isis."

He was patient, knowing she was groping with her own thoughts.

"A girl without a family is nothing," she said quietly, surely thinking about herself.

"Do you think the old woman loved her?"

"Love!" He sensed her confusion.

"The love of a mother," he explained. "A father."

He heard her swallow deeply, and he was silent for a long time.

"What choices would she have?" he asked suddenly.

"Choices?" It was purely rhetorical, since they both knew the answer. "There were no choices," she said. It seemed the bedrock of her knowledge, and he knew she could not resist the answer. "Not for her. She would simply have been grown, like a weed. She would not go to school. She would not be able to read." There was a long pause. "I can read. I have gone to school," she said proudly, as if to compare herself to the hapless Isis. She seemed reluctant to continue.

"And then?" he pressed, opening his eyes, looking at the ceiling. The stained and flaking plaster looked like a bas-relief of a lifeless planet.

"More than likely, a whore." She was hesitant, embarrassed. "A child whore. A plaything for men."

"For money," he asked. "That kind."

He knew that she was nodding, but he did not look at her.

"When? What age?"

"Sometimes very young," she said. "But there could be other choices," she said, quickly. "Labor. Like an animal. Or marriage. Babies. It is the same thing." He caught a glimpse of her own aspirations in the answer. She was engaged in her own struggle. It was, he understood now more than ever before, easier to be a male in this land.

He tried to relate it to his own experiences. But it was futile.

"Could she have risen above it?" Si asked. "Not gone that way. Become educated? Lived a better life." He checked himself. Better was a concept with many definitions. *Education* in his context could mean many things to her.

"Do you know what I mean?" he pressed.

He felt himself focusing on her, Abdel. He was sure it couldn't be her name. They were talking, he realized, in her language but not on her terms. She might have been on another planet. Perhaps, after all, America was the illusion and Egypt was the real world. He wanted to ask her more about herself, her life. She merged with Isis in his mind.

"Do you think she's alive?" he asked. It was another question impossible to answer. Perhaps he was asking it really to the ibis-headed god engraved on the glass panel that separated the toilet? He was surprised when she answered him.

"I hope so. For your sake."

He wondered what she meant, but decided to remain silent. There was also an inexplicable hint of waspishness in her tone.

Again, he remembered the old woman's words. *I brought her to him at the university.* To whom? If only he had pressed her further.

Fatigue finally gripped him and he felt his mind flicker. Outdoor noises faded. He assured himself that he was sleeping. Something touched his forehead, a tiny gust of cool breeze, barely touching. A kiss, perhaps.

CHAPTER TWENTY-ONE

H E WOKE UP WITH the idea bubbling on the surface of his consciousness, alert immediately to his surroundings. Abdel slept like an embryo, balled against the side of his body. She did not stir when he rose. Cautiously, he opened the balcony shutters a crack and peered out into the street. As always, people patrolled the pavement like walking phantoms. He sensed that he was being watched and closed the shutters.

Gathering his clothes, he stuffed them in a shirt, which he buttoned, closing off the neck to make a hollow sack. He signed a traveler's check for the approximate amount of his two days' stay, and using an end of moist soap, pasted it on the chipped mirror that hung beside the open shelving.

"What is it?" Abdel said, rubbing her eyes.

"Alexandria," he said. "Isis was born in Alexandria in 1951. December first. My mother was explicit about that. There must be a record of the birth. Some clue."

"They'll follow us," she said. The possessive pronoun jarred him. Now he was using her shamelessly.

Ignoring his guilt, he rummaged among the litter of clothes and pulled out a pair of faded jeans and a cotton shirt. "Come here."

She obeyed him, standing as he measured the jeans, ripping them at the legs to conform to her size. "Now put these on. And this shirt as well."

She was confused, hesitating as she stared at the altered jeans.

"I'll turn around," he said, smiling at her delicacy. He listened to her movements as she changed.

In her new outfit, she seemed metamorphosed, almost a woman, although the oversize clothes made her seem lumpish. She held the jeans at the waist, looking distraught, and the cotton shirt hung on her like a loose shroud. He took off his belt, redundant with his own tight jeans, and fastened it around her. When he finished, he stepped back and could not resist a smile.

"You'll do," he said, shaking his head.

"For what?" she asked, showing a flash of belligerence.

"Where does the train leave from? To Alexandria?"

"The main station. In Ramses Square. Not too far. A fifteen-minute walk."

"Good."

He pressed his clothes into her arms. "I want you to climb down that balcony. Then cut out. With any luck, you might look like me in the dark." He smiled again. "A smaller version. But they've got to be watching and probably won't make the distinction. If anyone can lose a pursuer, you can." It was a thought dredged up from the plot of an old movie. She nodded.

"We'll take the first train out for Alexandria. I have no idea when it leaves. But I'll buy the tickets."

"What class?" she asked. The question seemed to attack his smugness. "There are three. Buy a third class. More crowds."

"Okay, I'll meet you. Near the gate."

He felt a pang of concern. What she was doing was dangerous. They would be inflamed by the deception, especially if it worked.

"Let them see you at first. Then disappear." He gripped her shoulder, rubbing the frail blade under the oversize shirt. "Can you do it?"

"Yes," she said.

"You're mad," he muttered, watching her open the shutter, walk out onto the balcony and climb over the ledge, the stuffed shirt tied to a loop of her jeans like some giant bustle.

Hidden in the shadows, he watched the street below as she descended slowly enough to ensure detection. As she reached the street and headed in the direction of the river, he saw two men move simultaneously after her. In a moment, they were all running.

Without delay, he slipped into the corridor and quickly descended the stairs. The untidy lobby was deserted, except for a clerk who banged away intently on a noisy, old-fashioned adding machine while an old man slumbered in the cab of the elevator. He passed them without detection and headed for Ramses Square.

Light was edging along the sky when he reached the antiquated railroad station. An elevated overpass ran past the giant seated statue of Ramses II. Cairo was awakening and the crowds were thick on the overpass. The square below was choked with traffic. A line of droshkies, their leather bonnets glistening in the first rays of the morning sun, waited in a line at the station entrance for the initial fares of the day.

Inside the station, people seemed on the edge of hysteria as they crowded around the ticket kiosks or fought for space on benches or the station floor. They were a motley, overburdened populace of every imaginable shade of skin, in costumes of endless variety. The smells, a mixture of rotted fruit, garlic, sweat, hash, urine, and lubricating oil, formed its own special effluvia, permeating everything. He felt a nagging concern for Abdel. It was, he knew, wrong to involve her, wrong to endanger her, wrong, too, to be saddled with her. He bought two third-class tickets and proceeded to the departure platform.

The first train for Alexandria was scheduled to leave at seven. A crowd had begun to gather on the platform.

Women in black malayas sat cross-legged on the platform floor clutching their offspring. *This country is a swamp of fecundity*, he thought. Soldiers in sloppy black uniforms stood around with fixed bayonets watching the crowd with disinterest and boredom.

Settling at a place near the gate behind a man who stood waist-high in a pile of caged chickens, he observed the main waiting room, a whirlpool of humanity. Obviously, the British engineers who designed the station had not foreseen it being used by so many people.

The train was already in place, although the doors had not yet opened. Growing impatient, he surveyed the unruliness, noting how easily the concept of the British queue had dissolved in the Egyptian ferment.

He purchased two brioches and a Turkish coffee from a vendor, quickly returning to his vantage point, eating one brioche, sipping the tepid coffee. He put the other brioche in his pocket, anticipating Abdel.

Something disturbed the chickens and they began to cackle. Occasionally, eyes turned toward him, but they seemed more curious than predatory, more evidence that he had not fully stitched himself into the Egyptian fabric.

He watched the main entrance to the station, hoping he might see her coming. The minute hand of a large battered standing clock jittered toward the top of the hour. Its reliability was suspect. His own watch was six hours ahead of it.

The train door shuddered open and the carriages sucked up the assorted passengers like a gigantic vacuum cleaner. A loudspeaker blared an incoherent announcement, although he caught the words *Alexandria* and *leaving*.

When he felt he had waited for the last possible moment, he moved into the train, slipping into a crowded shabby interior. All the seats were quickly taken, and the overflow passengers sat on the floor. He edged himself through a wall of grumbling bodies. Continuing to stand, his height gave him the advantage of being able to continue to view the station platform.

The train grunted forward, spilling him against the passengers. Regaining his balance, he pushed his way through the crowds to keep the entrance gate in view. His anxiety grew. Where was Abdel? The wheels creaked, stopped, then squeaked forward again.

"Filthy louts," an unshaven man dressed in a wrinkled white shirt and bow tie said to him in broken English, obviously trying to impress him. "Not like in the old days."

Si ignored him and moved away, elbowing through a knot of firmly planted black-shrouded women. The train began to pick up speed. He yearned to resolve his apprehension about Abdel, to put it away the guilt, hoping he might prod himself to indifference. Perhaps they caught up with her? Hurt her? He had no right to expose her to such risks. The entrance gate moved out of sight.

Then he saw her. She was sprinting along the platform, her face tense and glistening with perspiration, the shirt bundle still attached to her belt, bouncing as she ran. He waved frantically. She saw him. Straining to reach the carriage door, he had to elbow his way through the crowd, sprawling across grunting bodies.

A chorus of shouts tried to stop him, and by the time he reached the door, he was nearly horizontal, but he managed to turn the latch, and Abdel bounded into the carriage. Her success in getting onto the train softened the complaints of those who had suffered by his actions, and as everyone righted themselves, the mood became good-natured.

"Sorry, everyone," he told them, as Abdel scrambled upright. The sweat had soaked through her shirt and she gasped for breath.

"You should try out for the Egyptian track team for the next Olympics."

She nodded, smiled, and tried to calm her breathing. He managed to find a clear corner of the car, where they squatted on the floor. She leaned against him.

190

"And here's your prize," he said, presenting her with the brioche he had stuffed into his pocket. She took it with a shaking hand.

"Did they follow you into the station?"

"I had to hide. They were very persistent." He was proud of her, happy that she had made it. The train rolled past the drab outskirts of Cairo, gaining speed as it reached the flats of green farmland, dotted by small villages along the river's edge.

"Nothing changes them," Abdel whispered. Women in black malayas walked gracefully along paths beside the Nile, carrying water jars on their heads. Barefoot men on little gray donkeys rode the trails through the fields. Naked children watched their mothers beating clothes on the river's stones. A blinkered water buffalo walked his perpetual circle around an Archimedes' screw.

"I grew up in a village like that," Abdel said, as they rode past a ramshackle row of mud-brick huts. "Not far from here."

"What was it like?" he asked.

"Beautiful," she said, mystifying him.

"Do you ever go back?"

"It is impossible."

She waved suddenly at a group of smiling villagers. "One of them is me," she said.

He thought about what she meant, remembering Thomas Wolfe's wise title, *You Can't Go Home Again.*

The tracks eased slowly downward, then suddenly were lower than the river, then rose again to the surface of the fields. He was amazed at the slenderness of the green strip on either side of the Nile. Not far, the desert began abruptly. Abdel was silent for a long time.

"Are you glad that I showed up?" she asked. She had closed her eyes. He thought she was asleep.

"Yes," he whispered. She smiled.

"I'm glad," she said.

She closed her eyes again and, after a while, despite the crowds, the heat, the smells, the bumpy track bed, they slept.

CHAPTER TWENTY-TWO

.

H IS FIRST IMPRESSION OF Alexandria was that it
seemed only half finished.

He counted more than a hundred unfinished buildings until
he gave up. The buildings that were finished needed repairs.
Every edifice needed a coat of paint. The street crowds were
thinner than in Cairo, which could have been because most
of the residents clogged the beaches, an arc of yellowish sand
edging the blue Mediterranean. After the stifling journey, the
taste of the sea tang was refreshing.

His plan, which seemed less defined than it had been in
Cairo, was to find some record of Isis's birth. He had no idea
what such information would reveal. His mother had told him
that Isis was born December 1, 1951. It seemed essential that
he find the record of her birth, a point of reference.

They found the city hall, an antiquated building built around
the turn of the century, now a dark cavern, a monument

to stultifying bureaucracy. Every college graduate, he had learned, was guaranteed a government job, albeit low paying. The system, he knew, had to be riddled with inefficiency and make-work. Because of this, indifferent clerks moped about the large open space, bored and disinterested. Even the occasional tin beat of an old model typewriter seemed grudging and unwilling.

It wasn't easy to get someone's attention, but he finally stirred up a junior clerk who looked sleepy and illfed. Si posed the question as succinctly as possible.

"December 1, 1951," the young man repeated with, "Maybe you should write a letter."

They haggled back and forth for a while, until it was apparent that baksheesh was the only way to get the clerk to act. Si slipped him a pound note.

"It will take a few hours," the clerk whispered.

"And another when you get me the information."

The clerk nodded.

"We close at four," he said.

He gave the clerk his mother's full name and the first name of his half sister. He felt uncomfortable and embarrassed when he could not give a father's name. The clerk looked at him with a wry smile.

They walked aimlessly about the main thoroughfares of Alexandria. Both people and vehicles moved at a slower pace than in Cairo. Soon they found themselves on the Corniche. The sea glistened invitingly in the sunlight.

"We owe ourselves that treat," he said. They found a stall that sold bathing suits.

She changed behind a curtain, visibly pleased as she shyly displayed herself.

"I never had a bathing suit," she said.

"You are a girl," he whistled with genuine admiration. She frowned for his benefit but blushed with pleasure. Her breasts were small and high, her waist narrow, and her buttocks were shapely, bulging sensually in the tight outline of the one-piece suit. "I don't think you can get away with it much longer, Abdel."

They crossed the Corniche to the beach. She poked him playfully and ran toward the water. He followed her, throwing down his clothing bundle. Running like a young deer, her feet flew over the sand, kicking up tiny sand fountains.

At the water's edge, she stopped short. But he dragged her, squealing, into the surf.

"I can't swim," she cried.

"You'll have to learn in a hurry."

When he was waist-deep, he flung her into the surf and watched her scramble to her feet, spitting water and rubbing her eyes. She was frightened and, groping toward him, grabbed him around the neck. The surf was mild, gently lifting them, the waves rippling toward shore.

"Feels good," he said, moving farther out, helping her float. He looked upward at the endless blue on which small white clouds, like puffs of cotton, moved lazily across the dome of the sky.

"So clean," he said. "So different from back there."

Rising gently on the ocean's rhythm, he held in an embrace. Her skin smelled sweet and her flesh was smooth and cool.

195

Without thinking, as if it was the most natural of acts, he cupped a breast and felt her nipple harden under the tight material. She didn't protest, but held him closer and continued to watch the vast expanse.

"You come from there?" she asked, lifting her chin as a pointer to the vast horizon.

"A long way from here," he said. He felt suddenly deceived by distance. "Or maybe not." He sensed the odd pull of his mother's blood.

"I don't understand."

He didn't either, not fully. Only that he felt oddly displaced, as if he inherited his mother's lost sense of place.

"Its a lot more than I bargained for," he said as if to himself.

They came out of the water and let the sun dry them. Later, they changed behind a wall, returning to the hall of records exactly at four. The young clerk was scowling.

He would not give him the document until Si had slipped him another pound. Si did not try to read it until he got outside. Holding it with shaking fingers, he read:

"Born. December 1, 1951. Given name Isis. Mother's name: Farrah. Father's name..." He swallowed hard. "Benito Mussolini!" he exclaimed. "Mussolini."

He felt a sense of spoilage, as if the ridicule was meant to defile. Abdel looked at him with confusion, not comprehending.

"He was the Italian dictator during World War II."

She took the paper from him, puzzling over it. He felt assaulted by despair. The gulf between him and his mother widened. Was she capable of such black humor?

"The Dancing Dolphin," Abdel said, reading from the paper. Isis was born at the Dancing Dolphin. She held out the paper for him to see.

Abdel jogged beside him. *Mussolini? Dancing Dolphin? Was it the same Farrah? The same Isis? Surely, someone is mocking us.*

The sun was now in the lower part of its descending arc, bathing the city in soft pink tones, hiding its blemishes. They stopped at a broken-down café with battered tables under torn umbrellas. It overlooked a crowded stretch of beach, from which people were now emerging in droves. In the distance, the ubiquitous call to prayer sounded from the loudspeakers in the minarets.

Si ordered himself a Stella, a labeled beer popular even in a country where Moslems are commanded to drink no alcohol, and a cola for Abdel. He felt worn out, frustrated.

"Nothing makes sense here," he growled. Abdel shrugged. A few Stellas later, he spoke again. "Not her either."

"Who?"

"Farrah. My mother. I feel..." He groped for the right word. "...shit... betrayed. I mean to be honest. Why should she have led a whole other life without telling me? She coddled me, smothered me. I choked on it. All that so-called love. But she had this whole other fucking life." He gulped down his beer. "Mussolini?" he fumed. "They killed that bastard after World War II. Forty-five. Six years before Isis was born." He ordered another beer and fell into a deep brooding despair.

"She was a god-damned whore. And she deserted her own kid," he mumbled, the words choking him.

Finishing his beer, he paid the waiter and stalked off, walking swiftly, stopping only to brood over beer after beer at the ramshackle outdoor cafés that lined the way. By the time the sun came down and the lights went on, he was in an alcoholic haze and his black mood had accelerated. Abdel tagged along like a forlorn puppy. Once, she tried to stop him from drinking.

"Don't mother me."

She retreated into silence.

At every café, somber men looked at him with scorn, as if his obvious alien presence was an affront to their sense of privacy. Growing loud did not help the situation, although he managed to keep just below the edge of obnoxiousness. The fact that he spoke Arabic may have given them some excuse for toleration. As the night wore on, the narrow streets exploded with lights and people, many of them foreign seamen, dark, swarthy individuals bent on relief from the boredom of the sea, lured by the beat of the belly dancers' music.

He moved from café to café falling into the stream of aimless wanderers. He felt at home here with these rootless men, their eyes glazed, seeking a moment's respite from the sewer of their bleak reality. He joined them eagerly. Abdel hung back, watchful.

Abdel saw it first, a flashing neon outline of what barely resembled a fish, but the words confirmed the illustration. She tugged at his arm. Misinterpreting, he shrugged her away.

"There," she persisted. "The Dancing Dolphin."

He turned and saw it and the electrification transmitted itself across the space, partially sobering him. Running drunkenly, he pushed through the crowds. It was a small place, smokefilled and jammed to the rafters. A belly dancer was performing.

"Who owns this place?" he asked the bartender, who motioned toward a bone-thin ascetic man sitting near the cash register. Jostling his way through the crowds, Si confronted the man.

"You the owner?"

The man showed a broad smile, filled with gold teeth.

"You want to buy this place?" the man said in halting but efficient Arabic. "They steal you blind." He laughed, snapping open the register and making change.

"How long have you owned this place?" Si asked, forcing a tone of humility.

"Ten years," he mumbled. For some reason, his openness had turned inward and he had become obviously suspicious.

"It's important to me," Si said. He struggled to convey his sincerity. "I need to know who was here around the end of 1951."

The man smiled, as if the idea was both amusing and ludicrous. He thought for a minute.

"Farouk. He was around." The knot of customers within earshot laughed uproariously.

"Please," Si said, touching the man's arm. Perhaps it was the touch of the flesh that softened the man. He looked at Si and shrugged.

"Try the old hag. She was here then. Vivanti. She still owns the damned building. Miss a minute in paying the rent and she's down on me like an avenging angel. And she's a wop like me."

"Where can I find her?" Si pressed, though the man, making change for another customer, seemed to have come to the edge of his reservoir of goodwill.

199

"Try her flat." He gave Si the address. "See, it's engraved in my head."

Outside, he found a policeman in a rumpled uniform smoking a cigarette in an alley. He seemed annoyed by the intrusion, but finally offered detailed directions.

Abdel had listened carefully and absorbed the directions better than Si. They were quickly lost in a labyrinth of narrow streets.

"Left," Abdel said when he took a wrong turn. "The policeman said left."

Finally, after more argument, they were on the right track again with Abdel leading.

"Sorry, kid, I've been a shit," he said, when they found the right address, an old three-story building struggling to retain some air of respectability. There were a number of flats in the building.

"Vivanti." He read the name in both the Arabic and Roman letters. Under the nameplate was a tiny buzzer, which he pressed. When he got no response, he rang again. A curtain moved on the ground-floor level and he saw the flashing light of a television set. He rang again. Someone was moving slowly in the hallway, and finally the door opened. A woman's surly voice croaked, "Who are you?"

He hadn't expected the tone.

"Osiris Kelly," he said, politely, knowing that it would have no meaning for the woman. Politeness nearly always works with strangers, he knew, but this woman was obviously a hard case.

"Go away."

"I must talk with you."

"Talk then."

"Not out here." He resisted the impulse to push the door open.

"Then go away."

"Please." He moved his head closer to the crack, but the interior was dark and he could not make out the woman. "You owned the Dancing Dolphin in 1951?"

"Who are you?" she snapped.

"Nineteen fifty-one," he repeated.

"You looking for back taxes," she sneered.

"No," Si said. "I'm the son of a woman you might have known then. Farrah was her name." There was a long silence. He could hear the woman's heavy breathing.

"You're a liar," she challenged. "The child was a girl."

His heart leaped. He looked at Abdel and gripped her arm.

"She knows," he whispered.

"Isis," he said, spitting the name out joyously. "Isis was her name." He hesitated.

The woman grew silent, and he sensed she was debating with herself. She thrust open the door, looked them over suspiciously, then walked heavily through the dark corridor, slippers flapping on the stone floor. They followed her into a tiny room filled with furniture and the heavy must odor of old age. She lowered the sound on the TV. The program was *Hawaii Five-O* with Arabic subtitles.

Then she turned on a lamp with an old-fashioned beaded shade, angled it, and inspected his face.

"And you? Say again."

"Farrah's son. Osiris Kelly. She died last week in America."

"So she got away from them," the woman said, shaking her head. "Landed in America, eh." She fixed the lamp shade and waved the visitors to an overstuffed couch, while she sat in a straight chair facing them.

"Who is this one?" she said in a direct, arrogant manner.

"A friend," he said.

Abdel nodded. The old woman seemed only barely convinced. Si studied her face, dark, wrinkled, with a gaping toothless mouth and steel-gray hair tied in a heavy bun. The room, stuffed with possessions, offered a fitting complement to the acquisitive, predatory air of the woman, which smacked of greed and penury.

"So she died," the old woman said, shaking her head. "Like my Vivanti, that alcoholic bum. That lazy bastard." She seemed to be gaining a good head of indignation. "That Farrah. Couldn't dance worth anything, but a good body. That Vivanti. Never a single moment's peace. Nothing but aggravation." She clucked her tongue and twisted old arthritic fingers in her lap. There seemed no end to her indignation.

"She named you Osiris. Of course. That had to be." The woman's old eyes continued to probe him.

"Farrah," the woman said, beginning a new round of vituperations. "She was a stupid fool. Pride." Her eyes narrowed and she squinted into Si's face. "Too proud. Then when she got smart, it was too late." The woman's internal wanderings confused him.

"Her birth certificate said the father was Benito Mussolini."

The woman's face seemed to puff up with air. The toothless mouth gaped.

"Mussolini?" She seemed to be struggling for recall, then finally, her head rolled back and a strident cackle, like a rooster's morning cry, rose from deep inside of her.

"Mussolini. That fool, Vivanti. That sly dog. He died just to escape me. I wouldn't let them put the coffin in the ground until I was sure he was dead. Benito Mussolini. Another dirty bastard."

He was puzzled, but the woman's eccentricities were alarming and he did not want to inhibit the flow of information.

"Then who was Isis's father?" Si asked, when her vitriol had subsided. She looked at him as if he had lost his mind.

"You mean she never told you?" she said, contemplating him archly. "Who is your father?"

"An American. Mike Kelly. Mother married him in 1953. They met in Tripoli."

"Married?" She nodded, acknowledging what seemed like admiration. The grim facade, he saw, was a pose. He was sure of that.

"I am looking for Isis," he said. "For some reason, my mother left her in Egypt, in the summer of 1952."

"So she did abandon the baby?" The woman grew silent. "Finally. She should never have let it be born." She appeared to be saying more to herself, not for his ears.

"Why are you looking for her?" she asked.

He had dreaded the question, remembering his explanation to his father: *She wanted me to go, Dad.* It seemed, suddenly, shallow, incomplete. Was it really something that his mother had urged? Or something he demanded of himself? He groped for a believable answer.

"It's something I felt I had to do... to understand the..." He felt himself stumbling. "Mother never... Not until she was about to die. Suddenly, a link." He was growing irritated with himself. The old woman seemed embarrassed by the explanation. She nodded and looked away.

"I think about Farrah," she said. She was softer now, confirming Si's suspicion about her. "It was Vivanti. He made me send her away." A note of guilt intruded. "Then, later, I saw her picture and the baby. The newspaper story." She looked up and confronted him sharply. "She told you nothing? Nothing?"

Si looked at Abdel. Newspaper story? They exchanged puzzled glances.

"Then you have no idea who Isis's father was?"

He shook his head.

"Worse," he said. "There seem to be others looking for Isis as well. Some shadowy figure. A man named Zakki." The name made a strong impression on her.

"That one."

"You know him?" He thought of the old woman at the City of the Dead. She had spoke of a man named Zakki as well.

Abdel stirred beside him. A wave of fear washed over him.

"He came once. Also looking for Isis. We knew who he was. He had been Farouk's chauffeur, a mean bastard. Vivanti didn't know where Isis was. How would he know, the dirty dago? Zakki beat him, cut him all over. It took him months to recover. But he didn't know."

"When was that?"

She thought for a moment. "Sixty-seven. I always remember. Vivanti died in sixty-eight."

"But why? Did he say why?"

She shook her head.

"I have never seen a greater rage." She sighed. "Vivanti was never the same." Behind the mask of enmity for her dead husband, Si saw her loneliness.

"He was her father?" Si asked.

"Vivanti?"

"That toad. Of course not."

"And Zakki?"

The woman got up from the chair and went to a shelf piled high with papers. Snapping open an eyeglass case, she carefully put on her glasses and began to rummage through the papers, stirring ancient dust.

"Zakki is still searching for her," Si said. The woman ignored him, continuing to carefully sift through the papers, occasionally holding one to the sparse light. They watched her. From time to time she mumbled something incoherently.

After a while, she came back to the chair and sat down, spreading a yellowed clipping on her lap, pressing out its folds. Then she handed it to him. Abdel came closer while they read it.

"King Farouk..." He felt his throat constrict and his lungs seemed to close. "Teenage mistress." The words swam before his eyes. "My god." He could not recognize the young woman who stared out from the badly faded clipping. Some of the type had been obliterated, leaving large gaps in the story. "I can't believe it."

"You think I could believe it. That's why I must have kept it all these years."

He was totally confused. Was this his mother? Surely not the woman he had known. The face of the baby was featureless.

Mrs. Vivanti seemed to observe him closely, then rose and moved to a cupboard, taking out a bottle of Scotch and a tumbler, which she half filled, handing it to him. He drank it greedily, feeling the liquid burn, jolting him.

"I had no idea," he whispered. Images of his mother crowded in on him, an indistinguishable jumble. Then the wall of the musty room seemed to compress, while the woman's body enlarged and he felt the beginning of some awesome feeling of strangulation. Suddenly, he stood up and slowly the feeling went away. The woman watched him.

"You look like you saw a ghost," she said.

"I did," he croaked. "This is my mother. I hadn't a clue." He cleared his throat. "Then where is my sister?"

The woman shrugged.

"And the man, Zakki. Did he ever find her?"

"The mother or the baby?" the woman asked, her mind obviously still shrewd and alert. She shrugged her answer and remained silent.

"Can I keep this?" he managed to say. The woman nodded assent. Although he tried valiantly to control his emotions, he could not. He felt a sob rise in his chest. *I have got to get out of here, quickly,* he told himself, moving toward the door, Abdel beside him. Questions choked themselves in his brain, like flames sputtering into life, then extinguishing themselves like trick candles. He felt slightly dizzy, nauseous.

He held up the clipping which shook in his hand. "My mother..." he began, then could no longer speak.

"Your mother? Crazy. She was beauty. That I will say."

"Thank you so much," Si croaked, barely able to speak.

"Go. Go. Go find your little princess."

"Princess?"

Outside again, he headed for the beach. It was pitch dark. He needed to clear his mind. Abdel said nothing. He wondered if she understood. *My sister is a princess*, he thought.

For a long time, he sat cross-legged at the surf's edge, watching the ocean's eternal rhythm, spangled by the million chips of light from the canopy of stars. The vastness seemed appropriate to his own state of mind. He was, after all, a minuscule grain of matter in the infinite cosmos. Why hadn't his mother told him about Farouk? Why had she kept such a secret until the end? Shame? Fear? That was a mystery that he would never solve.

He lay back, resting his head on his arms, and looked up at the flickering sky. Losing himself in its infinity soothed him. What was he looking for, he asked, wondering if it was a question directed at God or himself. God? Allah? Knowledge beyond comprehension?

Abdel squatted beside him. Suddenly he felt the need to touch something alive. He put his arm around her. She leaned against him.

"It's coming too fast," he said. "I can't grasp it. My view of her is so different. Like she was another person." He paused, shivering, holding Abdel closer. "She was my mother. How could I not know my own mother? And that article. So... so damned tawdry, a filthy little scandal. Maybe she just had to get away from here. Maybe the embarrassment... Yet it seems so out of character. Not the woman who bore me and loved me. Who was she really?"

Abdel shivered and leaned against him for warmth.

"Why did she tell me? She could have died with it all hidden. That's the enigma..." He sat for a long time, pondering the relentless flow of the ocean's tide. "Maybe you were right, what good will it do to stir up old ashes?"

He released her and lay supine, watching the stars.

"It's too late," he muttered. "I've already bit the damned apple. I must see this to the end. I need to know. Now more than ever. Is she alive?"

He closed his eyes, feeling his fatigue. His energy dissipated, he slipped into sleep. It seemed his only defense.

CHAPTER TWENTY-THREE

H E AWOKE AT DAWN. A sliver of light on the eastern horizon lit up the sea. He apparently had turned in his sleep into the fetal position, and he was surprised to find that Abdel was stretched along his back, her arm wrapped around his midsection. Removing it gently, he rose and walked to the sea's edge. The tide had receded. He brought his toilet kit from the stuffed shirt, lathered up and shaved by touch, then brushed his teeth with the salt water. He felt clean and fresh.

When he turned, Abdel was sitting up, rubbing her eyes, and the top arc of the sun was poking above the horizon. In the distance, he could hear the muezzin's call to prayer. Alexandria was stirring.

Abdel stood up and walked to the sea's edge, her graceful body silhouetted against the light, looking like a long-stemmed flower, caught in a puff of breeze. Watching her stirred memories of last night's revelations. People were arriving at the beach, their presence jarring him back to reality.

He knew he had to go back to Mrs. Vivanti. He reached into his pocket and unfolded the faded clipping that the woman had given him. He read it again with disbelief then noted the byline, Arthur Thompson, and the name of the newspaper, *Al Akhbar*. Perhaps this fellow, Thompson, was still around? It annoyed him that he had let his emotions rule his mind last night. He wanted the woman to empty her mind of everything she had known about his mother and sister. He felt the depths of his inexperience. Confrontations required better reflexes. Mrs. Vivanti could have offered insights, more clues.

Abdel came closer to him. Her hair was damp and the water had curled it. Watching her broke the tension and he smiled.

"Why are you smiling?" she asked.

"That outfit," he said. She smoothed her clothes. His comment had triggered her vanity. "We'll have to get you some decent clothes." He put his hands in his pocket, withdrew his packet of traveler's checks and counted them.

"You spent too much last night," she scolded. "Drinking."

"At least the hotel was the right price," he said, waving his arm to take in the beach. Others, too, had used the beach for the same purposes and were stirring now. Not far, a band of naked children were already squealing in the surf and he could see joggers moving in the distance.

On the Corniche, they bought a round loaf of bread from a vendor and washed it down with a cup of tea in a tiny café that had just opened. Abdel was unusually quiet, brooding. He tried to josh her into better spirits. Her response was enigmatic.

"If she's the daughter of a king, that makes her a princess."

"I hadn't thought of that," he lied. The fact of her paternity had considerably altered Isis's image in his mind. "A lot of good it did." It was like a painting being slowly filled in by a brush from an unknown hand.

The information eruption had subsided and he was able now to pick among the debris. His mother had been a belly dancer, mistress to a king, the subject of a scandal. But the idea of the anarchic term did not amuse him. Had his mother been a whore? The generational gap widened. A whore? What was that? So Zakki had been Farouk's chauffeur. He suddenly recalled the danger, remembering, too, what Madame Vivanti had said about Zakki beating up her husband. He thought, too, of the dead woman at the City of the Dead.

"I hadn't expected this," he said, shaking his head.

"Nor I," Abdel whispered, looking despairingly into the teacup.

"You can get off the train anytime you want," he said, annoyed now with her gloom.

He got up, paid for the tea, and stormed off. Abdel, hesitating at first, quickly caught up with him.

They passed through the narrow streets in the direction of the woman's flat. His movements were deliberately slow, as his mind catalogued the questions he would ask. Merchants were just opening their stalls. A gnarled little man was carrying out a rack of skirts and blouses. He suddenly felt guilty about Abdel.

"Let's get you something that fits right," he said. She frowned, but he rifled through the racks, measuring clothing against her body. Picking out a skirt and a white blouse, he gave them to her. The gnarled man pointed to the back. Abdel went behind a curtain, clutching the clothing. While Si waited, he poked around the stalls, finally buying her a cheap pendant, a piece of coral on a chain, bargaining with the man. It made him feel good to get the price down to half what the man was asking.

"I'm half Arab," he told the man, smiling.

The clothes he had picked out for her fit her surprisingly well, clinging to her youthful but now visible curves. Looking at her approvingly, he made her turn around and fastened the chain on the back of her neck. When she felt it, her eyes filled with tears.

"We don't need your blubbering," he said. "And don't look so damned grateful. A simple thank-you will do."

She nodded, unable to speak.

"At least you look like a girl now."

There is no mistaking that, he thought. An errant awareness of her sexuality intruded on his consciousness, but he dismissed it. *She's just a kid.*

He picked up speed. She hurried beside him, continuing to finger the coral pendant.

He had forgotten the address, and they made a number of false turns, although he regained the direction by recognizing a familiar sight here and there. He hadn't realized he had been so subconsciously alert. Finally, he was sure that he was on the right street and he hurried toward where he knew the house would be.

Even as he smelled the first whiff of acrid smoke, he knew what it was. A group of curious onlookers had clustered around the still smoking ruin. He did not have to ask what had happened.

"We're the kiss of death," he murmured, stopping briefly, then turning. Abdel seemed rooted to the spot, her eyes searching the crowd.

"How the hell could they know?" he said.

"They know," Abdel responded, her voice quivering.

CHAPTER TWENTY-FOUR

ZAKKI SAT ALONE ON the terrace, enveloped in darkness. The air was heavily perfumed by the moist verdancy. His power of hearing was a vast sensor. He listened, letting the sounds engulf him. He heard the insects pursuing their calamitous existence, the heartbeat of the roosting birds, the inchoate whelp of the desert puppy, the relentless tide of water emptying out of Africa. When he concentrated, he was sure he could hear the tremulous hum of the bottom fish in their river nests.

He rarely slept. It was a habit he had picked up when he had worked for Farouk. Once, the monarch's restlessness had been an enigma. Then Zakki had finally understood. There was no terror like the terror of dreams. And no comfort greater than the comfort of greed. Beyond that was the snake pit.

Triggered by the thought, he felt the cobra of agony stir inside of him again, the cobra of agony, a scaled, slithering cold-blooded serpent, coiling again around the soft center of

213

himself. Nothing, he knew, would ever satisfy that. Nothing but Isis.

Please, soon, he screamed inside of himself, feeling the beast squeeze its warning. *Soon!*

The young man's arrival had quickened the beast's hunger. Not that he had ever given up, but the scent had simply gotten colder. Then the boy had come. Farrah's boy!

He raised his bulk from the chaise and moved to the edge of the terrace. Between the palm trees, he could see the tiny lights that edged the outer wall of the villa. Men guarded the compound day and night, oblivious to the central truth that the enemy was inside, had crawled from the snake pit, into him, through the wound.

He moved back to his chaise. Next to it was a small table filled with cakes and sweets, an exact replica of the foods on which his old boss had gorged. His body had become a gelatinous mass, a balloon of oily flesh, as if all the remaining glands and ducts were discharging inside of him. Puddles of fat rolled over his bull neck, dripping downward, like melted wax, over his belly and thighs.

So he had thrown yet more bodies into the pit. He would throw more, a thousand, a hundred thousand, to reach Isis. The young man's sudden presence was a miracle, the miracle he had prayed for. Allah would guide him. He had become a beacon. He had only to track its beam. He had lost the mother forever. But it was the child that had become his obsession, Farrah's child.

Breathing deeply, he felt the faulty pumping of his over-burdened heart. He was certain that it could endure the rigors of the remaining journey. Hadn't he, after all, come to know the truth of Allah's grand design, eye for eye, tooth for tooth, pain for pain?

He was certain, too, that Farouk had metamorphosed his tissues, in the fat-clogged cells, in the flat bald head of the cobra, fueling the brain that directed his agony. That, too, would die with Isis's pain.

He heard the door open and Ahmed's whispering tread as he moved across the terrace. In the dark, the black Nubian was as featureless as smooth onyx. Zakki lifted his head and waited for the soft voice to begin.

"The young man..." he cleared his throat lightly. "And the other one are on the Luxor train. We have people on the train and waiting at Luxor."

The news did not startle him, although earlier he had been puzzled by the youth's actions. He had gone to the offices of *Al Akhbar*, the newspaper, then to Cairo University. At the paper, the boy had talked with an old copy editor. That, Zakki decided, had been a logical deduction. His men had extracted from the Vivanti woman that she had given Kelly the clipping of Farrah's story. So he had certainly tried to contact... he had to dig deep in his memory for the name of the man he had murdered. Thompson. But he was puzzled why the youth had proceeded to the university, where he talked with the head of the Department of Antiquities.

"We can find out," Ahmed had said, responding to his query.

Zakki had decided against that for the time being, although he filed away the names of the people in his mind.

"No need for that, Ahmed," he had replied, "as long as we follow the young man." Only later, when it was over, would he retrace his steps. Everyone in the chain must be swept away. Everyone!

When Ahmed had gone, he lay back on the chaise and sipped mineral water. He had only to be patient. He praised himself for having learned this trait. It buttressed his faith in his instincts. Farrah's boy, he knew, would lead him to Isis.

At first, he had denied this instinct. But at each stage in his life, he had looked back and seen the moving finger of fate.

As a boy, watching the young king in the open carriage, sharing the joy and tumult with a million ecstatic Cairenes, he knew that some day their destinies would be intertwined. He had, from that moment, been obsessed with the idea of one day being in the presence of the king, to serve him, to love him. Hadn't destiny put his father's donkey cart in the path of the young king's speeding sports car?

"Is he dead?" the driver had asked. He stood over them in the lonely moonlit road. His father had actually expired without a word, his eyes open to the star-studded sky. The donkey lay howling in a ditch, its hind legs crushed, helpless and pitiful in its agony, still attached to the upended, splintered cart.

By some miracle, Zakki was thrown clear and had scrambled to his father's side, embracing the dead man. Grief had not yet turned to anger. Behind him, he heard footsteps, the slam of the car door, then quick steps toward the shrieking donkey.

"Poor bastard," he heard the driver murmur, followed by the sharp crack of a pistol and the death gurgle of the donkey. The pistol shot had also exploded his anger, and he had lunged at the man and wrestled him into the ground.

Their bodies rolled in the mud of the ditch, and his hands had instinctively reached for his neck, gripping it, pressing his thumbs against the windpipe.

The man struggled, but he was no match for the strength of frustration. Surely, in a moment, he would have been dead. The life seemed to be running out of him. He had ceased to struggle. Then Zakki looked down at the face, saw the eyes pleading, open and bulging.

"You," Zakki said, releasing his grip. The king sat up and rubbed his neck. It was then that Zakki saw the pistol still in his hand.

"I nearly pulled the trigger," he said, struggling to his feet.

"Forgive me," Zakki had sputtered. Forgive him? Recalling that would always sear his guts.

"I didn't see you," the king said. "These damned carts should have taillights." He walked back to the sports car and kneeled near the headlights. Both casings were cracked and the grill had been bashed in.

"Brand-new. I was just trying it out." He looked up at Zakki, who stood behind him, filled with contrition and confusion. For the moment, he had actually forgotten about his dead father. "Ruined," the king said. "It's English. I'll have to get the parts sent. Tough luck."

He stood up and lit a cigarette, puffing deeply. The match light had illuminated Zakki's face.

"Who was he?" the king asked, with a shrug of his shoulder.

"My father," Zakki murmured, looking toward the heap at his feet.

"Shit," the king said, shaking his head. "I couldn't see you."

He threw the lighted cigarette at his feet and stamped it out.

"Look..." Zakki could see the king's hands pat his pockets. "I'd like to make this up to you. Really. I feel like hell about it. I can make it up to you."

"Why are you alone?" Zakki asked, stupidly. It had been inconceivable that the king could ever be alone.

The king looked at him shrewdly, the sense of superior majesty restored. He ignored the question. They were about the same age, but the space between them was an ocean.

"Come to the Qubbah Palace tomorrow," the king said, the air of command abrupt. He grabbed the handle of the car door and pulled. The door seemed stuck.

"Damned door's out of line," the king huffed, shaking his head. Without thinking, Zakki rushed to the rescue, grabbing the handle and tugging until the door squeaked open. The king bent and moved into the seat, Zakki holding the door open, then closing it.

"No need to mention this," Farouk said, touching Zakki's arm. Zakki could see the king's smiling features clearly. He nodded.

"Good boy," the king said, patting his arm. Zakki felt an uncommon flush of pleasure as he looked toward the ground. "What is your name?"

"Ashraf Zakki," he mumbled.

"Speak up, boy," the king commanded.

Zakki repeated his full name.

"Tomorrow then, Zakki."

The king waved, gunned the motor, and backed up until the car could be maneuvered around the wrecked cart. It did not quite clear his father's body, bumping over the dead man's legs.

He had, of course, obeyed the king. It would have made little difference in any event. And yet, he had loved his father. Even now, he was grateful to him for the opportunity of meeting the king. He had always said, *You must do better than me, Ashraf.*

CHAPTER TWENTY-FIVE

S LOWLY, AWE HAD BECOME merely admiration, and that had turned to disillusionment, then dislike, contempt, and finally hatred. But in the years with the king, Zakki had acquired wisdom. What he had learned from Farouk was that there was no end to man's hunger. "Get it all!" Farouk had burned the message into his brain. At first, he had been amused by the assertion. But later, under the playboy guise, he watched the relentless greed become the king's sole motivation.

The weak fools had let him go into exile in Italy, along with a great deal of his wealth, much of it in whiskey cases filled with gold ingots. He had carted that off right under their noses. They had tried to recoup by auctioning off his precious collections, but for a fraction of their worth. He suspected that Farouk himself had actually bought a great deal of it. If it had been up to him, he would have blown up Farouk and every one of his lackeys.

Less than a month after the abdication, the king's agent arrived at the brothel where Zakki had made his temporary home. The man, Bordoni, brought him a letter from Farouk, who had set up business headquarters in Italy. The letter announced that Bordoni was his Italian business manager and also laid claim to the "various enterprises" that were the king's conception, thanking Zakki for his "temporary management," which was now to be "relinquished forthwith."

"So he still thinks he is king," Zakki told the man. In his tailored, pinstriped suit and white-on-white shirt, Bordoni looked remarkably cool and confident.

"Frankly, he is still willing to allow you to run things," Bordoni said, picking his teeth with a gold toothpick. "Providing your accounts are accurate and your production increases steady."

Zakki assessed the man, dark hair, swarthy skin, a southern Italian. Zakki had, by then, taken over the brothels, and was still consolidating his hold over the hashish trade. This had proven enormously difficult and complicated, and had depleted almost all of the value of the gold ingots he had stolen from Farouk. They had covered the shipments already in the pipeline. In fact, he had overpaid to show his strength, but there was still a lack of confidence among many of the people in the long chain of distribution.

The hash moved over time-honored Sinai smuggling routes, through the Levant and Syria, over the infamous Via Maris. Bedouin smuggling families had moved their contraband over this route for centuries. Whatever nation claimed the Sinai, it was always the indisputable turf of the Bedouins, who owed no allegiance to anyone but themselves. The bridge of dreams, Farouk had called it.

Zakki had previously accompanied the incognito king to the Sinai, participating in the elaborate transaction between the king and Salah, the sly Bedouin chieftain who, with his family, controlled the smuggling route.

It was 1946. The war was over, and Egypt had been given, under the benign hand of the British, nominal control over the Sinai. In Farouk's eyes, it was a wasteland, good only for what it had always been, an avenue for invading armies going somewhere else, or a smuggling bridge between the Levant and Egypt.

Not content to receive a mere commission, Farouk could not resist the temptation of acquisition. He wanted it all. En route to the Sinai, the king had sat beside him in the truck, disguised as an ordinary workman, enjoying the charade immensely. They had crossed into the Sinai by launch, loaded to the gills with gold, jewels, exotic foodstuffs, and three frightened, eleven-year-old virgins that the king had inspected personally to ensure their certification.

"One busted hymen and our credibility goes down the drain," he had said, roaring with laughter.

They were met on the Sinai side of the Suez Canal by a motley band of Salah's armed henchmen, complete with camels and salukis to carry them on the long hot trek to Salah's camp. The king was in good humor all the way, bouncing along on the camel, energized by the journey.

Not far from Salah's camp, the king changed into his grand-est uniform, that of an admiral in the British navy, an honorary title that he had embellished with lines of decorations and elaborate gold braid, designed especially to impress Salah. Then, mounted on the lead camel, the resplendent Farouk entered the scruffy campsite, a conglomeration of filthy tents and arishas, a kind of temporary arbor booth, used as a make-shift shelter.

Salah was a tall, fierce-looking man with a face of crinkled tar paper from which crafty eyes darted covetously under the ragged rim of his red-checked kaffiyeh. Obviously, Salah felt he was the equal of the king, and both engaged in an astonishingly elaborate round of salamats and handshakes.

Finally, the king offered his gifts, including the three girls, whom the chieftain inspected with undisguised lechery. Farouk had an enormously good time, reveling in the character of a king play-acting a king before this selfpossessed megalo-maniac who ran his moving empire with absolute control over the life and death of the men, women and animals under his care.

All of the men carried guns. To the untrained eye, they appeared to be a pack of impoverished rabble, although it was well known that Salah and his family had sequestered vast wealth in this barren wasteland.

The deal was agreed to and validated by a mutual shower of shukrans, again to the king's vast joy. The two men, gulfs apart in background and breeding, understood each other well. To Zakki, it was a firm lesson in the affinity of greed and lust.

In a gesture of extraordinary hospitality, Salah even offered the king the first choice of the virgins, which the king quickly obliged, performing the deed in an adjoining tent. Salah and Zakki had sat cross-legged outside the tent, listening with pleasure to the girl's cries of pain. The king himself, emerging from the tent, showed his understanding of the niceties of this type of hospitality, waving a bloodstained handkerchief to prove the virgin's penetration.

As a further gesture, Salah himself provided a second penetration, as if it were a final sealing of the pact between the men.

The deal was struck and, thereafter, as an annual ritual, Zakki had made this hegira by himself, although Salah, observing the protocol of kings, never offered Zakki quite the same hospitality.

By the time the king had been deposed, the deal had been going for nearly six years. The only tender had been gold and hashish, and an elaborate distribution system had been carefully constructed. It was, of course, common knowledge that this was, among other things, the king's domain, and no one had dared interfere.

One of Zakki's first acts, after the king had abdicated, was to cement his own relationship with Salah, who wisely continued as before, his shrewd eyes observing that the tribute had been tripled, which was enough evidence for him that Zakki had indeed inherited the king's mantle. Loyalty transferred automatically with the gold.

As for the steady supply of the traditional young virgins, Zakki had worked that out with what he boasted to himself was incredible ingenuity, establishing a network of "farms," like the one at which he had deposited Isis, to serve his purposes. Even when, later, Nasser outlawed the brothels, Zakki had shown his reverence for the law, by closing them down, although the "farms" continued to operate. Lust and money were, as Farouk had shown him, man's most basic motivation.

"There are three ways to a man's heart," Farouk had told him, his eyes sparkling with amusement. "Through the pocket, the balls, and the stomach. It is the primary rule of life."

Oddly, the king had not trafficked in boys, as if some puritan instinct or, perhaps, some insecurity in his own sense of manliness did not allow that. Zakki, on his own, had violated that condition occasionally, when it was necessary to achieve his purposes. Indeed, he prided himself on having embellished the king's lessons, and many an official, even in the supposedly incorruptible regime of the revolutionary idealists, was not without his price among the triumvirate of temptations. Under Sadat, the process continued, but by then it was practically institutionalized. As long as it did not interfere with politics.

But at that early date, the king's confidence was unshaken. In his own mind, Farouk had simply given up the throne of Egypt, not its commercial prerogatives. Italy, after all, was as good a base as any.

"Farouk believes, too," the unflappable Bordoni had continued, "that the hash trade can be considerably increased with export markets opening everywhere, particularly with friends in the Americas...." Bordoni paused. "We... are prepared to be generous."

They had been sitting on cushions in a parlor of the now outlawed bordello currently used for Zakki's business transactions. Between them was a little table on which were a bowl of dates that the men ate as they talked.

225

"I am in control here," Zakki said quietly. "The king is gone." Zakki cleared his throat. "In these humble enterprises, Zakki is king."

Bordoni smiled, a confident sardonic baring of teeth. "But, you see, there are partnerships now. This is not a freelance business anymore." Bordoni moved in his chair and dipped his fingers into a side pocket, drawing out a black glove and putting it on the table. Bordoni's eyes had narrowed and the smile disappeared. The symbolism was not lost on Zakki. He knew its meaning. The Black Hand. Sicilian Mafia. So, the king was paying for his passage, Zakki thought.

"So you see, the king's servant must always be the king's servant."

Zakki nodded. Bordoni must have taken it for consent.

"You are very clever. Farouk said you were very clever. There simply is no choice in the matter."

Zakki nodded again, sensing the man's basic weakness. If the situation was reversed, Zakki would have simply slit the other's throat. The man put too much of a premium on human life. He was ignorant of Egypt. Thousands could be lost, building a pyramid for an ancient king. A hundred thousand could be lost building a canal for Muhammad Ali. Farouk could run over his father and mourn for the dents in his sports car. Egyptians do not fear death. They welcome it. The man was a fool.

Bordoni stood up, looking downward at Zakki, another symbol that was not lost on him. Zakki liked that. It was a fine point. Farouk must have been giving them lessons.

Bordoni rubbed his hands together.

"Well, then we had better get to work," he said, smoothing the pinstriped suit, taking the black leather glove from the table and replacing it in his side pocket. He reached out his hand. The man, Zakki observed, was a stickler for these little niceties.

From under his jacket, Zakki drew a curved dagger lodged in his belt, fashioned in the perfect shape of a half-moon, with a jeweled handle, one of those geegaws that Zakki had spirited from the Farouk collection years before the abdication.

Bordoni had just time to see the metal flash as Zakki thrust it upward, entering the flesh just below the breastbone, lifting it until it could be imbedded directly into the heart muscle. Bordoni staggered backward, stumbling against the wall and sliding into a squatting position. Zakki let him fall, relieving his grip on the jeweled handle. Bordoni, the life ebbing with the beating gush of blood, watched it dumbly.

"Beautiful work, don't you think," Zakki said, watching the man's confidence wane in his now alabaster face. Unfortunately, death did not hurry and his features reflected the long painful struggle.

Not to be outdone in symbolic gestures, he had Bordoni, dagger intact, transported back to Farouk's new home in Naples, the black glove stuffed into the man's mouth. Surely, Farouk would appreciate the act. Zakki was sure it would amuse him.

CHAPTER TWENTY-SIX

B Y THEN, TOO, ZAKKI had permanently donned what was to become his permanent mask. Never again would he reveal the vulnerability, the inner mechanism of weakness and sentiment, that he had shown to Farrah. That had taught him the futility of revealed truth. One must never show other people the truth of oneself.

Yet the memory of Farrah persisted in mocking and humiliating him again and again. It was especially virulent when it surfaced in his dreams. It was partially because of this that he trained himself to avoid sleep. Sleep was an enemy. It allowed the mind's defenses to crumble, dredging up hidden myths, weakening one's foundations. In his waking brain, he could devise a thousand ways to denigrate Farrah. A worthless cunt, the king's toy, a shallow-minded, inconsequential whore, good only for a passing mindless pleasure with only the tiny after-taste of a ripe olive. It was much more difficult in his dreams.

She had been thankless, ungrateful. Yet all that vituperation had never erased the festering wound of his humiliation.
Nothing in his life up to then had ever made him suffer with
such incomprehensible pain. He could never erase the intensity of his longing, the terror of his anguish, as he had waited,
twisted with jealousy, for her to finish her ministrations to the
king.

Never once had she glimpsed the full measure of his passion.
Even when it had surfaced, even then, when she had mocked
him with her power, did she know the true extent of his vulnerability. She saw him only as a clumsy ape, the king's lackey,
showing as much interest in him as in the droppings of a camel.

He could have destroyed her. He regretted not having
done that. Would that have destroyed the mind's terrors, the
dreams? He doubted it. What he had devised for her was a
lifetime of fear. It gave him a special joy to watch the growing
Isis, reminding him of his own special hidden innocence, the
once pure love he had borne for both Farrah and the king, and
the ransom he had extracted for their betrayal.

The thought of Isis awoke the snake of agony again. If only
he had killed her when he held her that day in the City of the
Dead. But he had yielded to the enigma of his passion, the illusion that softness would endear him to Farrah, bond them. He
had paid the price for that folly, paid for it with his substance,
his manhood.

To the child, he had been a pariah from the beginning. She
had shrunk away from him, shivering with fright, like a dog
who remembers the torture inflicted by a stranger. In his mind,
he laid away special plans for the girl, waiting for the day when

nature would make her a special prize. With her mother's green eyes and what would eventually be her lush figure and her father's smooth, white skin, she would be the emerald in his diadem. It would delight him to present her to the greediest maw of them all.

As Zakki expected, the visit of Bordoni would not be Farouk's last attempt to recapture the lost domain. But even in Nasser's sanitized Egypt, the reality of human fallibility was observed, as always, in the breach. Nasser was too absorbed in his pan-Arab fantasies and, finally, his own megalomania to look too deeply behind the curtain of internal reality. Man needed even more manufactured dreams to escape his dismal reality and, as always, officials well-lubricated by baksheesh looked elsewhere for culprits. It became impossible for Farouk and his Mafia henchmen to gain a foothold in Egypt, although they had greater success in setting up a rival to Salah in the Sinai.

The '56 war was a brief annoyance, although it politicized Zakki, to the extent that he was not anxious to see the Israelis spread their self-righteous, justice-ridden influence. They were too intense, too incorruptible, too efficient.

"Nasser had better keep them out of here," Salah had complained to Zakki during the latter's visit to the Bedouin chieftain in 1957. "They are bad for business."

Salah was having his own troubles by then. One of his sons, Malek, had thrown in his lot with the Farouk-supported Mafia and, using his father's connections, had established his own smuggling operation.

Malek was, if it were possible, greedier than Salah, certainly crueler, with a lust for gold, power, and fleshly pleasures more gargantuan than his father's. Farouk, of course, knew the way to the man's heart and, advising his Mafia mentors, was making the going difficult for Salah. More insidious, as well, Malek was aware of where his father kept his secret caches of gold and weapons, and had attracted a band of cutthroats whose loyalty was well assured by these spoils.

No government authority dared to penetrate the morass of the Bedouin world in the Sinai. It existed as a kind of special dispensation of history.

Like wild animals, they had never been domesticated by any government. They existed as if no other world existed, living out their lives in their own timeless way, carting their families and their animals through the wastes of the Sinai, pitching and unpitching their tents, nesting briefly in the sparse shadows of any scrubby oasis, oblivious to the march of history or technology. They were a monument to their own stubborn self-denial, and were, therefore, allowed to operate in their own isolated orbit.

Their durability gave them a concession to be left to their own devices. It was one of the great oddities of their history that they did not increase in numbers, despite the obvious fertility and maturity of their women, who were as much chattel as the scrubby animals given to their charge. One could only assume that they practiced a mysterious kind of population control. No one dared speculate how this was done.

During the ritual of their annual meetings, Salah would hint at confrontations, but only in vague, sometimes mystifying terms. Zakki saw signs of it in the armed guards that ringed the camp, even in the site that had been chosen, no longer on open land, but deep in the low hills where men could scan the horizon from high vantages. There were also more obvious signs in the depletion of hashish bales carried by the caravans, despite increasing demand and a sophisticated distribution system that reached southward into Black Africa, westward across the Sahara to Libya, Tunisia, Algeria, and Morocco, and northward to Europe and beyond.

In a few years, it became apparent that, somehow, Farouk and his partners were besting him. This was, he had learned, a business that could not operate except by monopoly, and he decided that the time had come to take some definitive action. He had to make a deal with Malek.

Isis's time had come.

CHAPTER TWENTY-SEVEN

ISIS WAS SURLY AND sullen, mocking him with her green eyes. As was the practice, Herra had given the girls sleeping pills and they had slept under the truck's canvas during the journey from Cairo to Suez, dozing fitfully on the launch from Suez, awakening finally as they were transferred to the waiting camels in the Sinai.

Seven camels moved them for hours through the dry, barren land. Malek's men, somber in their checked kaffiyeh, their automatic weapons held at the ready, brought up the front and rear. Ahmed, the one Nubian bodyguard allowed for Zakki, eyed them with sinister annoyance.

Isis sat with him on one of the camels. Behind him on another camel sat the other two girls, frightened and confused. They were ten years old. Isis was eleven, already showing the first signs of her female maturity.

"Where are we going?" she asked. She had, Zakki knew, become attached to Herra, too attached, and Herra had given her up with obvious reluctance. He had repeatedly warned her of undue sentiment.

"They are human beings," she had protested whenever she had to part with any of the girls.

"They are merchandise," Zakki had responded, signaling to the men who watched over them that it was time for another persuasive lesson. Sentiment, Zakki knew, was the enemy. Who knew that better than Zakki?

He had not given a second thought to any of the girls he had provided as gifts to Salah. Some he had recognized on later visits. Others had disappeared, perhaps bartered for food and animals, absorbed elsewhere into the Bedouin society. Oddly enough, they were a commodity never in short supply, and he never ceased to marvel how easy they were to acquire. Some he used for his own purposes, but never the best of the lot.

"For you, my little princess, we have a special treat in store," he told her.

She looked at him with abject detestation. He would have preferred her to be rebellious or visibly frightened, yet he was comforted by the thought of what she was about to become. "Soon, Farrah," he told himself, regretting only that Farrah would not be there to bear witness. Farouk, he knew, would have enjoyed the impending spectacle.

Yet he refused to let himself be carried away by this satisfying little act of retribution. Revenge, of course, had its psychic pleasure, but he must not let it interfere with his alertness. He was here, after all, to pursue a sensitive business transaction.

They arrived at Malek's camp after nightfall. Carpets had been laid on the floor of his commodious tent. Malek seemed to live better than his father, or was simply showing off to Zakki, who presented him with a chest of gold ingots and a bag of precious stones. Malek looked at the cache with greedy joy. As always, they went through the elaborate ritual of salamats and handshakes. Food had been especially prepared. A roasted lamb within a roasted goat, bowls of rice, and sliced oranges were laid along the carpets. Both men exchanged shukrans and blessings, and Malek spent much time kissing his right hand, a sign of humility for his guest.

After they had eaten, Zakki called for Ahmed, who helped bring in two large crates, which he opened with a crowbar.

Zakki drew out a Russian gun and hefted it in his hand.

"Something from the big bear," Zakki said. "Nasser wanted you to have them."

Malek laughed, playing with the gun's mechanisms, caressing the barrel.

"Does my father have this?" he asked, abruptly.

Zakki shook his head, knowing that was where the bone of contention lay. Malek, obviously, was trying to best his father.

"So, he is getting too old," Malek said, leaning against a pillow and dipping his dark fingers into a bowl of plump olives.

"That, too," Zakki said, implying that his father was no longer the man he was.

"The wops say they are very powerful now."

"Not here," Zakki countered. "In the States. Only Malek makes them seem powerful here. You should stay with your own. Make it up with your father."

Malek spat out a pit on the carpet, a tangible reaction. But Zakki pressed his plan.

"You are his blood," Zakki went on, appealing to Bedouin vulnerability. Tribal blood feuds went on for as long as five generations. A family quarrel carried with it an element of guilt, which Zakki exploited. Zakki watched him contemplate the impact. It was, after all, just a charade now. Malek was ready for a reconciliation on his own terms. The only catch was that Zakki had never discussed this with Salah. Malek must be induced to eventually believe that his father had betrayed him. Zakki had learned the protocol of these strange people. The confrontation, Zakki reasoned, would almost certainly end in bloodshed, with Malek victorious.

"Besides, I will raise the price," Zakki said. Already, he had raised the price to his wholesale distributors. The objective was monopoly, to force out Farouk and his Mafia.

"And my father will retire as leader?" Malek asked. Distrust was endemic in this society.

Zakki nodded. "Have you ever known Zakki to lie?"

Malek looked at him shrewdly, rubbing his bristled face. He stretched, lay against the carpets, and smiled, putting aside thoughts of business. Zakki knew what that meant.

"I have a special gift," Zakki whispered. "Farouk's daughter. His blood."

Malek's eyes opened wide. His tongue washed over his lips, which formed a broad smile.

Farouk's exploits with women were legend, worthy of deep respect in this milieu. Zakki made an obscene gesture with his fingers and Malek sat up, his body rigid in anticipation.

"Farouk's daughter?"

"Better than the soup of a thousand pigeons," Zakki said, enjoying the buildup of suspense. He called to Ahmed, who had been waiting near the entrance of the tent.

Isis suddenly appeared. She was washed and perfumed and dressed in a red veil, a deliberate harbinger of excitement. Zakki was pleased with her preparations.

"Come here," Zakki ordered. The girl came forward obediently. He caressed her tight young buttocks. "Surely, she has her father's hot blood." He watched the color rise in his host's face.

Malek reached out and pinched her. Startled, crying out with pain, she pushed his hand away. She started to back away, but Malek was after her like a lion, gripping her arms and holding her helplessly against his body. She squirmed and struggled furiously.

"Farouk's daughter," Malek squealed, grabbing her by the hair and bending her head back.

"I told you," Zakki said. "The best." *Farrah, you cunt,* he cried within himself, remembering his humiliation, fueling his sense of retribution. He stood up, but Malek reached out and held his arm.

"Stay," he said. "Are we not brothers?"

Zakki nodded, smiling at the trapped Isis, caught in the vise of Malek's grip.

She continued to struggle, although Malek had, by now, pinned her down with his legs as well. Quickly, he ripped the veil from her, then the rest of her covering, leaving her naked. Her flesh glowed pink in the light from the kerosene lamps.

"Delicious," he cried, inspecting her fledgling womanly parts. "Not a hair on it yet."

He took one of her arms and roughly twisted it behind her back, making her wince with pain. Inexplicably, she did not cry out, perhaps fearful of greater harm. Then, he lifted his robes and, leaning against the pillows, displayed a large, erect organ, its head moist and glistening, revealing his advanced state of excitement. Isis looked at it, then turned toward Zakki, her green eyes misted with anger and humiliation, imploring help.

Zakki's response was to show her his own erect organ, which he thrust in her face. She turned her head away, but Malek had increased the pressure on her arm, making her groan with pain.

"You must taste it, my darling. It will be good for you," Malek said, his throat gurgling with pleasure, as he thrust her mouth against Zakki's organ. Instead of kissing it, she gagged, and Malek laughed uproariously.

Zakki grabbed her arms and, holding her head tight against his organ, watched as Malek kneeled between her legs and rubbed the head of his penis against the hairless opening.

Isis closed her eyes tight and bit her lip as Malek pressed against her, grunting and shoving, until he had forced himself into her. He drove his body forward in a quick thrust. Isis screamed and shivered as the organ entered her to its hilt. Resting, momentarily, Malek looked up at Zakki in triumph, then began oscillating his buttocks.

Resigned now, Isis's body slackened. Malek's pleasure came swiftly, accompanied by noisy gasps. He seemed proud to be showing off before Zakki.

"Sweet," he said, withdrawing his spent organ.

Blood seeped from the girl's vagina, and Malek tapped Zakki's naked thigh, offering the girl, who now lay, legs spread, her thin chest heaving with pain and humiliation. In a moment, Zakki was in her, watching the girl's green eyes, open now in horror, as she watched him. Every pore of his body had opened as he battered her insides, feeling his body fill to overflowing with the pleasure of his victory, the joy of this vengeance.

"Farrah." He could not keep the word from ejecting itself, along with an excruciating eruption of pleasure. It rolled over him in long, delicious waves. This, he was sure, was the ultimate reward of revenge.

The process, repeated a number of times that night, never quite reached the awesome heights of that first time. Exhaustion and pain had taken the fight out of her and, by morning, she lay in a whimpering heap by the side of the tent, like a discarded piece of rotted fruit.

CHAPTER TWENTY-EIGHT

JOURNEYING TO CAIRO THE next day, he felt expunged, as if he had finally shed some terrible disease. He was also delighted with the business results, certain that Malek, better armed now than Salah, and goaded by the prospects of greater wealth, would reach the ascendant position.

Zakki, in his new role, thrived on turmoil, welcomed it, courted it. His own wealth was multiplying, and he was laundering the profits from the hash trade in a variety of investments throughout the world. He was able easily to buy his protection and confederates. He also enjoyed the excitement of it. He had, after all, added another dimension to greed, had embellished the game by once again besting Farouk.

But Farouk, licking the wounds of his defeat in Italy, and apparently pressured by his partners, would not or could not give it up. Nor could he woo the Lebanese dealers, masters of intrigue and dissimulation, into a Mafia alliance. The Lebanese, particularly the Maronites, had parceled the business out among themselves, and, protected in their enclaves, had successfully warded off attempts by the Mafia to make inroads, at least at that level of the distribution process.

As a protected species, the Bedouins moved at will across the old overland routes. Salah had apparently accepted his fate, unwilling to risk a direct confrontation with his son, refusing, as Zakki knew he would, any movement toward détente, inflaming the son.

Malek's reaction was complicated. He had, as he had agreed, shaken the mantle of Farouk and his Mafia confederates. Then, he had attempted a détente with his father, who, as Zakki had imagined, refused. He would never abdicate his role as leader.

Indeed, Zakki had told Salah that his son was ready to assume a secondary position. Thus, each felt betrayed by the other, a fact that suited Zakki's purposes. For the sake of business, the feud had to be resolved, and it could only be resolved by violence. Each believed that Zakki favored the other's ascendency, and Zakki continued to follow the time-honored protocol of visitation and gift giving.

On his next visit, he had asked Malek what had happened to the green-eyed girl. A broad smile lit Malek's face. The memory of their frolic had bonded their relationship. But he was fuzzy on the question of the girl's present whereabouts. He had, he remembered, passed her on to a cousin, who had traded her for two goats to another Bedouin family.

Malek reached over and grabbed Zakki's genitals in a traditional ancient Arab show of affection.

"It was the best sport ever," Malek said. Zakki nodded, returning the affectionate gesture. Later, they repeated the performance with another of Zakki's "gifts," but it was not the same.

Early in 1965, a wave of hit-and-run raids between Salah's and Malek's men had temporarily disrupted the trade routes. Zakki had been expecting it, requiring him to return to the Sinai with more arms for Malek's men, to assure his victory over his father. It was the kind of mission that had to be done, both clandestinely and in person.

With three men, a dozen crates filled with Russian automatic weapons, and thousands of rounds of ammunition, Zakki arrived in the Sinai, oblivious to the impending events that would subsequently change his life.

Malek was less playful, more harassed. There had been a series of murders. Some of his hidden caches had been robbed. He had captured and tortured one of his half brothers, still loyal to his father, and learned that Salah had made contact with Farouk's agents.

"He is a stubborn old man," Malek said sadly. "I should have killed him years ago."

It was obvious that the man was depressed. He had other complaints as well. Nasser was sending waves of fedayeen, a euphemism for saboteurs, into Israel, and building up his Sinai armies. It was disruptive, although the Bedouins were rarely bothered by the soldiers. Israeli patrols, too, were roaming the border areas with greater frequency.

"The damned desert is getting too crowded," Malek told Zakki gloomily.

Zakki spent most of his time trying to cheer the man up, recalling their moments together. But that night, Malek was beyond redemption, and finally both men retired together in Malek's tent.

He would always remember the first shrill cry of pain, entering his dream as if it were part of the scenario of some sub-conscious terror. Because of that, he did not awake instantly. Not that it would have helped. Salah's men had swarmed over the encampment, cutting the throats of the guards on the high ground. By the time he and Malek realized what was happening, most of the men in the camp had been killed and the women and children rounded up and herded together with their animals.

Zakki was lifted roughly to his feet. His hands were tied behind his back and, with Malek, he was taken outside.

Salah was waiting for them. He had grown older, the lines etched deeper in his dark, leathery face. Zakki noted that many of his men carried Israeli-made Uzi machine guns.

Standing in the circle of Salah's men and the women and children that comprised Malek's family, Zakki felt for the first time in his life the true taste of fear. His legs nearly buckled, although he was determined to show his courage and face down his attackers. Besides, despite the competition in the Sinai, he was a valuable business asset at the distribution end.

"The fat one sends his greetings," Salah mocked, spitting on the ground. Turning to his son, he struck him a glancing blow across his face.

"Camel dung," the old man cried. Malek dropped to the ground, prostrate before his father.

"We must end this, Salah," Zakki rebuked. "These feuds are not good for business."

"They are ended," Salah said, smiling now, showing a mouthful of rotted teeth.

"Then release me," Zakki demanded.

"Soon."

Behind Salah, partially veiled in a white gossamer fabric, a mark of special distinction, her green eyes peering above cheekbones burnished copper by the sun, he saw her. The eyes watched him, flashing their spite. It was only then that the facade of courage cracked, and he struggled to break free of his bonds. Salah signaled to two men who held him, stripped away his clothes, and tied his arms and legs to two split railroad ties.

"No. Kill me," he pleaded. Sensing his fate, he tried to will his mind to return him to the terror of his dream. He could at least wake up from the horror of it.

Building up supports of stones, the men lifted the railroad ties and sat them in a position that lifted him off the ground. He dangled helplessly, spread-eagled between them.

"You must not do this," he cried. From somewhere, a glint of steel caught the sun and he could see the long knife in Isis's hand, her grip tight and sure.

"Kill me instead," he screeched, but they were the last words to reach outside of him. Salah himself stuffed a gag of cloth in his mouth. He tried to stop himself from breathing. He writhed on the rails, feeling the bonds cut into his arms and legs. He stared, helplessly at the dusty ground, feeling the free swing of his genitals.

Tell her not to, he begged Farrah in his heart, knowing that he could never earn her pity, not now or ever. He felt the burning slice of pain, the shock of agony. Finally, oblivion.

When he opened his eyes again, there was only the pain, a terrible, all-encompassing sense of despair, beyond physical hurt, another dimension of excruciation.

He lay on the ground. Malek had disappeared with Salah, Isis, and their group, and the mourning sounds of the women rose up in a loud ululation that expressed his inner feelings as well.

He wanted to die, vowing that he would kill himself when he found the strength. He heard Ahmed's voice.

"They have gone," he said. "Only the women are left. The other two are dead as well." So they had left him, he thought, and had spared him his life to continue their business. He felt the sun's heat in the tent where he lay. The pain gnawed at him, vibrating through his body.

"She will pay," Zakki said, turning to Ahmed.

He lay there wishing for death, but the memory of Isis, her green eyes shining, the large knife in her clenched hand, the slicing motion, the pain, the blood, fixed itself in his mind, burning into his brain. But first her, Farouk's daughter, Farrah's little whore, he told himself. First Isis, he vowed, then Allah will provide.

So his manhood had died, but miraculously something else was being born inside of him, something growing, rooted deep, fed by a rage so powerful that it created its own verdancy, a lushness of hatred so rich and fertile that it infused him with renewed life. He felt it surge, felt the tide pull his new persona into its vortex, a new incarnation. He would postpone death for a while.

In a few days, he found the strength to travel. He was determined now to spend whatever he had, money and energy, to satisfy this monumental maw of revenge, hungering with the power of its own self-propelled greed. There it was again, the joy of greed. Allah's vengeance would be nothing compared to the vengeance of Zakki. Life became purposeful now, more focused. Once again, they had humiliated Zakki. But Zakki was alive. He would give them his own private hell.

CHAPTER TWENTY-NINE

H IS IMMEDIATE PLAN WAS clearly defined, first to settle the score with Salah, then to find Isis and destroy her. Vengeance had given him the will to survive. The power of hatred had replaced the loss of his manhood and his hunger for revenge.

All his energy was devoted to preparing his path of action. Through his Lebanon connections, he got word to Salah that he was once again prepared to do business, to consider the debt paid, the slate washed clean. Nearly a year had gone by.

Word came back that Salah would be willing to talk. Once again, the protocol of the Bedouin world had become operative. Salah would be prepared to accept the obeisance. An enemy who acknowledges his defeat is no longer an enemy.

It took months and considerable expense to work out his plan, knowing that the wily Salah would be on his guard. Treasure and sex would conquer squeamishness, and large amounts of it, unlimited amounts, could find its way to the root of conscience.

Assembling the usual array of gifts, he also collected twelve prepubescent girls to present to the Bedouin chief. This, he knew, would be a sure sign of his total capitulation. The girls were not sedated during the trip, their nervousness allayed prior to entering the launch that would bring them across the Suez into the Sinai. With childish delight, they fingered the unusually heavy, but gaily decorated jewelry Zakki provided.

"It will make you all even more beautiful," he told them, as he carefully fastened ankle bracelets, neck and waist decorations, and earrings on each of the girls. It pleased him to see how much enjoyment the trinkets gave them.

He had recruited a number of well-paid Nubians. They were armed to the teeth, and carefully hidden during the journey into Salah's redoubt. Technology had not made even the remotest inroads into their society. The camels moved with their special grace along paths that their ancestors traversed for centuries, oblivious to the crated arms and explosives that they were hauling into the heart of Salah's camp.

Nor could they possibly understand, even if they had known, that Zakki had outfitted another caravan with men and weapons, who waited in the shadows of a nearby wadi, a reserve force to ensure Salah's destruction.

Salah greeted him as if nothing had occurred between them. The old man, Zakki knew, hid his contempt with the same craft that Zakki hid his hatred. In the crowd milling about the encampment, he saw Malek, who nodded, his eyes ridden with defeat and the same hint of naked contempt, as if Zakki had violated some immutable law of nature by willing himself to continue living.

Zakki ignored the unspoken insults of father and son. He would prove to them that the measure of a man was not merely in his cojones.

Isis, as expected, was nowhere to be seen. It was obvious to him that Salah would be hiding her out of sight at such a critical moment of reconciliation. Zakki understood. This was business and there would be no point in providing a living memory that might induce the rupture to continue.

Sooner or later he would attend to the matter of Isis's fate. But he did not linger long over this. Nothing must destroy the pleasure and precision of his plan. Isis's moment would come. He was certain of that.

The men sat cross-legged, facing each other across the carpet, as always strewn with the symbols of mutual hospitality. In front of them were heaping plates of lamb and rice.

"We must put all differences behind us, Salah," Zakki began, after they had performed the obligatory rituals. Through the entrance of the tent, he could see that Salah's men had relaxed their guard and were mingling with the girls, ingratiating themselves, although observing the strict protocol of the camp. Salah chooses first. Zakki, as always, had picked the prettiest girl child for Salah's pleasure, and after they had sparred in the time-honored business way, he got up and had one of his men bring in the girl.

Salah nodded, pleased with the choice, although he could not resist the opportunity to remind Zakki of his loss. Zakki's expression gave no hint of his inner feelings.

"I am sorry, my friend," Salah said solemnly, although his eyes could not hide his amusement. He patted the carpet beside him and the girl sat down next to him. The little gifts had placated the girls considerably. Salah continued to talk while he fondled her.

"The wops do not understand us as Zakki does," Salah said. "They only understand money. There is more to life than that." He turned toward the girl and, bending over, kissed her hair.

"Does Farouk ever come?" Zakki asked, innocently. Salah looked up at him.

"Never," he said. "Not like in the old days. Only Zakki knows how to do business." It was, Zakki knew, convoluted reasoning. The cost of doing business had just risen considerably, but Zakki had paid little attention to the matter. His mind was elsewhere.

"I am very tired, Salah," Zakki said. "The journey was tiring. I am not as well as I was." The remark was pointed, a deliberate reference to his own aborted manhood.

Salah nodded, dismissing him with a profuse display of thanks. He was pleased with the interview. Any suspicions Salah and his men may have harbored had dissipated.

Outside, the desert air had cooled. The girls had been divided among the men, and the women and children were bedded down near the animals for the night. He moved freely now that his guards were involved in other pursuits, joining his men in a tent at the periphery of the encampment.

Earlier, they had unloaded the crates from the camels and placed them in what seemed like a helter-skelter pattern. Zakki had rehearsed them well.

He looked at his watch. By now, the caravan in the wadi had begun to move toward the encampment. The men in the encampment would be taken by surprise. Everything had been coordinated to the second. They would see the hot blue tongue of Zakki's rage.

Inside the tent, the Nubians squatted around a smoking fire, waiting for the moment. The explosives were in place, the fuses ready.

In an odd way, he welcomed the confirmation that Isis would be hidden somewhere outside the encampment. There was cause for rejoicing even in that. Pursuing her would extend the purpose of his life.

What else was there to live for? Death to Farouk. Death to Salah! Death to Isis? He had lost the trail of Farrah, who had miraculously escaped. But her blood had returned to him with the sudden arrival of her son. It was a gift from Allah.

Salah provided him and his men with the hospitality of tents for sleeping and they repaired for the night while the enemy in the encampment frolicked until satiation. The operation had been costly. But what was money for, if not for this?

Inside of himself, he felt the familiar tingle of his excised sexual energy, certain that in the shuddering moment that began the planned attack something similar to an orgasmic tension would be released. He did not sleep, but waited for the agreed deadline in the first light of false dawn.

In the half light, he watched as the second hand of the watch made its last circular journey. His caravan of men and arms were poised to erupt. The moment had come.

The fuses were lit and the encampment exploded in an ear-splitting cacophony. Shrieks of human and animal pain rang in the air, partially drowned out by the sound of gunfire as the armed men poured round after round into whatever living thing moved.

The staccato sputtering of the guns had a calming effect on Zakki as he sat cross-legged on the carpets waiting for the last note of this blood ritual to sound. Yes, he acknowledged, the pleasure was as he had imagined it.

The gunfire grew more sporadic, then ceased completely. Zakki glanced at his watch. No more than twenty minutes had elapsed. He looked out of the tent. Most of the men were poking around in the carnage, scavenging. An occasional cry of pain was answered with a quick round of gunfire. Then all was quiet. Men, women, and animals were all dead.

Zakki went on a round of inspection. He observed the corpses of Salah and his son, and carefully inspected the faces of the men, women, and children laid together in rows, their faces uncovered for viewing. As he had suspected, Isis was not among them. Zakki then ordered his men to create a huge pyre of the bodies, soaked them in gasoline, and watched them burn.

Soon, only the sound of shovels poking in the soft, sandy earth could be heard, and by morning, those bodies that were left, along with dead animals and all of the worthless possessions of the group that could be found, were either burned or buried in a shallow mass grave.

Mounting a camel, Zakki marveled at the beauty of the operation. Nothing remained. It was as if the earth had swallowed them up. But even the exhilaration of the moment could not diminish the joy of expectation.

Zakki felt it fitting that Farouk's destruction precede Isis on his list of priorities. The father before the daughter. It was the natural rhythm of life. Besides, Farouk was stationary, conducting, as always, his dissolute existence and nefarious business affairs with the same cunning greed displayed when he was the King of Egypt. Finding Isis, he knew would be his ultimate challenge, but in that case fate had brought him the young man, his heaven-sent guide.

Farouk now lived in Rome, still surrounded by his ubiquitous Albanian bodyguards. Reports of his agents informed Zakki that Farouk had grown heavier, his health had deteriorated, and he was spending frequent visits at a Swiss clinic for treatment of a weak heart.

Zakki had learned, too, that his Italian partners, faced with the mysterious disappearance of their supply routes in the Sinai, had become increasingly disillusioned with Farouk's ability to deliver. The business vacuum offered a bonus of opportunity, but first he had to settle this part of his mammoth personal debt.

But it was one thing to massacre a band of Bedouins, and quite another to kill a well-known ex-king on foreign soil. The Egyptian government had little interest, and little authority, over the bands of Bedouins that roamed its deserts, concentrating its energies primarily on the people in the 4 percent of arable land that lay on either side of the narrow strip of the

Nile. To ensure the government's disinterest, their little sortie had been neatly executed, the evidence destroyed.

The elimination of Farouk, on the other hand, might stir up the hornets of nationalism, particularly among the emotional Italians, and lead to snooping by police agents. Naturally, he would have loved to confront the fat bastard at the last moment of consciousness. What joy that would have given Zakki. To make up for such a deprivation he would have to plan Isis's destruction so that he would be present as a witness.

Keeping track of Farouk's habits was simple. The man was highly visible and predictable. Women and food were his chief delights. Narriman and her mother had, by special dispensation, returned to Egypt. Not that Narriman's presence would have mattered to Farouk. The man's insatiable appetites were all-consuming, beyond control.

Sadly, he had to reject all scenarios that might lead to suspicion. It would be death by remote control, a necessary but hardly exhilarating effort.

It troubled Zakki, too, to know that he was probably offering Farouk oblivion almost as a gift. Reports informed him that the man had become deeply religious, further diminishing his joy.

Not that Farouk had ever been truly afraid of death. His belief in Allah had been a pose. Now it was supposed to be genuine. The bastard had armored himself with faith. Indeed, there were moments when Zakki nearly abandoned the operation. I am being sentimental, he told himself, remembering the early days when the image of Farouk, the boy king, shined in his mind.

But the more recent memory of what Farouk's offspring had done to him rekindled his resolve. And his hatred. He would have to settle for a quick, passionless murder. He would have to comfort himself with his own secret knowledge.

Death by poison was easily arranged. A busboy at the Isle de France, a roadside restaurant near Rome, accomplished the deed by placing the poison in a dessert of Monte Bianco. Zakki enjoyed this little irony immensely, eagerly absorbing the report of Farouk's last supper, rendered in the minutest detail in the press: a dozen oysters, Evian water, leg of lamb, fried potatoes, ginger ale, two oranges, and, naturally, the restaurant's specialty, Monte Bianco.

So Zakki had been kind, he thought. At least the bastard died with a satisfied belly. Perhaps, when they met in the netherworld, Farouk would thank him for this last meal.

But the flame of memory had grown cold in the nightly retelling. The joy had turned to ashes. Zakki reopened his eyes to the first signs of dawn, puffs of river mist floating over the terrace. He always greeted the first rim of light with hope that today would reveal some clue to Isis. He had convinced himself that the young man would find her. And then? He dared not project the pleasure on himself. Too many false starts and blind alleys had angered the reptile of vengeance that slithered in his gut.

He heard the servants stirring in the villa, the bodyguards changing shifts. Ahmed's footfalls moved along the stones of the terrace, and Zakki raised his huge bulk to a sitting position. He had learned to fathom the language of the Nubian's eyes, which could not hide what the passive features did so well. He was warmed by its foreshadowing.

"You are amused, Ahmed?" Zakki asked.

Ahmed nodded.

"They have taken elaborate steps to elude us," he said in a monotone, only his eyes betraying his pleasure. "They are dressed now as fellaheen. I am sure they think they have escaped us."

Zakki listened with some excitement. His heart palpitated, and he forced his calm.

"And their destination?" Zakki asked.

"There is a design to it," Ahmed responded. "They have engaged a felucca."

"Then they must have found a destination."

"It would seem so."

"Do you think they have evaded us?"

"Never. You must not lose patience."

Zakki felt the snake of agony loosen its grip. He rose with effort and crossed the terrace. From its edge, he could see the river, running slowly at its timeless pace, leading in the opposite direction of his thoughts. He strained to reassemble the fading image of Farrah in his mind. Oddly, it had never lost its grip on his heart.

"Soon, Isis," he whispered. "The fishes of Mother Nile will eat your flesh."

CHAPTER THIRTY

T HE OLD EDITOR, A gnome of a man with a back
humped from years of leaning over his desk, was surprisingly alert. He worked in the musty library of the newspaper
office now, a hodgepodge of moldering pulp. He delighted in
proving that his memory was intact.

"Thompson was more of a freelancer than a staffer," the old
man recalled effortlessly, the remembrance belying his ancient
appearance. He had been a subeditor at the time.

"Gloomy fellow. Long in the mouth. Always huddled with
the editor." He studied Si over his glasses, then looked down
again at the faded clipping that Si had spread on his desk.

"That piece made quite a stir."

"And Thompson?"

The old man shrugged.

"Never saw him again. An American. I presume he went
home."

Si nodded. The morass seemed to close in on him again. Yet
they had taken elaborate, extravagant precautions, a hired taxi,

the desert road from Alexandria. The driver had dropped them at Mena House in Giza, where they took another taxi, getting off in the heart of old Cairo, then moving on foot into the thick crowds, through the backstreets and bazaars to the newspaper office.

Si searched his mind for some inquiry that might offer a next step.

"Did he do other stories?" Si asked. The old man paused and stroked his chin. He knew the man's curiosity was building, but he deliberately held back any further explanations.

The man stirred and rose from his cluttered desk. He walked slowly past rows of file cabinets to a series of dusty, unused shelves. The room was disordered, with no apparent plan to the filing system. Typically Egyptian, Si thought. But not without a sense of grudging respect. Coping with chaos seemed instinctual, a national trait. He knew the man would find what he was looking for.

He pulled a manila envelope from a pile, stirring a cloud of dust. On its face, someone had scrawled in big, black letters, "Thompson Stories."

Si resisted his impatience. The old man seemed to relish both the attention and the mystery. Returning to his desk, he opened the envelope and spread a small pile of yellowed clippings on a space he cleared with the heel of his hand. Slowly, he read through each one.

"He seemed to have some interest in the preservation of our antiquities."

Si hesitantly reached over and quickly read through the headlines. "The Lost Obelisks," "The Politics of Pyramids,"

"Museums of Plunder." On the surface, it seemed far afield from the lurid story of Farouk's teenage mistress. Then Si read the body of the clippings. A clear pattern emerged. The antiquities were a metaphor to discredit colonial domination in general, and British domination in particular. They were more political than archaeological.

Embedded in the stories were also some telling swipes at Farouk, and his apparent indifference to Egyptian culture.

"Quite outspoken, don't you think?" Si asked, although he had shied away from dialogue with the old man.

"They had just come off wartime censorship. The independence movement was just flexing its muscles," the old man said, winding up for what seemed a long explanation. Si let the old man drone on as he read and reread the clippings.

"Only five obelisks left inside Egypt... More outside than inside... The nose of the Giza Sphinx in the Berlin Museum... pieces of Karnak and Abu Simbel carted off to far away places." His mind circled in the maze, mulling and backtracking. The main quotations seemed to come from a Dr. Ezzat, Cairo University. Si's memory was jogged.

"...the concept of National Treasure has always been a rallying point for the intellectuals." Si felt the man's faded myopic eyes watching him. "After all"—the man lowered his voice—"what holds it all together? Certainly not the mess you see outside."

But by then, old Herra's words echoed in his brain. She had taken Isis to the university. He felt the exhilaration of discovery. Thanking the man, he departed, leaving him, literally, in midsentence.

Outside, he found Abdel gloomy and frightened.

"You were so long," she said, as they hurried along the crowded streets. He explained what he had learned, surprised when she didn't reflect his enthusiasm.

"I feel we're getting closer," he said, ignoring her depression. "To Isis," he added.

"And then?" She moved out in front of him, heading for the university. Her tone annoyed him. Again, he remonstrated with himself for ever getting her involved. *I can do without her,* he told himself. Somehow, his words carried no conviction.

"Ezzat," the professor said, raising his eyebrows, offering Si instant recognition. "One of our most respected authorities." He drew deeply on a cigarette and puffed smoke out of both nostrils. "His monographs are essential, germinal to our understanding." He seemed to be growing pedantic, and Si interrupted him. Abdel sat beside Si on a battered leather couch.

It had been terribly disappointing to find that Dr. Ezzat was no longer associated with the university.

"I would like very much to see him," Si said.

"So would we all, young man. So would we all."

"He's not dead?" Si blurted, feeling again the collapse of optimism.

"Haven't heard that," the professor said, taking another deep puff on his cigarette. "He was also a bit on the eccentric side. A bit too political as well, an occupational hazard in our business. But very able. Very able." The professor looked at the ceiling.

"And courageous." His eyes darted toward Si. "You know he opposed the big dam at Aswan. Hated the Russians with a passion. Of course, if it wasn't for him, Abu Simbel would have been underwater, lost for eternity. Nasser didn't think it could be done. But Ezzat could be persistent. And abrasive. In the end, Nasser had him sacked. Something like that. He simply disappeared. It could only have been that."

He shook his head. "Nasser," he said with contempt, clearing his throat as if he were about to spit. "He ruined us. Of course, Ezzat was one of his greatest initial supporters. Also, the first among us timorous scholars to oppose him." He raised a finger as if ready to deliver a lecture. "The protocol, you see, is for an archaeologist to transcend the exigencies of contemporary fortune..."

"Do you know where he is?" Si asked, annoyed now with his own impatience. The professor frowned. He was apparently not used to being interrupted.

"Why, anywhere from Memphis to Abu Simbel," the professor snickered, restoring his sense of self-importance. He punched out his cigarette in the ashtray and looked at Si again. "More than likely anywhere from Thebes to Aswan. Wherever there are digs. Old archaeologists never die, they just haunt digs." The professor laughed at his little joke, his joviality disintegrating into a coughing fit.

"Is there any way you could be more specific?" Si asked, when the professor had quieted himself. The man took out his handkerchief and blew his nose. Shuffling among his papers, he found a map and pointed to red markings. "The Poles are here in the Valley of the Kings. The Brits over here. And a joint Anglo-Egyptian team here. And, of course, this one, near

Aswan that the Israelis are negotiating to start. Quite important. Eighteenth Dynasty, we think one of Thutmose III's sons. You see, there is every reason to believe that..."

"And you think he might be found in the vicinity?"

"I didn't say that," the professor countered sharply. "I said, more than likely." He lit another cigarette. "I also said he disappeared." He looked at the ceiling, as if some clue might be found there. "I seem to remember someone saying he saw him poking around some digs, somewhere." He paused. "But, he's completely out of the mainstream. There were some rumors that he was living in Upper Egypt... but who knows?"

"Has he family? Perhaps his family might help?" Si asked.

"A daughter. I saw her once when I visited the Abu Simbel project..."

"And his wife?"

The professor inhaled deeply, holding the smoke in his lungs interminably before exhaling.

"Don't know. Never met her. Poor woman, whoever she was. Ezzat was brilliant, but rather intense." Beneath the facade was a trace of jealousy.

"It will be like looking for a needle in a haystack," Si said, turning to Abdel.

"More like a needle in a stone stack," the professor said, quickly smothering his own chuckle. He was, apparently, used to having his students respond to his humor. He scowled.

"May I copy the map?" Si asked.

The professor looked at it, then at Si with an accusatory stare.

"You're not one of those efficiency experts from the fundraisers?" the professor snapped.

Si was perplexed.

"Always snooping around to tell us we do things too slow, that everything costs too much. We are paying the price for our ignorance of the past. Archaeology is the pursuit of truth. A buried pot can tell us more about humanity than an army of contemporary philosophers..." He was wound up again. Si traced the map on tissue paper. It was crude, but serviceable.

"I appreciate it," he said, standing up. Abdel rose in tandem.

The professor ignored the movement, his face tilted toward the ceiling, as if he were reading from cue cards of knowledge.

"What will anyone remember of us? What will they find in our rubble?"

"Thank you," Si said politely, quietly closing the door of the professor's office, his words muffled in the smoky chamber.

CHAPTER THIRTY-ONE

O N T H E L O N G R I D E on the Cairo-Luxor train, Si wrestled with his choices. He did not share his feelings with Abdel, if only to avoid her concern, and her warnings.

They were being pursued by people, not phantoms. He could not understand it. To complicate matters, he had unwittingly fallen into the role of Abdel's protector. And she had become his needed confidante and advisor. Of course he was grateful, but equally confused.

He had bought a map at a kiosk at the train station, and spent part of the journey studying it and copying the dig sites from the tissue map. Brief legends explained the areas and he made mental notes as he traced a potential route. Deir El Bahri in the Valley of the Kings was the logical first stop, near the three-tiered Temple of Queen Hatshepsut, on the Necropolis side, the West Bank of the Nile, opposite Luxor.

Abdel lay against him, cuddled like a cat in the crook of his arm. She had fallen asleep, and he absentmindedly stroked her hair. Feeling her warmth beside him, despite his misgivings, comforted him. But the comfort did not dispel his confusion.

Nothing he had done or seen in Egypt had the remotest resemblance to his romanticized image. Only now could he acknowledge his expectations. He had, he admitted, fantasized a soul-stirring, tearful reunion with his half sister, the validation of blood, the commonality of genetic magnetism. Finding her would mean new beginnings, the lifting of the veil of uncertainty, the discovery of purpose and identity. He was, he had led himself to believe, obeying some mysterious matriarchal imperative, goading him, as if Isis was his Holy Grail.

In the metal capsule of the jostling train, he wrestled instead with the hard realities of this headlong plunge into an unmarked wilderness. *It is the compulsive, irrational, romantic Irish side*, he decided, chuckling to himself. On the other hand, he was part Egyptian, a people imbued with spiritual mysteries and ancient blood myths, a strange DNA potion that drove him forward beyond his ability to restrain himself.

He did not like the turn of his thoughts. Letting his mind wander, he leisurely observed the people who swarmed around them in the carriage. They were a limitless variety; dark, smooth-featured women huddled in their black shrouds with children clutched to their bosoms; old men with tired faces; young fellaheen smoking endless cigarettes. In the air swirled odors of sweat, feces, urine, ripe fruit, and, unmistakably, hashish. Cooped chickens cackled and fluttered their wings. Finally the sensations faded with fatigue and he fell asleep.

Abdel awakened him. Apparently the train had stopped.

"We should go now."

He looked out of the window. No station was visible.

"We are still north of Luxor, but it is a good time to leave."

"Here?"

In the dim light he could see endless fields split by the river. Of course, he thought, as a new idea emerged. River travel would be safer. Besides, most of the "digs" on his map were close to the river. They stood up and moved past sleeping bodies to the train's door, opened it quietly, and jumped to the ground.

Moving swiftly across a maturing field of beans, they reached a tiny agricultural village.

There, much to the amazement of the villagers who eyed them curiously, they bartered the clothes they wore for a torn djellaba and turban for himself and a black malaya for her. The village elder who supervised the transaction was smug in his certainty that he had gotten the better of the deal. But he was helpful in advising them where they might rent a felucca for the journey up the river.

"My village was like that," Abdel said, as they crossed a bean field on their way to the river's edge. Her face was hidden in the folds of her black malaya. He had caught in her tone a sigh of longing. The village had been no more than a cluster of mudbrick huts equipped with makeshift fired cooking stoves and little furniture. Each family literally slept adjacent to their animals.

A fleeting picture of Abdel's earlier life intruded on Si's musings. He had seen a young girl sleeping on a straw pallet in a corner of a tiny room.

"Unfortunately, there is no going back," Abdel said with a sigh, as if reading his mind.

266

The felucca moved quietly against the tide, tacking frequently as Hassan, the boat's owner, maneuvered the prow as close to the wind as possible. The boat heeled, and Si and Abdel braced themselves against the gunwale. Hassan's young son, Anwar, hung on the foredeck, ready to untangle any fouled lines. Moshe, the boy's dog, a large black spot surrounding one eye, slept at their feet, unconcerned by the precarious angle. Si and Abdel watched Hassan's village fade from sight.

Hassan grinned at them, using his foot to manipulate the tiller while he peeled an orange with his teeth and spit the rinds into the Nile. Abdel had bargained with him, smiling at Si, showing her pleasure in the arrangement, enjoying the exhibition of her street smarts. In Cairo, she had advised him to cash in his traveler's checks.

"The fellaheen know only cash," she had warned. He had obeyed her and now could be grateful for the advice.

The negotiations were elaborate and, in the end, Hassan had accepted only on the condition that he was accompanied by his helper, his son, eight-year-old Anwar, named for Sadat. Anwar, in turn, would not go without his dog, Moshe, obviously named in a rare moment of political awareness of new events.

Si was considerably brightened by the prospect of the journey with this odd triumvirate.

"We are the best on the river," Hassan assured them.

They also took aboard a supply of beans, onions, carrots, oranges, and bananas, and a few jars of treacle and curdled milk.

"You will like it," Hassan said. Si had looked at the treacle with distaste.

He did feel safer on the Nile, although the rising light showed a few feluccas off their stern, plying the waters gracefully, tacking against the wind and tide. Occasionally, Hassan would wave, and the men on the other boats would return the greeting. They watched as the sun rose beyond the fields on the east bank.

Abdel made them tea over a kerosene stove, which they drank along with bananas and oranges. After the uncertainties of the night on the train, and warmed by the tea, Si felt calm and confident that somehow, without any real evidence to stoke his optimism, their journey would lead to Isis.

"I know we're on the right track," he whispered, as they sat in the wooden cockpit, listening to the music of the wind and the counterpoint of the squeaking mainmast.

A frown shadowed Abdel's face.

"For you, I hope so," she mumbled, lifting her face into the breeze.

"Well, the old woman said that she had taken Isis to the university. And Dr. Ezzat was connected with Thompson." It seemed a rebuke, and he touched her arm. "I mean it seems logical. I can't think of anything else." She apparently caught the drift of his appeal, and she looked at him and shrugged.

"Maybe," she said, studying the wake of the boat. "The important thing is that we are not followed," she said. "Hassan, I am sure, knows the river. He will be able to tell if there are strangers."

Seeing them watching him, Hassan nodded happily. Si had made a copy of his map and given it to Hassan, who had explained to him that the workers at the archaeological sites started at dawn and, because of the heat, usually stopped well before noon. Even the tourist traffic started and ended early, he told them, pointing out that they were lucky that July was not the height of the season, implying that he would not have then been available for hire.

"My father always dreamed of owning his own felucca," Abdel said. She had been looking into the distance, lost in a familiar kayf.

"And now?" Si asked gently.

"He is dead."

"I'm sorry," Si said. She shrugged and the glaze receded. She had been, he realized, reticent to show him any bit of her background. Nor had he been overwhelmed by curiosity. Suddenly he had the knowledge. The hush of the light-spangled river seemed to stir her recollection.

"They took him for the war in '73. He did not come back. I remembered I could not understand why he went away." She sighed. "I understand now." He let her relish the silence. "For nothing," she said bitterly, her eyes misting. "He felt only that the river, a felucca, would give him his freedom. He loved the river."

"And your mother?" Si asked, drawn deeper into her recollection.

"She became the wife of another man."

"Did you run away?"

She shook her head, as if the inquiry were obscene.

"My father had insisted that I stay in school. It was a long journey, but I went happily. It was very important to him. And to me. Only a handful of the villagers knew how to read. My father was very proud of me." She grew hesitant again, and he felt her shiver, although the heat had begun to penetrate the breeze. "My mother's husband wanted me to stop. Ordered me. He said he needed my labor at home. My mother was helpless. What could she do?"

"So you went away."

"I didn't want to leave my mother," she protested. "I was sorry that I had been born a girl. There was really no solution. If my father had lived, it would have been different." She turned toward him, her chin high, showing him her pose of pride. "So you see, I was able to survive. I found the City of the Dead." She pointed a finger at him. "You'll see. Someday I will go to the university."

Considering her predicament, it seemed like a hopeless wish. But his heart went out to her.

"Perhaps, someday, I will help you," he said, reaching out his hand to touch her. She must have interpreted his gesture as pity and disengaged herself, moving toward the prow. He turned toward Hassan, who smiled provocatively.

"What the hell are you grinning about?" he snapped.

But Hassan continued to smile.

The river became more crowded as they neared Luxor, its high buildings glistening in the sun. A string of barges and large tourist boats were moored along the banks. Ubiquitous wild dogs slumbered on the river slopes, while an occasional droshky could be seen clip-clopping along the river road.

"The Temples of Karnak," Hassan said, pointing to a clutter of stones and an obelisk poking into the sky.

Si acknowledged the reference, and ducked as the mainsail shifted and the felucca tacked toward the opposite bank. Guiding the tiller, Hassan pointed the prow toward the bank and headed to shore on a gust of breeze, jamming the boat into the mud. Si and the girl jumped ashore and walked along the river trail to the large dock provided for the tourist ferries.

Abdel inquired as to the specific location of the Polish dig on the map and arranged with an old man for the use of two tired-looking gray donkeys. The man also insisted that he accompany them, obviously to earn more money. There was no dissuading him.

Mounting one donkey, they followed the old man on the other. Abdel sat in front of Si, holding the reins, while he clung to her back. His legs nearly reached the ground, and he had to hold them outward, making the journey difficult. Tourist busses passed quickly on their way to the tombs. Their occupants observed them and waved and smiled. They managed to wave back.

"See," he said. "They think I'm a fellah."

"You should ask for baksheesh for the privilege of observing you," Abdel said sarcastically, showing her antagonism for the tourists. Oddly, he actually shared the feeling, resenting the sense of his being on exhibit. When another tourist bus came by, he turned his head.

They followed the old man's donkey along the winding roads to the Valley of the Kings. The desert began abruptly, and the donkeys climbed upward through the dry, hot dust, past the mudbrick village that seemed placed there deliberately as a tourist attraction. Hassan had told him that the village derived its sole income from trafficking in phony antiquities, which they hustled to the tourists with a mixture of exasperating pressure and craft.

"Don't believe what they seem," Hassan warned with a tinge of jealousy. "They are rich."

Only the women seemed to occupy the village, while the men were out hawking their wares. Wearing black malayas, they carried earthenware water jars on their heads or sat listlessly along the slopes, like roosting ravens, indifferently observing the parade of tourists. In the distance, he could see the flat cliffs, glowing reddish in the blazing sun. As they moved closer, the old tombs and temples defined themselves, like chipped jewels in a diadem of uncertain settings, the centerpiece of which was the beautiful and awesome threetiered Temple of Queen Hatshepsut.

Watching it as they came closer, it struck Si how arrogantly it had defied time.

"A woman built that," he whispered to Abdel, his lips brushing against her ear. She said nothing, although he sensed that she felt some flush of pride.

"There," the old man pointed out, urging the donkey toward the temple. Beside it, they could see workmen digging at a nearby site. In a lean-to on the side of a hill, a group of men pored over drawings. They moved closer, then stopped before a fence beyond which was a carpet of numbered stones. Si dismounted and moved over a sandy path to the men. A bearded man, wearing a white wide-brimmed hat, greeted him warily, but his face softened when he heard the name of Ezzat.

"A storehouse of knowledge," the man said. "Had a genuine feel for how those old buzzards did things." Si listened patiently as he described the site and its future. "...with computers, we'll have this temple reconstructed in half the time. Half the time."

"But have you seen him. Ezzat?" Si interrupted.

"Not since Abu Simbel." The man scratched his beard. "Someone saw him around two years ago. Brilliant fellow. Eccentric as hell. Wouldn't acknowledge who he was, but I once heard him speak in Warsaw. When I confronted him with that, he denied it. He was dressed rather odd. Like a peasant, a fellah. But he didn't fool me. Poking around here as if he were someone else."

"Do you know where he lives?"

The bearded man shook his head.

"I'm afraid not," he said. "Chances are, someplace in Upper Egypt. Near the digs." Si pressed him, but nothing seemed to spur any further recall.

"They don't understand how important this work is," the bearded man said, bending toward Si and lowering his voice. "The fact is that us scholars and those parasites who make a living off this are the only ones who care. Most Egyptians don't give a shit."

"Well, you can't blame them for that," Si snapped, surprised at his own anger. "You can't eat history, and these damned stones won't till the land. What has all this got to do with them?" His arm swept the surrounding countryside in what he knew was a grandstanding gesture.

"Not a damned thing," the bearded man said. "Not even then. Nothing changes for them."

Si glared at him, nodding a farewell. The man had been standing, facing westward, his back to the rising sun, which suddenly popped over one shoulder as he moved. Si turned away to avoid the sudden beam. He walked through the path between the numbered stones. At least, he thought, the man had confirmed his own theory. Ezzat was somewhere out there. The ultimate question still gnawed at him. With Isis?

CHAPTER THIRTY-TWO

T HE SUN BORE DOWN relentlessly, slowing the donkeys' pace. Si was drenched in perspiration. The old man
led them through narrow paths, past abandoned tombs and
ruins to the other active digs in the valley. Those in charge
acknowledged their familiarity with Dr. Ezzat and his work,
but could offer no clue to his whereabouts. The older archaeologists had not seen him since Abu Simbel, and the younger
ones knew him only by reputation.

By early afternoon, the heat was scalding, and Si felt com-
pelled to offer the old man additional baksheesh to press
forward. The tourists had disappeared, and the village peddlers
had moved to any shade they could find.

The information that the bearded man had given him had
excited him. The heat was a mere detail now. Nothing could
stop him, he knew, trying to transfer his excitement to Abdel
who, at first, had seemed indifferent.

"Don't you see?" he argued. "The man is hiding. That can only mean one thing."

"If he hides from Zakki, how can you find him?" she said sullenly, kicking the donkey's haunches. She seemed to be taking the position of the devil's advocate, and this annoyed him.

"I'll find her," he said, with exaggerated bravado, as if it was necessary to convince himself.

Even when they had exhausted the various sites, he would not allow his enthusiasm to wane. Nothing would shake his faith, he told himself, remembering his mother's agonizing confession, recalling it now to buttress his sense of purpose.

His mouth was parched, and they stopped in front of a mud-brick hut to purchase water for themselves and the donkeys. Bending to dip his face into a bowl of still water, he saw his reflection. He had to touch it, as if the reflected gesture was the only thing to assure him that it was his. His sloping eyes peered back at him under his brown turban. His heart pounded as he contemplated his image.

"What is it?" Abdel said, startling him. He had apparently stiffened into a frozen pose.

"Nothing," he lied, dipping his face into the cool water, splintering the image.

But when they had mounted the donkeys again, he kicked the donkey's haunch and the animal pulled up beside the old man.

"Tutankhamun?" he asked.

The old man looked at him with exasperation. Si quickly gave him an additional pound. Nodding, the old man took it and struck the tired donkey with the flat of his hand and they moved at a swifter pace along the trail.

Except for a few peddlers who slept in the shade of their stall awnings, the entrance to the area of the tomb was deserted. Above them on a high knoll was a modern rest house with high glass windows, from which faces peered with mild interest. But, when they dismounted, a man in a brown djellaba came out. Si began to count out the admission charge.

"Would you like to come?" he asked Abdel.

She seemed hesitant, but he paid for her anyway, taking her hand and following the signs up the hill to the tomb. As they approached, a man stirred from a squatting position against the wall and lifted a mirror to catch the sun's reflection, lighting the staircase to the tomb. They followed the old man down the stairs to the main chamber. It was dank and empty, but to the right was a small staircase leading to a vantage from which they could look into another, well-lit chamber.

In it was the huge, perfectly preserved sarcophagus of the boy king, a supine golden statue in regal headdress, the eyes open and serene, the lips curled in a joyous smile of content-ment over its false beard of kingly office. Beyond were the frescoes he had seen in photographs in New York. He recalled the legend depicted by the figures and how he had been moved by them.

Abdel stood beside him, her gaze fixed on the figure of Tutankhamun.

"He is in there," Si whispered.

"In there?" She gripped his hand.

"The body mummified." His eyes rose to the frescoes.

"The spirit alive." She shivered beside him, and he put his arm around her.

"There," Si whispered, surprised at his detailed recall, knowing that it had lain embedded in his subconscious, ready for retrieval at this moment, "is Ay, Tutankhamun's successor, wearing the blue crown of the reigning Pharaoh, performing the open-the-mouth rite on the mummified boy king. And there"—he pointed—"is Nut, mother of Osiris, who receives him as her son. You see, he carries the club and staff, symbols of his power. And there..." He felt his excitement rising. "There, the mummy form of Osiris greets him and his Ka... conscience. See the ankh in her hand, symbol of life. And those symbols, hieroglyphics, they are saying 'given life forever and forever.'"

He wanted to shout for joy, to hear the sound of his voice echo in the tomb.

"Don't you see," he cried. "The connection." He looked at her and held her close. "Of all of us. The endless river of blood. You and I. My mother. Isis."

He felt the exhilaration, an epiphany.

"From there to now is more than three thousand years. Don't you see? It is important to know that. The human link. Nothing dies. Nothing ever really dies." Perhaps, he thought, that's why he had come, to prove that his mother had never died, a part of her was still planted in this land.

"Please," Abdel whispered. "Take me out of here."

He wanted to stay, but her fear was compelling, and he soon led her out of the tomb. The sunlight blinded them, and the mist of heat enveloped them like a hot bath. When his eyes became accustomed to the light, he saw the old man napping in the shadow of the donkeys, who stood drowsing head down in the heat, oblivious to the flies that swarmed on their flanks.

His excitement left him in a state of euphoria, and although he had mounted the donkey and felt the movement of its hooves against the asphalt road, his mind was still in the tomb. He was sure his experience was not unique, but that did not diminish his wonder. They followed the old man on his donkey over the main road.

He felt the strangeness in the way Abdel held herself, the silent transmission of fear as his body moved against hers. At first, he thought it had to do with the tomb. She did not turn toward him, but he heard her voice.

"What is it?" he asked.

"They are following us," she said.

He heard the low purring of a car's motor behind them.

"They may be tourists."

"I wasn't sure," she said. "I saw this face in the big windows of the rest house. It struck me then as familiar. In the tomb, I was certain."

"I thought it was Tutankhamun."

"No. I am not afraid of the dead."

He kicked the donkey's haunches, and they pulled up beside the old man. They were still on high ground. In the distance, they could see the beginning of the green fertile land, beyond which was the river. Below them, the road wound downward.

"Perhaps we can save time by going over the side."

"It is dangerous. The rocks are loose. Even the donkeys find it difficult."

They let the old man move ahead. Glancing back in an off-hand gesture, he caught a quick glimpse of the car moving slowly. They must have been following them on the train, he realized, and picked up their trail again at Tutankhamun's tomb. *Damned fool*, he castigated himself silently.

"We have no choice now," he whispered. "They will follow us to the river."

Ahead, they could see the bend in the road, a sharp turn, sure to slow them down. He gripped her tightly. She understood the signal, braced herself, and headed the donkey down the hill, slapping and kicking its haunches. They heard the sudden acceleration of the car's motor. The donkey picked his way downward over the rocks, miraculously surefooted. Then, near the edge of the road, the animal slipped, and they tumbled downward for a few yards. Recovering quickly, they remounted the stunned animal and resumed the flight.

The car zoomed toward them. They crossed the road into the field, pushing the donkey to its maximum speed. Behind them, they heard the screech of brakes, the sound of running men. There were two of them in pursuit.

Heading the donkey into a copse of palm trees, they drove him parallel to the river, over a narrow path beside an irrigation ditch. What Si feared most was that they would give away the location of the felucca, leaving them, literally, a moving target on the river.

Suddenly, the donkey faltered and fell. It remained at the edge of the ditch, unable to rise. They tugged at the reins until it was obvious that it was too exhausted to move.

Grabbing Abdel's hand, he crouched and they moved across the field. In the distance, Si spotted a field of high corn, and they headed toward it, no longer bothering to see if they were being followed. Reaching the cornfield, they crouched low in the security of the stalks, hoping that they could pass between the neat rows without ruffling the high stalk peaks.

Perspiration soaked through their clothes. The heat was oppressive, and he felt that his lungs would burst. Finally, they had to rest. They lay on their bellies, listening. They heard the river surging nearby, but no sound of pursuit. Si's heart pumped wildly. The sun was slipping over the western cliffs, laying long shadows on the ground. Earlier, he had fixed the boat's location by a landmark on the eastern bank, the distant obelisk of the Temple of Karnak, its tip still glistening in the reflection of the falling sun.

Soon they were fighting time, as the darkness began to descend. At last, in the distance, they saw the mast of Hassan's felucca. Hassan and Anwar, crouching on the shore beside the boat, were busy preparing the evening meal on the alcohol stove. Moshe lay asleep on deck.

Their anguished faces told Hassan everything, and with Anwar's frenetic help, he quickly doused the fire and gathered up the stove and pot and stowed it in the boat. Si and Abdel threw themselves on the deck as Hassan, reacting to their panic, pushed the boat smoothly into the river. He and Anwar quickly unfurled the sail. The wind caught it and moved the felucca to the center of the river.

Lifting his head over the gunwale, Si could see the car's headlights, like giant eyes peering into the river. He felt, suddenly, a terrible twinge of pity for the old man. They would certainly harm him, if only out of frustration.

"Just head upriver," Si called to Hassan. He nodded, smiling. He had enjoyed the excitement. Although he did not understand the reason for it.

They passed the lights of Luxor and tacked forward. The breeze quickened, and they were able to make some headway. Soon the lights were left behind, and the boat moved soundlessly through the tunnel of darkness, the river glowing faintly by the light of a tiny sliver of moon.

CHAPTER THIRTY-THREE

W HEN HE AWOKE, THE air had cooled. He had lost any sense of time, but it was still dark. Abdel was sleeping beside him on the deck. Hassan sat slumped beside the tiller, moving mechanically as if he sensed the wind's action. Anwar and Moshe slept on the foredeck. Si shook Hassan's shoulder.

"Where are we?" he asked.

Hassan lifted his head and looked around him, peering into the murky darkness. Both sides of the river seemed exactly the same. Not a single light dotted the shore. Then he looked up at the canopy of stars shining down through the soft air.

"About thirty miles south of Luxor," he said hoarsely, moving the tiller hard to lee and heading toward the western bank. The boat slipped through a tangle of bulrushes and grounded itself in the mud. Anwar rose as if on cue, and he and his father pulled down the sails and unbolted the mast, swinging it downward over the cockpit. They were now invisible to the river traffic.

Carrying a rolled canvas over his head, Hassan, followed by Anwar, waded through the bulrushes to the shore. Si heard him roll out the canvas and cough lightly. Then all human sounds ceased. Waterfowl, insects, and animals stirred lightly, offering a restless babble of soft lilting sounds.

Lying down on the deck, Si stretched out and put his hands behind his head, watching the vast display of stars. They were a hive of activity, other worlds in ferment. Once again, he sensed his connection with the past, the universe, the endless flow of life and death. Beside him, Abdel whispered his name and moved closer to him.

"It feels like there is only us," Si said. "But it's an illusion. We are in the thick of life." He reached out and she rolled close to him, her arm passing over his chest. He could hear her beating heart. It recalled the beat of his mother's heart. He could not remember exactly when, knowing only that he had listened to it, concentrating on its mysterious rhythm, as if it were music. It struck him that he had not listened to other hearts, had not lain this close to any other human being. Not this way. The reaction of his body was not brotherly, and he moved in a subtle separation.

In the enveloping darkness, he felt oddly secure, lost in the joyous warmth of a great womb. He wondered about Isis, where she was, what she dreamt. Was she also looking at the stars? He tried to summon up the physical characteristics of her face, her body. Did she walk erect, with soft padding steps like his mother? Did she know she was a princess? What did she long for? It was a question that drew him back to himself.

It had puzzled him as a boy, and later as a man, that he had never craved anything, never could find a demand in himself, a passion. Nor was it something that he ever felt was missing in him. Not until now. Nothing was more important, more passionate and invigorating, more obsessive, more stirring of all his inner needs than what he felt now. The road to Isis.

"I'll find her," Si said, knowing Abdel was listening, as if his original objective needed restating.

"But suppose..." He felt her hesitation.

"Suppose what?" he pressed.

"Suppose she does not want to be found. By you. Certainly not by..." Again, she hesitated. "By them."

"But I must find her," he protested.

"Why?" she asked. He had not wanted to confront that question, and it annoyed him to be asked. He searched his mind for the one definitive answer, remembering his mother's confession, his own original romantic view.

"Because she exists," he said, finally.

Abdel moved away from him. Reaching out, Si coaxed her toward him. His hand touched her face. He felt her warm tears.

"I hope you never find her," she said, stifling a sob, which perplexed him.

Before dawn, they breakfasted on the treacle and curdled milk, which, Si was surprised to discover, tasted delicious. They moved upriver under good winds as the sun rose over the low hills of the east bank. Although Hassan couldn't read the words on the map Si'd given him, he had no trouble discerning the geography of the Nile.

"It is my river," he said, proudly. "There is not a bend from Aswan to Luxor that I don't know like this..." He raised his hand and showed his palm.

He kept the felucca as close to the wind as possible, and in the strong morning breezes, the boat heeled precariously, making it difficult for Si and Abdel to keep hidden. They passed Esna and headed south toward Edfu, following the markings on the map.

Abdel said little, huddling under the mast. Occasionally, Si would poke his head above the gunwale, surveying the river. A number of feluccas plied their way in either direction. Sometimes, tourist boats passed and barges loaded with crates. Hassan and Anwar waved to every boatman that passed, sometimes shouting their names. Even Moshe barked a greeting.

"You seem to know everybody," Si said.

"The river is my home."

He was gregarious and friendly, obviously content with his life on the river. In addition to Anwar, he told them, he had four children with his two wives, and because he owned the boat he considered himself prosperous, although he admitted that it had taken two generations to save enough money to purchase the boat.

His contentment was enviable. Both wives got along well, he explained, another validation of his success.

"It is not easy to please two women," he said, winking and puffing out his chest. With Anwar, he was alternately severe and affectionate, and father and son caressed each other without shame, with Moshe joining in. When he was severe, Hassan did not hesitate to strike his son or the dog.

"With the exception of the disease of the snails, Allah has been good," he said, a paper-rolled hash cigarette between his teeth, the smoke curling out of his mouth as he talked.

"The what?" Si asked.

He was startled at Si's ignorance, and shook his head. The information was common knowledge in his world. But to Hassan, the world was the river.

"It lives in the snails and comes in at the feet." Nonetheless, he was barefoot, but showed the bottoms of his soles, hardened like leather. "There is no medicine for it."

"You mean people just die."

"Slowly," he said. "They sicken and die. My father died from it." A shadow of gloom crossed his face. "And the big dam has made it worse."

Si looked at Hassan's feet. Anwar, too, was barefoot.

"Allah watches over us." Hassan shrugged, responding to the unspoken inquiry.

"He also watches over the snails," Si said, but it seemed to make no sense to Hassan and again, he shook his head and smiled.

"I suppose you think I'm stupid." Si laughed. Behind Hassan, scraping out pots on the deck, Anwar nodded with a big broad smile flashing across his coppery face. Si envied them their world, their river, their Allah, their harmony with nature.

"What makes him so happy?" Si whispered to Abdel later. The sun had gone down, and they sat up at the prow just under the boom with Moshe between them.

"He has his place," Abdel said, caressing Moshe's mangy coat. "Not like us," she whispered. His instinct was to protest, but he reconsidered. Hassan was primitive and uneducated and superstitious. But he was content. He belonged to something. It was a state of mind that Si had never attained, and he envied the man.

Hassan pointed out the village of Edfu on the east bank, a tiny cluster of lights, which he knew from his map, marked the halfway point between Luxor and Aswan. A French team was excavating about two miles upriver, not far from the bank, and Si instructed Hassan to put the boat in about a mile from the site.

"No fires," he said. Hassan nodded, slapping Anwar's hand as the boy lit a match to ignite the kerosene stove. Dogs barked in the distance. Moshe barked in answer to what struck Si as a generic welcome. The dogs seemed as plentiful as people. Si quickly stepped onto the shore. Abdel jumped after him.

"Where are you going?" he asked.

"With you."

"No, Abdel."

"My name is Samya," she whispered. Even in the darkness, he could see the familiar pout. He was momentarily confused. Why did she choose that moment to tell him that? He studied her face, seeing the subtle difference in her, and she lowered her eyes in embarrassment.

"Well, you're still Abdel to me," he said. During the long sail, she had been mostly silent, brooding, and he had deliberately left her alone, remembering his mother's long bouts of kayf. *Perhaps she is reevaluating her stake in all this*, he told himself. But he could not find the courage to chase her away.

Annoyed with his hesitation, he grudgingly nodded consent, and she followed him along the narrow, hard dirt trail that ran parallel to the river toward Edfu.

The town was stirring as they arrived in what passed for a main street. Merchants were preparing their wares and those who plied their various cottage industries and services were putting their tools in order for the day's work. He asked specific directions to the site from a man ironing a djellaba with a device strapped to his foot. The man gave them elaborate instructions, although the site was no more than a quarter of a mile from the Temple of Horus, a Hellenic version of an Egyptian temple, which dominated the village. The legend on the map had indicated that the temple had begun under the reign of the Ptolmies, the dynasty that came after the death of Alexander the Great.

At the dig site, they were directed to a self-absorbed Frenchman sitting under a tree, smoking a pipe, and inspecting a piece of broken pottery. A group of Egyptians squatted nearby, painting numbers on bits of stone. The excavation site was smaller than the others he had seen.

"Ezzat? Vaguely," the Frenchman said, biting hard on the stem of his pipe, making his Arabic difficult to decipher. He was not interested in being helpful.

"A well-known archaeologist," Si said, trying to jog his memory. The Frenchman removed his pipe. "My interest is in what the Greeks did here," he snapped with patronizing restraint. He seemed inordinately touchy, inspecting Si carefully.

"You don't look like an Egyptian," the Frenchman said, after a blatant inspection.

"American," Si said grudgingly.

The Frenchman nodded.

"I thought so," he said, looking suddenly at the workmen.

"Can't get the bastards to work. Merde! Sometimes, I think it is revenge."

Si resented his criticism, but resisted telling the man he was half Egyptian.

"My field is the Ptolmies. The authorities are a bit paranoid about anything foreign. The fact that Napoleon invented their bloody Egyptology cuts no ice. It took me ten years to get this dig going—" He might have gone on, but Si cut him short.

"Well, it's their country," he murmured.

"Look around you. See what they did to it."

"Looks all right to me," Si responded defensively.

"It's in the eye of the beholder," the Frenchman snapped, fixing his pipe between his lips and dismissing them with an arrogant glance. Si, frustrated and annoyed, started to leave. The Frenchman ignored them. As they moved away, one of the workmen stood up and followed them. He was an old wiry man with gray hair, set off against almost jet-black Nubian skin.

"I know who you mean," the man said, his eyes peaceful and alert. "I worked with him in the old days. And in Abu Simbel." Si's interest perked up. "A fine man. A great scholar."

Si nodded, his pulse quickening, letting the man ramble on.

"When you see him again, please send him Abdul's greetings. He always praised my work." The man hesitated, showing pleasure in the memory. "'Mamoud,' he would say to me. 'You have a great instinct for history.'" The man smiled, showing a sparse line of ruined teeth. "I saw him last year in Kom Ombo."

Kom Ombo? It was unfamiliar, and Si's frown must have indicated his confusion.

"The Temple to the Two Deities: Hawar, with the hawk head, and Sobek, the crocodile," Mamoud explained, proud to display his knowledge. "A restoration project. Some of the reliefs are fading. He would sit on the high wall and watch us. He has become quite old. I did not recognize him. But you see, they were making an error in one of the figures." He kneeled, and with one of his fingers, drew a figure in the dust. "The eye, you see, they had confused the shape…"

Si did not interrupt him, absorbing little of the explanation. Then the man stood up.

"He signaled me to come up, and I recognized him instantly. 'It is wrong, Mamoud,' he said to me, pointing out the error, and explaining the correction." Mamoud's smile faded and he grew morose. "He tried to deny that he was Dr. Ezzat. But, you see, he had called me by my name. Beyond that, he did not acknowledge anything more. But I knew him, you see—"

Si interrupted what seemed like a much longer explanation.

"Did he live near there?"

"I was not sure. Then I saw him again in the village some time later. He was sitting on a donkey cart with, I suppose, his family. A woman. Small children. There was a young woman with him, I think."

Si looked at Abdel, who was also concentrating on the man's story.

"Mamoud." It was the Frenchman, booming out the man's name with irritation.

"I had better go now," he said, politely. "But if you see him, you must send my regards." The Frenchman stood up, glaring at them with anger.

"Is there anything you might tell me about the young woman perhaps?"

Mamoud shrugged.

"I am very bad at modern people," he said, breaking into laughter at his little joke.

"...the way she looked."

Si waited for the laughter to die down. The man scrutinized Si's face, and his laughter ended abruptly.

"Yes, something," he said, scratching his chin, sprouting with tiny gray hairs. His face lit with the sudden glow of recollection. He studied Si's face.

"Her eyes. Green. Like yours."

CHAPTER THIRTY-FOUR

T HE SUN HAD RISEN higher, the heat falling like a shroud over the village. Crowds had filled the main street lined with the usual stalls selling indigenous foods, the same offerings wherever he went in Egypt, oranges, bananas, beans, flatbread loaves, goat cheese, flyspecked lamb carcasses. They moved through the effluvium to the river's edge. The town reflected a ravaged sense of time, clearly reflecting his own mood. Time seemed a personal enemy now, as if the abrupt knowledge had clotted its passage, leaving him suspended in a cloud of indecision.

Had Si secretly wished that the search might not end? He had observed this letdown in himself at other times, like finals week at school, at that moment of greatest expectation when the test papers were handed round, or when he first touched the flesh of a tired prostitute in the off-campus brothel. It was less disappointment than an unmasking, showing the sudden brutality of reality that intruded on his scrim of fantasy, hastening the cruel dismantling of delicious suspense.

He watched a group of women kneeling at the river's edge, pounding clothes on the moist rocks, smiling and chattering, surrounded by naked children, their ancient burdens lightened by the company. It frightened him to think about the mission's end, remembering the old drifting, the plethora of choices and alternatives that had confused him, the causeless, uninspiring bobbing and weaving from one dead end to another. How he envied the purposefulness of these fellaheen and their families, spared by definitive hard labor from the confusion of perceived uselessness.

"The worst thing that I can do now is to lead them to her," he said, suddenly. It was, he knew, perhaps an unconscious wish to abort the pursuit.

"I told you that from the beginning," Abdel said.

"Whatever she did, she at least managed to remain safe."

He looked around him, studying the faces that passed along the trail at the river's edge.

"So far, we have not been so clever," he said gloomily.

She lowered her eyes, perhaps contemplating the illogic of her own involvement.

"It seemed so simple at the beginning," he said. "All your life you're searching for something. You don't know quite what it is, but you know it's there, nagging at you, biting at your insides. Then, suddenly, it seems to appear. You grab at it. You push for it. You'll do anything in the world to get at it. Anything. No one can stop you. You're invulnerable. No hardship, no pain, no danger is too much to get at it." He watched her, but she turned her face away and looked toward the river. "When she told me about Isis... you must understand that her love, her protection, was fierce, smothering. I used to wonder if I hated her..." He paused, asking himself now, *why am I telling her this?* "...So you see, Isis became the missing key..." *The key to what?* "...to the thing I was searching for."

"Isis..." Abdel jeered, her voice rising. She moved suddenly, climbing the bank, regaining the road, heading back in the direction of the boat. Her action confused him, and he tried to dismiss it. Why should what she did concern him? He shrugged and rose, walking slowly along the path toward the boat, deliberate in his pace, trying to decide among the alternatives that rose in his mind.

When he saw her running toward him, he expected it was some gesture of contrition, but her face was pale, and a stiffness in the way she held her body as she came closer told him otherwise. She was out of breath as she reached him.

"What is it?" he cried, running to meet her.

She reached out and grabbed his hand, dragging him in the direction of the boat. They ran through the palm grove at the riverbank. He saw the mast poking above the bulrushes. Hassan squatted gloomily on the deck. Anwar, like a discarded wet bundle, lay beside him, not moving. Si's first impression was that he was dead, but then he coughed, and his thin little shoulders shook with sobs. Si jumped into the boat.

It was then that he noticed the waterlogged, bloated dead dog, its coat encrusted with mud, its snout open, its dead eyes frozen in a paroxysm of terror. Hassan looked up at Si lugubriously.

"They drowned him. They held him by his hind legs over the boat and put his head in the water. There was nothing I could do. Nothing." He bit his lip to stop it from trembling.

"Who?" Si asked, but it was a question that needed no answer. Them! Of course, he knew.

"They wanted to know where you were, where you were going. Anwar nearly went mad. They would put the dog's head under water. 'Tell them,' Anwar shouted. Tell them, what? There were three of them. Mean, cruel men. Finally, they would not bring the dog up." He looked toward the shivering Anwar. "'Give them the map, Papa,' the boy had cried. What was I to do?"

Si patted the man's shoulder.

"It's all right," he whispered. "It's all right."

Abdel kneeled on the deck and stroked the whimpering boy's back.

"The next time, it will be the boy," Hassan said. "They made me promise that I would tell them everything. What could I do? They held the boy as they held the dog." He shook his head sadly, obviously confused by events. "So you see. There is little choice now."

"I know," Si whispered, sure now of his own choice. And theirs, as well. "You must go back," he said. "They will keep their promise." He looked around him at the deserted shore, knowing that they were out there, watching. "They must see that you have left me ashore and gone on. And they must see that it is my decision."

Hassan looked disconsolately at the dead dog. Si understood their loss. The dog was part of the harmony of their lives, with his own place in their extended family.

"And you must take Abdel with you," Si said. Hearing that, she disengaged from the boy and stood up. Her nostrils flared with anger.

"That is not for you to say," she snapped.

"I'm sorry. I've thought about it. It can do you no good. These people are killers. I have no clue to why they are doing this, but that is a piece of the puzzle I am determined to find..." He looked at the dead dog. "Remember Herra. Mrs. Vivanti. Now this. I have no right to expose you."

"That's not it," she cried, exploding with anger. "You don't want me anymore. Now that you are about to find her. Your precious Isis... I hate her."

Her reaction confused him further.

"Dammit," he shouted. "You just get the hell out of my life."

He jumped over the gunwale into the bulrushes and pushed the prow free from the bank. The force of his push slid the boat quickly into the river tide. Reacting instinctively, as if a felucca out of control was an affront to the river, Hassan grabbed the tiller, paid out the sail until it billowed over them, and swiftly cut into the tide on a downstream course. Moving with the tide, the wind in her favor, the felucca slid swiftly away, the figures on her deck fading into the distance as seen through the blinding mist of his tears.

CHAPTER THIRTY-FIVE

L ONG AGO, ZAKKI HAD learned to distrust elation, as he had learned to distrust love, friendship, honor, and loyalty. Elation, with its mindless promise of reward and optimism, was an enemy. Yet he could not deny himself its tiny luxury now that he scented culmination. Soon he would be able to concentrate on the full measure of his revenge, the mechanism of its inflicted horrors.

Death, he had learned, bore only the promise of an infinite void, the end of pain and fear. He had also learned to distrust, perhaps to disbelieve their precious Allah. Allah was the hashish of guilt. He wondered if he had freed himself from that scourge.

Allah would not save her from the infliction of his special revenge, a form of maiming that would require for her a lifetime, a long lifetime, he hoped, of endless remorse. He had dreamed of cutting out her tongue, plucking out her eyes, puncturing her eardrums, locking her into the prison of herself forever. Such fantasies satisfied him, left him limp with a special kind of ecstasy.

Below him, from his vantage in the first-class compartment, surrounded by his handpicked men, he watched the thin green strip of the Nile moving on its inexorable course. In the distance, in the clear air, he could see the high dam and, below that, the earlier dam and the first cataract with its little patches of islands. Kitchener's. Elephantine.

There the Aga Khan was buried in his elaborate tomb, a further waste of his subjects' wealth, which they had weighed out in diamonds to match his absurd corpulence. How Farouk had envied him. "I would have done much better than that bastard," the king had bragged, patting his huge, swollen belly. But the Aga Khan was a proclaimed deity, which rankled Farouk. "The god business has always been better than the king business."

Poor Farouk. He had actually tried that ploy, getting himself appointed a direct descendant of the prophet Mohammed, a genealogical absurdity. Unfortunately, the idea came too late. If it had been done at the beginning of his reign, it would have changed the course of history. Perhaps, even he, Zakki, would have also believed it and lived out his life as a lackey to the king-god. A painful nostalgia gripped him. Perhaps it might have been better, after all.

The plane banked and circled, moving out over the desert, and finally to its approach to the Aswan airport. There was no doubt in his mind now that the boy had picked up the scent, a vindication of his own instincts. Unfortunately, the communications made it impossible to learn how things were going from 750 miles away. He had demanded frequent responses and, as always, he suspected that there were gaps in the reportage. He had, therefore, despite his infirmities, come to see for himself. Besides, in the scenario of his vengeance, he had to be there.

His villa in Aswan was used infrequently. It was a huge structure, surrounded by a high wall. It was built from blocks hewn from the timeless stone quarries nearby, from the same hard rock used to build the ancient temples and pyramids. Primarily, it served a pleasure palace for officials and businessmen who had traded their integrity for Zakki's largesse.

He was, after all, a protected species. Someone had to ply the hashish trade, take the risks, coordinate the complexities. Wasn't hashish as essential as bread? It gave the illusion of satisfaction. In a special way, Zakki also had convinced himself and others that he was a national hero. After all, he had kept the price down, kept the dream weed in reach of the masses. The laws created by governments were for show, not for obedience.

A wheelchair met Zakki at the bottom of the ramp, sparing him the effort to reach the cars, and soon they were speeding toward the villa.

"The boy?" Zakki asked Ahmed, who sat up front beside the driver.

"He is still traveling upriver," Ahmed said, turning. "On a barge carrying wheat sacks." He took a map out of his pocket and gave it to Zakki. He studied it carefully.

"What are these marks?"

"Archaeological sites."

"And he is still looking for that man? Ezzat?"

"Yes."

They had explained earlier what they had done to get the information, an overreaction to his own impatience. Where is the young man going, he demanded to know. And why? He berated the clumsiness of his own men. Typical Egyptian inefficiency. It had been Farouk's favorite complaint.

Despite himself, he was intrigued by the young man's moves, admiring his logic and tenacity. Farrah's boy, he smirked, remembering his own humiliation, knowing, too, that he would soon have to devise a special fate for him as well. That, of course, would be a simple matter. In this case, an eye for an eye would do nicely. Revenge in kind would provide him with the greatest satisfaction.

"We must keep our distance," Zakki warned. "Let him think he has lost us."

The dark-skinned man nodded.

"The destination of the barge is Aswan," he said. Then he looked at his watch. "It should arrive at dawn." Leaning over, he pointed to a site on the map.

"We have men waiting there."

Zakki studied it and nodded assent. He could sense that the end was coming.

He spent the night as always, sitting in his chaise on the terrace, avoiding the nightmare terrors of the darkness, trying to plumb the secrets of his triumphs and keep the snake of his agony at bay.

Impatience, it seemed, made the dawn hesitate. His men, he knew, would be on the quay waiting, an elaborate operation, now a test of ingenuity and will. He tried to probe the mystery of the young man's tenacity. His obsession seemed without motivation on the surface, a missile guided by an unseen hand. Perhaps, he thought, this was what was meant by providence. Or was it Farrah's blood returning to find nourishment in her roots? Such speculations amused him.

Ahmed's familiar step broke the silence. He was moving at twice his normal speed, footfalls pounding the stone, previewing the urgency. When he appeared in the half-light, his face glistened behind a mask of perspiration.

"He was not on the barge," he announced, somberly, accustomed to being the conduit for any news, good or bad. Zakki would not suffer obfuscation, rejecting the elaborate facade of Arab subterfuge.

"We saw him get on board in Edfu. We followed the barge by land on both banks. It did not dock anywhere."

Zakki's mind groped at questions. Ahmed would be accurate to the letter, supplying only facts. He had neither the subtlety nor the deviousness to form self-serving conclusions. Not that Zakki would have believed them. After all, he trusted no one, and would trust no other interpretation than his own. Command demanded that. Power depended on it. Ahmed simply obeyed.

"And the bargeman?" Zakki prompted. He felt the snake of agony tighten its grip.

"At first he denied that the young man was ever on the barge, afraid that he would lose his job. It took some persuasion to get to that point." Ahmed grinned. "We had to break both his legs. But he swore he did not see him after he had ordered him to get to the front of the barge and make a spot for himself among the wheat sacks. He operated the barge from the rear and it was dark."

"The young man said nothing, gave no hint?" Zakki asked, determined to keep his rage in check.

Ahmed shook his head vigorously. Zakki leaned back against the chaise and looked up at the lightening sky. The stars were rapidly losing their luster. To lose sight of Farrah's son, his beacon, now verged on the catastrophic. His breath grew short. His heart palpitated and beads of icy sweat poured out of his soft, heavy body.

"Are you certain?" Zakki hissed. Ahmed cleared his throat, nervously.

"First we broke his legs," Ahmed said. "Finally, the man fainted."

"And now?"

"He is on the bottom of the Nile."

It was, he knew, futile to berate Ahmed. The poor bastard had proven his loyalty. And he had assured Zakki that the men were busy along the entire length of the Nile from Edfu to Aswan. Was it possible that the young man had outsmarted him? Was he destined always to suffer Farrah's humiliation?

With great difficulty, he rose from the chaise and shuffled through the glass doors, followed by the gloomy Ahmed to the drawing room. Earlier, he had placed the map in a drawer of a desk. Now he drew it out and opened it, studying it carefully. With his finger, he traced the Nile from Edfu to Aswan.

"Did they bother to check here?" He pointed at a mark, indicating the archaeological site at Edfu.

Ahmed lowered his eyes, revealing his answer. *So*, Zakki thought, *when the young man came back to the boat, they*

assumed that nothing of moment had occurred at the site, and
since he was in the snare again, what did it matter?

His mind cleared and the drying perspiration cooled him.
He had to assume, too, that the bargeman was telling the truth.
The barge was, he was sure, quite long, piled high with wheat
sacks, and the night was dark. The hum of the motor would
mask any other sounds, particularly if the young man was
determined to keep his actions hidden.

Ahmed forlornly leaned against the wall. He had lit a cigarette and was puffing deeply, letting the smoke curl from his
lips.

Suddenly, Zakki felt a throb of excitement and the snake of
agony relieved its pressure. Apparently, the young man had
learned something of importance at Edfu and was no longer
in any doubt of his destination. And he had sent away the girl.
More confirmation. But where was he headed? Zakki looked
at the map until his eyes could barely focus. Beyond Edfu, the
river made a sharp bend at Kom Ombo. Coming upriver in the
dark would make most landmarks valueless to an unseasoned
eye. The banks would be bathed in darkness. Only the thump
of the motor and the gentle turning of the barge would provide
evidence of movement and hint at the change of direction.

Zakki's basic assumptions had been confirmed every step of
the way. Farrah's son needed to find Isis. Zakki could understand the concept of need. No logic could define it. Need was
need, mindless, driven, powered by a mysterious force, like a
car's engine with a stuck accelerator, heading relentlessly forward or backward, moving only for the sake of itself, beyond
reason or explanation... And yet, he had begun to suspect that
need, even need, was finite.

Such thoughts could frighten him. What happens when need burns out? Love. Hate. Revenge. Good. Evil. The need for these could end, disintegrate in the cosmos of the mind. What else would sustain him, give him nourishment? The end of need was death. He tore his mind from dwelling on such a catastrophe now. He must husband what remained of his need.

Suppose the boy's need should falter, just at the rim of the caldron. He must concentrate now on the boy. His beacon!

He had never assumed that the young man was clever, but he knew that need had a subtle effect on cunning. Cunning could explode into craft. So he has reached that stage, Zakki surmised, sure now that Farrah's boy, like a hunter's pointer, was nearing his prey.

"Of course," he said suddenly, rising slowly from the table, the map held to the light. "Here," he pointed to Ahmed with his stubby finger. "The river makes its wide bend to the west, an unmistakable turning. A subtle landmark. He would need no other beacon." He banged on the table with his fist. "Here. Right here. We must go there. At once."

Ahmed followed Zakki's finger. Bending, he peered at the spot. He could not read.

"Kom Ombo," Zakki said, dead certain of his intuition. "I am sure of it."

CHAPTER THIRTY-SIX

S I HAD MOVED THE wheat sacks, piling them in such a way as to make a burrow on the forward deck of the barge. He could view both banks of the Nile through spaces in the sacks without exposing his head. The little bargeman suffered from his own paranoia. He feared an inspector would spot the passenger. "No passengers" was a strictly enforced rule, and it had taken a formidable sum to induce the bargeman's risk.

"You must not be seen," he had warned, explaining how Si might circumvent the potential problem. He lay now, sprawled in his burrow, on a pallet of wheat sacks, surprisingly comfortable and looking up at the star-filled patch of sky and waiting for the barge to sail.

The self-righteous martyrdom he had felt in forcing Abdel (he deliberately avoided thinking of her as Samya) to leave had quickly turned to loneliness. He hadn't expected it to be so corrosive to his concentration. Now that he had determined to proceed, he needed all his mental energies for the pursuit of Isis. He tried to summon up a picture of Isis, peering into the vast canopy of stars, as if he could create her outline in the constellations.

Longing shattered the sparse image. All his feeble effort could do was recreate the face of Abdel. He smiled ruefully, remembering the silent grace of her movements, the shallow breathing of her body beside him. Trying to shake the pervasiveness of her image, he argued himself into the assurance that he was protecting her. This thought triggered additional guilt. Isis! Would he be the instrument of her death? Or worse?

How different his life would have been if his mother had died suddenly. He would have graduated from Cornell, blithely ignorant of any dark, maternal secret, pursuing a far less dramatic objective. Yet compared to this, anything else was bland, colorless, without meaning.

He had always envied people with certitude and goals, especially those among his classmates who knew what they were after, or thought they knew. The rest, like him, merely floated on an endless river, going from nowhere to nowhere. He had told himself that this was only the normal uncertainty of youth, that life would create its own natural goals. Well, he had one now.

And after? Well, he would cross that bridge when, and if, he came to it.

Despite the dry warm night, he shivered, and listened to every sound. Water flapped rhythmically against the barge's wooden hull, rocking it gently like a giant cradle. The inevitable bark of a wild dog split the air with its shrill appeal. Human sounds faded. He heard the low neigh of a donkey and the light baa of a sheep.

At last, he heard the first click of the barge's motor, its hacking first gasps, and soon the steady turnover as it nosed forward away from the shore. It was too dark to see any but the barest outlines of the shore. He forced himself to maximum alertness as he mapped in his mind the barge's movement, sensing its turns as it reached the river's center and puffed its way upstream.

He had calculated it would take five hours at the outside to reach that spot where the river bent westward and where he would swim to the east bank at a point contiguous to Kom Ombo. It was essential he not be seen. He was sure, if he concentrated and was cautious, that he could accomplish the subterfuge. Beyond that, he dared not speculate.

A vague movement on the sack just above his head alerted him. He presumed at first that it was the bargeman, but it seemed illogical that he could leave the wheel. The sound had an animal-like quality, a movement in fits, as if each portion of energy needed a quick reassessment.

He determined to remain still, muscles taut in case of attack, while his senses strained to track the sound. Whatever it was moved closer to his burrow, where he crouched now, ready to spring. He was sure now it was human, although he could decipher little else. Then the sound was directly above him and he could see the depth of the shadows change as it moved across the burrow and padded lightly onto the wooden deck.

He could not restrain a cautious look at the space between the sacks. Instead of the expected fear, his heart beat with elation. It was Abdel. Samya! She seemed baffled as she crouched and surveyed the line of wheat sacks. He let her watch, amused by her tiny perplexed sighs.

He stirred and pushed aside the wheat sacks, reaching out to drag her into the burrow, a hand clasped over her mouth. Terrorized by the sudden movement, she struggled, relaxing only when she saw his face. He smiled at her, unable to mask his joy.

"You're crazy," he said softly, releasing his hand and caressing her shoulders as she bent toward him.

"You sent me away," she said, the words falling like small coins from a torn purse.

"You came here to tell me that," he said, feeling the pulse of her excitement. Her nearness made him shiver and he hugged her to him.

"You had no right to do that," she said, unable to stop the tinkle of the little coins. They stretched out along the wheat sacks, embracing, savoring the joy of reunion. He wanted to ask her how she had managed it, but somehow it seemed irrelevant. Longing had become desire now. He no longer feared to disguise his need.

"Samya," he whispered.

Her flesh smelled sweet, and her hair seemed perfumed by the soft river breeze. He saw her eye whites above her cheekbones, the pupils that peered back at him offering a bottomless mystery of attraction. His lips did not have to search as they found hers and drank deeply into the softness. The warm dart of her tongue caressed his.

Beyond thought, his body stirred, the blood surged through him. Undressing her, his hands roamed her body, the contours womanly, yielding. Her flesh was smooth as alabaster,

his fingers noting that there was not a hair on it, as if she had
secretly prepared herself in the Egyptian way, expecting what
was about to occur.

"Am I beautiful?" she whispered as his fingers, then his lips
explored her. "Am I a woman?" They were questions that
words could not answer. He kissed her small, high breasts,
her belly, her thighs and between them, tasting the sweetness.

Then he disengaged and, feeling a special joy in exhibiting
himself, undressed and showed her the fullness of his body
kneeling beside her. She embraced his sex and he felt the gentle
throb of her caressing lips, feeling the goodness of her suffuse
him. Such feelings had, thus far, eluded him. Now he was grateful. *This is joy*, he screamed inside of himself.

Then she lay down under him, guiding his sex to the center
of her, reaching upward to receive him, pressing him to
her. He felt the barrier of her girlhood yield, then the tremor
of pain as she shivered. For a moment, he held back his
weight, uncertain. But she drew him in, his fullness burst-
ing into her, feeling the ecstasy of her response, shivering
with waves of pleasure, culminating in a final explosion of
joyousness.

They held each other, merged together in the inevitable
response. Her thighs engulfed him, caressing his body with
its strong female energy. They did not disengage, holding each
other in silence, hearing only the rhythm of their pounding
hearts and the distant purr of the barge's engine.

"When you left, I felt like a piece of me had disappeared," he
whispered.

"I felt that, too," she said, kissing his eyes, finding his lips,
sucking his tongue, staking her claim to his body, which he

returned in kind, feeling tumescence begin again and a slow undulating pressure, assuring him of her need. Her body opened itself to him, cleft in two, as he felt now the full joyous depth of her, lingering in the connection until their bodies melded into a syrup of mutual physical love.

"From the moment I saw you," she said, "I could no longer playact at being a boy. I wanted you to make me a woman."

The matter of her age, too, had disappeared, as if he had plucked the flower at the moment of its greatest beauty.

"I have never felt such joy," he said, remembering flashes of the tawdry experiences that left him dry and gasping with humiliation. He could see her eyes watching him quietly.

"You are so beautiful. Osiris. My Osiris," she whispered, her breath soft and tingling musically against his flesh. "I prayed to Allah that I would please you."

"More than pray," he said, unable to resist the recognition of her ablutions, feeling the smoothness of her shaven woman-hood. It did not embarrass her, and she held her hand there, reaching gently for his sex.

"I was not afraid," she said, proving to him that he had unlocked her from the fear of all men. She continued to caress him. "I prayed, too, that you would love me forever."

He had seen the gulf between them as impossibly wide, unbridgeable, yet this surprise in discovering their sameness moved him deeply. Beyond language and time and culture and education, they had come to each other in this mysterious primordial human dance.

"I will love you forever," he told her, plumbing the infinite well of his passion. Love, expressed by others, had always puzzled him. No longer.

"You must never go away from me again," he said, his lips nipping her ear, as he caressed her hair, noting that its curls had lengthened.

She moved tightly against him, her arms enveloping his waist as she pressed her body along his length, her legs opening to caress his thighs.

"Never?" He resented the intrusion of his own sense of doubt, knowing that the resolution of future plans was in his hands.

"I'll take you to America," he said, testing his bravado, feeling the uncommon strength of his manhood. "We'll start a whole new life. After all, America is the land of opportunity." It seemed suddenly to have the ring of truth, no longer the cliché of a tired slogan. "Now that I have something to live for." He knew the statement had needed a qualifier. What good was opportunity without inspiration? So this was what had plagued him, he thought suddenly, absorbing the impact of awareness.

Their little burrow, it seemed, had become a vacuum, eschewing everything but love and joy, creating the illusion of an abstraction, as if their bodies had disappeared and the only thing that remained was the melded spirit of a single entity.

He must have briefly slipped into some current of the subconscious, a dream, perhaps. The sensation of floating movement was clear. He was on a boat. Had he died? He saw his face on the sarcophagus, gold-painted, the eyes open, clear, alert. And the boat, in his dream, was a sacred barge with a ram-headed prow, both fore and aft. He was, like the ancient god Amun, being taken through the river of night to be reborn.

The cough of the barge's motor chased the image and his mind lurched into the present. They lay like twin fetuses, he draped along her naked back, arms engulfing her. Without disturbing her, he disengaged and peered into the spaces between the wheat sacks. The blackness of the night had softened, and he could see the outlines of a hill along the eastern bank. He wondered if he had passed the spot, resolving that if he had, it would be a sign to retreat, proof that the need to find Isis had diminished as a crucial cause.

Why endanger what he had found, he thought, with Western practicality. What did it matter now? The pull of his mother's guilt was losing its fascination. He wished with all his heart that the barge had passed the spot.

He felt her stir, her arm reach across his shoulder.

"What do you see?" she whispered.

"I think we passed it," he said, kissing her fingers.

"Kom Ombo?"

He nodded.

"And if we did, that will be the end of it."

He sensed her hesitation.

"After you have come so close?"

He turned toward her, embraced her, and whispered into her ear. Her response confused him.

"But you were the one that protested all along. What is the point of it... especially now?"

At that moment, he felt the barely perceptible turning of the boat, the creak of its boards as it strained to follow its course midstream.

"It's turning," he said. "We must be there now." He wrestled with irresolution, tormenting himself.

"You must go," she said.

He tried to mount a protest, searching among the rubble of his confused motivation.

"She will always be between us."

The boat continued to turn, pressuring his sense of time, goading him to decide. Logic seemed to disintegrate. He felt the inertia of his cunning, the old challenge of his courage. She was right. He would always regret not having bridged the final narrow gulf.

He willed a deliberate suspension of his doubt, and they quickly gathered up their clothes, which he tied in a bundle and fastened with his belt onto the small of his back. Silently, they moved aside the wheat sacks, and crouching along the deck, moved to the flat edge of the deck riding low on the water. He gripped her hand, and they dropped silently into the river. Although the water was cooler than the air, it was surprisingly comfortable, and they remained underwater until the sound of the moving barge ebbed.

Surfacing, they bobbed in the barge's wake, watching it move smoothly upstream.

The current was strong, and they let it carry them downstream as they pushed closer to the eastern bank. Her stroke was stronger than his and she made greater headway, although she would stop and call to him occasionally in the darkness. He would have preferred silence, but he answered her reassuringly as he struggled to maintain enough forward motion to keep himself heading toward shore.

The effort winded him. Fortunately, his feet touched the muddy bottom, and he was able to slog forward to the bank, where she waited with an outstretched branch.

Crawling to the dry edge, he lay on his stomach, exhausted, waiting for the pounding of his heart to recede. Loosening their clothes, she wrung them out and hung them on a nearby shrub.

Then, with a handful of moist grass, she wiped his body, considerably diminishing his sense of protectorship. He recalled her self-assurance when he had first met her in the City of the Dead.

"Maybe I can't do without you," he said.

"I am sure of that," she answered, recalling her earlier attitude of mock rebuke.

Grasping her hand, he used the first vestige of his returning strength to pull her next to him.

"I don't ever want to be without the need of you," he said. She placed her hands on his face and kissed his eyes.

"Never," she said. "That is a promise."

"Samya," he whispered. In the quiet air, the sound of her name rang like a strong musical note. "Samya," he repeated. "I love you."

It was then, like a drumbeat emphasis to a plaintive string note, that he felt the first clear tremor of fear.

CHAPTER THIRTY-SEVEN

WHEN THEY PUT ON their moist clothes, the eastern sky was alight with the promise of another hot, cloudless day. He was certain that they had escaped the net of surveillance, although he had learned that he must distrust that sense of freedom. He had been certain before, only to be proven wrong.

She explained that she had swum back to shore at a point downstream from Edfu, and made her way back to the village dock in the darkness. Actually, she had guessed that he was on the barge only because she saw them watching it. There were three of them, burly men, clumsy in their attempt to fade into the population, but unmistakably them. She had hidden in the grass on a small knoll, watching the barge, then moving upstream and into the river when it became apparent that the barge was getting ready to sail. She was certain that no one had seen her get aboard, explaining that she had grasped

316

a dragline and not hoisted herself aboard until the boat had reached mid-river.

Having seen her swim, and observed the ways in which she had adapted to survival, he was buoyed by her explanation, which buttressed his optimism.

"We must be very cautious," she said. "No one must see us."

Sooner or later, Si knew, their pursuers would retrace the course of the barge, combing the villages for any sign of him. Faced with that reality, his confidence ebbed.

"They saw me go away in the felucca. They will not be looking for a girl. It would be wiser for me to search for Dr. Ezzat."

He knew what she meant.

"It is too dangerous," he said, shaking his head.

She looked at him with an unmistakable sense of possession. He felt pleasure in it.

"We are together," she said.

"For always."

He had not intended to reinforce whatever actions she was about to undertake, but he had lost the sense of authority that age and manhood had earlier suggested. Love, ironically, had brought equality.

"I can't let you do this, Samya," he said, gently. It seemed like the old refrain on a soundless instrument.

"There is no choice," she said.

Again, he rushed through the alternatives in his mind. He could turn back. He could go himself. Turning back would bring inevitable self-recrimination. She was right in this. That stigma would haunt him always. As for his going alone, or even with her, he was increasing the risks of Isis's discovery.

Nevertheless, his objective seemed quite clear. He must see Isis, identify himself, validate their connection, fulfill the silent promise to himself and his mother. In that act, he was certain, he would confront his truth, test his courage.

It was, he knew, a convoluted sense of nobility. And yet he could not deny himself the moment, a grand gesture, beyond logic or safety, a slap at reason and balance, but carrying with it a sense of priority that superseded all else. What was life without courage? He would have to find Isis, see her, touch her, feel the genetic pull of kinship. Was he merely fantasizing some new way to actualize an ancient rite of manhood? He wondered. Perhaps.

If he had insisted, he knew Samya would not have gone, but then the shadow of indecision passed, and his silence gave her permission.

"All villages you see are like a fortress," she said. "Even bitter enemies unite against strangers. I do not appear threatening. An innocent young girl." She blushed. The humor had been accidental. "The village mullah is sure to know everyone and everything about this place."

"And how will you find him?"

She looked at him and shook her head.

"He is always in the shadow of the minaret."

She stood up and he came toward her, gathering her into his arms. He held her, kissed her face and lips, until she insisted on her release.

"You must wait here," she said, as his hands slid from hers. The tall grass prevented him from seeing her receding figure, and he obeyed her admonition to stay hidden.

Sitting there, he grew restless and impatient as the sun rose and burned off the layer of mist that hung over the river and its banks like an opaque shroud. That image and the pervasive sense of Samya's loss reminded him of his mother's death, the mask of her frozen face as the lifted sheet provided a last glance. He had looked at that face and it had struck him that in death it was as impenetrable as in life. Was it the loss of her, or the knowledge of her, that had provided the gnawing grief?

"We didn't know her, Dad," he had said to his father, turning away from the mask to view his father's runny face, like a glob of shapeless clay.

"I knew all I wanted to know," the grieving man had replied.

Yet, he knew his father. There were points of reference. The innumerable Kellys, supernumeraries in the vast Irish-American drama with its incessant rituals, its moody brooding alcoholic eruptions and stupors, its endless talk, its books and plays and poets that propagandized the Irish myth. Pride in it had become a cliché.

"It's all right," his father told him and his mother at Kelly gatherings, when the level of alcohol had risen in the blood, reddening their noses and cheeks, and all the highs and lows of the Irish mood erupted at once. "They're Irish."

The landmarks were common and colorful; the mysteries had been exploited by novelists and poets and actors and playwrights and politicians, burrowing into the American conscience, like some persistent, spreading weed.

"But what was Egypt like?" he had asked his mother. He knew the Irish. The monotony of the inquiry seemed to elicit a flash of futility in his mother's eyes. Perhaps even she could not explain it. Egyptology, he had learned, was not Egypt. Nor were the cruel caricatures and endless military defeats. Nor the muezzins proclaiming the one god from their minarets, nor the Copts and their Christ worship, nor the blindfolded beast walking the eternal circle, pushing the Archimedes' screw. Where, then was the real Egypt?

It was as impossible as comprehending why Zakki, a mysterious, evil, obscene force, was pursuing Isis, or why Isis existed in his mind as a child abandoned, deprived of love by a bereaved guilt-haunted mother, this offspring of the king, the fairy princess.

Stretching out, he pulled out stalks of grass and sucked them, remembering his hunger. Occasionally, groups of people and animals passed along the river trail. He heard their voices and high-pitched laughter. In the distance, a dog barked.

The chatter of river birds drew his attention to the water, rippling forward on its serpentine path, proud and arrogant in its timelessness. It mocked man and all his vanities. It had witnessed the follies of a thousand generations, bestowing the sustenance of its bounty on countless nations that rose and fell in its moist embrace. It survived every contrivance of man's imagination, his greed, his joys and sorrows, his agonies. Nor did it fear man's potential for extinction. What did it matter? It would continue its endless journey from deep Africa to the Mediterranean until the end of earthly time.

Samya's voice startled him. He had not heard her approach, but her alert, eager eyes told him that she had met with success. As if in celebration, she carried two pita loaves filled with ful, and an earthenware jar of cool milk, which she set on the ground between them. He attacked the ful with salivating fury.

"He is here," she announced. Si stopped chewing, his mouth filled, unable to ask the questions that stumbled in his mind.

"The mullah was very cautious," Samya said, "very suspicious. He is not known here as Ezzat. But it is unmistakably him. He is known as the professor. He knew very little about him. I told the mullah he was my father. Fatherhood is a very important thing in these villages." She sighed, remembering, he was sure, her own sad experiences. "He questioned me very carefully. I told him about the university and the man we had met in Edfu. I was very convincing. The mullah, too, is curious."

"And Isis?"

"The professor has a wife and children. Beyond that, I was afraid to inquire."

The caution seemed sensible and he nodded agreement.

"He said the professor lived about three miles from here. His directions were elaborate, much more than the information he had about them." They finished the ful and the milk.

He wondered if his feeling for her had invested her with inordinate wisdom. She had undone the black head covering of her malaya, showing her youth again, and he moved toward her to kiss her lips, which were soft and tasted milky.

"We had better go," she said.

She stood up, peeking cautiously at first over the high grass. The heat had begun to nudge a light sweat out of his pores.

"There is a narrow road," she said. "But we must not risk that. We will go through the fields." With her instinct for direction, he did not dispute her. "I will go first. Just follow me at a distance."

She set a pace that seemed, at first, almost leisurely, cutting into the fields when she saw a group of people approaching at a distance. Once, she squatted against a shade tree at the edge of a field, waiting until a worker in the distance had finished weeding a row of beans in slow, back-creaking motions. He followed, obeying her actions to the letter, trusting her instincts.

She moved to the edge of an irrigation ditch, following its trough of muddy water, almost to the point where the desert began. Crouching in a copse of palm trees, she waved him forward, and he joined her. In the distance, they saw some young boys harvesting the low-growing bean crop. The land was flat. Where the desert began, he saw a cluster of mudbrick structures attached to each other. They appeared ramshackle, their walls not quite plumb.

A black-clad woman moved along the shade of a wall. She held a baby in her arms while two small children played in the brown dust. A black goat and two scruffy sheep were tethered to a post near the entrance to one of the houses. Nearby, a gray donkey stood impassively, its front legs tied together by a rope staked to the ground. She nodded.

"Here," Si whispered, incredulous. "He lives here?"

He watched as Samya's eyes surveyed the landscape. A narrow, rutted road bisected two fields. It was a breezeless day and the dust of the road seemed too heat-exhausted to rise, giving her a clear view of its straight line to the river in the distance.

"It must be there," she said. "As I said, the mullah was quite elaborate with his directions."

"Ezzat is an educated man, a scholar. He couldn't be living under such circumstances," Si said.

She gripped his arm. "You must go," she said. He started to move forward, but her grip restrained him.

"I will go and watch in the village," she said, recalling the sense of danger. His resolve seemed to drain away. *It is pointless,* he told himself, frightened for her. "If I see them in the village, I will come back to warn you."

"And then?" he added, pointing with his chin to the forlorn houses.

She shrugged. One had to assume, he decided, that Zakki's men would be in the village sooner or later. Yet he did not want to go alone.

"I shouldn't go," he said. "If it is them, I can only risk doing them harm. And I'm not sure that Isis is there."

"It is what you want," Samya said, offering an odd reassurance.

"I want you," he said, reaching for her hand. "The other doesn't seem to matter anymore." His eyes searched hers, finding the doubt.

"Come with me," he said, tightening his grip on her fingers. He knew, of course, that she was too practical for that. Schooled in survival, she knew instinctively the methods of self-protection. In her black malaya, she could lose herself among the village women, for whom to display public individuality was an affront to society. Considering the passion of the predators, the precaution offered an undeniable layer of extra protection.

"I will be very cautious," she assured him.

He fought his reluctance to release her, feeling suddenly the abstract terror of her loss, flailing himself for his inability to control circumstances. It was more than caution that moved her. She knew that this was his obsession. Not hers. It had to be resolved by him alone.

"When will you come back?"

"Soon."

He could not find the will to resist. He watched her move along the edges of the green fields until the heat shimmers destroyed any focus on the far distance. When he could not see her anymore, he turned toward the brown monochromatic landscape, watching the motionless scene, as if all life were suspended, lost in a single flat dimension, timeless and inert.

He stepped from the green river-fed carpet of fertility to the parched, deadened earth. A swarm of desert flies, like a friendly military honor guard, escorted him forward.

CHAPTER THIRTY-EIGHT

A S HE DID EVERY morning, Dr. Ezzat placed his ancient field glasses against his pale, dim eyes to watch the birds. Observing these creatures streaking across the sky, in the changeless patterns of their breed, had become more ritual than curiosity. The process gave him reassurance, conclusive evidence of continuity.

Continuity, he knew, was the obsession of all archaeologists, as if the proof of the past was necessary to validate the future, about which he had lost all confidence. He was convinced that when the ultimate holocaust arrived, the birds, in some aberrant species, would survive in the wasteland of the future, as the radioactive waste settled its deadly blanket over the earth's crust.

In the flight of the birds, the wagtails and onyx swallows, the spur-winged clover, even in the massed squadrons of Nile ducks, pochards, teals, mallards, and the indigenous Egyptian geese, he was convinced he saw the future of life. He was also convinced that the ancient Egyptians, with their herons and falcons and egrets carved into the timeless stone, offered another clue to this surety. Wisdom was finite, a lifetime of study had concluded, and the ancient Egyptians knew it. There was, indeed, nothing new under the sun.

Secure in this knowledge, he removed the field glasses from his eyes and placed them on a plank beneath the paneless window of his tiny abode. The plank was cluttered with chipped pottery, dog-eared books, crumpled papers, bits of dry uneaten food, the tin cup, still moist with the dregs of the herbal leaves that Isis used to prepare his morning tea. She had not bothered to rouse him, but placed the cup of tea on the plank, not realizing that, although he lay supine and unmoving on the pallet, he rarely slept. But he did not want to spoil the sense of her consideration, which presupposed that it was better for him to remain in the void of sleep rather than face the day with his myriad infirmities.

He hadn't expected himself to live this long, to nearly eighty. Both his parents had died in their fifties, softened perhaps by the affluent life of that era. He placed his longevity squarely on the shoulders of Isis, who had, unwittingly, proved necessary to his long life.

Isis had always been the supreme test of his humanity. He knew that almost at once, facing the near hysterical woman who pressed her on him, as if she were a debt that had to be paid.

"You must take her and hide her," the woman had begged as the girl squatted on the floor of his office, a huddled, pitiful figure, a far cry from the memory of the fat, pink baby whom Thompson had jostled on his knee. The girl had listened with indifference as the woman recycled her story, stunning him with its graphic, painful images. The woman, it was obvious, had relished the telling of it, as if she herself had wielded the castrating knife. Looking at Isis, he was certain the girl's reportage was far more matter of fact.

How she had managed to steal away from the Bedouins and find her way back to the City of the Dead, the only home she could ever remember, was nothing short of a miracle as if she had received some secret instruction from her own mother, who had found her own path of escape from the pursuing monster.

Indeed, finding safe passage for the woman's offspring seemed to Ezzat as if it was necessary for her belief in a personal salvation, a way to neutralize the horrors of her own evil acts and soften the judgment of Allah in the realm of the afterlife. Finding a safe haven for this much abused girl child, he supposed she believed might assure her a place in paradise. For him, that was hardly a consideration.

Zakki's reputation had, by then, penetrated even Ezzat's own sphere. By then, too, the silver chalice of the revolution had tarnished considerably and there were even those in his own circle who agreed that the people needed their dream weed as much as bread. He was, he knew, unmoved by the girl's plight, although aghast at the horror of the story.

And he was not without fear. Reprisal seemed almost a necessity to avenge such an atrocity. He could feel, too, the urgent shaft of pain in his own crotch, discovering that even he, who had wrestled to subvert the urge, while channeling energy into other pursuits, could not shed the penultimate fear of a lost manhood.

What could he do, he had protested? He was involved now with the monumental international effort to move the Temple of Abu Simbel from the inevitable flood to be caused by the construction of the big Aswan Dam that the Russians were building. But, then the woman had dredged up Thompson. Not his name. But the deduction was inescapable.

It was Zakki who had brought Farrah and the baby to her on the day of Thompson's death. She had recounted the threat, Farrah's terror and flight. Ezzat knew instantly what she had meant.

Thompson's death had left a residue of guilt. It was he who had found the body and notified the Americans, who efficiently disposed of everything, including the man's existence. It continued to haunt his memory.

The woman pleaded, while the girl sat nursing her terror behind a blank mask. She seemed so unlikely a prey. And yet, her instinct for survival was formidable, considering the distance she had to traverse.

Perhaps he had nodded assent or given some other sign of compassion. He would never be sure. He had deliberately created a life without human ties, without obligations. Then, suddenly, the woman was gone and he had acquired this albatross. The next day, he left with Isis for Abu Simbel.

He established housekeeping in a modest villa near the site, letting others assume that she might be his daughter or, maybe, his mistress.

He had his work, although even the enormous concentration required could not relieve him of the ever-present gnawing fear of discovery followed, surely, by some form of horrible death.

It was not in his nature to be cruel. An abstract idealism and a certain self-righteous piety about human degradation in its most blatant forms, poverty, disease, repression, had prompted him into a brief foray of political romanticism. Deposing the monarchy seemed to satisfy both his own need, and the larger purpose. But once that had been done, the spectacle of Nasser seemed a worse travesty, and he had turned away from activism with disgust. Better to poke around in the relics of yesterday's megalomania, he had decided.

Abu Simbel had been a godsend, marred now by this obscene irony of his brief political past. Isis actually reminded him of some stray dog, scruffy, unaffectionate, teeth poised to snap at the tiniest hint of a hostile act. Except for her fear, which was in itself doglike, she showed barely a trace of a human persona. He had, he assured himself, tried to extend to her the hand of kindness, but she had treated the effort with indifference.

"I knew your mother," he had told her, remembering vaguely the pretty girl with the green eyes, like hers, who had joyfully attended Thompson. He remembered, too, the obvious involvement, berating Thompson for it as if it had been some crime. It filled the overflowing beaker of his guilt to be reminded that it was he who had prevailed upon Thompson to get moving with his story. He tried to explain this to Isis and to justify Farrah's actions. The girl was indifferent.

"You don't care?"

The girl shrugged. It seemed beyond the periphery of her consciousness and her reaction was to absorb herself in an interminable kayf.

"What choice had your mother?" he told her. "She traded her absence for your life." Perhaps, he was ascribing a nobility to her act. Why the devil was he defending her?

"All right," he said, drawing no reaction, pulling down the curtain. He had tried other ploys as well to draw her out, finally withdrawing himself to pure recrimination.

"Some fix you got us into." He would bombard her with that more out of pique than brutality, and she would skulk away as if he had slapped her. Finally, he ignored her completely, letting her live a kind of protected pet life, roaming around the temple construction sites on the psychological tether of their mutual fear. That she understood.

"Just make yourself invisible," he told her. "Don't talk to anyone." He didn't really have to tell her that, and she seldom left the villa except in early morning or at twilight, when the army of foreign workers left for their ethnically segregated encampments. He had toyed with the idea of dumping her somewhere, sending her abroad, boarding her in some remote Nubian desert village, but he declined for a variety of synthetic reasons. The effort was too time-consuming, and he did not want to bring strangers into the orbit of these events. Nor did he have any illusions about his own culpability. He was harboring someone who had, for whatever the reasons, committed so grotesque an act that vengeance was an absolute certainty. Even the fact that Zakki had killed Thompson in cold blood could not, somehow, equalize the atrocity. Death he could understand, but the loss of one's manhood...

Perhaps it was his study of the ancient Egyptians, who had begun to seem more real than contemporary people, that added to his revulsion. To them, nothing was more sacred than their sexuality and the attendant joys of procreation. The frenetic replication of themselves, the awesome and devoted worship of the male erection, artfully hewn out of the Aswan quarries as obelisks, was embedded in the genes of the people, his people. Zakki, he knew, would stop at nothing to find this killer of his manhood and all who might willingly abet the culprit. *Like me*, thought Ezzat. He was as marked as if he had worn a skin of blood-red stripes in a white-duned desert.

But he couldn't keep her locked in a cage. Actually, she was so uncommunicative she seemed in a cage of her own making. Imprisoned in her somber cocoon, she drifted, furtive and alien, in some secret dank impenetrable swamp of anger and fear.

Thankfully, the enormous task to which he was committed, helping to supervise the moving of four hundred thousand tons of temple from its perch in the sandstone rock cliff to another spot ninety feet above it, was enough to absorb his every waking hour, and he was able to shove Isis and all her consequences to an obscure corner of his mind. It was enough that he was hindered in this task by the jabber of conflicting opinions, arguing engineers and archaeologists, an army of heat-crazed workmen and platoons of flat-faced, implacable Russians who considered the task theirs alone.

He despised Nasser for bringing the Russians to Egypt, with their overbearing, bureaucratic joylessness and paranoia. To them, Egypt was exile, and they expressed their frustration by maintaining themselves in superior and antiseptic isolation. Bringing in the Russians was the final betrayal of the revolution, Ezzat had decided, another alien occupation that Egypt had to endure.

But the saving of Abu Simbel transcended everything. At least present-day Egypt would not fail the ubiquitous spirit of Ramses II and his crowning masterpiece, this temple to the imagined glory of the three great enduring gods of that millennium, Ptah, god of the Underworld; AmenRa, patron god of Thebes; and Ha-Rakhte, the sun god. The sly old bastard had placed four sixty-five-foot statues of himself at the temple's entrance and, as if to assuage his regal loneliness, two smaller statues of his mother and his favorite wife.

In the press of events and all its attendant aggravations, his interest in Isis paled and, although the fear was an ever-present specter, they both settled into a routine of indifference.

Then, suddenly, the long-lit fuse sputtered to the point of impact.

CHAPTER THIRTY-NINE

T HE WALL TO PROTECT the temple had been fully erected, and the laborious and painstaking task of dis-assembling the ancient temple had begun. They had already reached the second hall and had begun removing great chunks of the beautifully preserved wall reliefs, showing a heroic Ramses on his chariot, speeding to some mythic battle.

Ezzat had fallen into a schedule of daily rounds in the late afternoon, but some endless meeting to arbitrate a petty squabble made it impossible to proceed on his round until dark. Lantern in hand, he traversed the wall, and moved past the coherent rubble of marked stones scheduled for transport and reassembly. The watchmen were squatting around a stove, sipping the coffee that topped their evening meal, and puffing on their hashish-loaded water pipes, talking in low voices punctuated by occasional laughter.

Not wishing to disturb them, he switched off the lantern and moved deeper into the site by the light of a thin, crescent moon. Toward the rear of the second hall, he paused at a point where an acoustical aberration collected low hushed tones, the unmistakable babble of a small crowd.

Carrying his unlit lantern, he moved deeper into the chamber, where he could make out the outlines of the four giant Ramses, at the base of which he could see a huddled line of squatting figures. He watched them until he could distinguish a pattern of movement. At intervals, someone would rise and move to the darkest recess of the chamber, where muted sounds could be distinguished, like the lowing of animals.

It was strictly forbidden for anyone to be inside the temple site at this hour, a rule, like many in this baksheeshridden land, easily broken with the collusion of the caretakers. The objective of this security was to prevent the theft of artifacts.

But the leisurely indifference of the squatting figures dismissed that possibility, and he proceeded toward them without fear.

"Back of the line, mister," one of the men grumbled in a hushed, urgent whisper. Ignoring the caveat, he proceeded toward the darkest part of the chamber following the sound. In a corner, he could make out what seemed like a thrashing animal, although the sounds of exertion and the outline of a dark shape indicated a human in the throes of some compelling seizure.

When what he was watching became comprehensible, he waited until the movement ceased, either out of some pathetic sense of delicacy, or forewarning of imminent horror. Finally, a man stood up and in the vague light he could make out his movements clearly, the hitching up of trousers, a low clearing of the throat, then the sound of his footsteps against the ancient stone floor.

It was only then that he dared flick the switch of his lantern, catching in the circle of his yellow spotlight that which he had dreaded, the supine form of Isis, alabaster thighs spread, revealing the raw, moist open womanhood. She lifted her face to the light, the green eyes glazed and glinting like gems, glowing with rapt indifference.

"Damn you, Isis," he called. Then, louder, as he moved the circle of light across the walls and into faces of the squatting, hungering men. The light, acting like a catalyst to their fear, roused them and soon their footsteps beat swiftly along the stone floor as they scrambled through the temple, lifting a cloud of stone dust in their wake.

Switching off the light, he felt the rising bile of his anger, choking off the words that froze in his throat. She had risen, and was slumped now against this four-thousand-year-old wall, showing, for the first time since he had known her, a genuine outpouring of emotion.

He came toward her, not knowing which side of the razor's edge his inclination might fall. His mind wanted him to be angry, but she seemed so forlorn, devoid of defenses, her vulnerability like a cold stench in the dusty cavern, that he discovered himself moved to pity and he gathered her in his arms. She moved into them, shivering but tearless, offering only the mute explanation of her helplessness.

In this sea of deprived men, she had become, as he should have seen, a logical target of their primordial urge, an accomplice in her own gang rape. He knew she was groping for an explanation amid the poor tools of her articulation. She was illiterate, and had been raised with such conversational indifference that she could barely summon the words to describe her feelings.

"They wanted me," she said, finally, leaning against him as they moved back toward the villa. For the first time in his life, ever since his mother had died when he was ten, he felt a sense of involvement in another person, responsible.

Not that she wasn't wary of his sudden affection. He could feel that, along with this epiphany, as he laved her mortified flesh with cool water, even those parts that had been more directly abused, with paternal, sexless piety.

"We must not let this happen again," he whispered to her, surprised at his use of the collective pronoun. It was then that she shook her head and the tears came in big shivery blobs, drowning her cheeks.

"From now on, I will never let you out of my sight," he said, hoping that she would see through the superficiality of the words to the core of his sincerity.

That night, they moved the pallet that she had been using as a bed from that spot in the corridor where he had first put it to his bedroom. He knelt beside it, embracing her shoulder and kissing her eyes closed.

"Will you love me?" she asked, lids fluttering open, pupils big as saucers in their green rims.

"Of course, child," he replied, gently, overwhelmed by this sense of possession.

CHAPTER FORTY

H E WAS IMMEDIATELY AWARE that this relationship
provoked profound changes in the way he measured his
life. He had bounced between looking backward and forward,
vacillating like a roller coaster on an endless track, reversing
himself in mid-loop, hurtling both forward and backward in
time. After his disillusion with Nasser, the gears engaged to
bring the conveyance to a sharp stop, reversed themselves, and
brought the focus of his life back to the contemplation of what
had occurred in past millenniums.

By being a detective of the past, poking around in the
relics of past manias, he could both sustain and refresh himself. Each new clue to the past encouraged the reverse action
of the roller coaster, offering the surprises and satisfactions
that were supposed to be the harbingers of the future. Now,
suddenly, spurred by this new relationship to the future, he
felt the damned conveyance shift gears again and start rolling
upward toward the summit of the looped track.

She rarely left his side now. He would take her on his twilight rounds of the temple, deliberately ignoring the empty-faced guards, dismissing what he knew must be their obscene fantasies of this relationship. He offered her a running account of the progress of the temple movement, but she seemed to show little interest in that, more curious as to why the figures were so big, wondering aloud if the people of these long ago times were actually as big as these images.

"He wanted to be remembered," he told her, unwilling to complicate the reply by a long rendition of why the obsessive, megalomaniac Ramses II had gone berserk, with his orgy of defacement and construction.

"But why?" she asked, puzzled.

"He believed that the gods would favor his being granted eternal life."

"You mean he thought he would live forever."

Ezzat nodded, knowing that the explanation was both mystifying and abstract. What he could not tell her was that Ramses' persona did indeed have a kind of eternal life, that his spirit had taken on the hue of a living thing through the crazy genius of these monuments.

"But who built these places?" she asked.

"People," he had answered, his mind wandering in the contemplation of those vast faceless minions whose toil had made these constructions possible.

The explanation did not satisfy her. She had no response to broad abstractions.

"They were the people," he tried again, the pedant in him aroused. "They lived along the banks of the Nile. They tilled the soil, lived in the rhythm of the twice-yearly flood. When they were needed, the old Pharaohs would summon them to do the work, thousands of them, pounded into work gangs of common fury."

"But who were they?" she persisted. "What were their names?"

How were such questions to be answered? What would she make of an explanation that dealt only in statistical estimates of countless thousands, hundreds of thousands, millions, who had given the last ounce of their strength for these geegaws of civilization, these fanciful offerings to some self-chosen maniac determined to actualize his greedy fantasies of immortality?

They were ferociously possessive of each other, and their fear increased proportionately. Zakki manifested himself in everything, like some gelatinous, consuming, impersonal mass moving downhill from the high cliffs overlooking Abu Simbel. He saw potential Zakkis in everyone and everything, watching them like the germinal Egyptian eye. The gang rape was not simply a foreshadowing. It appeared now as an act of aggression, rooted in revenge, perhaps promulgated by Zakki, the first, surely, of many planned terrors.

Isis announced the suspicion of her pregnancy at about the same time that the Israelis swarmed over the Sinai borders to destroy the Egyptian army that Nasser, in a paroxysm of vainglory, had rattled like a saber down the nose of the trigger-nervous Jews.

They heard it on the shortwave radio, the velvet Oxfordian tones of the BBC announcer providing an eerie counterpoint of dispassion to what Ezzat knew was cataclysmic. The Russians, always arrogant and inert, became surly and contemptuous, and the workmen, many of whom had been spared military service by this monumental toil, became unstuck by the national mortification.

Tension and arguments increased, as the Russians tossed epithets at the Egyptian workers, including the archaeologists, stripped of their reticence to declare that the Egyptians were a pack of lazy assholes. Ezzat suffered the indignities out of fear that any reply on his part would call attention to himself and Isis. In his heart, although the logic was tenuous, he was almost convinced that the debacle, like the pregnancy, was more of Zakki's handiwork to torment them.

Yet he stayed on, if only to underline his conviction that what they were doing at Abu Simbel was a truly Egyptian enterprise, not like Nasser's debacle, rooted in the miasma of some pan-Arab fantasy. The idea that the purity of the Egyptian heritage was somehow tied to the destiny of those Arabian primitives who had lived like wild goat herds while the ancients were inventing paper galled him.

In his mind, Zakki became illuminated as the ultimate transgressor, the penultimate foreign body stuck in the bloodstream of the Egyptian race, the embodiment of all its evils. Nothing seemed safe from his centipede onslaught, each infested leg carrying the germ of some Assyrian, Nubian, Libyan, Persian, Mameluke, Circassian, Macedonian, Roman, Arabian, French, British, German, or Italian aggressor.

As her belly blossomed with its nameless embryo, he brooded on some plan to escape from this inferno of ignorance and evil. Oddly, it was Isis's naive innocence that pointed the way out. "But who were they? What were their names?" she had cried. Of course. There was only one true place to hide in this accursed land, to lose one's fabricated identity and swim anonymously, at last, in the great flesh pond of Egypt's life-giving excrescence.

Trusting him implicitly, she did not ask where they were going as they moved out of the villa in the dead of night, loading only portable possessions, clothes, a few books, and some bits of light artifacts on a donkey cart. There were no formal resignations from the project, not a single good-bye, as the donkey cart rattled away from the half-displaced temple, caught four-cornered in limbo between proliferating technology, godhead fantasy, ancestor worship, and national vanity.

She sat stoically in a corner of the cart, which jiggled and bounced over the stony, parched road heading northward over the ancient caravan route, sparsely lined by ramshackle but immaculate Nubian villages.

They traversed the 168 miles from Abu Simbel to Aswan in the blazing heat of late June, sleeping under the cracked boards of the donkey cart and buying food from the Nubians along the way. They also acquired a goat and another donkey, which they tethered to the cart's rear, using the goat for milk and the new gray donkey to spell the other. By then, too, he had eschewed Western clothes and donned a brown djellaba and white turban.

Schooled by Bedouins and much younger, Isis was more attuned to the hardships of this nomadic life, while he had to harden himself to its effects. The hothouse of civilization had softened him, and soon he followed her example.

They traveled mostly at night, escaping from the sun by camping in the shade of palm copses or reclining under the boards of the cart. She prepared meals of fava beans, softened in a mush and inserted into pita bread, which they washed down with goat milk.

They talked little. She had grown up in silence, and for hours they could sit facing each other, locked in bottomless kayf, although he found it difficult to train his frenetic mind to empty itself. Knowledge had sensitized it to hum with energy and curiosity, and instead of floating in a maze of emptiness he used the silence to recall and unify the bits and pieces of past learnings, and to calculate his plan of anonymity.

They would become fellaheen. That had all been determined in advance. What he must find now was a few hectares of land, enough for self-sustenance. Unfortunately, and he was amused by the image, there was no vengeful Judaic God to point the way to the promised land. He would have to find his own real estate, and he did not plan to spend forty years wandering in some haywire plan to destroy the generational memory of enslavement.

They reached Aswan in a few weeks. There, he sold the artifacts to an underground dealer. He had already converted his savings to cash in Abu Simbel. In Aswan, he consulted a farm broker. His method of operation seemed slightly devious, but since he was also being devious in the method of his new identity, both parties were able to wink at the joint deception.

After nearly a month of trudging through the countryside, they found an abandoned place of six hectares outside the village of Kom Grobe, thirty miles downriver from Aswan. The cluster of mudbrick houses were roofless, the fields were in need of care, the creaky Archimedes' screw that provided irrigation was in disrepair. He had picked the place, not for

its condition, but for its relative isolation, his prime consideration. The fields on either side of him were, he learned, in a
cooperative venture, which the previous owner had apparently
rejected and which eventually ruined him, forcing a migration
to the slums of Cairo.

But Ezzat, with his cache of money, and ability to absorb
the facts of agricultural mysteries from books, was certain that,
considering there were only two, potentially three, mouths to
feed, he could make it work.

That first night on their own land had an air of expectancy
for both of them. She had begun to call him father, and he,
in turn, called her daughter. He brooded about this relationship. In truth, it existed in just that way, and he thought of
her in those terms. Yet there were practical considerations,
and he was faced, ironically, with the single most pervasive
consideration of a fellah's survival. Progeny. He had not really
confronted that immutable fact of life, determining and dis-
carding options as quickly as they arrived in his mind. He had
the means to purchase her a husband, but the thought of a
stranger entering their conspiracy seemed more perverse than
the course that persisted in his mind.

He was over sixty, but his health was good, and although
he had willfully submerged his libido, he knew from unmistakable physical signs that he was quite capable of reversing
the process. Indeed, the recall of her bare, blatantly exhibited
womanhood revealed in the circle of light had tugged at this
protective veil of celibacy. Often now, when she moved
close to him, soliciting what seemed like a fatherly embrace,
he felt the beginning tumescence, distinct stirrings of an
"incestuous" lust.

He was not, after all, her father. Not that that would have mattered, he decided finally. The manic Ramses himself had fathered children from among his ninety-six daughters. He had 105 sons as well. It was argued by scholars that it was this propensity for incest that eventually watered down the genetic strength and capacity of the ancient Egyptians, a subject open to debate.

But the die had been cast. Besides, he was engaged in what he believed was a compelling idea, to reverse the tide of his own history, which, centuries before, he was certain began in some nameless patch of fertile earth just like the one he had purchased.

It was not lost on him, as well, that she was in actual fact the living daughter of the last dynasty of Egypt. Slipping backward in time was the last refuge, the final hiding place. To be a fellah was the ultimate connection with the living history of the human race, the primordial urge to find harmony and life in the rhythms of the land and the seasons.

On that first night, he prepared a pallet for them in one of the roofless buildings, the largest of the group. Tomorrow, they would go to town and purchase food, seeds, tools... the currency of a fellah's life. He had discussed this with her at great length.

"This is your place, too, Isis. Yours, forever."

The idea seemed to thrill her, and she moved closer to him on the pallet.

"It will be hard work, backbreaking." He felt foolish, explaining what was so self-apparent. "It will be home to all of our children," he whispered, feeling the swell of her pregnant body, as his hands roamed its fullness.

"I felt it move today," she whispered. What did it matter how the random seed had been implanted, and by whom? he thought. The fact was that nature had spoken, and that, in itself, was the root of all knowledge, all mystery. He hoped, too, that he might one day empty his mind of all its science and logic, and believe, finally, in the mysterious, immutable force of Allah. There is no god but Allah! Could he ever believe that again?

"Be fruitful and multiply," he whispered, mocking the Koranic inflection. Lifting her malaya, he felt her moist womanly parts. The mysterious response of his own sexuality made him draw her close to him. Entering her, he felt certain that the offering of his seed would bond him to her. Perhaps, too, he thought, it would stake his own fatherly claim to the unborn fetus stirring inside her warm, honeyed womb.

CHAPTER FORTY-ONE

E ZZAT WATCHED THE FIGURE as it emerged from the copse of palms that edged the field, stepping into the brown dust. Lifting his field glasses, he surveyed the bronzed face, sun-darkened, not the natural dark skin of this racial noman's-land.

It was a habit now, this reflex of surveillance, that made it impossible to be open-handed with strangers. In the man's carriage, in the high cheeks and strong brow of his face, he tugged at his memory for some shred of recognition. As always when a stranger approached, he took a quick inventory of the family. Isis would be squatting in her usual spot in the shaded eaves of the animal house, nursing their youngest, while the twins, brown and naked, tugged at her garment, tormented by being usurped by this new arrival. The three oldest, all boys, would be in the fields harvesting the fava beans.

Allah had, indeed, been bountiful, he mused, alerted by a sudden hesitancy in the stranger's movements. Who was he? What did he want?

It had been years now since the steps of a stranger could stir the intensity of the old fear. That, he thought, had passed into oblivion, as the stamp of the fellaheen etched themselves on the fabric of their lives. As he had suspected, it had come naturally to Isis. For him, the best he could manage was to construct a warm cocoon around his educated, denatured interior, sometimes unable to resist the urge to poke around the old relics of ancient times. Once or twice, he had even ventured to Luxor, unable to thwart the lure of that old urge to plumb the crust of history.

Occasionally, Isis would rise from some terrible shred of dream, a convoluted rearrangement of her earlier living nightmare of abandonment and violence, but even that did not disturb the quiet harmony of this adopted life. And other things had occurred to ruffle the tranquility of the early fellaheen years. Knowing he could read, the boys had begun to bring old newspapers from town, tourist cast-offs in Arabic and English, which he steadfastly refused to read to them, although he could not resist them for himself.

Also, television had come, marching to the tune of government edicts that established television centers in the villages. Kom Ombo had one, and it was with difficulty that he had restricted Isis and the children from visitations, compromising finally on a monthly ritual. They were exposed to American programs of police violence, which, except for the images aping humans, were worlds beyond Isis's and the children's sense of reality.

WARREN ADLER

The edict, Ezzat believed, was one more clue to the coming putrefaction, an attempt to, once again, break the eternal cycle of the fellaheen. Nasser had done his work, giving the fellaheen the land they worked, a gift, really, although it changed nothing. Now Sadat was attempting to link this land with the star of technology. More futility lay ahead. More pain. The fellaheen had endured the five thousand years of Egyptian history. They would endure another five thousand, long after the relics of these new monuments to new gods had been buried in the sands of time.

The figure drew closer, and Ezzat put down his field glasses and walked slowly out of the hut toward the stranger, his eyes squinting to focus on his approaching face. The man waved, a traditional sign of peace, but it struck him as contrived, furtive, as if the man needed the assurance of this effort to continue his advance. Ezzat goaded his tired body forward. He did not want the man to move closer.

"Salaam alaikum," the man said, halting tentatively a few yards away.

"Salaam alaikum," Ezzat whispered hoarsely, struck by the vague and persistent familiarity. He had resisted the ancient traditions of honorable hospitality, knowing it had characterized him as mean-minded and eccentric. But it had also protected them.

"What do you want?" Ezzat asked cautiously. He noted that the man's manner and voice confirmed the youthful image he had seen in the field glasses. As the young man came toward him, Ezzat squatted to receive him, preferring the barren, sun-drenched emptiness of the parched earth to the darker shadows of his hut's interior.

348

MOTHER NILE

"I am looking for someone," the young man said, squatting
beside him as a measure of respect. He had taken a position
where the sun bleached the air between them with its brightness and Ezzat's dull eyes had to squint their curiosity. The
young man's accent was unmistakably foreign, another harbinger of danger. And, there was something else, but the slant
of the sun made it illusive, unable to confirm.

"Are you Dr. Ezzat, the archaeologist?"

The young man had lowered his voice. It passed the distance
between them as a low whisper, but it had the timbre of crack-
ling thunder, and Ezzat forced himself up abruptly, ignoring
the uncertainty of his aging joints. He had long dreaded this
moment, although even when he did summon up the possibility, logic told him that the link to Isis might never have been
established.

"There is no such person here," he mumbled, turning his
back on the startled young man and proceeding toward the
mudbrick huts. He had, he realized, lost all subtlety in dealing
with people, and it annoyed him now to think that he had been
too precipitous. But he could not bring himself to confront the
young man.

Behind him, he could hear the crunch of the young man's
sandals on the hard ground. Abruptly, Ezzat stopped and
turned.

The young man, he suspected, would not be easily deterred.
He searched his tired mind for some plan to deflect the intruder.

"I'm sorry," he said. "You have come to the wrong place."

The young man looked down and kicked the hard ground
with his sandals, then turned to survey the little patch of
buildings. Ezzat could sense his uncertainty and his own fears

calmed. For a moment, the old fright receded as the young man continued to hesitate.

"Perhaps I have made a mistake," he said.

Ezzat reined his curiosity. An echo of Herra's words bounded through the cavern of years, "They will turn heaven and earth to find her. They are very clever." Years ago, he had exhausted the vein of speculation on how they might come, in what form of Trojan horse. A sweet-tongued inquiry, a harsh invasion, an elaborate subterfuge.

Through the years, he had shown his face, had been recognized, but the connection with Isis seemed safe in the primal ooze of the fellaheen's world.

"I have never heard such a name," Ezzat said, pouring fuel now on the young man's uncertainty, sensing the mounting hesitation, finding his own courage. "I am sorry," he said gently, lifting his gaze on to the man's face.

The sun's arc had altered its reflection and what he saw left him speechless with foreboding. The resemblance was an acute attack on the core of their security. Could they have been that clever? The resemblance was uncanny. Watching him were Isis's eyes, unmistakable in their special hue and peculiar innocence. Like Farrah's and, in retributive mockery, like his oldest son, the errant seed.

"No," he said, abruptly. "You have definitely come to the wrong place."

"I have come so damned far," he said with a sigh, his face reflecting the hazard of a long journey, the connective link a positive confirmation of the long-smoldering pervasive fear. Ezzat felt the tentacles of some inner holding power. He fought to mask his terror, sure that he was confronting the ultimate subterfuge.

"You see, I'm looking..." the young man began, his words a clarion of danger.

"You must be mistaken," Ezzat said, turning his back and moving swiftly toward the shelter of their now threatened life, determined not to listen.

It was then that one of the twins stumbled precariously from the rear of the animal shelter, his unsure three-year-old step careening him forward on the slightly sloped ground, a foreshadowing of Isis's protective motherly presence.

Ezzat watched, terrified, since the child had also arrested the young man's interest. Ezzat froze. They watched as the child stumbled and fell, then squealed, more in confusion than pain. The young man moved swiftly toward the child. At that moment, he saw the floating form of Isis, moving gracefully as the black malaya caught the breeze of her movement. He saw them move in tandem toward the fallen child, stooping, in an astonishing symmetrical configuration, looking up suddenly, confronting the unmistakable stamp of blood relationship.

The unfamiliar grumble of a car's engine ripped at his attention, the audibility confirming the descending presence of the incarnate predatory terror.

CHAPTER FORTY-TWO

S HE HAD LOOKED BACK at him with a mingled flash of
recognition and indifference, more concerned about the
sunbrowned naked child who nestled now in her bosom. Her
fingers, strong and blunt with blackish half-moons under the
fingernails, were a laborer's, but her wrists were narrow and
the soft flesh above them smooth and white, protected by the
black material from the sun's devastation.

Everything visible of her flesh was deeply sun-browned,
the eyes gleaming like emeralds in soft silk jewel pads. She
watched him with suspicion and hostility, frightened by this
unexpected mirror image she saw in his face.

"Isis," he whispered, the one word stifled, gargling in his
windpipe, like a cry from a bottomless pit. But her gaze had
moved upward over his shoulder, following the sound of the
car's engine. He stood up swiftly, like a lifted marionette, and
saw the swirl of dust in the narrow road as the big four-wheeled

beast lumbered determinedly over the donkey-cart ruts, its snout pointed relentlessly in their direction.

For a long moment, the three adults and the tightly clutched child stood mesmerized by what appeared in this setting as an apparition of some alien force. Moving forward, the car made angry, grunting noises as its tires clawed at the uncertain earth.

"Them," Si said, the terror gripping him, arrested by the knifed stare of the old man's hate as it descended on him, accusatory and raging.

"You brought them here," the old man said. "Brought Zakki."

At the word, Isis sucked in her breath and, covering the child with her hands as if to protect him, ran toward the mudbrick shambles, emitting a shrieking tongue-vibrating ululation, the traditional eerie wail of both mourning and defiance.

Ezzat seemed pinned to the ground like a specimen butterfly, and Si had to drag him, stupefied with fear, toward the huts. Actually, Si knew, he should be heading for the fields. A flash of images saw him in a crouched military run along the palm copse, like some actor in an old war movie. Instead, he moved with Ezzat toward the dubious protection of the huts.

Rounding the ramshackle wall, which shielded them from the road and the oncoming juggernaut, he watched as Isis gathered her brood, which included all visible living things, beast and human, into the dank turd-piled animal shelter. She crowded them into it as if were the entrance to Noah's Ark, two dull-eyed gray donkeys, three mud-spattered black wool sheep, a mangy rust-colored dog, a shaggy, muttering cud-chewing dignified goat, all followed by a moving cloud of buzzing flies. Three older boys had also suddenly materialized, dressed in filthy pajama-striped djellabas, summoned from the bean-harvesting chores by their mother's eerie ululation.

An ill-fitting half door was clamped shut in some ridiculous pose of protection. Yet, inside, a pall of silence descended as if the fear had been transmitted by the common language of terror, clubbing the entire ménage into silence.

As the door of the shelter closed, Ezzat shook off Si's gripping hand with surprising strength, moving across the expanse of open ground in the direction of the approaching car. By then, it had avoided the unpassable section of the road and was proceeding along the rim of the field, mowing down the mature plants in its path. Si stayed out of sight behind the wall of the animal shelter, crouching to observe the scene through a gap in the crumbling mudwork.

He knew, even then, that he could still head out unseen over the parched desert wasteland. But the thought left him with an excruciating pang of betrayal. He cursed himself, eyes welling with tears of frustration. Swallowing, he tasted a metallic bile, bitter and nausea provoking, reflecting his mood of despair and frustration. So he had found Isis. What difference could that make to anyone, especially his mother, whose maggot-ridden body could only be mocking him now?

What he had felt when he saw Isis was, remarkably, nothing at all, except a fleeting stab of recognition. There was no sentiment in it, no nostalgia, no hint of a summoned cataclysmic event or an epiphany of awareness.

What cause had he pursued that drove him across the world in search of some vague blood connection? In fact, her visage, and the environment in which he found her, was so depressingly different than what had charged him forward that he felt denuded of purpose, disillusioned, disappointed. No sense of victory or achievement or of high realized purpose masked the bleak reality.

The glorious Isis was merely a primitive peasant woman.

He was afflicted with an overwhelming sense of embarrassment. If he had found her under different circumstances and brought her back to Brooklyn, even in Brooklyn, with its own social stigmas and disappointments, he would be embarrassed to acknowledge the relationship. Perhaps, even their mother would feel the same way.

The car, a large black Mercedes, moved to the field's edge, the tires gripping the harder earth as it rolled toward the old man, who, like a madman, was flaying his arms and moving directly into the path of the oncoming car. Suddenly, the brakes squeaked to a jarring halt, and three dark men brandishing automatic weapons got out and surrounded him.

Si could hear the panicked singsong of the old man's entreaties. It was a pitiful, fruitless performance.

In the front seat of the car, beside the driver, he saw the grotesque, bloated image of a man who, he was certain, was Zakki. Logic again told him to run, but he seemed rooted to the ground, bludgeoned into inaction by a pervasive sense of detachment. What had he to do with all this?

It was only when the shots rang out, a long tattoo exploding in the dry air, that the instinct for personal survival gripped his consciousness. Yet he continued to crouch, immovable, gaping at the tableau of death. The shots, carrying the message of pent-up rage, exploded into the supine figure of Ezzat, giving the corpse an afterlife of twitching limbs and tiny fountain bursts of blood. The sound, like a thrown switch, triggered a disparate chorus in the animal shelter, mingling the screams of frightened animals and humans. Above it, rose Isis's vibrating tongue-clucking ululation.

Si started to run, but his legs felt like rubber and he fell, then rose, and, for some absurd reason, headed instead for the animal shelter, fumbling with the roped latch and throwing himself into the foul interior.

His sudden entrance froze the sounds for a moment. But they began again as the animals stamped and struggled against each other, coats lacquered the pungent ooze of fear. Squatting against the far wall, Isis sat surrounded by her panicked, trembling children. The twins lay burrowed in her arms, while her hands clutched her infant, lodged against her bosom, as if she were trying to insert it between the mounds of her protective flesh.

The three older boys huddled together, terrorized, uncertain about Si's presence. The heated air in the enclosure was a gaseous inferno, and the life forms, people, animals, insects, seemed rooted in some primeval stench.

He could not understand why he was here. His feelings now seemed inert. Will Allah take care of this, he suddenly thought, his body racked with a hideous giggle, which ceased abruptly as he saw the shaft of outside light lengthen as the unoiled hinges squeaked and the door opened.

Dark faces peered inside, waiting for their pupils to focus, the barrels of their weapons glistening, the muzzles still smoking from earlier messages of death. The men crouched, peering through the bars of the animals' restless legs at the huddled group against the wall. The goat was closest to the door, and they pulled sharply on its tether to move him from their path.

Si watched as the sweating men cajoled the animal out into the sunlight. When he was free of the entrance, they calmly spattered him with bullets. The poor animal dropped with a thud, with little time to be startled by this uncommon death.

Through the entrance, Si could see the metal skin of the Mercedes coated with dry dust, the front door open, revealing the seated figure of a grotesquely fat man, his pallor as yellow as mustard, the skin moist with unhealthy sweat. He was certain this was Zakki. Zakki, the tormentor. The man's swollen eyelids blanched in the sunlight, moving with tremors of excitement as the men, with feverish efficiency, poked at the animals with their gun barrels.

The woman's wails had become a whimper. The clucking ceased. Only the painful braying of the persecuted animals rent the air. They moved the donkeys out next, and the bullet bursts could be heard thudding into their carcasses as they fell to the ground with a slow-motion crumbling of their front legs. Rivulets of ocher blood began to form on the earth. The sheep, with some instinctive presence, tried to make a run for it. Two were cut down in flight almost as an amusement, with long bursts of gunfire, but one, the mangiest of the pack, was still to be seen scurrying in the distance.

Zakki presided over the animal massacre with an expectation that was pervasive as his eyes squinted into the darkness of the animal shelter. When the way was cleared, the men entered, three huge, dark forms filling the tight space with the omnipotence of authority, as faceless as anyone who had the dispensation of God in a trigger finger. The mangy dog, who had somehow been overlooked, snapped at one of the men, who quickly stitched off its head with an even line of gunfire, his features alight with the killer's pride of accuracy.

"Don't kill them," Zakki ordered from his perch on the seat of the open car, his voice oddly tremulous and weak. Hitching the weapons over their shoulders, the men's meaty, dark hands grabbed the three boys, the oldest about twelve, the youngest no more than ten, and dragged them out to the cluttered and blood-soaked arena of death.

Stooping over the anguished, squatting form of Isis, Si helped lift her. He managed to unlock the twins from her grasp, the baby's arms flayed at her breasts as its hungry lips searched the black expanse for its nipple of nourishment. Outside, she tore away from his grasp, her face cast in a hard mask of defiance.

The sun was momentarily blinding, and they were herded by rough hands into a huddled, squatting mass before the bloated man, who sat watching them through glazed eyes. The edge of his tongue darted nervously at the edges of his thick lips as his eyes turned on Si.

"I knew you would find her," Zakki said, the sweat cascading over his cheeks in long oily blobs. He looked sick, spent, near death himself.

"Farrah's children," Zakki said, spitting into the ground. He surveyed the group huddled around Isis. "Farouk's filthy brood." Isis, in a movement that seemed to symbolize her contempt, bared a heavy milk-filled breast and placed its nipple in the baby's mouth.

Si, squatting next to Isis, watched as the three, thick-featured dark men stood arrogantly around the motley group,
their impatient authority inscribed in glazed eager eyes. He
looked across the wide expanse of umber earth, still confused
as to why he had not run. *To where*, he thought suddenly, as if
that might satisfy his disappointment in himself.

Then his eyes suddenly shifted, affording a view of a wide
pie-shaped chunk of green field in which, at that moment, a
black spot, like some restless fly, was moving. Samya! He had
not yet come to grips with his own fear, but her emergence
shocked him into the inevitable reality of their impending
slaughter.

"You can't do this," he shouted at their captors, shattering
the tableau as the sweating Zakki confronted the waiting
helplessness of his victims. He said the words in a high-pitched
shriek, hoping they might carry to the advancing figure of
Samya, whose pace accelerated as she grew closer.

From where she approached, he knew she could not see
the Mercedes. Si tore his eyes away, knowing their direction
would give her away. *Please, Samya*, he begged her in his heart.
Save yourself. There was nothing he could do.

The three oldest boys sat cross-legged in the dust, the oldest
glum but still defiant, obviously misunderstanding his vulnerability. As Zakki's face beamed down at him, he spat insolently,
observing the bubble of his dust-laden spit, while his eyes rose
to meet Zakki's look with contempt.

"Strip them," Zakki ordered, the action clearly defined for
the brutish men, who grabbed the boys and tore their clothes
away, revealing slender, reedlike white bodies, unburnished by
the sun. The oldest struggled against the man and it took two to

hold him. Observing her children in this moment of terror, Isis began a piercing ululating endless shriek, whipping through the shimmering air like a tornado.

Si caught the glint of metal stakes. One of the men was hammering them into the ground with the butt of his weapon. Zakki watched, his eyes deadened by the monotonous efficiency. The oldest boy was pushed to the ground, belly down, his face pressed into the ground. He spat the dust from his air passages, as his legs and arms were tied to each stake, leaving him spread-eagled, his fledgling testicles hanging from his middle like two wrinkled, overripe plums.

Watching the boy, squirming and grunting helplessly on the ground, Si could not find his voice, and his limbs felt heavy and inert, rooted to the ground. The staking process was repeated on the other two boys, the three of them resisting the tethers in an undulating dance macabre.

Si felt the transference of helplessness, although his mind struggled to codify the events. A shaft of light pierced the veil of his confusion and, seeing the moving steel in Zakki's puffy fingers, the knowledge of this terrible obsessive retribution transmitted itself instantly. He knew now what Isis had done.

Almost at the exact moment of this understanding, the black-clad figure of Samya intruded, amplifying his horror, magnetizing his eyes. She was moving in a crouch, oblivious to their having spotted her. A burst of gunfire, like some hideous counterpoint to Isis's frenetic ululation, split the air, freezing the advancing black image.

Si stood up, shouting, "Go back, Samya. Go back."

The figure hesitated, seemed to heed the warning, started to move away. Another burst of gunfire rang out, halting the receding image, which disappeared from sight in the bean plants of the green field.

The volcano of his anger erupted, destroying logic, concentrating every morsel of fettered energy in his body, which became a weapon as it shot forward to grasp the soft throat of the clammy Zakki. Operating as a separate intelligence, his hand clutched the soft knife hand, which released the handle instantly, as if he had simply surrendered and willingly handed it over. From behind, one hand grasped a handful of pinched flesh from Zakki's belly, the other the knife handle, the point of the blade held to the throat, the skin dented to the brink of its tenuous point of entry at the jugular vein.

All sound ceased. Even the nursing child had stopped the smacking, greedy gulps of sustenance. Si felt the sweat of Zakki's body oozing like mucilage from the pores of his yellowed flesh. Even the dark men had frozen, the muzzles of their weapons pointed unsurely toward the shield of Zakki's body.

"Tell them to put their guns down," Si said. His voice uttered the words with cool, almost disembodied indifference as the point of the knife moved a millimeter more into the soft flesh.

"It doesn't matter," Zakki whispered. The heart in his bloated body seemed to fibrillate, and he felt the man's strength ebb, the will disintegrate.

Without a definitive order from Zakki, the men moved in choreographed unison, pointing the muzzles of their weapons at Isis's temple, then moving them, roaming over the children like camera sentries. He had to impress upon himself that it was indeed him, Si, involved in the scene, not a screen image of himself playacting some fictitious danger.

361

He felt Zakki's flesh puddled in his hand, while his sweat-rimmed eyes groped for some logic in this moonscape of horror. He saw the writhing, staked young bodies, the twins huddled and trembling, their faces hidden in Isis's lap, the baby pressed in the billowy white, lightly veined blob of breast, the dark hard-faced ice-blooded thugs.

Beyond mere vision, he absorbed the image of Ezzat, his blood-sodden body crumpled like a marionette on the umber ground. And Samya! A vibrating sob escaped from someplace deep in his chest, like a harsh pleading protest against this personal holocaust. Outside himself, he watched the scene helplessly, unable to find the will to design some response beyond this melodrama of violence so foreign to his life's experience.

Isis suddenly stood up. The twins continued to clutch her black skirts. She moved toward Zakki, the emerald eyes like dead green beads, lips clamping all sounds shut, the flesh paling under its bronze patina. The fat man's body stirred beneath his grip, but Si's arm held his neck rigid. Zakki's breath came in quick gasps as he tried, it seemed, to shrink inside his vast cocoon of flesh. The three men tensed, waiting for some sign from Zakki.

"If they touch her, I will kill you," Si said. He saw Zakki's wrist flex in a staying motion that kept the men frozen.

Isis came close, as if she were stepping into some invisible spotlight. Zakki lifted his eyes, locked onto hers, the commu-nication between them silent, intense. Si could sense their kinship of hate, a life flow so tangible that it seemed to electrify the overheated air. In Isis's glazed eyes, he saw his mother's mysterious kayf, that look beyond life, observing suddenly what had eluded him, at first, the real connective link, unexplainable, the immutable alliance of blood.

Her lips poised as if to speak. Instead, the ululation began again, shrill, piercing, transmitting the anguish and pain of any dying life form able to protest in the face of impending death. The cry rose and became unbearable to hear as it belched out of her mouth like a sheet of hot blue flame. He felt Zakki squirming under his grasp, oblivious to the knifepoint that had broken the skin's surface, showing a single bubble of oozing red blood. Si would have gladly shoved the knife forward if it could cut off that sound.

But something else was happening in the midst of this cacophony, something that had been lost in the onslaught of visual and auditory imagery. She had been holding the child still attached to her breast, one browned hand supporting its small pink rounded buttocks. With her other hand, she held the back of the child's head, pressing it against her breast. The small frame quivered and struggled, its little feet kicking helplessly, its hands tearing at the material of the black malaya. *My God*, Si screamed within himself, *she is killing the baby.*

"Isis. Please," he shouted.

But the ululating wail drowned out his shout. He wanted to drop the knife and reach out to snatch the baby from her grasp, torn now between impossible alternatives. The dark men stood watching, mesmerized, their eyes fixed on Zakki, poised to obey.

She stood there, defiant, standing on the outer rim of the human abyss, as the baby struggled and pawed at her, fighting for its life.

"You can't do this," Si screamed at her, but again his voice was lost in the eerie sound. Inexplicably, as if his own godlike role of potential death-giver bonded a relationship with Zakki, he hissed his plea into his ear.

"You must make her stop."

He saw the fat man's wrist flick and the three men act in unison, grabbing the baby, who had begun to turn blue, and wresting it from her grasp. One man held the gasping baby, with surprising and experienced gentleness, while the two others struggled with Isis.

As if the act signaled its own special alliance, Si relieved his hold on Zakki's neck and one of the men, as alert as a predatory bird, moved quickly to reach out and grab Si's hands, twisting the knife from it. He heard it clatter to the ground and, with the sound, the total ebbing of his energy, as he grew limp and dropped to his knees.

The man who held the recovering child put it on the ground, where it squirmed on its back, its arms reaching out for the lost breast, oblivious that this life-giving flesh had just been designated the instrument of its death. The muzzle of his weapon was poised now at Si's head. Isis's clucking wail subsided into a whimper, and her emerald eyes reflected the hopeless resignation of defeat.

Si moved toward her, ignoring the gun muzzle, engulfing Isis in a brotherly embrace. As the men released her, she fell against him. He felt her body shiver with hysteria, her tears moistening his djellaba.

Behind him, he heard Zakki breathing in short gasps like a faulty bellows. Turning, he saw a moist, yellow face, puffing and gasping. The knife had again materialized in his hand. With the help of one of the men, he staggered to where the three young boys lay naked and spread-eagled, their exposed fair skin reddening in the relentless noonday sun.

Turning quickly again, Si buried Isis's face against his chest. He felt her heart beating against his own.

"Forgive me," he whispered. "What have we done to you?"

He had expected screams, but none came. Time was suspended. He sensed he had entered a vacuum of chronology. Behind him, he heard shuffling footsteps, then saw what was unmistakably Zakki's shadow, hovering over them like an enveloping black cloud. When he turned, he was looking directly into Zakki's face. Something had changed. A strangely different demeanor seemed sculpted out of the clay of the old features. An element had disappeared. Hatred!

It was gone now. In its place appeared only the ravaged mask of anguished resignation.

Zakki shook his head. Perhaps it was compassion or understanding, but what he saw in this new face was some primitive acknowledgment that it was possible to transcend vengeance.

Si watched him, sensing his struggle to find words to communicate this transformation. Their eyes searched each other. Was it compassion Si saw? Finally, Zakki could only nod and turn away.

"Thank you," Si whispered. Zakki could not have heard. He watched him being helped into the car by the three men. He appeared ravaged. Spent. Isis, too, turned to watch the spectacle. Zakki slumped in the seat beside the driver, his eyes glazed, watching them.

He seemed exorcised of all evil, almost benign now, perhaps already turning inward to face the ultimate darkness. Was it possible, Si wondered, for evil, too, to burn out, to end? The sharp anger of the croaking engine startled him. He watched the greedy grasp of the tires' treads as the car shot forward over the timeworn landscape.

CHAPTER FORTY-THREE

FOR A LONG TIME, the survivors remained paralyzed with disbelief. Zakki had cut the bonds of the three boys, covered their bodies again with their tattered djellabas.

The twins had taken refuge against their mother's flanks, and a stunned and weary Isis recovered the baby and cradled it hungrily in her arms, kissing its face.

"Allah is just," Isis said. The statement needed no reaction from the others, as they stirred and began moving.

Si held back, sitting in this blood-soaked arena, strewn with dead animals, a visual harbinger of what he might expect if he went to find Samya. The lower rims of his eyelids puddled with tears as he rose and walked toward the field where he had seen her fall. He walked slowly, haltingly, postponing the agony of discovery. Already, he could taste the bitter bile of his own guilt. He had brought this down on them. They were the victims of his own self-indulgence, his own egoism. Did he have to suck their blood to sustain his own life? Suddenly, he wanted to vomit, but could only gag and dry heave, picturing Samya's pain-distorted death mask.

Along the edge of the field, sprawled in a bed of broad-leafed mature plants, he saw the blob of black. Starting to run toward it, his legs buckled and, he fell.

For a long moment, he could not summon the energy to rise from his knees. It was only when he thought he saw the black blob move that he stood up and ran toward it.

"Samya," he shouted, sure that he had imagined it. "Samya."

She was moving. He reached her as she rose, her face reflecting both bewilderment and relief. Assured that she was alive, he examined her clinically, noting that a bullet had apparently grazed her temple, a fraction from certain death, and its force had providentially knocked her unconscious. Beyond that, she seemed fine.

"Isis?" Samya whispered, her alertness returning as her face brightened under his gaze.

"Isis is fine," he whispered, kissing her forehead.

"I am happy for you."

"For me?"

He wondered what she meant.

"It's you that is important to me," he said.

She rubbed that spot that the bullet had grazed, then sat up and looked toward the mudbrick huts. Isis and her children kneeled around Ezzat's body. They could hear her ululation of mourning, a plaintive, anguished cry of loss. She turned to him in confusion.

"I don't understand it either, Samya," he said, gathering her in his arms.

It was dark by the time they had put the place in some reasonable order. The dead donkeys and the dog were dragged over the parched earth some distance from the huts. By tomorrow, the oldest boy assured him, their bones would be picked clean by vultures and other small desert animals. The carcasses of the sheep and goats were hung from hooks in the animal shelter, and the body of Ezzat was sewn into a sheet and placed on boards in the main hut. They would, he knew, bury him tomorrow.

Samya helped Isis prepare the evening meal, and they squatted around a kerosene stove on which a pot of fava beans simmered in a watery mash. He watched Isis's face in the muted fire's light. She looked considerably older than her years. Deep lines were etched in her face, and she showed the fatigue of the grueling day.

"Will you be all right?" he asked gently. She looked up vaguely and shrugged. It seemed an alien idea. She would endure, he knew. She had always endured. Nearby, lying on a ragged carpet between the twins, the baby gurgled in its sleep.

"Do you ever think of her?" he asked, explaining, "Our mother." When she did not respond, he whispered, "Do you forgive her?" He wanted to have this forgiveness, if offered, extended also to him. He felt Samya watching him.

"Forgive?" She repeated the word and he knew she could barely understand its meaning. She was as far removed from such concepts as if she had lived on another planet.

All those symbols and values by which he lived seemed meaningless in this place. *You are the granddaughter of the last dynasty of Egypt,* he wanted to remind her. But that, too, seemed meaningless and inert.

Beyond now, for them, was nothing. No past. No future. The rhythm of life remained unperturbed. The world here was circumscribed and finite with no possibilities beyond birth and death, planting and harvest, the inevitability of good and evil, and its frail division. He felt the ultimate intruder. The gap between them was aeons of space and time. It was a relationship of blood. Simply that. There was no meaning beyond that, he knew now, a mere coincidence.

Then Isis rose, lifted the baby, woke the twins, and they moved drowsily into the main hut. The boys rubbed their eyes and followed, after first shutting off the kerosene fire.

Si lay down on the ragged carpet just vacated by the children, and Samya joined him. She laid her head in the crook of his arm and embraced his chest.

"I should never have disturbed them," Si said. "I did them no good." He knew she was listening, but she didn't respond, and he caressed her hair.

"As soon as it's light," he whispered, "let's get away from here. You and me." His tongue grew heavy. "I have my place."

"Where?" she asked, her body tensing.

"With you," he said, feeling her body relax, "and yours with me." It occurred to him then that the only real place was here, rooted to the land. Out there was only wandering, a perpetual search in the mysterious jungle of the world. Perhaps love was also a place, he thought. Only time would give him that answer. Then he grew drowsy and fell asleep.

ABOUT THE AUTHOR

Acclaimed author, playwright, poet, and essayist **Warren Adler** is best known for *The War of the Roses*, his masterpiece fictionalization of a macabre divorce adapted into the BAFTA- and Golden Globe–nominated hit film starring Danny DeVito, Michael Douglas, and Kathleen Turner.

Adler has also optioned and sold film rights for a number of his works, including *Random Hearts* (starring Harrison Ford and Kristin Scott Thomas) and *The Sunset Gang* (produced by Linda Lavin for PBS's American Playhouse series starring Jerry Stiller, Uta Hagen, Harold Gould, and Doris Roberts), which garnered Doris Roberts an Emmy nomination for Best Supporting Actress in a Miniseries. You can follow Warren Adler's current stage/film/TV developments at www. greyeaglefilms.com.

Adler's works have been translated into more than 25 languages, including his staged version of *The War of the Roses,* which has opened to spectacular reviews worldwide. Adler has taught creative writing seminars at New York University, and has lectured on creative writing, film and television adaptation, and electronic publishing.

CPSIA information can be obtained
at www.ICGtesting.com
Printed in the USA
LVOW08s0204100217
523814LV00003B/288/P